Mr. Laurence, I Presume...

Mr. Laurence, I Presume...

a novel by

Joseph Sciuto

IGUANA

Front cover design: designplayground.ca

ISBN 978-1-77180-588-9 (paperback)
ISBN 978-1-77180-587-2 (epub)

This is an original print edition of *Mr. Laurence, I Presume*....

Dedicated to my very close friends Rod Lynch and David Martin.

You can read a preview of one of Joseph Sciuto's short stories, "Close Friends," from his forthcoming collection of short fiction, at the end of this book.

CHAPTER ONE

Joe

The last thing I remember is falling over a railing in a Bronx apartment building and tumbling down multiple flights of stairs.

The next time I opened my eyes I was in a hospital bed with an excruciating headache. I was hooked up to a bunch of machines and, when I was finally able to focus, I caught sight of the rear end of a sweet-looking nurse.

I asked, "Where am I?"

She turned around and, let me just say, her front was as nicely proportioned as her backside.

"Oh my God," she said. "You're awake!"

Within minutes I was surrounded by doctors checking my heart rate, my reflexes and my pulse, looking in my mouth and up my nose, and flashing a light into my eyes.

As they were doing this, I kept a blurry eye on the nurse. I had to squint to make out the name on the tag pinned to her shirt.

"L-U-C-Y," I said, proving I could still spell. "Lucky?"

"Loo-*see*," she giggled.

One of the doctors leaned across and felt my forehead. "How do you feel?" he asked.

"Terrible."

"That's to be expected. You've been unconscious for four days. Do you remember what happened?"

I paused. "The last thing I remember is tumbling down a flight of stairs."

"Anything before that?"

"No."

"Your name?"

I thought about it and shook my head.

"Your parents' names? The president? What year it is? The school you attend? Your age?"

"Nothing! I remember nothing."

"It's to be expected. You've experienced severe trauma to your head."

"Oh yeah?" I asked and felt my eyes close involuntarily.

"Yes," he said. "Memory loss is common in cases like this, but with any luck it should all come back. If not, we'll just have to re-program you." Everyone laughed, and as quickly as they arrived, they left, except for Lucy, who said, "Your girlfriend is here. Would you like to see her?"

"Sure, but first can you tell me how old I am?"

"Eighteen."

She opened the door and the most gorgeous young woman I'd ever seen walked in. After looking at her I knew this had to be a dream. She had the kind of long, dark, silky hair that you only see on models, and her face looked like it had been stolen from an angel. Flawless olive skin, plump lips, adorable button nose. Perfection. I just stared at her and watched her glare at Lucy as the nurse left the room. Then the goddess with the big brown eyes sat down beside me and asked, "How do you feel?"

"Except for this terrible headache, not bad. Are you really my girlfriend?"

"Yes Joe, I'm really your girlfriend, Angie."

"No! No way a girl like you would ever be my girlfriend. This is either a dream or some type of cruel joke."

"You really don't remember me?"

"I don't remember a thing, and if I don't remember a girl like you, I'm in a lot worse shape than I thought."

"You're not just pretending to not remember me so you can break up with me later?"

"No! Jeez. Why would I do that?"

"I don't know. I guess you wouldn't."

"I would have to be crazy to do that. Am I crazy? Is this a psych ward? Are you even real?" I reached out and touched her forearm and she laughed nervously and covered my hand with hers.

"Yes Joe, I'm real, and no, you're not in a psych ward."

"Okay. Good."

The girl who claimed to be my girlfriend smiled through her concern. "Do you remember who your parents are?"

"Nope"

"How about your friends?"

"I have friends?"

"Wow! To think that something good might have come out of this terrible … accident…"

"What makes you say that?"

"Because your friends are a bunch of degenerate drunks who are intent on destroying our relationship," she said with such a flash of anger that I was taken aback.

The next moment, two police officers walked into the room, handcuffed this beautiful creature, read her her rights, and told her that she was being charged with second-degree murder and attempted manslaughter. I watched in stunned silence, and when they were finished, they escorted her out of my room.

One of the officers hung back and asked if I was ready to give a statement.

"Concerning what?"

"You really don't remember?"

"I really don't remember."

"Seriously."

I glared at him.

"She killed her brother — stabbed him twenty-seven times — and then we suspect she tried to kill you by pushing you over a railing and sending you down eight flights of stairs."

"Wow. A little thing like her? That seems unlikely."

"Believe it."

"I don't remember anything. The doctor told me I suffered a severe trauma to the head. I don't even remember my name."

"I'll be honest with you, I'm surprised you're alive." He fished in his wallet and handed me a business card. "If you do get back your memory, give me a call. The quicker we put this psycho away, the better it'll be for everyone."

Suddenly the headache went from an eight to a twelve. I called for Lucy and begged for relief. A few minutes later I was hooked up to a morphine drip.

It didn't do much to kill the pain, but after a little while I became pleasantly unconcerned with the throbbing in my skull. As for the psychotic chick who was supposedly my girlfriend, I was becoming even more convinced that the whole thing had to be a hallucination. I couldn't remember my name, what school I went to, or who the president was, but I was damn sure that a girl who looked like her I would never forget.

I closed my eyes, feeling as buoyant and carefree as a feather. Suddenly I had an image of my brain as a jukebox, with EPs plucked out of a stack and dropped onto a turntable. Weirdly, it only played songs by one of my grandmother's favorite singers, Jimmy Durante. "Smile," "Make Someone Happy," and "Young at Heart" kept playing in my head, one after another, and naturally I started moving to the beat. Soon I was snapping my fingers and lip syncing to the songs. I have no idea if I was getting the words right or jumbling the lyrics, splicing the sun with the girl and the love with the fame. I just remember feeling like I was aging backwards in a field of sunflowers. My heart was young. I was happy to be alive. A morphine-soaked survivor, spilling over with good will towards everyone and everything.

I was grooving along, feeling good, when a chorus of shrill voices pierced my bubble of bliss. When I opened my eyes, there were three people standing over my bed, looking super worried. A woman, a man, and some kid. At first it sounded like they were speaking in tongues. They kept making references to God and Saint Joseph and saying that their prayers would be heard, that it was miracle, and that that bitch would burn in hell. When I asked them who they were, they introduced themselves as my mother, father, and little brother. The woman burst into tears and turned away. The kid shot me a dirty look, and the old man just looked lost. They wouldn't stop with the questions, and they couldn't get it through their thick heads that I didn't remember anything. So I closed my eyes and turned the volume on the jukebox up higher, and just like that, the groove came back.

CHAPTER TWO

Joe

It was about a month before my memory came back, and yes, the psychotic bitch who stabbed her brother twenty-seven times was my girlfriend. And here I was at Rikers Island, in the juvenile section of this illustrious shithole of a prison, being patted down by a guard. When he was sure I wasn't packing a shiv or a pistol he escorted me to a room where my beautiful Angie was seated.

Despite it all, I still loved her and was determined to marry her one day. And that was after seeing her stab her brother repeatedly with a kitchen knife.

To be fair to Angie, the scumbag had it coming. Like any caring and loving brother, he'd tried to rape her — again. I had kicked the shit out of this lowlife a number of times, but once an asshole, always an asshole … or in his case, a dead asshole. I'd walked in on this brutal act of self-defense just as she sent the knife through his limp and lifeless crotch. It was chilling, to say the least.

I sat across from Angie in a bare room with two chairs and a table and a guard just outside the door. Angie looked pale and seemed to have lost a few pounds, which took her from skinny to skeletal. It was the first chance I'd had to visit. She'd been sick in the infirmary for most her time here, which was too bad for her but a good thing overall. It kept her out of the general population and away from the real criminals. Despite the seriousness of the act she committed, I wouldn't classify her as prison material.

"My God," I said, "this place is depressing."

"You think so? Well, you should try being a prisoner here."

"They're not treating you very nicely?"

"You know, that might be one of the stupidest questions you've ever asked me, and my God, there have been a lot."

"You know Ang, you're not really in a position to be a wiseass, so why don't you just cool it."

She rolled her eyes and stayed silent, so I tried to make conversation. "I thought we'd be sitting across from each other talking on a phone through plexiglass, like in the movies."

"Maybe that part of the prison is being renovated," she said. "I'm sure they're filling it up with white couches right now. I wonder if they have a budget for fresh flowers…"

I folded my arms and stared at her. "You know, I did an independent survey of fourteen individuals and I asked, 'Do you think my Angie is guilty?' Twelve people said yes, and not only did they think you were guilty, but they also thought that you should spend the rest of your life behind bars. One voted not guilty, and one was undecided."

"Who voted not guilty?"

"My little brother, but that little slimeball is in love with you, so there's some bias one has to take into account."

"Who was undecided?"

"Oh, that was me…"

There seemed to be a bit of steam coming out of her ears, but her gorgeous mouth curved into a smile. "You, who know my story better than anyone, voted undecided?"

"Well, to be fair, my memory was still a bit dodgy at that point."

"And now?"

"I'm still undecided, but leaning toward guilty."

She shook her head and closed her eyes. For a minute I thought she was going to get up and have the guard escort her back to the infirmary. I leaned in closer and whispered, "I talked to the prosecutors a couple of times and told them that I fell over the railing and down eight flights of stairs all on my own."

She looked surprised. "How did you explain that?"

"I said I threw the knife down the stairs so hard that I fell over the railing."

"They're supposed to believe you're that clumsy?"

"That's my story and I'm sticking to it."

"Hmm."

"They're dropping the attempted manslaughter charge against you, and after I gave them a complete history of your brother's behavior toward you, backed up by my parents and my baby brother, they are also going to drop the murder charge."

"Are you serious?"

"Dead serious. Your lawyer will come by later today to have you sign a bunch of paperwork."

"So am I going to be set free?"

"Not exactly. There were some stipulations."

"What stipulations?"

"You'll spend some time at a women's correctional facility on Long Island. You'll be living with another lady and seeing a psychiatrist five times a week." When Angie just stared at me, I said, "I asked if that could be bumped up to seven days a week. They said they'd look into it."

"You didn't."

"No, I'm joking. You're seriously in need of a sense of humor."

She gestured around herself. "Have you seen where I am?"

When she looked like she might cry, I decided to take it easy on her. "The new facility is supposed to be nice," I said. "It has a movie theater and a library. You'll be able to finish high school and apply to colleges. And you'll be able to wander the grounds freely."

"I will?"

"Well, you'll have an ankle bracelet that'll set off an alarm if you try to escape, but other than that, yes."

"What about the other women who live there?"

"A bunch of deranged criminals. You should fit in perfectly."

She clenched her hands into two little fists. "I swear, there are times I wish I'd pushed you harder over that railing…"

"Please Angie, finish your thought. I'm listening."

She started to cry and lowered her head. "I'm so sorry. I lost control."

I let her cry and plead for me to forgive her, and after a while I said, "Shut the fuck up, Angie. Do you really think I want to listen to this crap?"

"I don't know how you can even sit there and look at me."

"That's the easy part, Angie. Despite everything, I'm still madly in love with you." She stopped crying and blew her nose softly while I kept talking. "And as hard as it is for me to admit, I feel somewhat responsible for what happened. I promised not to drink on Christmas Eve, and I did, and when we got back to my parents' apartment you overreacted, as usual…"

"I overreacted?"

"Yes … and then you stubbornly refused to continue to stay with us, where you were safe, and you went back to that nut house."

"You hit me," she said.

"Bullshit, Angie! You knocked me over the coffee table and while I was trying to get back up you came at me with that porcelain thing. All I did was push you aside."

"You hurt me!"

"Seriously? You were going to crack that stupid figurine over my head, and *I* hurt *you*?" I got up from the chair and started pacing.

She watched me and seemed to shrink into her chair. "I'm sorry," she said.

I looked at her and thought to myself that it was useless being mad. It wasn't like I was going to break up with her. I sat back down and stared at her. "Okay," I finally said, "let's put all that aside for now. Promise me you won't do anything stupid."

"Like what?"

"Like try to kill yourself."

"I would never do that. Suicide is a mortal sin."

"Great! It's good to know that some nugget of your Catholic upbringing has stuck with you. I try to tell my friends that you're not all evil. That in some ways, you're the purest of the pure."

"Do they know we haven't…"

"Well, I might have mentioned to one friend that we've been going out for over a year and still haven't kissed on the lips."

"We can do that stuff after we're married," she said. "Maybe even on our honeymoon."

"You think?"

"Definitely, but we have to go slowly. Is that all right?"

"Of course. Have I ever forced you to do anything that you didn't want to do?"

"No." She bit her lip and looked at me. "You've always been a gentleman, and you're the only man I've ever loved. I want to spend the rest of my life with you."

"That's sweet, Ang."

"It's the truth."

"First you're going to have to wriggle out of this mess."

She nodded and said, "How?"

"Play ball. Tell them what they want to hear."

She nodded again as I continued. "If they offer you everything they said they will — dropping the charges and having you go to that home — just agree. No arguments. The last thing you want is a trial. In all honesty, a jury might not find you so sympathetic. You can come off as a real sourpuss."

She glared at me. "Are you taking any medications for your concussion?"

"Just aspirin when I need it. But the morphine they had me on for two days was amazing."

"It sounds like you might have lost a few IQ points."

"Not at all. Since waking up it's like my IQ has shot up about two hundred points. Suddenly, all these complex equations have been going through my mind."

"Complex equations?" She looked doubtful.

"Yes. Like $E = mc^2$. I'll just be sitting around and it'll pop into my head."

She stifled a laugh. "That's the most famous equation in the world."

"Maybe so, but I never knew about it, and without looking it up I knew what it meant."

"Oh yeah? What does it mean?"

"The E stands for energy. M is for mass, and c^2 is the speed of light, squared. It's Einstein's theory of relativity. It's basically the idea that mass and energy are the same physical entity and can be changed into each other."

She looked at me as though I'd lost my mind. "So now you know what the most famous equation in the world means. That's great, but it doesn't mean you're a genius."

"But now I know hundreds of equations I never knew before. Newton's second law of motion, Newton's law of universal gravitation, the Schrödinger wavefunction, Maxwell's laws…"

She raised her hand and said, "Enough."

"Now do you believe me?" I asked.

"I'm undecided," she said, with a wry smile.

"And what is that supposed to mean?"

"You tell me, genius."

I shook my head. "And I was going to use you as the subject for my first painting. I'm calling it the *Mona Lisa II*."

"So now you're not just the next Einstein, but the next Leonardo da Vinci?"

"You know Ang, sometimes you can be a real downer."

"I'm sorry. It's just that you're hitting me with a lot." She sat up in her cold metal prison chair and looked at me earnestly. "So tell me, when did you realize you were an artist?"

"When I was still in the hospital. I asked the nurse for a pen and paper. I was going to write you a letter telling you that I forgave you for trying to kill me, and that I didn't see any reason why that should interfere with our plans for the future. But I couldn't get the words down, and suddenly I was doing a sketch of the nurse … the pretty one that was there when you came to visit. Do you remember her?"

"Vaguely," Angie said, suddenly frosty.

"Well, after about ten minutes I was finished with the sketch … my first one ever … and I showed the nurse. She was stunned, and couldn't stop telling me how great it was."

Angie rolled her eyes, but I kept going.

"She gave me more paper, and I started drawing everything in the room. The IV pole, the machines, the flowers from my parents. I was able to draw everything, down to the smallest details, like I'd been doing it all my life. After I was discharged, I went to the bookstore and bought every book they had on da Vinci. I studied all his pictures, diagrams, and sketches and started trying to copy them in my own hand. Mine weren't as good as his, obviously, but they weren't bad. My mother was so shocked that she thought someone else had sketched them.

"So I went out and bought an easel and a canvas and a bunch of paints. That's when I decided that you would be my Mona Lisa … even though you're a million times prettier than her. We just need to work on your smile."

"What's the matter with my smile? Everyone tells me I have a beautiful smile."

"You do, and you have those amazing dimples, but smiling doesn't come naturally to you, if you know what I mean."

"No, I don't…"

"Okay, let's forget about the smile for now. Do you want to be my subject? You could live on into eternity like Mona Lisa."

"I don't know how I feel about posing for a portrait. It's weird!"

"Fine, don't do it," I said, waving my hand. "I'll just find someone else. It won't be easy to find a girl as beautiful as you, but I'm sure if I travel to Italy or Spain I'll come close."

"I didn't say I wouldn't do it. I just said it seems weird. And you're not going to Italy or Spain to find another girl. You're all I have in this world," she said, suddenly choking up.

I looked at her, and then at our surroundings, and I started to think that maybe I *had* lost my mind. Before the flight down the stairs, I had always tried to keep in mind the horrible conditions that Angie had lived under since her mother's death five years earlier. Very few girls would have survived being in that hellhole with a drunk father and a bastard brother who was constantly trying to rape her. She was lucky she got out alive.

I reached over and gently pushed her loose hair back behind her ears and apologized.

She shook her head. "There's no reason for you to be sorry. You've always come to my rescue." She looked at me fiercely through eyes brimming with tears. "Do yourself a favor and walk out of here and don't look back. I'm just an albatross. You should go. Seriously. Please, just go."

"It's not that easy, Angie. I love you, and not having you in my life is unacceptable. I'm sorry, but I'm not going anywhere … even though I'm sure my jerk brother would love nothing more than for me to disappear so he could take my place."

She wiped her nose with her sleeve and laughed. "He's just a baby," she said. "He doesn't mean anything by it."

"Yeah, right. That little creep is obsessed with you."

"Okay, but he's also obsessed with his baseball cards."

"That might be true, but if he had to choose between you and them he'd throw the cards to the wind."

"He's a cutie."

"Yeah, he's a cutie all right. Let him find his own girlfriend. The little bastard wanted to come with me today. I told him you're only allowed one visitor at a time. He accused me of lying and said I was just scared you would pick him over me. I told him to stop dreaming and go play with his baseball cards."

"I think you might be exaggerating just a bit."

"Nope. He has pictures of you hidden in his card collection so he can pretend to be looking at Derek Jeter and really be staring at you."

"Really?"

"Yes, and it's not funny. I've decided, if you agree, that we shouldn't wait to finish college to get married. We should do it as soon as you get out of the women's center."

"Is this your way of proposing?" She started to cry again.

"I've said all along that I have every intention of marrying you. I just want to move the date up by four years. If I had the money I'd buy you an engagement ring, but I'll have to save up."

"But I don't know if I'll be ready to get married that soon."

"Why not?"

"You know why," she said, as tears flowed down her cheeks.

"And how many times have I told you I don't care?"

"You will at one point. It's not fair to you."

"Why don't you let me decide what's fair or not? I've never forced you to do anything and I never will, unless you're doing something to harm yourself. Then I would stop you."

She kept her head bowed as she continued to cry. I reached over and took her hand. "Angie, please. If I'm willing to take the risk, all I'm asking is for you to take a chance."

The guard knocked on the door and indicated that we had two minutes. Angie looked up at me and said, "Okay."

"Angie, please, please stay on script when you meet with the lawyers."

"I will, I promise."

CHAPTER THREE

Joe

I stepped onto the train and took a seat. The car was nearly empty. I leaned back and closed my eyes. As soon as I did, the same three Jimmy Durante songs that I'd heard in the hospital started playing in my head. Something about his voice made me smile. I liked to hear him sing about the simple ways people could make each other happy and stay young at heart. I even loved the old-timey string section and the soaring background vocals.

This little concert in the brain was exactly what I needed after seeing the girl of my dreams behind bars. The sight of her had been a shock. She was already skinny, and she must have dropped another ten pounds during her time at Rikers. Her lovely olive skin was lacking its usual high-density glow.

The songs suddenly stopped, and though I kept my eyes closed, it was like I could see the doors of the train opening and shutting at every stop while passengers came and went. I imagine I was dreaming or hallucinating from the concussion I'd suffered.

The train came to a stop and I was sure I saw Angie get up and exit the car at a stop I didn't know. I got up but not in time to leave the train before the doors closed. I started banging on the door, trying to get her attention, but she just kept walking and disappeared into a crowd.

I either woke up or the hallucination disappeared, and I could feel my heart racing. It was all so real, something I had feared since meeting the love of my life. I had always worried that one day, Angie would come to her senses and walk away from me and into the arms of another man.

None of my friends could believe that I wanted to stay with her. Even before she tried to kill me, she wasn't that well-liked by any of them. It didn't help that she called them a bunch of drunken losers, occasionally to their faces.

They thought she was good-looking, but not so special that any guy would give up his sanity to deal with her drama. And when I made the mistake of telling them that she'd never "put out," they laughed their butts off. I didn't mention that I'd never tried to get into her pants or for that matter ever really kissed her. There would have been no end to the teasing then.

It wasn't that Angie was asexual. I could see that anytime we went to a movie. She was obsessed with Paul Newman and Robert Redford. We would go to the repertoire theatre to see their movies, and if both of them were in the film, like in *The Sting* or *Butch Cassidy and the Sundance Kid*, she was pretty much a puddle. At first I got a bit jealous, but then I realized that if those two were on screen I got to eat more popcorn. That girl is a real hog when it comes to popcorn, but if she was staring at either of those hunks she'd forget to dig her hand into the bag until I was most of the way through it.

So yes, Angie had a sexual side, even if I'd never actually seen it, let alone benefited from it. And she could attract as many guys as any girl I've ever seen. But she went out of her way not to flirt, and if you saw her from behind you might think she was a little boy. She literally had no butt. In fact, my Angie looked best in her Catholic school uniform. At least in a dress there was no denying that she was a girl, and a beautiful one at that.

If it weren't for pure luck, I never would have had a chance with her. I just happened to be passing by when a grocery bag she was carrying broke open from the bottom and the food went all over the place. I helped her pick everything up and carry it home.

It wasn't the first time I'd seen Angie. I'd seen her plenty of times. If the rest of her was camouflaged by little boy clothes, at least she didn't disguise her face, and it was miraculous. If da Vinci asked me to describe the girl of my dreams and then painted her from my description, it would have been Angie before I ever even laid eyes on her.

I had passed her in the neighborhood a bunch of times, but I was too shy to say anything, and she walked right past me like I was invisible. This would have hurt if I was the only one she ignored, but I noticed that she didn't seem to pay attention to the other guys at school either. If someone had told me she was a lesbian or a nun-in-training, I would have believed it.

On that first day we talked, when her groceries went everywhere, I was thanking the Lord for weak paper bags and for putting me in the right place at the right time. We collected all the food off the ground, and I held onto most of it while she dealt with the other bags. She kept repeating, "Thank you so much, thank you so much…" as I cradled her loose groceries in my arms. I remember at least two bags of potato chips, a bunch of celery, a bunch of Kit Kats and a bag of apples.

At first she was going to bring the bags she was holding up to her apartment and come down to get the rest of the food, but I offered to follow her up so she wouldn't have to make two trips. She looked nervous but allowed it.

We got into the elevator and she pressed the button for the fifth floor. The whole way up, we looked everywhere but at each other. She opened the door to her apartment and I followed her in and she went back to repeating, "Thank you so much…"

"Don't mention it," I said, as I stood in the cramped entrance looking for a place to put down the food.

"Here," she said as she led me over to a card table in the living room that was set up in front of an old TV. She pushed aside a bunch of dishes and unopened mail to make room on the table, and as I put the food down she just stood there smiling at me stiffly like she wanted me to leave as soon as possible.

I finally asked, "Are you okay?" Just then her brother, Brian, stepped out of the bathroom into the living room. I could still hear the toilet running, which meant the pig didn't wash his hands. I could smell booze on his breath from three feet away, and by the way he was walking I could tell he was already drunk. He looked at me, then at Angie, and asked, "So who's your boyfriend?"

"This is Joe and he's not my boyfriend. He helped me carry the groceries upstairs after one of the bags broke..."

"Don't give me that shit, you little whore. You brought him up here to fuck you because you didn't think anyone was home. Isn't that right, bitch?" Then he pushed her so hard that she tumbled into the table and knocked everything over. The apples were heading for the floor when I shot out my hand and caught the bag in midair before gently setting it back on the table.

Angie's brother let out an evil little laugh as he looked at me and back at Angie. He raised his hand as though he was going to slap her, but just as he was about to make contact I grabbed his hand and pulled it back. This threw him off balance, and I hit him with a one-two combination to the face that sent him to the floor. He scrambled to his feet and started swinging at me and swearing and frothing at the mouth, but I overpowered him easily, and from there I lost all control. As he struggled on the floor I bent down and started punching him until blood was flying all over the place. Suddenly I stopped and yelled, "You cowardly motherfucker. You touch her again and I'll kill you. Got it?" He didn't say anything, so I kicked him and repeated the question, and he finally replied with a meek, "Yes."

I turned around and grabbed Angie's hand and led her out of the apartment and into the elevator. When it lurched into action, I looked at her and said, "Does he always treat you like that?"

She nodded silently.

"What about your parents? Do they put up with that?"

"My mother's dead."

"And your father?"

She just raised her eyebrows and looked off, which spoke volumes. When we stepped out of the elevator and into the lobby she looked at my shirt. Her eyes filled with worry. "There's blood all over you. I'm so sorry."

"Don't apologize. The asshole had it coming." She still looked worried but I thought I saw a little smile. Then I remembered what we'd left behind. "We should have taken the apples, at least," I said. "Want me to go back and get a few things? I could give him another smack in the head while I'm at it."

"No, that's okay," Angie said.

We walked in silence from her building to mine, which was less than five minutes away. We rode the elevator up and when I opened the door to my apartment and walked in, she stayed in the hallway. I reached across the threshold and took her hand and said, "Please, Angie, come inside." She looked uncertain but finally walked into the apartment, and I closed the door.

I guided her to the living room, gave her a glass of water, and left her sitting on a couch while I went into the bathroom to clean up. I tried to wipe off the blood with a hand towel, but there was just too much of it, so I took a quick shower and put on clean clothes. As I threw my blood-stained clothes into the hamper, I thought of the questions I'd be getting from my mother when she did the wash.

Back in the living room, I found Angie sitting in the exact spot where I'd left her, with her hands folded on her lap.

"Would you like something else to drink?" I asked.

"No, thank you. If I had money I'd buy you new clothes to replace the ones that got all bloody. I'm so sorry."

"Don't even worry about it! My mom is a champ when it comes to getting tough stains out of my clothes."

She stood up and said, "I've got to go."

"Where?"

"Home. I have to put the groceries away."

"Are you on drugs?"

"No, why would you think that?"

"Because if you go back there that asshole brother of yours will probably kill you. You're not going anywhere. You have as much chance of me letting you go back to that apartment as I do of becoming Walt Frazier."

"Who's that?"

"A famous guard for the New York Knicks during their glory years. It's been a long, frustrating ride ever since. You don't follow basketball?"

"No, but I'm sorry your team sucks."

"Considering all the problems in the world, it's pretty meaningless."

"I really can't stay here."

"Did you not hear anything I just said? You *have* to stay here. And if you have a problem with that you can call the police."

"I can't…"

"Oh yes you can, unless you have an aunt or uncle or a friend you can stay with?"

"I have no one," she replied, and at that moment I had a strange sense of relief. No one probably meant no boyfriend.

The door opened and my mother walked in pulling a wagon full of groceries. She looked at Angie and then at me and said, "Hope I'm not interrupting anything?"

"Not at all. This is Angie. If you don't mind, she's going to be staying with us for a while."

"Why?"

"Because her brother likes to beat the shit out of her and she has nowhere to go. He's a cowardly piece of garbage and I taught him a lesson he won't soon forget."

"Of course you did," my mother said suspiciously.

"You always taught us to stand up to bullies, especially the ones who hit girls."

"I'm proud of you, son," she said, then looked at Angie. "You can stay here as long as you like, Angie. I hate to think of the terrible situation you have been living under."

"Your son is the first person to ever help me out, but if I'm an inconvenience I can go somewhere else."

"Where?" I said. "You just told me you have nowhere to go."

"Sweetheart, you're going to stay right here," my mother said.

"Thank you," Angie said. She looked at the wagon near the door. "Can I help you put away your groceries?"

"No, sweetheart, why don't you just relax," my mom said, just as that little shit, also known as my baby brother Stephen, walked into the apartment. My mother introduced him to Angie and told him she would be staying with us for a while.

I should have known from that first moment that he would be my chief rival for the girl of my dreams. Right out of the box he was already hitting on her. He perched on the couch and asked her, "Would you like to see my baseball card collection?"

Angie looked at my mother for approval and naturally my mom, not suspecting anything, said, "Go ahead, Angie."

She followed my brother down the hall to our room and a second later I could actually hear the love of my life laughing. I could barely get a word out of her, and already he had her in stitches. My mother turned to me and said, "She's a beautiful girl. Is what you told me the truth?"

"Yes. Why would I lie about such a thing?"

"Because you want me to let her stay. Because you're in love with her."

Well, there was no denying that, but it didn't take long for my parents to decide that she was greatest thing since sliced mozzarella. Angie cooked, cleaned, and was a great student. And to top it all off, she got to sleep in my bed in the room I shared with the little shithead, while I took the couch. Surely, my parents would never even consider letting a teenage boy and girl sleep in the same room, even with the door wide open. Instead, the ten-year-old pervert got to sleep in the room with her.

I was thinking about all of this during the train ride home from Rikers, and then suddenly I was at my stop. I got off the train and started walking toward my building. Every step felt like a chore, and when I saw a bench I took the opportunity to sit. I closed my eyes and tried to empty my head of everything, but as soon as I did, those three Jimmy Durante songs started up again. They were so clear it was like I was hearing them on the radio. With my eyes still closed, I started to sway to the beat of "Smile," and then suddenly the music stopped and my cellphone rang, and it was my psychotic girlfriend.

"Hello," I answered.

"Hi Joe, I did exactly what you told me and they've already moved me to the new place on Long Island. I just got here. It's real nice and I share an apartment with a lady named Gloria who's very sweet. She killed her abusive boyfriend by cutting his you-know-what off and then sticking it in his mouth."

"Testicles, penis, the whole thing?"

"Yes, and she videotaped the whole thing, but they confiscated it. She'll tell you about it when you come and see me tomorrow. You're coming, right?"

"Of course…" I said.

"You're not going to go out with your useless friends and get drunk and forget about me, are you?"

"No!" I exclaimed, suddenly irritated.

"You promise? I need you more than ever. I love you so much. They have visiting hours from eleven in the morning to eight at night. If you come at exactly eleven we can spend the whole day together. It's pretty easy to get here. You take the number six train to Penn Station, and at the station you buy a round-trip ticket on the Long Island Railroad and get off at Stony Brook station. It's about a mile and a half from the station on foot, but since you love walking it'll be a breeze for you. I figure if you leave there by eight and don't fiddle around you should get here by eleven."

"What's the name of the place?"

"Women's Correctional Center," she said. "I'm only allowed one phone call per day for the first two weeks I'm here, so please don't make me use it up trying to track you down tomorrow."

"I'll do my best."

"Joe, please. I need you…"

The nerve of this girl, after trying to kill me and having me cover for her ... Now she was making demands that were outrageous. "Make sure you don't go out with your useless friends," and "Don't make me use up my one phone call trying to track you down."

If it weren't for me, she would be serving twenty years at Rikers. "Please, I need you, you're all I have." The girl was simply amazing. Whoever said love is bliss never met my Angie. God, if I wasn't so in love with her I'd show up an hour or two late tomorrow, just to piss her off.

She sounded so desperate. I closed my eyes and shook my head. At first, I'd had my doubts about Angie being in love with me, but as time went on I was fairly sure she was. Certainly not with the same intensity that I loved her, but after what this girl had lived through, it was no wonder she was suspicious of men.

Usually, after walking out of a movie theater she would talk excitedly about our future together. She wanted to live by the ocean, in a place like Malibu or Santa Barbara. Of course, we never thought about how much money you needed to live in such places. But then, they were dreams ... happy dreams ... and the cold realities of life did not figure into them.

Now those realities were hitting me in the face. My lovely Angie was stone cold nuts. And why should this surprise me? Could it actually be any other way? She had fit so neatly into the tapestry of my life; I fell madly in love with her, based solely on her looks. Did I actually think such wondrous beauty would come my way without a price? Of course not. I never gave it any serious thought. And why? Because from afar she was perfect? I had already endowed her with a lovely, caring, and charming personality, even though I had never even seen her smile or acknowledge the existence of anybody else on the planet.

I closed my eyes and remembered what my grandmother used to say: that God would "never put anything before you that you cannot overcome." I wonder if she'd still say that if she'd met Angie. Then again, I did beg and pray to God to give me a chance with her, and he gave me what I asked for, so I couldn't blame Him. He was off the hook, and I was seriously screwed.

CHAPTER FOUR

Joe

The following morning, I left for the correctional center at 7:30, took the number six to Penn Station, boarded the Long Island train to Stony Brook Station, and arrived just before 10:00. A passenger gave me directions to the center, which he said was about a half-hour walk, or a ten-minute bus ride. Since I had plenty of time, I walked.

It was an unusually warm day in early March, and the scenery was quite beautiful. I arrived at the gate at 10:30, but the guard wouldn't let me in until 11:00. Through the chain-link fence surrounding the center, I could see housing units that looked like rows of army barracks from a war movie. The grounds were neatly landscaped, and in the distance I could see a pond and a park. This was already a million times better than Rikers.

At exactly 11:00, the guard checked my name off a list and told me the expecting inmate was in room number 33. I knocked on the door and a tall, Black lady opened the door almost immediately. She was extremely pretty, with high cheekbones and a regal air, and she was dressed in a silk blouse and black jeans. I couldn't tell how old she was. Maybe late twenties or early thirties.

"Hi," I said. "Are you the psychiatrist?"

"No, silly. I'm Gloria." She extended one manicured hand and as I took it I felt my hand disappear inside her confident grasp.

"Angie's roommate?"

"That's right. And you must be Angie's prince charming."

I laughed and told her my name.

"Well, come on in, Joe, unless you'd rather stay on the stoop."

I walked into the apartment, which was a simple but pleasant space with a tiny kitchen and a living room with two love seats and two chairs.

Gloria gestured to one of the love seats, and I sat down. She brought me a glass of water and sat across from me on the other sofa, crossing her legs and sizing me up with her placid gaze.

"Your princess is cleaning up. She said she wanted to look especially good for you today."

"I love her just the way she is."

"That's sweet."

"It's the truth."

"Good."

"You sure you're not the psychiatrist? I feel like I'm being studied."

"No, Joe, I'm not the psychiatrist. But I do know you've got your hands full in this situation."

"What do you mean?"

"Only that if you really love Angie, you'll need to be very gentle and patient with her—"

"I am—"

"Joe, listen to me," she said. "I've been here nearly two years. I've seen a lot of girls come and go. Some of them in body bags. I'm here to tell you that your little Angie is a fragile flower whose roots don't run very deep."

"Is this place not safe?"

"No, it's plenty safe, but it doesn't stop some girls from doing themselves in. Just be supportive of her because, as of now, you're all she has."

"I know."

"Good."

I reflected for a beat and tried to change the subject. "So, you've been here quite a while?"

"You could say that. I refuse to repent for my actions or see the error of my ways. The day I cut off my boyfriend's penis was one of the happiest days of my life."

"Is that so?" My throat went dry, and I took a sip of water.

"Yes, and it was also a service to others."

"How so?"

"Well, I thought I was the only one he was drugging and raping, but it turned out he had a taste for much younger girls. They found thousands of pictures on his computer, including videos that he shot himself with girls under thirteen."

"Jesus."

"That's right. I did it for Jesus," — that got a laugh, which I think she appreciated — "and for my own peace of mind. I couldn't have lived, knowing what I knew and having suffered what I suffered, if I let him stay in the world."

"How did you end up with him in the first place?"

"We met in the ER at Harlem General. He came in with a gash on his neck, and I was the poor sucker who patched him up and fell for him, all in about fifteen minutes."

"Wow."

"Now, of course, I wonder if the cut was put there by one of his victims. If only she'd managed to slice open his jugular, I would never have met the bastard. I'd still be living my life."

"You couldn't tell he was a monster when you first met him?"

"Oh gosh no. That's the thing about psychopaths. They're charming as hell. In fact, I know now that if someone seems incredibly special within the first five minutes of meeting them, that's a reason to run."

I nodded, and asked, "What was so charming about him?"

"Oh, everything. The crooked smile, the Armani suit, the way he love-bombed me from the get go, calling me a goddess, complimenting me on my stitching technique, my jawline, my décolletage … he was relentless."

I nodded and she continued. "He also had a great job as a senior analyst with one of the big investment houses in New York. I thought he was the whole package. My parents even liked him. My dad, who worked for the New York Stock Exchange, said he thought Darian was a lion in his field."

"So he managed to pull the wool over their eyes, too."

"Exactly."

"Your dad sounds like an influential guy. Can't he get you out of here?"

"Let's just say my parents are both still 'processing' what happened. My father has started drinking a lot, and my mother said she understands my motives but not my methods. I think she found the whole episode a bit … grisly."

"I see."

Gloria smiled, got up, and slid down next to me on the love seat. Then she took out her cell phone.

"I taped the whole thing, but the feds took my only copy. One nice officer from the child sexual exploitation division let me keep a few screen shots. He told me privately that he thought I should have been given a medal."

She called up an image of a very handsome and fit looking man lying spread eagle on a four-poster bed. Both arms and legs were tied to the railings, and he looked like he was out cold. Gloria held up the image for me to admire, then scrolled to a close-up of a cart covered in surgical instruments.

"Wow!" I said, looking at the cart, with its neat rows of scalpels and scissors. "You were well prepared."

"I was the head nurse in the ER at Harlem General for ten years," she said. "I pride myself on organization."

The third image was too blurry to really make out what was going on, but it looked like the man had been given a tattoo around his privates.

"What's that?" I asked.

"Well, mapping out the surgery is very important."

"Was he ... awake for any of this?"

"Oh, eventually, yes. After the first deep gash he woke up screaming. I believe his exact words were, 'What are you doing, you fucking bitch?'"

"And you filled him in?"

"Yes. I told him I was just performing a little surgery to help remove the stain of his existence from the planet."

"Wow. Was it hard to do?"

"Was what hard to do?"

"The surgery, I guess. All of it."

"Not at all. Cutting along the line was as easy as cutting through a New York steak. But it did get messy. There was quite a lot of blood, and he was screaming and cursing and frantically trying to break loose. Then he went quiet as I lifted his entire genitals off his body and the blood stopped gushing forth."

I couldn't help it; I closed my eyes tightly and waved off the images with my hands until Gloria finally stopped talking.

"The bastard deserved it," she said, a little haughtily. "I only wish he hadn't checked out so soon. I wanted him to suffer long and hard like he made me and those other girls suffer."

She put the phone down and held my gaze. "I hope you realize that this isn't just a casual case of show and tell."

I was feeling a little woozy, but I managed to say, "It's not?"

"No, Joe. Please keep up."

"What is it, then?"

"I've grown very fond of Angie in the short time we've been here together."

"That's good. I'm happy—"

"I also have very little to lose."

"Is that so?"

"Yup. And here's the point, prince. What I did to that psychotic pervert could be exactly what's in store for you if you ever abuse the clueless, skinny-ass child who has been in there making herself pretty for you for well over an hour."

"But I'm the one who saved her—"

"Stop it! Just stop it."

I shut my hole, as instructed, and felt myself sinking further into the couch. I took a drink of water to keep my mouth occupied.

"I've seen plenty of saviors turn into abusers. You touch that child and I will gladly use my superb skills on your precious shrimpy, and that's not a threat but a promise. Understand?"

"Yes," I said meekly.

I was sitting there in obedient silence when Angie walked back into the room and Gloria tucked her phone by her side.

"It's about time, baby girl," Gloria said. "Come on over here. Let me see."

Angie walked into the center of the room and turned around.

"Hmm," Gloria said. "You would think with all the time you spend dolling yourself up you would look like Grace Kelly."

"You don't think I look nice?" Angie asked.

"Sweetheart, with a face like yours, you are always going to look beautiful. It's the rest of you that needs work."

"Work?" Angie asked.

Gloria continued to tease her. "You're just a bit on the scrawny side."

I turned to Angie and said, "Well, I think you look gorgeous."

"Thank you, Joe," she said as she kissed me on the cheek. Then she turned to Gloria and said, "Joe's going to paint a portrait of me. That's why I took so long."

"A portrait?" Gloria asked suspiciously. "What kind?"

"What type of portrait is it, Joe?" Angie asked, as I tried to wiggle out of the conversation.

"Whatever type you want," I said.

"Oh, for God's sake, don't give her a choice," Gloria said.

"Well, I think it might be better if we start by painting my face and see how that goes."

"Sweetheart, I didn't bring my easel and tools with me. I thought you wanted to wait until you settled in and got used to your new surroundings."

"Oh," she said, lowering her eyes.

"For gosh sakes, Angie, your prince charming traveled two and a half hours to see you. Surely, you have plenty to talk about and a whole bunch of smooching to catch up on."

"She's right, Joe. I have a lot to show you, and we can sit by the pond and watch the ducks. Would you like to come, Gloria?"

"Not this time, angel, but thank you."

Angie went back into the bedroom to get a jacket, and Gloria turned to me and leveled me with her gaze.

"Remember what I told you?" she said. "Gentle and patient. And if you lay a hand on her you'll end up like my ex-boyfriend. Except, this time I'll do the surgery quicker and stick your manhood where the sun don't shine."

CHAPTER FIVE

Joe

I didn't want to tell Angie that my intellectual prowess and creativity had been flagging over the last few days. I was hoping they would make a comeback, and that I could at least do her portrait. That's what I get for bragging about myself.

Angie showed me around the center, and I had to admit that it was a pretty sweet setup. It had a nice-sized library that was equipped with plenty of computers for students like Angie who wanted to finish high school and come out with a degree. Angie only had one semester to go, and it was a relief to know that she could finish while serving her sentence.

They also had a movie theater that showed mostly old movies, a restaurant, a small clothing store, a drugstore, and a medical facility. We walked to the drugstore and I bought Angie some granola bars in case she got hungry at night and two boxes of sanitary pads. Then I bought an outdoor blanket that we could sit on as we watched the ducks.

We took the blanket over to the pond and spread it out on a grassy slope next to where the ducks were waddling around. It was quite pretty, and we were by ourselves, except for a few inmates walking by. I asked Angie what she had done that morning and she told me she'd seen the psychiatrist.

"And how did that go?"

"Okay, I guess. I told her about my crazy family and about how bad things were at home after my mom died."

"You didn't happen to tell her about pushing me down the stairs, or about going after your father when you finished off your brother?"

"No, we didn't get that far," she said.

"Good. You can't mention any of that, do you understand?"

"Why not? She said the only way I'll get better is if I'm honest."

"Because if you tell her either of those things, you're going to be here for a very long time."

"But why? She said everything we talked about was private and just between her and me. There's doctor-patient privilege…"

"Yes, but she'll have the final say on when you're able to leave here, and if you tell her the whole story, she's not going to want to authorize your release. What you tell her might be privileged, but it'll have a huge effect on the evaluations she submits to the center. Angie, you can't mention it. Do you understand?"

"But she's going to bring it up. What do I do then?"

"You tell her I slipped and that it was you who called the ambulance, which you did, and that by doing so you saved my life."

I could see that Angie was getting stressed out. She stared at me like she was about to share a big secret.

"I have terrible nightmares every time I fall sleep. They're all about that night, and they always end with me pushing you over the railing. I wake up covered in sweat."

"Sweetheart, I forgave you. I know the type of stress you were under. You understood you did the wrong thing, and you called the ambulance. You saved my life."

She went quiet and leaned against my chest. Then she fished through our bag from the drugstore and took out a granola bar. She unwrapped it, broke off a little piece, and threw it into the pond, and at least twenty ducks went after it at the same time. Angie sat up and watched them.

"Maybe I'm better off staying here and never leaving," she said, not looking at me. "That way I can't hurt anyone else."

"And what about our dreams and plans for the future? Are you going to let your brother and father rob us of those, too?"

She started to cry as she put her head back on my chest. I edged back and lay down on the blanket and she literally climbed on top of me and lay there, still crying. This was the most intimate we had ever been, and without sounding too much like a pervert, it was the first time I could verify that she actually had breasts. Granted, they weren't very large, but they were definitely there.

After about ten minutes of nonstop crying, she fell asleep. She was so light that it was more like having a blanket on top of me than a person, and after a few more minutes, I dozed off, too.

We woke up at what seemed like the same time, and looked into each other's eyes like never before, and before I could say a word her lips were pressed against mine and we were seriously going at it. And then the most bizarre thing happened — bizarre only because it was Angie. She started to pull down her pants, and then went to work on my buckle.

I don't know what came over me, but I grabbed both her hands and asked, "What are you doing?"

She looked at me and said, "You deserve to have me. I've never given you anything. You shouldn't have to wait any longer."

I didn't know what to say, so I just wrapped my arms around her and held her loosely as I patted her back with one hand. Apart from that I was as still as a statue.

"Angie, honey, I'm going to need you to pull up your pants."

"What? Why? Did I do something wrong?"

"No, Ang, you didn't do anything wrong. Please, just get dressed."

She hovered there for a few seconds, then let out a little sigh and rolled over and pulled up her pants. I stood up and tucked in my shirt and re-attached my belt.

She sat on the grass, staring down at her hands. "Do you not find me attractive anymore?" I had never heard her sound so pitiful.

"Angie, shush. You're the most beautiful girl I've ever seen. But this is not the place or time that I want to remember as the first time we made love."

"Is it because I have no ass?"

"You're joking, right?"

She laughed nervously and I took her into my arms again and said, "I don't deserve you. I'm blessed that you're in my life."

We rolled up the blanket and I took her to the small restaurant that had been set up for visitors. It was quite clean, with six tables, and its menu consisted of burgers, hot dogs, salads and French fries.

The waitress was a fellow inmate who looked like she was a few years older than us. She took our order and walked away. Angie just sat there with her head lowered, running her hands up and down her thighs. I had never seen her do this before, but then today had held several firsts. I ducked my head down to meet her eyes and said, "Hey, you."

"Hey."

"What's wrong?"

"I just feel so stupid and embarrassed."

"Please don't feel that way. You have nothing to be embarrassed about."

She flashed a quick look at me and said, "I really don't know what I would do if I didn't have you."

I sat on that, not knowing what to say. After a little while I said, "How's it going with Gloria? I like her. You two seem to get along really well."

"Gloria's great. But she can never be you."

"Well, no…"

"In that dream I have, after pushing you over the railing, I run down the stairs after you, and when I get to you, you're already dead. And they place you on a gurney and put a sheet over your face and roll you away."

"But that didn't happen."

"But it could have. I still don't know how you could forgive me so easily."

"I told you how," I said, my voice suddenly rising. "How many times do I have to tell you?"

"Please don't yell at me," she said. Her eyes were suddenly full of tears and her shoulders began to shake.

I pushed down a flash of irritation, then reached over and lifted her chin up. She looked at me again before averting her eyes like a dog about to be punished. The tears were falling hard now, and I remembered Gloria's words: "She's a fragile flower with weak roots. You have to be very gentle and patient with her." I softly wiped the tears away and waited for the storm to pass.

CHAPTER SIX

Joe

Angie had clung to me so tightly that in just the last few hours I had touched parts of her body that I wasn't sure I would ever see or touch, even after we got married. I wish I could say it was sensual, but it wasn't. It was more like suffocating.

I had always felt that of all the people I knew, Angie was the one most likely to commit suicide, despite her pledge that she would never do such a thing. It was like every time she sent the knife through her brother's lifeless body, she was also aiming it at herself. I seriously believed that if I had not wandered up there that night, she not only would have killed her brother, but also her father and then herself.

In an attempt to get Angie's mind off whatever she was thinking, I decided to go into the library and pick out a book. I went looking for anything I could find about our favorite coastal communities and ended up with a coffee table book called *Ocean Paradises in the United States*.

Back in her apartment, we sat down at a table and started flipping through the book together. She snuggled up against me as I turned the pages and stopped at a picture of a beach in Santa Barbara, California, with the Santa Ynez Mountains in the background. Angie had always said that of all the towns and cities in the US, Santa Barbara would be her first choice. She was certain that she could live happily ever after there. I said, "Look, our future home."

When she didn't respond, I looked at her and realized that she was sound asleep. It was like the life was sucked out of me, not so much because she was asleep, but because she looked so hopeless. I lowered my eyes and looked at the beautiful pictures and realized that even though both of us were only eighteen years old, it felt like we had no future. It was like the pain and fear that this beautiful girl had been living with for the last six years was trickling directly into me.

CHAPTER SEVEN

Joe

At 7:59 p.m. I walked out the gates of the center. They were very strict about visitors being gone by eight. I had decided earlier in the day to get a room in a motel about a half-mile from the center. I was physically and mentally exhausted and I didn't have it in me to travel three hours back to the Bronx only to turn back around in the morning and make the same trip to the center. She had made me promise at least ten times that I would come back the next day, and I figured this would be a lot easier.

As I walked to the motel, I was sure of two things: My Angie was in a bad place emotionally (how she survived one month at Rikers was totally beyond me), and it would be nearly impossible for me to make this trip back and forth every day from the Bronx to the center and back again. I had been working since I was twelve years old and had my own bank account with nearly $10,000 in it. I had to get an apartment, close to the center, and I really could not afford more than $500 a month in rent because when I added in things like food, transportation, clothes, and laundry, I would be spending at least $1,000 a month, and my savings wouldn't last long.

I also knew that when I told my mother of this plan she would go crazy, and rightfully so. Before Angie went on her killing spree, my mother thought that God, personally, had sent her to our family. She looked like an angel and acted like one, too. She cooked, shopped, cleaned, did laundry, and helped get my weirdo of a baby brother ready for school in the morning. Then everything changed, and she went from a godly angel to Lucifer. My guess is that she told my mother she pushed me over the railing, and that set my mother off. Not only did she never want to see Angie again, but the idea that I was still planning on marrying her was beyond anything she could accept.

I walked into my motel room, which was nothing to brag about. At eighty-five dollars a night I was just happy that I had a functioning bathroom and a bed that didn't seem to have any roaches walking across the sheets.

I called my mother and told her of my plans, and of course she read me the riot act. After raising me to be responsible, I was doing just the opposite. There were a million girls out there; surely I could find one that wasn't a murderer or a lunatic. She went on and on, and I never interrupted her or challenged her. Every point she made was valid, if somewhat exaggerated. Finally, she got tired of repeating herself in the void, and the call ended with both of us saying we loved each other.

While checking in at the desk, I picked up a free copy of a real estate newsletter. I scanned the rentals and from the start it was quite discouraging. Almost everything was either a house or a two-bedroom apartment and the cheapest was $1,200 a month, plus first and last month's rent and a security deposit. I would be wiped out in three months. Further down there were one-bedroom apartments, but they didn't list prices, which was never a good sign. The good thing about all of them was that they were close to Stony Brook University, and both Angie and I had already sent in our applications and both been accepted, with the possibility of financial aid.

I circled all the one-bedroom apartments, put the newsletter on the night table, and lay down in the darkened room. Pretty soon I was going over every detail of the day and starting to wonder what my responsibilities were when it came to Angie. She was a basket case, and it wasn't so much about love anymore as it was about pure pity and guilt.

She'd wanted that Christmas Eve to be special because, since her mother died over five years earlier, the holiday had become a nightmare for her, with her drunken brother and father at their worst. She didn't want any gifts from me ... just the gift of staying sober on that one holiday, and I failed.

Even after she pushed me over the coffee table in my family's apartment, I begged her not to go back to her father's apartment. Naturally, she had a different take on the whole episode. She said I hit her hard in the stomach while she was trying to help me up, and that the idea of smashing something over my head was absurd.

Whatever really happened, at some point she stormed out. I followed her to her father's apartment and begged her repeatedly not to go in there and she replied, "Why? Either way, I get hit ... either by my drunken boyfriend or my drunken family."

The six months she'd lived with us were some of the happiest times of my life, even if my younger brother got to spend more time with her than I did. Waking up every morning and seeing that beautiful creature walking into the kitchen was like heaven and coming home from school knowing she would be there was miraculous.

I tried to do what she asked. I drank less than I had at any point since I started drinking at fifteen. I spent less time with my friends, and since she had no friends that I knew of, it was just the two of us. I always let her choose the movies we went to, and sat there silently while she got off looking at Newman and Redford, knowing that I wouldn't even be able to kiss her at the end of the night.

My friends thought I was crazy. "Sure," they would say, "she's pretty, but then there are a hundred pretty girls who walk by the basketball court every day ... who aren't stuck up and who enjoy drinking and partying."

In Angie's defense, there was no way she was stuck up. Traumatized, definitely, but stuck up? No way. Stuck up was for debutantes. I'd fallen for a girl with serious issues and a family that was as messed up as they get. And now, I was paying the price.

CHAPTER EIGHT

Joe

I woke up early, took a shower, and cleaned up as best I could considering my abrupt change in plans. I let the front desk know that I was keeping the room for another night, and before going to see Angie I planned on buying some new clothes and toiletries. But first I needed to go to the bank and take out money. After that I was going to hit all of the one-bedroom apartments I'd circled in the real estate newsletter.

Naturally, just as I was about to walk out of the room my phone rang. It was Angie, and as usual she was upset and worried. I lay back down on the bed and just listened. Since I wouldn't allow her to tell the psychiatrist the whole truth about that infamous night, she had to tell someone, so she told Gloria, who swore she wouldn't tell anyone. She also told Gloria how she tried to seduce me by the pond. Gloria was impressed with my restraint and said I was the type of man a woman could only dream of, but that she was quite sure Angie would screw everything up and that once I opened my eyes to how crazy she was I would be gone in a blink of an eye.

Even though Gloria said she was only joking about me being gone in a blink of an eye — after all, if I was this loyal to her so far, I was definitely in it for the long term — Angie wasn't so sure anymore. I tried to tell her she had nothing to worry about and that I would never walk away, but then I made the mistake of telling her I would be a few hours late getting to the center, and that set off another round of insanity.

Over and over, she said, "But you promised, you promised. You really do plan on leaving me, don't you?"

"No, Angie, I have no intention of ever leaving you…"

And she just kept cutting me off and would not let me explain. "This is the way it always starts, with little things like showing up late and then not at all."

Finally, I got so frustrated that I yelled at her to let me explain. That shut her up for a moment and I went on to explain that I was going to look at one-room apartments in the area so that I would be closer to her and cut down on traveling.

"And how do you plan on paying the rent and all the other expenses?"

"If I find the right apartment at the right price I'll be able to survive for quite a while."

"I don't want you spending all your money just so you can have an apartment close to me."

"Do you have a better idea? Because it costs me nearly forty dollars a day to travel back and forth to the Bronx to visit you."

"No, I don't have a better idea. I simply need you, Joe. I need you. I'm sorry."

"There is no reason to be sorry. I need you, too."

She started crying and then she realized that she was late for her appointment with her psychiatrist, so she hung up and ran off.

CHAPTER NINE

Joe

I stopped off at the bank and took out $500 in cash in case I found something reasonable and had to hold it with a down payment. I then walked past the Smith Haven Mall and turned onto Stony Brook Road. It was a beautiful street, and I could not even imagine how much the homes went for in this area. The lots were huge — the type one might expect in a more rural area like upstate New York. The landscaping was gorgeous, and the houses were all large and beautiful.

The first one-bedroom apartment I looked at was built above a garage, and it was very nice. It had that new-construction smell of freshly cut lumber. They were asking $1,400 a month, plus first and last month's rent up front and a $500 security deposit. I took the flyer and told them I might be back.

The next four apartments I looked at were also built over garages. The further I went down the road, closer to the Long Island Sound, the more expensive the apartments became. This made sense, because everyone wants to live close to the water and the smell of salty air. After my fourth and worst case of sticker shock I stumbled out onto the street, which was devoid of sidewalks, and suddenly realized that I was dehydrated. I tried to keep walking but finally sat down on the edge of someone's lawn.

I lowered my head. It was already past eleven o'clock and I just knew Angie was back at the center flipping out. It didn't matter how often I reassured her; if she got it into her head that I was lying to her, and that this was the beginning of an elaborate plan to finally leave her, she would obsess about it. It was hard to believe that not that long ago she'd seemed rational, logical and a million times smarter than me. From the way she was acting you would think that she was the one who tumbled down the stairs and suffered a concussion.

Suddenly I thought about my mother and saw the whole situation from her point of view. My mother loved her children as much as any mother could. She worked a full-time job, putting in as many hours as my father did, just to give us everything we needed. What loving mother wouldn't be worried about her son planning to marry an unstable, unpredictable girl who, in a moment of rage, had tried to kill her baby boy?

It was hopeless, and as I lowered my head and closed my eyes I could feel my eyes filling with tears. And then suddenly I felt a presence behind me — an indefinable presence that seemed to want to freeze me in the position I was in forever. I was struggling to move and couldn't even lift my own hand off my leg when I heard a man's voice say, "Are you okay, young man?"

The voice was gentle and pious and seemed to release me from my bondage. I turned — relieved to be able to move — and looked up at a tall man with neat silver hair and a chiseled face. His eyes were a deep blue, and in their reflection I could swear I saw a history of the world.

I quickly stood up and began apologizing for sitting on his property, but he held up his hand and smiled.

"It's not your fault they forgot to put sidewalks on this road. Are you all right? Would you like something to drink?"

"No! No! I'm fine," I said as I folded the real estate newsletter in my hand.

"Looking for a place to rent?" he asked.

"Yeah, but not in this neighborhood. It's much too rich for me."

"Come," he said. "I have a place out back that I feel you might really like."

For a second I wondered if I had stumbled upon a Long Island axe murderer, but his manner put me at ease, so I followed him, even though I knew I could never afford what he had to offer. We passed by the main house, a colonial style mansion that had a view of the Long Island Sound from the back deck.

The apartment he had for rent was behind the main house and was its own freestanding structure. It looked like a Cape Cod style cottage, with newer cedar shingles and a pair of window boxes out front, full of blue flowers. He opened the door and we entered a bright, open-concept living room with high ceilings and two large bay windows overlooking the front lawn. He told me to look around as he sat down on a couch in the living room and flipped through a newspaper that was sitting on a side table. As I moved beyond the large living room I discovered that the house was fully furnished, with three large bedrooms, three bathrooms, and a modern kitchen with French doors that overlooked a large swimming pool.

"This place is absolutely beautiful, but believe me, it's so far out of my price range that there is no way."

"Why don't you take a seat, Joe?"

"How did you know my name?"

"You have it written on the top of your newsletter: 'Joe's apartment search,'" he said as I looked down at the newsletter and there it was.

"And what's your name?" I asked.

"Laurence," he replied as we stood up and shook hands. "How does two hundred dollars a month sound?"

"You're joking, right?"

"No!"

"You could easily get three thousand a month for this place. I've been looking at one-bedroom apartments, all built above garages, and they've been going for fourteen to seventeen hundred a month."

"That sounds awfully high."

"It's the neighborhood. It's beautiful around here."

"I'll tell you what, two-hundred and twenty-five dollars a month, and I'll pay for all the utilities and that's my final offer."

"What's the catch?" I asked suspiciously.

"There is one catch," he said.

I let out a small sigh and muttered, "I knew it," then immediately felt like a jerk and apologized.

He laughed and said he understood. I noticed that the light coming through one of the bay windows was creating a halo effect around his silver head. The sun was glowing all around him when he said, "It's less of a catch than a job."

"Okay…" I said, eyeing him nervously.

"I would expect you to drive me to the cemetery each morning to visit my wife. I'll introduce the two of you. I have no doubt you'll get along great. You do have a driver's license?"

"Yes, but I don't have a car."

"Not a problem. You can use any one of mine you like. And another thing: When you go shopping, I'd greatly appreciate it if you took me along. You see, I failed the eye test when I went to renew my license. Personally, I don't think there's anything wrong with my eyes, but I don't want to break the law."

"And this is all on the up-and-up?"

"Most definitely, Joe," he said as he handed me the key to the house.

"Well, at least let me pay the first month's rent."

"Don't worry about that. We can settle up later. Why don't you buy your girlfriend a nice bouquet of flowers?"

"My girlfriend…"

"Surely, a guy as good-looking as you has a girlfriend."

"Yes, but after I tell you about her, you might want to back out of this deal."

"I doubt that, but why don't you tell me about her anyway."

I was sure that this law-abiding man would want me out of the house as soon as he found out about my psycho-killer girlfriend. It was better to rip the Band-Aid off now.

"My girlfriend is an inmate in the Women's Correctional Center about a mile from here. Her brother tried to rape her, and she stabbed him like twenty times…" When his expression barely changed, I looked in his eyes and added, "…to death. She's a killer. She killed her brother."

Mr. Laurence nodded and said, "But you still love her?"

"I do. I'll always love her. From the moment I saw her I prayed to God for a chance to meet her and talk to her. Her father and brother abused her for years before she snapped. I'm all she has. Her mother died, and there's literally no one else."

"Well, it's a good thing she has you, isn't it?"

"I guess so."

He just stood there looking at me with such a mild expression on his face that I felt like he was waiting for me to keep talking, so I did.

"She's in a bad place, emotionally," I said. "I'm always scared she'll hurt herself. I have daydreams where I find her—"

Mr. Laurence closed his eyes and nodded as if he knew exactly what I was saying. I shook off the emotion and got to the point. "If they ever release her, she'd have to come to live with me, and I don't know how wild you'd be about that."

Mr. Laurence — I was already thinking of him as *Mr.* Laurence, even though he hadn't told me whether it was his first or last name — raised one hand as if to quiet my fears. He spoke slowly and deliberately. "My wife, who I was married to for an eternity, came from an abusive family, and eventually she was placed with a loving and caring foster family. In fact, the large house where I live now is the same house she was raised in by her foster parents. You're a good man, Joe, and you and your girlfriend are lucky to have each other. Whenever she's set free she is more than welcome to come live here."

"That's — wow." I shook my head in disbelief. "Thank you."

"Of course."

"I'm sorry about your wife. I can't imagine how hard it must be to be in love for such a long time and then lose that person."

"I haven't lost her, Joe. I visit her every day."

"At the cemetery?"

"Yes, at the cemetery. After we got married, she and her sister decided they wanted to move back here to be with their parents. I'm referring to their foster parents, of course, but they were Mom and Dad, without question, and the house that this one is attached to was the first place they felt safe and loved."

"Where did you live before moving back here?" I asked.

"In Southern California."

"Along the coast?"

"Santa Barbara."

"That's where Angie wants to live, in Santa Barbara. Every time she sees pictures or video of it she gets so excited. In her mind, it's paradise. It's the one place where she believes she can find peace and happiness."

"She'll only find peace and happiness there if she has you beside her. The sunrises and sunsets might be beautiful, but they'll only remain beautiful as long as she has someone to share them with."

I looked into his eyes and saw reflected in them the most beautiful, seductive, dark-haired goddess I had ever seen. She had green eyes that sparkled like emeralds, and yes, she was even more beautiful than my Angie from before she jumped into that swirling pool of insanity.

I was so mesmerized that I didn't hear Mr. Laurence speaking. Finally, I snapped out of it and heard him ask me if I wanted to drive one of his cars over to the Women's Correctional Center. I replied, "Have you always been so trusting with strangers?"

"You're no stranger, Joe. I knew you were trustworthy the moment I found you sitting on the edge of the lawn. You were about to burst into tears, and a strong, young man from the Bronx just doesn't burst into tears unless he's filled with compassion."

I didn't bother asking him how he knew I was from the Bronx. At that moment, I was beyond asking why or how when it came to Mr. Laurence. In fact, I wasn't even sure I was awake.

He opened his garage door and there before us were two Ferraris, one black and one red, a Rolls-Royce, and a blue Malibu Classic from the seventies in mint condition.

"Which one would you like to drive?"

"The Malibu, please."

"Good choice. The other cars might be more stylish, but the Malibu is like a desert tank. It's reliable, and it gets you to your destination and back without any problems."

He handed me the keys and I got into the car as he leaned in through the open window and said, "Don't forget to stop by the flower shop at the corner. I recommend a bouquet of white lotus for your beautiful Angie, and maybe six yellow roses for her roommate. Yellow roses symbolize friendship, so Angie need not get jealous, and in turn, it will make her roommate feel good."

I drove slowly out of the garage. Yes, I had my driver's license, and had driven my father's car a number of times, but in no way, shape, or form was I a polished driver. I turned onto the street, and it suddenly felt like I had been driving for twenty years. I stopped at the florist and bought a bouquet of white lotus for Angie and six yellow roses for Gloria. I had the owner put the flowers in vases for me because I didn't know if they had vases at the center.

I drove to the center and parked in the lot across the street. The guard announced my arrival and I walked to Angie's apartment but found only Gloria there. I gave Gloria the yellow roses and said, "To celebrate our friendship." She was stunned and said, "That is the sweetest thing anybody has ever given me."

I jokingly replied, "Seriously Gloria? You're so beautiful, I just assumed guys had been giving you flowers since you were twelve."

"Not so much," she said. "I haven't had the best luck with men."

"That's sad," I said.

"What's sad is that I put up with it," she said.

I was going to ask her if she wanted to elaborate when she shook off the subject and thanked me again for the roses, then told me that Angie was down by the pond looking at the ducks.

I thanked her and headed over to the pond, where I found Angie sitting on a bench reading a book. When I called her name, she turned around and smiled at me innocently.

"Hi Joe," she said. "I'm so happy you were able to come."

I handed her the vase full of white lotus flowers and she asked, "For me?"

"Of course, for you. Who else would they be for?"

"I don't know, you never gave me flowers before. White lotus is my favorite. How'd you know?"

Before I could answer, she placed the vase safely on the bench and stood up and flung her arms around me and we kissed. "I love you so much," she said as she took my hand and we sat down on the bench.

I told her all about Mr. Laurence, except for the stuff I couldn't explain or simply didn't know enough about. Like talking to his dead wife, and him telling me that he was sure that the two of us would get along really well. Angie was really excited about everything I told her. "It's like a miracle," she said. She was genuinely happy, and I had not seen her like that in what seemed like forever. When she was like this — smiling, happy, her face aglow — her beauty was magnified to a level similar to that of the woman I saw in Mr. Laurence's eyes.

I ran my hands through her hair and said, "You are so amazing. I could never live without you." It was like words were coming out of my mouth without me fully knowing where they came from or why I was saying them. Maybe that's what's meant by true love? The unconstrained feeling of emotion toward another person. I reached over and kissed her passionately. It was quite possibly the first time I had initiated such passion, and we kissed for a long time. Suddenly I became extremely lightheaded, and I collapsed across the bench with my head resting on Angie's lap.

Angie ran her hands through my hair and said, "My beautiful boy is so tired. You've been working so hard."

I lifted my arms up and wrapped them around her waist as my head rested against her lap. I could feel her lower stomach muscles, the place that if we ever had a baby would be the baby's womb. It was as though we were one person, united by feeling. Suddenly I heard her reciting from the book she was reading.

But our love it was stronger by far than the love
Of those who were older than we—
Of many far wiser than we—
And neither the angels in Heaven above
Nor the demons down under the sea
Can ever dissever my soul from the soul
Of the beautiful Annabel Lee;

For the moon never beams, without bringing me dreams
Of the beautiful Annabel Lee;
And the stars never rise, but I feel the bright eyes
Of the beautiful Annabel Lee;
And so, all the night-tide, I lie down by the side
Of my darling — my darling — my life and my bride,
In her sepulchre there by the sea—
In her tomb by the sounding sea.

I woke up hours later, my hands still wrapped around Angie's waist, and my head resting on her lap. She stroked my hair and said, "It's almost time for you to go."

"I'm not going anywhere," I mumbled, never wanting to be apart from her, and fell back asleep.

"Joe," she exclaimed, "in a few minutes they are going to throw you out."

"Let them throw us both out," I said, and she laughed as she ran her hand through my hair.

"That would be wonderful, but that dream is just going to have to wait for a little while," she said as I lifted myself up slowly and looked into her lovely eyes. The setting sun cast a warm glow across her face as our lips touched and fused into a passionate kiss … and just like that I found myself behind the wheel of the blue Malibu Classic listening to Sinatra singing "Moonlight Serenade."

CHAPTER TEN

Joe

I pulled into Mr. Laurence's driveway and parked. I had had no recollection of walking to the car in the lot across from the center. It was like I'd blacked out. It could be that I was just exhausted, but that seemed unlikely, since I had just spent four hours sleeping on the most comfortable pillow known to mankind, my beautiful Angie's lap. All of my senses were filled with her aroma, her warmth, the taste of her lips and the softness of her hair.

I opened the car door and started walking toward the house in the back when I heard Mr. Laurence ask, "And did you have a nice time with your lovely Angie?"

He was sitting on the front porch of the big house. I was so distracted that I would have walked right past him if he hadn't spoken. I apologized for not seeing him, but he waved it off and said, "Come, tell me about your day."

I sat down beside him and immediately started talking about the amazing time I'd had with Angie … possibly the best day ever, and easily the best day since that nightmare night. I told him how much she loved the flowers, and that she'd been so loving and passionate that I hadn't wanted to leave. The idea of being apart from her felt like torture. It was the type of day I'd always dreamed of having with her from the first time I laid eyes on her.

"I'm sorry if I sound like some teenager in love for the first time, but I've been so worried about her. Since we first met, when she first moved into my family's apartment, she was like the adult in our relationship, and then just like that … after that horrific night … I became the adult … and I've just been hoping and praying to get her to a safe place where I didn't have to spend every day and night worrying that she might…"

I suddenly stopped talking and looked up at the full moon. As I did, one of the stanzas from the poem Angie had recited to me ran through my mind. I came up with a few of the words and images and mentioned the name Annabel, and Mr. Laurence quickly figured out that it was Edgar Allan Poe's poem, "Annabel Lee." He ducked into the house and came out with an old volume of Poe's collected works. Together we found the poem and I recited the passage that she'd read to me:

> For the moon never beams, without bringing me dreams
> Of the beautiful Annabel Lee;
> And the stars never rise, but I feel the bright eyes
> Of the beautiful Annabel Lee;
> And so, all the night-tide, I lie down by the side
> Of my darling — my darling — my life and my bride,
> In her sepulchre there by the sea—
> In her tomb by the sounding sea.

As I read the last line, its meaning struck me like a bolt of lightning. The author, Mr. Poe, was talking about his lovely bride who had died and was now buried in a tomb by the sounding sea.

It was eerily similar to a recurring nightmare I'd been having ever since I got my memory back. In the middle of the night, I saw myself visiting Angie's grave, and in the background I could hear the hammer of waves against a nearby beach. It was like the poem was an omen.

"Joe," Mr. Laurence said, "Don't let crazy thoughts intrude upon the lovely day you had with your darling Angie."

It was like the man knew more about me than I knew about myself.

"You're right," I said. "And before I forget, Gloria loved the flowers. She said it was the first time anyone had given her flowers, which I found hard to believe. She said the men in her life have treated her horribly. No one should have to put up with that. Especially not a woman like Gloria, who worked as an ER nurse for ten years, saving lives."

Mr. Laurence just nodded and listened as I continued my story. I might have been babbling a little, but I was starting to feel quite protective of Gloria, and for some reason I wanted Mr. Laurence to know more about her.

"At her criminal hearing, the police officers who arrested her testified on her behalf and told the judge and prosecutors that what the world needed was more women like Gloria, and that the man who was abusing and hitting her might not have deserved to die, but, that being said, the world was better off without him."

Mr. Laurence stood up and gently patted me on the back and said, "I left some clean clothes on the kitchen table and put some food and drinks in the refrigerator."

"You didn't have to do that. I already feel guilty for paying such cheap rent for such a beautiful place."

"You're a good man, Joe ... a good man. I'll see you tomorrow morning at eight."

Mr. Laurence walked into his house, and I got up off my chair and walked to my house in the back. As I opened the door and walked inside, I was again struck by the beauty of the place. It was hard for me to fathom that I was living in this beautiful home, twice the size of my family's apartment back in the Bronx, for virtually no rent.

I turned on the kitchen light, and there on the table were five pairs of pants, five shirts, underwear, socks, a new pair of sneakers and a couple of jackets with removable lining that one could easily wear in the spring or winter.

I tried on one of everything, and they all fit perfectly. The strangest thing of all was that I was not one bit surprised.

I hung up the shirts, pants, and both jackets in the large closet in the bedroom I was going to sleep in, and put my underwear and socks in a drawer in a large bureau across from the bed.

I walked back into the kitchen and sat down and called my mother. I told her all about Mr. Laurence, the house, and the use of a car. All in exchange for driving him to the cemetery to visit his wife's grave each morning, and taking him along when I went shopping.

She was immediately suspicious, and said she would be doing an internet search on this Mr. Laurence once we were finished talking. She asked me if I'd told him about my psychotic girlfriend. I told her yes, and that he'd said his wife was also the victim of sexual abuse as a child.

She then went off on Angie in a way that was very hard for me to listen to, yet I tried as hard as I could not to argue with her. As it continued, the diatribe got more and more nasty. Somehow, over the course of this rant, Angie went from being a cold-hearted lying whore to a disciple of the devil.

Finally, I couldn't take it anymore. "Mom," I said, testily. "Just a few months ago you thought she was an angel sent to us from God. Never in your wildest dreams did you think I could ever find a more perfect girlfriend and future wife. That's what you said."

"The devil's followers wear many masks. We were all fooled."

"Seriously, Mom? Angie, a disciple of the devil? Her brother tried to rape her. She fought back and killed him. Would you look more kindly on her if she'd let him rape her?"

"Don't you play stupid with me! You know exactly what this is all about. She also tried to kill you."

"And how do you know that? Did she tell you that?"

"No, she didn't tell me that, and the conniving little bitch certainly wasn't going to tell the police that, but they didn't believe her story either."

"Well, I was there and I'm telling you, she didn't push me over any railing. My momentum took me over that railing. End of story."

"You're weak, Joseph. You're letting a pretty face cloud your judgment. I just pray to God it doesn't come back to haunt you."

"I love you, Mom."

"And I love you," she replied as I hung up.

I sat up and walked over to the sliding door and looked at the swimming pool, and then up at the full moon. The final lines from Poe's poem kept running through my head:

> For the moon never beams, without bringing me dreams
> Of the beautiful Annabel Lee;
> And the stars never rise, but I feel the bright eyes
> Of the beautiful Annabel Lee;
> And so, all the night-tide, I lie down by the side
> Of my darling — my darling — my life and my bride,
> In her sepulchre there by the sea—
> In her tomb by the sounding sea.

I turned away from the door, closed my eyes, and pressed my hands against my ears in a futile attempt to drown out the haunting, passionate voice that was like the song of a siren.

I collapsed on the floor, and could feel my body being dragged out through the sliding door and along the patio stones, toward the pool. Suddenly I was in the water, being held under the surface by an unseen force. I struggled to free myself, my hands and legs flailing futilely against the force, and then my body went limp and lifeless as I floated to the surface. In the end I was drifting across the water, on my back, my eyes still open as I looked up at the moon. At the "moon that never beams, without bringing me dreams of my beautiful, my darling, my life and my bride..."

CHAPTER ELEVEN

Joe

I woke up hours later on the floor where I had first collapsed, drenched in what I could only hope was sweat. I stood up, and not seeing a trail of water from the pool to the spot where I'd found myself, I assumed it was all a bad dream. It was already getting light outside. The birds were chirping, and I could swear that in the distance I could hear Sinatra's voice.

I opened the refrigerator and to my delight, right in front, was a half-gallon bottle of freshly squeezed orange juice. I don't normally like orange juice unless it's mixed with vodka, but when I saw that bottle, it was like I'd discovered fresh water in the desert. I grabbed the container, whipped off the top, and guzzled the juice right out of the bottle. Within seconds, I felt refreshed and renewed. This led me to wonder if my blood sugar level had been low. I'd never had that problem before, but I was looking for anything to explain what had happened the night before.

I jumped into the shower and let the water splash against my body for what could have been ten minutes or an hour. All I wanted to do was stay there, getting clean and soaking in my new surroundings — the gleaming white subway tiles, brushed nickel fixtures, and the perfect water pressure, raining down on me from a giant shower head like the kind you see in magazines.

When I'd finally had enough, I gave myself a blast of cold water to try to wake myself up. I can't say if it worked or not. As I toweled off and wandered around pulling on the clothing Mr. Laurence had left for me, I looked around at the house in the daytime and began to feel strange. Everything in this supposed guesthouse seemed to be new; the refrigerator, the stove, the TV, even the faucets in the shower and sink, the toilets, and the furniture all looked like they had been installed within days or weeks of my arrival. It all felt like an elaborate façade. I suddenly wondered if I'd wandered onto a film set.

I walked to the front of the big house and found Mr. Laurence watering plants. He looked at me and said, "You're early."

"I figured it was better to be early than late on the first full day of my job."

He laughed and asked, "Did you sleep well?"

"Yes. And thank you for the clothes. As you can see, they fit perfectly." I had chosen khaki chinos and a blue button-down shirt, and I had to admit, they looked good. But I must have been self-conscious because when Mr. Laurence just stood there, smiling and watering his rose bushes, I started babbling about money.

"I'm not totally broke," I told him, for no good reason that I can recall. "I've been working side jobs since I was twelve and I do have a savings account."

He looked at me for what felt like an eternity, then smiled and said, "How about we get going? I have a few places I need to stop at before we visit my lovely wife."

We got into the car, and the first place we stopped was at the florist. The lady behind the counter was different than the one who'd helped me the day before.

Mr. Laurence greeted her like they were old friends, addressing her by her first name, Francine, and asking how she was doing on this beautiful morning.

"Wonderful, Mr. Laurence and you?"

"Splendid, thank you."

"The usual, sir?"

"Yes, except this morning can I get my usual set of three, and another with two roses?" He turned to me and said, "This young man has a beautiful girlfriend who I'm sure would love them."

Francine picked out the most beautiful red roses I think I have ever seen. They glowed. She wrapped the roses separately as Mr. Laurence turned to me and said, "When you give a lady two red roses that means mutual love like you and your beautiful Angie share."

"That will be twenty-four dollars, Mr. Laurence."

Mr. Laurence handed Francine a hundred-dollar bill and she asked, "You wouldn't have anything smaller?"

"No, I'm sorry."

"Would it be okay if I just put the change aside and give it to you tomorrow? I have only a few small bills in the register."

"I have a better idea. You keep the change and buy yourself something." Before she could object, he added, "I insist. Thank you, Francine."

He picked up the flowers as Francine said, "Thank you so much, Mr. Laurence."

Our next stop was a confectionery shop. We entered the cozy little store, which had a bell on the door that chimed softly as we went in, and Mr. Laurence asked me if Angie had a favorite type of chocolate.

"She loves the chocolate-covered cherries, but I wouldn't buy them because she's only going to get mad."

"And is that because she's worried about her weight?"

"Yes, even though she's super skinny, especially after her incarceration at Rikers Island. I swear, I don't know if she weighs a hundred pounds."

"Well then, let your beautiful Angie get mad at you. And how about her roommate, Gloria?"

"I have no idea, but she has the body of a model and the face of Halle Berry."

"I'm going to guess she also loves chocolate-covered cherries."

The salesperson approached us and asked, "Can I help you gentlemen?"

"Yes," Mr. Laurence said. "We're going to need two large, heart-shaped boxes of chocolate-covered cherries."

"You're going to get me in trouble with both of them," I said.

"*Good* trouble, Joe. Good trouble."

The total came to a little over forty dollars and Mr. Laurence paid with two twenties and a ten-dollar bill ... after he had told Francine he had no small bills and left her a seventy-dollar tip. He put the nine dollars and change in the tip jar on top of the counter.

On the way to the cemetery, we travelled south and up a hilly road that seemed to go on forever. It felt like we were driving up a mountain road, but I didn't know of any mountains on Long Island.

We reached a gilded, wrought iron gate that was very tall and wide. It was the type of gate that kept people out. Engraved within it was a family crest, but I couldn't make out the name. Just as I was about to ask Mr. Laurence what the crest stood for, he opened the gate with a small electric gadget on his key chain.

I waited for him to tell me to drive through because I wasn't so sure. He simply told me to stay on the road and try not to stray onto the lawn ... a lawn so perfectly manicured that it looked like the outfield at Yankee Stadium. The property was huge, as big as a football field. On the left and right sides, huge, flowering hedges glowed with a radiance that I have never seen before, not even at Disney World.

The road cut the property in half. On each side was a mausoleum the size of the small house I was living in. We didn't stop at either. Instead, we stopped before the only outside grave, which included one large gravestone and a small garden.

There were no names engraved on the stone. On the right side of the stone was a laser-engraved, color picture of Mr. Laurence's wife. I recognized her immediately from the woman I'd seen reflected in his eyes. She was mesmerizing, with dark, wavy hair, alert green eyes, and a perfect, oval face. She was the most beautiful woman I have ever seen … a combination of Hedy Lamarr, Grace Kelly, and Gene Tierney. On the left side of the stone was a laser-engraved, color picture of her sister Rachel, who was also beautiful but in a very plain and innocent way.

I could not take my eyes off the picture of his wife and kind of went into a trance. Then I heard a woman's voice … a voice so hypnotic that I would have done anything it asked. "It's such a pleasure to meet you, Joseph," the voice said. "My husband has told me so many wonderful things about you."

I had a couple of options. Running was one of them. I could have hightailed it across the lawn and through the gate, leaving behind the car and Mr. Laurence and the house and the clothes. I could have stripped off these haunted coverings piece by piece as I ran to find the nearest bus back to the Bronx. I could have run for my life and never looked back —if my feet were working. They were not. In the nanosecond or eternity that passed after her greeting, I realized that my entire body was being held captive by her voice, or whatever spectral presence lay behind it. That voice — spellbinding and pure — was addressing me by name, as though this was the most normal thing in the world. My only real option was to answer it.

"It's a pleasure to meet you," I said. Easy. Conversational. "And your husband is the kindest and most generous person I have ever met."

"Yes, he is," she said. "I picked the right guy."

"He's wild about you."

She laughed. I made her laugh! It was the purest sound I'd ever heard. A mountain stream, cascading over rocks.

"And I'm wild about him. He's my hero and guardian and we'll forever be as one."

I continued to look at her picture, focusing intently on her eyes. The music of sirens seemed to fill the air as I felt a soft breeze pass through my body. And then the sound of her voice again, saying, "You take care of yourself, Joseph, and I look forward to many more visits."

I came to my senses and looked around. At first I couldn't see Mr. Laurence, but then I noticed him sitting on a nearby bench overlooking a beach. I walked over to him and sat down. He was still holding the roses he had bought for his wife and her sister. A stone staircase, with railings on both sides, led down a cliff to the beach, where waves crashed against the shore.

At first I didn't even acknowledge him. Then I looked at him in silent amazement and could tell from his expression that he knew what I was thinking. *How? What just happened?* He offered no explanation. We sat watching the waves until I could finally speak again. It was easiest to speak of tangible things.

"Did you and your wife come here often?"

"Only a few times. She loved to walk along the beach and feel the ocean spray against her face."

"That must have been a stunning sight. Not to take anything away from Angie, but your wife is the most beautiful woman I have ever seen."

"I think so too, Joseph. It *was* astonishing to see her walk along the shore, arms outstretched, bare toes in the sand, feeling the sun and spray against her face. What makes this memory even more precious is that it's one I almost didn't get to see."

"Why?"

"After surviving D-Day, seeing the bullet-riddled bodies of my friends washing up on shore, and the bodies of other friends being swept further out, never to be recovered, I swore I never wanted to see another beach again if I survived the war."

He gazed out at the water and tightened his grip around the flowers.

"She told me to give her a chance. That she understood the terrible trauma I'd suffered, but that she believed she could make me see a beauty so breathtaking that when I looked at the ocean I would never want to look away."

"And did you? I mean you must have," I said.

"Not at first. I laughed and told her the only way that was possible is if she was a real sea goddess, and the only way I would ever get to see her is if I looked for her rising high above the water, then diving back under."

"Very creative. She must have loved that. What did she say?"

"She smiled and asked, 'And would it surprise you if I were a sea goddess?' I looked into those green eyes and said, 'No, it wouldn't. Nothing as beautiful as you could possibly be of this earth.' She laughed and said flattery would get me nowhere, unless I gave her a chance to show the ocean to me in a different and more beautiful way."

I'd shifted my whole body and was perched on the edge of the bench, waiting for him to continue with his story, which he did.

"I was powerless against her," he said. "I had seen many beautiful women while I was fighting in Italy, and many when we were liberating Paris, but she was in a world all her own … if she was even of this world. It was as though she could read my thoughts, my dreams, the life history of a twenty-two-year-old, recently discharged from the marines."

"What made you think she could read your thoughts?" I asked.

"She would say things like, 'And what part of the Bronx are you from, marine?' — without having been told anything about my past or where I was from. And when I asked her what made her think I was from the Bronx, she laughed and said, 'Because with an accent like yours, you're either from the Bronx or another planet. I'd guess up by Fordham University.'"

"How could she have known that?"

"That's what I asked her," Mr. Laurence said. "She explained that her father owned a chain of newspapers, and that she would travel all around the city with him. Whenever they were in the Bronx, they would stop for pizza at Arthur Ave., just down the street from the university. She said it was the best pizza she ever had. She teased me and said, 'Surely, you must have had pizza from one of the many Italian restaurants in the area?'"

As he spoke, I felt the bluff and the bench and the cemetery fade away, until I was somewhere else — in the mists of their life together, watching them talk and flirt, the way young lovers do. My body was no longer my own. I was a spectator, watching Mr. Laurence's story come to life, and he was a young marine, standing before a sea goddess, exclaiming on their shared love of pizza.

"There were times when I ate pizza for breakfast, lunch, and dinner ... seven days a week."

"And you don't remember seeing me? I'm insulted!"

Her twinkling smile told him she wasn't, but he rushed to explain himself anyway. "My vision back then wasn't very good. I was always bumping into things. A real embarrassment."

"Yet, the marines had no problem taking you?"

"Desperate times called for desperate measures."

"I see. Yet your vision seems to have markedly improved."

"A real miracle. So, what newspapers does your father own?"

"A lot, across the entire country, and he has even picked up a few radio stations. Some call him a tycoon, but to me he's just Daddy. The most kind, generous, loving and caring human being I have ever met."

"Do you have any brothers and sisters?"

"Fifteen sisters, no brothers."

"Fifteen sisters! And do they all look like you?"

"No! We're really a mixed bag of girls."

"Has your father been married and divorced a number of times?"

"No! He married his childhood sweetheart and has been married to her for over twenty-five years. They make such a handsome couple."

"Your mom has had fifteen children?"

"No, silly. She couldn't—"

"Couldn't?"

"Conceive."

"Ah."

"We're all adopted. Our home was sort of like a big, fun-loving orphanage. Both my mom and dad were raised in orphanages. Both abandoned and abused by their biological parents. They've treated all us girls like we're made of gold. We live in a large estate on Long Island."

"You know, it's not nice to lie to a wounded war veteran."

"But you were shot in your right thigh. If am not mistaken isn't that one of the best places to get shot, if one is unfortunate enough to get shot?"

"How in God's name do you know where I was shot?"

"You have a slight limp on your right side, and you seem to favor your left." She pointed to her temple and widened her eyes comically. "Daughter of a newspaper man. Trained to observe."

"And are you trained to read minds?"

"Yes. Right now you're thinking how lovely my eyes are, and how quickly you're falling in love with me."

"Oh?"

"That's right. You're also thinking that a rich, beautiful girl like me would never fall for a poor slob from the Bronx."

"You never would fall for a poor slob like me from the Bronx, would you?"

"That depends..."

"On what?"

"If I could get that poor slob to see the beauty in the ocean after all he has been through."

"So, when do we start, teacher?"

"Tonight, at the house my father has rented for us to live in while we get acquainted with the staff and editors of the new paper he bought ... the first on the west coast."

"I get to meet your dad tonight?"

"Yes, surely you don't have a problem with that? You'll also get to meet two of my sisters who are out here with us. But you do need to be careful because my daddy is better at reading minds than I am. So, whatever illicit thoughts might be wandering around that brain of yours, I would bury them deep in your unconscious before meeting him."

"I don't have any illicit thoughts running around in my head."

"Oh my God, you're adorable."

"And why would you say that?" Laurence asked as her emerald eyes twinkled and she smiled, revealing a pair of dimples that were like orbs of light.

A limousine pulled up and parked beside them. The chauffeur got out and opened the back door and she slid into the back seat. The door lay open as young Laurence looked on stupidly. Suddenly, the tycoon's daughter leaned forward and asked, "Oh soldier, are you waiting for an invitation, or have you decided to skip dinner on the off chance you might get a better offer?"

Laurence slid into the limo as the chauffeur closed the door and got into the driver's seat. The driver turned and asked, "Where to, Miss. Isabelle?"

She looked at Laurence and asked, "What motel are you staying at?"

"The Hollywood Estates. It's about five miles down the boulevard."

"Did you get that, Adam?" Isabelle asked the chauffeur.

"Yes, miss. If I may say, it's not the type of place a girl like you should be seen entering."

"Oh, I have no intention of going in. We can take a drive around the block while my friend collects his belongings. He might be staying with us for a while. You won't be long, will you?"

"No, I never unpacked."

"By the way, what's your name?"

"Laurence."

"Like Laurence Olivier, the actor?"

"I guess. I don't know much about actors."

"You actually look like him. You could play his stunt double. What do you think, Adam?"

"That's who I thought you were talking to when I just picked you up."

She laughed as they proceeded to the motel, where Adam parked under a flickering neon sign that was missing the O in Hollywood. Laurence slid out of the limo, dashed up to his room, grabbed his duffel bag, checked out of the motel, and reappeared in the back seat.

"Wow! That was awfully fast, Laurence. Were you afraid we wouldn't wait?"

"No, just afraid I'd wake up from this dream," he said as he caught his breath.

"Back to the house, miss?"

"Yes Adam. Mr. Laurence will be having dinner with us and then I'll be tutoring him on oceanography and sea life."

"Wonderful! Have you been interested in oceanography for very long, Mr. Laurence?"

"Been getting more and more interested in it by the minute, you might say."

"Before you know it, he'll be a certified ichthyologist. Isn't that so, Laurence?"

He leaned toward her and whispered, "What's an ichthyologist?"

"A person who studies fish," she replied, as she patted his leg and said, "Don't worry, I'm a very patient teacher."

CHAPTER TWELVE

Laurence

Adam waited for the guarded gate to open and drove up the driveway to the mansion that Isabelle and her family were staying in. We both slid out of the limo before Adam had a chance to open the doors. I, Laurence — I was pretty sure I was still Laurence, and not some dream version of my former self — looked up at the mansion and said, "So this is what a Beverly Hills mansion looks like."

"Not quite as stylish as the French chateaus you're used to seeing?" Isabelle asked.

"I wouldn't know. All the chateaus we passed were so badly damaged by German bombs that you were lucky to make out their skeletons."

We entered the mansion, which was about fifty times the size of my parents' apartment back in the Bronx. Cathedral ceilings, spiraling staircases, crystal chandeliers, too many bedrooms and bathrooms to count, a screening room, a ballroom, a library, and the list goes on. I asked Isabelle where I should leave my duffel bag and she opened a closet by the front entrance and replied, "Right here is fine. Just in case we need to throw you out, we can do it with a minimum of fuss."

I put my bag in the closet and looked at Isabelle, who asked, "What's that awful smell?"

"Your sister is cooking dinner tonight," Adam replied.

Isabelle asked me, "You're not a vegetarian, are you?"

"No."

"Well, after tonight you might seriously consider becoming one."

I followed Isabelle into the kitchen, which was as big as a bowling alley. Rachel, the youngest sister, was frantically stirring dishes and keeping track of four different pots on the large gas stove that took up one wall. Isabelle took her aside as she lowered the flames on all the jets and opened the oven and said, "I think whatever you have in there might be done."

"No, it's supposed to be in there for forty-five minutes."

"And how long has it been in there?"

"I'm not sure. I've been so busy."

Isabelle wrapped her arms around her sister. "This is my beautiful sister, Rachel. She's practicing to be a gourmet chef. Isn't that so, sweetheart?"

"Yes," Rachel replied, as she looked at me and said, "Who's your friend?"

"This is Laurence. We met a short time ago. I'll be tutoring him in oceanography."

"Wonderful," Rachel said sarcastically.

"And what are we calling these splendid dishes you're preparing for us tonight?"

"French cuisine. I've prepared a number of different dishes, for variety."

"Laurence just came back from France. He was part of the Normandy invasion and the liberation of Paris."

"Wow! A war hero, and so good-looking," she said as she tried to break away from her sister to shake my hand.

"Control yourself, my lovely baby sister."

"I just want to properly introduce myself," Rachel said as Isabelle let go of her.

We shook hands and Rachel turned and looked at Isabelle and said, "You see? Innocent enough."

"Would you like a little help with supper?" Isabelle asked.

"That would be nice, but only if your boyfriend can help too."

"He's not my boyfriend."

"Really? Would it be okay if he was my boyfriend? That would give you extra time to concentrate on your fish."

"You're fifteen years old. I don't think Daddy would approve."

"Sixteen!" Rachel exclaimed.

"Fifteen! Your birthday was just a month ago."

"I lose count..."

"How about we all help out?" I interjected and we all agreed.

That's when I noticed smoke coming out of the oven. A lot of it.

Rachel screeched and I ran to the oven and cranked the main dial all the way to the right until I heard the flame go out. Rachel was standing by helplessly, holding her hands over her mouth, when Isabelle grabbed two kitchen cloths and handed them to me, saying "Open it, but be careful." I stood back, holding my arms out as far as I could, and slowly opened the oven door.

A cloud of smoke engulfed us, and there was a lot of commotion as Isabelle and I flung open a window next to the stove and started waving the towels through the air to try to move the plume outside. When this proved ineffective, Isabelle grabbed two cookie sheets and we used them to try to direct more of the smoke outside. Rachel was standing off to the side, whimpering. I asked her to go and shut the door to the adjoining dining room to keep the smoke from spreading through the house. When she came back, the three of us continued to wave cookie sheets through the gradually thinning smoke for another ten minutes. When we could finally see again, Isabelle peered into the oven and pulled out a roasting pan. In the center of it, a blackened lump, about the size of a baseball, was still giving off rivulets of smoke.

Rachel began crying heavily, and Isabelle took her younger sister in her arms and gently caressed the back of her head, saying, "Everything is going to be okay," over and over again.

"But I promised Daddy!"

"Doesn't he always understand?" Isabelle asked as I moved around the stove, checking the dials again to make sure everything was turned off.

"Come, let's go tell him what happened," Isabelle said, with her arm around Rachel's shaking shoulders. When I didn't move, Isabelle turned to me and said, "Do you plan on cleaning the dishes, or would you like to meet my father?"

"I don't know, you tell me," I said, as she reached and grasped my hand with her free hand and pulled me along.

We entered a large library where Mr. William Hamill was sitting at an enormous desk. He was holding one broadsheet in front of his face while his elbow rested on a large pile of other newspapers to his left. Rachel hovered in the doorway, sobbing, then ran to her father. He immediately put down his newspaper and took her in his arms. "What's wrong, sweetheart? Did you burn yourself?"

Rachel shook her head and cried harder until Mr. Hamill repeated his question, then reassured her that whatever was wrong, they could fix it.

He took out his handkerchief and tried to wipe her face, but she hung her head and sobbed. "I burned dinner."

"Oh my darling, is that all?"

"It's ruined! And I promised you the best dinner ever."

Mr. Hamill held onto his daughter and met her eyes with his own. "Honey, it's okay. It's nothing, in fact."

Rachel looked at her hands. "It's not nothing."

"Well, okay, it's not nothing. But the important thing is that you tried. I'll bet the next time it'll be great. I doubt Babe Ruth hit a homerun the first time he came to bat."

"Who's Babe Ruth?" Rachel asked.

"A very successful baseball player. I'm so thankful that you were willing to spend so much time cooking dinner for the family. You must love us very much." She nodded earnestly and he hugged her and pulled her gently into the chair beside his.

When Rachel had quieted down, Mr. Hamill looked up and noticed me standing next to Isabelle.

"Hello, young man," he said, a little warily.

"Oh Daddy, I have someone I want you to meet," Isabelle said as she pushed me forward until I was standing in front of his desk. "This is Laurence. He was in the marines. At Normandy…"

Mr. Hamill stood up and came around the desk to shake my hand. "It's a pleasure to meet you, Laurence. You look like you came back all in one piece."

"He was shot in the thigh, but that didn't stop him from helping with the liberation of Paris," Isabelle said.

"I have a reporter who works for one of my papers who was badly wounded covering the invasion. Thankfully, he's doing well after a long hospital stay. Did you lose friends? The casualties were mind boggling."

"Yes sir, I lost a number of my friends."

"I'm so sorry. After covering the First World War, I didn't think it could get any worse. Apparently, history has proven me wrong."

Isabelle took my arm in hers and looked at her father. "I'm going to teach Laurence about the beauty of the ocean. Hopefully replace some of those terrible images with wonderful ones."

"That's kind of you, sweetheart," Mr. Hamill said.

Rachel, who had regained her composure, said, "She's going to teach him about all the beautiful fish. She's says he's not her boyfriend, but I don't believe her, unless she needs glasses and we just never knew it."

Mr. Hamill laughed while I blushed and Isabelle rolled her eyes. Then Mr. Hamill said, "How about we order from Maestro's Restaurant? If Mr. Sinatra eats there, I imagine the food must be wonderful. Laurence, by now Isabelle must have persuaded you to stay for dinner. Do you have any preferences?"

"I eat just about anything," I said.

"Oh, no you don't," Rachel said. "Not if you want to marry my gorgeous sister you don't."

"Rachel, be good," her father said.

"I'm just telling him the truth. Let me see … stay away from all fish dishes or birds, such as ducks, who like to swim in water, and especially dolphins, who are actually mammals. Personally, I think anybody who eats a dolphin should be arrested."

"Are you finished, sweetheart?" Mr. Hamill asked.

"Yes Daddy, just trying to be helpful."

Isabelle smiled good-naturedly, as though it was perfectly natural that Laurence should want to marry her and get started learning about her dietary restrictions.

"I would be happy with pasta and a plain tomato sauce, or even pizza and a plain salad," I said, looking at Isabelle for approval, which she granted with a beautiful smile.

I would have eaten sand, if it gave me even the smallest chance of marrying that earthly goddess.

CHAPTER THIRTEEN

Laurence

Maestro's delivered six bags of food, and Rachel and Isabelle arranged the containers all down the middle of their enormous dining table. Isabelle put the pasta with plain tomato sauce and pizza near me.

We were just sitting down to eat when a third sister, Maureen, walked in. She kissed and hugged her father, Rachel, and Isabelle, then looked at me and asked, "And who's this?"

Rachel said, "This is Isabelle's friend, not her boyfriend, who she is going to tutor about the ocean."

"Well, it's nice to meet you, Isabelle's friend. I'm Maureen." She put out her hand and we shook, and I said, "Laurence."

Maureen had long, flowing red hair and blue eyes, and looked a bit like the actress Maureen O'Hara. She was the third-youngest sister.

Rachel, who was sitting beside her father with her head against his shoulder, said, "You know, Daddy, I think Isabelle might be a mermaid."

Mr. Hamill laughed and said, "What makes you think so?"

"Well, she's beautiful, like a mermaid."

Isabelle laughed and blew Rachel a kiss.

"All right," Mr. Hamill said, playing along in amusement. "Let's examine this. You and Maureen are beautiful, but I would never think you two were mermaids."

"But we're not crazy about fish and the ocean. That should have been my first reason. I'd like to change my answer and put that first."

"All right. Fair enough," her father said. "But mermaids have tails, and I don't see a tail on Isabelle."

Isabelle, who seemed to find all of this very amusing, turned around in her chair and checked her legs and backside for a tail. Finding none, she shook her head.

Rachel was too wrapped up in her theory to notice. "But with some mermaids their tails turn into regular human legs and feet when they come out of the water. When she takes a bath, I'll check and see if her legs and feet turn into a tail."

"That would be very rude, Rachel. Your sister is not a mermaid, and we all need privacy in the bath."

"You know, Daddy," Isabelle said, "I think your youngest daughter was testing the French sauces she was preparing, and you know how much wine they use in their sauces."

Mr. Hamill laughed and asked Rachel if she was drunk.

"I don't think so, Daddy."

"Let me check your breath," Mr. Hamill said and Rachel opened her mouth and Mr. Hamill leaned in and sniffed. "All I smell is toothpaste."

"That's because I brushed my teeth after I tasted the sauces."

Everyone laughed and Maureen said, "Speaking of sauces, what happened to the French cuisine you were going to make for us tonight? I'm seeing a lot of take-out containers."

Rachel's whole body seemed to crumple. Isabelle turned to Maureen and shook her head mournfully.

"Oh dear," Maureen said. She sniffed the air. "Is that smoke?"

Isabelle glared at Maureen as Rachel started to cry again. Maureen went to her sister and wrapped her arms around the younger girl's shoulders. "It's okay, sis," she said, then landed a kiss on Rachel's cheek. "It was your first try. I'm sure you'll do wonderfully next time."

"That's what Daddy said," Rachel said. "He said when I'm ready he'll hire a French chef to teach me properly, and then I can write a column about French cuisine for one of his papers."

"Splendid," Maureen said.

Mr. Hamill asked Rachel to say a prayer before supper.

"Thank you, God, for all of this wonderful food, which I did not cook," she said, opening one eye just long enough to look at her father, "and thank you for giving us the best daddy in the whole world." We were all about to dig in when she held up her hands as if she'd forgotten something important and added, "And thank you for bringing Laurence."

That put a smile on my face, and as we all started to serve from the containers, I followed Isabelle's lead; she transferred some pasta and a slice of pizza onto her plate, and I did the same. It was hard watching the rest of the family eating their steak, ribs, pork chops, and lobster. I could really have gone for some surf and turf in that moment. But I had to look at the bigger picture. Yes, the chances of a nobody like me getting to marry Isabelle were slim to none, but if staying away from meat and fish improved my chances at all, then that's what I would do.

After dinner we formed a line by the kitchen sink and cleaned and dried all the dishes and silverware. Mr. Hamill did the washing, using a slow trickle of hot water and a modest amount of dish soap, "for the health of the oceans," Isabelle explained. Rachel did the rinsing, Maureen dried, and Isabelle put everything away. I volunteered to clean the inside of the stove. It was filthy from the exploding roast, and it took a long time and a lot of sweat. By the time I'd polished the whole thing to a shine and listened to half an hour of amusing banter between Isabelle and her sisters and their father — adding the occasional one-liner or observation of my own to their well-oiled after-dinner routine — I knew one thing: I would have given just about anything to be the newest member of the Hamill clan.

CHAPTER FOURTEEN

Laurence

After the dishes were put away, Isabelle made a big pot of popcorn and scooped it into four paper bags, then handed one to each of her sisters and her father. She didn't hand me a bag, and said that since we were sitting together we could share.

I followed the clan into a big screening room. It was filled with rows of plush chairs that were bolted to the floor. Isabelle had already set up the projector and we were going to see a movie by Jacques-Yves Cousteau. It was his first underwater film, called *Par dix-huit mètres de fond,* made in 1943. It was in French, and it was a very grainy black-and-white film.

Maureen had given me a notebook and a pen as we entered the theatre, and I opened it, preparing to take notes. Isabelle looked at me and said, "What are you doing?"

"Maureen said you'd be giving me a quiz later."

Isabelle grabbed the notebook and pen out of my hands and put them on the empty seat to her. "That's the stupidest thing I've ever heard," she said. "I will be giving you a quiz but not until you've seen the film at least three times."

As the lights came down and the film began, Isabelle dug her hand into the bag of popcorn and took little bites. One could barely see anything, except for small fish swimming by, and to make it worse, there were no subtitles. I don't remember how long it was, but it seemed like an eternity, and before she could rewind the film and show it again, Rachel sat next to her and said, "Please, Isabelle, I don't want to see any more fish movies tonight." She lifted the armrest on her chair and laid her head on Isabelle's lap. Mr. Hamill and Maureen had already left the room.

"What's wrong, angel?"

"I don't feel good," Rachel said as she wrapped her arms around Isabelle's waist. Isabelle stroked her hair and asked, "Are you still upset about dinner?"

"No…"

She looked up at me and then Isabelle asked if she could have some private time with her sister. I immediately got up and walked out of the screening room.

Later, I would learn that Rachel was the last one to be adopted and that she had suffered serious abuse in her family of origin — abuse so appalling that it shut her down and robbed her of the capacity for speech. For the first few months after being adopted she didn't speak to anyone in her new family except for Isabelle and Mr. Hamill.

Rachel was very sensitive, and she often joked and laughed more as a defense mechanism than anything else. Isabelle later told me that, more nights than not, she slept in the same bed with Rachel, with her arms wrapped around the child.

I walked into the kitchen and found Mr. Hamill sitting at the table reading a newspaper and drinking a glass of wine. He offered me a glass, but I declined, so he asked me to sit down and said, "Tell me a little about yourself, Laurence."

"Well, you know I was in the marines. I enlisted at nineteen, after my sophomore year at college."

"You volunteered?"

"Yes sir."

"You didn't want to get a deferment and stay in school?"

"I could probably have done that, but so many boys from the neighborhood were being drafted, I was starting to feel ashamed that my friends were doing their part for our country while I was getting away easy."

"Where are you from?"

"You mean, you don't know? Isabelle got it on her first guess."

He laughed. "I'm a proud father who has no problem admitting that my daughter is smarter than me. My guess would be the Bronx."

"And you would be right. Up around Arthur Ave., above the zoo, and before Fordham University."

"Isabelle and I have been up that way quite a bit. She loves the pizza. What college did you go to?"

"Fordham. If I'd stayed, I was going major in English Lit."

"Fordham is a good school. Your parents must be very proud."

"They were, until I enlisted. Then they went crazy. I'm their only child. The first among all my relatives to go to college."

"Do you think you'll go back and finish?"

"That was my original plan, but I'm not sure. Everything feels different now."

"I imagine it does." Mr. Hamill thought for a moment. "How would you like to write for some of my papers?"

"I have no experience as a reporter."

"I'm not asking you to be a reporter. You could write a weekly column about your experiences during the war. We could call it, 'A Soldier's View.'"

"You could almost certainly get other soldiers who could do a much better job."

"But you're the only soldier who's going out with my daughter."

I smiled at the suggestion that Isabelle and I might be more than friends. "When would you like the first story?"

"I would have liked it yesterday, but how about in three days. No less than fifteen hundred words."

"Okay, and thank you so much for the opportunity, Mr. Hamill. I can't tell you how much I appreciate it," I said as I reached over and shook his hand.

"By the way, Isabelle is your boss. She's one of the best copy editors I have on staff. I hope that's all right with you?"

"That's an added bonus," I said, then I wished him goodnight, picked up my duffel bag, and headed up to the third floor, where Mr. Hamill had said I could choose to sleep in any room, except the last one at the end of the long hallway.

As I walked past the second floor I could hear Isabelle talking. I followed her voice and came to a door that was ajar. I knocked gently without pushing it further open and Isabelle emerged, wearing a white bathrobe over silky green pajamas. The hue was like the green that glints up through the ocean when sunlight hits the water.

"Hello Laurence! Are you on your way up to bed?"

"Yes, but I heard you talking and I wanted to check on Rachel," I said. She took my hand and walked me into another room where Rachel was sitting up in bed.

"My beautiful baby sister is doing much better now. Isn't that so, angel?"

"Yes," Rachel said. Then she looked at me and added, "Isabelle always makes everything better."

"That's good," I said, not knowing what else to say.

Rachel looked like one of those dolls that some people place on their beds after they make them up in the morning. She was petite, with a perfectly oval face, vivid blue eyes, and brown hair that grazed her shoulders. I couldn't help wondering what had suddenly made her so upset in the theatre, but I didn't want to pry or make things worse, so I pivoted to telling them about my new column.

"Your father offered me a job."

"Yes, I know," Isabelle said.

I looked at her and asked, "Do you know everything?"

"Yes, Laurence, Isabelle knows everything," Rachel said.

"I believe you, Rachel."

Isabelle picked up one of Rachel's delicate hands and swung it back and forth next to the bed.

"Rachel and I have an arrangement," Isabelle said. "She's my guardian angel, and I'm hers. It works out pretty well."

"It does," the younger girl said. She managed to smile at Isabelle before yawning and laying her head down on the bed. Looking up at me, Rachel said sleepily, "We protect each other. I could never live without Isabelle."

"And you'll never have to," Isabelle said, "because I could never live without you." Turning to me, she said, "And so, Mr. Laurence, fifteen hundred words describing what you felt and experienced during certain battles while fighting in Italy and France. He would like it in three days, which means what, Rachel?"

I looked at Rachel and she replied, "You should get it to him by tomorrow."

"Oh," I said, suddenly nervous. "Any advice?"

"Don't try to be Tolstoy or Conrad. Just write down what you felt at that moment, at the sight of losing friends, at being frightened about getting killed or badly wounded, of never seeing your parents again or never getting to enjoy another slice of pizza on Arthur Ave."

"Okay," I said.

"And by the way, I'm your boss. I'll copy edit all of your work and give the final okay."

"Your father told me."

"Lucky you, Laurence, you have the prettiest boss in the whole world," Rachel said.

"And the smartest," I added, not caring if I was sucking up. Isabelle suppressed a smirk but didn't contradict me.

I chose the first bedroom I walked into on the third floor. It was about ten times the size of my room at home in the Bronx, but simply furnished. One corner of the room was taken up by a large mahogany desk. On top of it was a massive version of the Oxford English Dictionary, a few other books, a typewriter, and a stack of paper. I could not imagine that I just happened to walk into the one bedroom that was set up for a reporter or student. Every room was probably set up similarly — though I'd noticed that Rachel's room wasn't. There was no desk or typewriter, but there were plenty of stuffed animals.

I sat down at the desk and fed a piece of paper into the machine, which was a tall black Underwood with gold lettering and keys faded from heavy use. Isabelle's words kept running through my brain: "Don't try to be Tolstoy or Conrad. Just write down what you felt."

I decided to start the story as we boarded the LCVP landing crafts and started across the channel to Omaha Beach. I talked about some of the guys in my unit, and about how we joked with each other about anything and everything to try and stay calm. I described the look on all our faces as the sound of gunfire from German positions in the hills grew louder. I described the click of the hatch on the craft and the shock of running down the ramp into neck-deep water, a considerable distance from the beach, which was not supposed to happen. I described how the first wave of soldiers off the craft were slaughtered by German machine gun fire, and how other soldiers drowned in the high, choppy waters. I wrote about the water turning red as I struggled toward the beach, pulling along a buddy of mine who had been shot, and how I didn't realize until I hit the beach that he was already dead, his chest ripped open by machine gun fire.

I explained how I found shelter with a group of other soldiers behind a sea wall and described the medic who came around and pointed at my leg and told me I'd been hit. I'd had no idea. A bullet had ripped into my right thigh. The medic cut open the part of my pants where the bullet went through and said, "I can get you an airvac out of here to one of the offshore hospital ships." I shook my head, and said, "Just take the bullet out."

He used forceps and a surgeon's scalpel to dig deep inside my thigh and remove the bullet. He cleaned the incision and covered it in sterile dressing. All of that took him less than three minutes. He wished me luck and moved on.

It wasn't that I was heroic. I was scared out of my mind, but when I looked down that long line of soldiers behind the sea wall, there was no way in hell I was going to take the easy way out. Shakespeare's line kept running through my head: "A coward dies a thousand times before his death, but the valiant taste of death but once." I was no hero, but I didn't want to live knowing that I was only alive because I had deserted my fellow soldiers.

Besides, I was fairly certain that all my friends on the landing craft were dead, and as it turned out I was just about right.

I read and re-read what I had written, making a few small changes, but for the most part I wrote it the way Isabelle told me to — straight, without flourishes. As I worked on my draft, it struck me that I might never be able to see the ocean the way Isabelle saw it. And if that caused any relationship we had to fail, I would have to notch it up as another casualty of the war.

It was nearly five in the morning when I went over my work one last time. I was exhausted, but I felt so dirty that I jumped in the shower and let the warm water run down my body for what seemed like forever. I shaved and brushed my teeth, and instead of putting on pajamas, I put on the clothes I was going to wear that day. I lay down on the bed and fell into a deep sleep. Then, just as suddenly, there was a knock on my door. Four hours felt like a few seconds.

"Laurence, are you decent?" Isabelle asked.

"Yes, come on in," I said and she entered the room. Any drowsiness I felt left me in a hurry.

She looked at me and asked, "Did I interrupt a nap?"

"Yeah, but one look at you and I'm wide awake. Please feel free to interrupt me anytime you see me napping."

"Very funny. I told them to save you some breakfast. In case you don't know, we tend to eat breakfast early around here. I figured a former soldier would have been the first one in the kitchen this morning."

"I was up all night writing the article."

"And did you finish?"

"Yes," I said as she looked over at the typewriter and my piece sitting next to it. She sat down at the desk, took a pencil out of the top drawer, and started reading, and just as quickly started crossing out line after line, word after word, and writing notations across the entire paper …. the whole time not saying a single word.

She then fed a clean piece of paper into the typewriter and started typing at a rate of about two hundred words a minute. The army secretaries couldn't touch her speed. She was finished in less than five minutes and asked, "Do you have your army ID with you?"

"Yes, would you like to see it?"

"Yes, please," she said as I handed her the ID, which she attached to her edited, clean copy of what was once my article. "Not a bad picture," she said. "I should have it back to you later this afternoon. All finished! Off to the presses."

"Do I get to read it?"

"Yes, on Sunday when it will appear in the Sunday magazine section of a number of our newspapers."

"I mean, don't I get to read it now?"

"No. Did you forget that I'm your boss, and that I get the final word?"

I shook my head slowly and she said, "I think you'll be pleased when you read it on Sunday. Very pleased." She took the clean copy, the edited copy, and my ID and said, "Rachel and I will be going to the beach in about an hour. We'd love the pleasure of your company unless you'd rather nap a little longer?"

"No, no, I'm coming. Just let me get some breakfast first."

"Great! In the meantime, I'll send this off. Thank you so much." She walked out of the room, leaving me somewhat dumbfounded. I put on my shoes and walked down to the kitchen.

On the second floor landing I ran into Rachel. She was dressed in a red checkered swimsuit that included a thin red belt. Except for the goggles on top of her head and the snorkel in her hand, she looked like a doll. A doll ready to explore the Great Barrier Reef.

I asked, "And how are you feeling this morning?"

"Wonderful," she replied with a big smile. She lowered the goggles onto her eyes, adjusted the strap, then raised them up again. "Isabelle always makes everything perfect."

"Is your sister a genius?"

"Yes, Laurence. You're just realizing that now?"

"Well, I only met her yesterday."

"It usually takes only a few hours, at most, to figure out that she's not only a genius but enchanting."

"Enchanting, like a mermaid or a siren, or just plain enchanting?"

"Wouldn't you like to know?" She turned and walked toward the kitchen and I followed.

Inside the bright kitchen, I noticed a plate with a metal lid on it and a little piece of paper next to it that said Laurence's Breakfast. I lifted the lid and found scrambled eggs, bacon, and three fresh strawberries.

I sat down and asked Rachel, "Have you already eaten?"

"Yes, we eat early. Were you up all night writing your article?"

"Yes, how did you know?"

"Just a guess," she said. "Are your parents really nice?"

"Yes, they're perfect."

"Were they very worried about you fighting in the war?"

"Yes, like millions of other parents, wives, and children."

"Did you see a lot of people get killed?"

I looked at her, and at that moment I had a vision of all my friends who were killed who would never get the chance to sit down at the kitchen table in their homes, or their friend's home, and eat breakfast. All the parents weeping at the loss of their sons. All the wives left to care for their children alone.

"I'm sorry," Rachel said after I didn't respond to her question.

I drank from a glass of juice that was sitting next to my plate and looked at her. "Has anyone ever told you that you look like a doll? I mean those Christmas dolls you see in the windows of department stores."

"Yes, Isabelle says it all the time. And my daddy and mommy."

"It's as though God made you so that anyone who was feeling sad would immediately cheer up when they looked at you."

"But I cry all the time because I feel so sad. I don't know how I can cheer people up when I'm always crying."

"Because even through the tears, the magic in your face doesn't disappear." When she looked down at the table, I added, "And then there are the goggles. If you can't cheer them up with your face, you can make them laugh with snorkeling equipment." She laughed and looked satisfied.

I picked up my empty plate and glass and walked over to the sink and washed and dried them both. Then I asked Rachel to put them away because I didn't know where anything went.

Isabelle walked into the kitchen dressed in a white robe loosely tied around the waist. Beneath the robe was a bathing suit like Rachel's: red, one-piece, checkered. A Peggy Sue suit. She was filling it out more than Rachel, and I tried hard not to stare.

"How was breakfast?" she asked.

"Delicious, and the company was great," I said, looking at Rachel and deliberately keeping my eyes on her.

"Of course it was. I put swim shorts on your bed and a shirt that is more appropriate for the beach."

"You don't miss a beat, do you?"

"Not often," she said cheerfully.

I nodded and left to go back up to my room, feeling ready to follow this woman to the ends of the earth.

CHAPTER FIFTEEN

Laurence

The three of us climbed into the back of the limousine. Adam tipped his hat to us and asked, "What beach will it be, Ms. Isabelle?"

"Why don't we go down to the Pacific Coast Highway and make a right? We could keep our options open."

We ended up parking just above Malibu, on a beach known for its sand dunes and crashing waves. Adam stayed with the limo while we walked down to the beach. Isabelle decided that we should lay out our blanket about twenty feet from the water.

I was nervous and pointed out that we would get overrun once it hit high tide.

"So we'll move the blanket back," she said. "After all, why come to the beach if you're not going to swim?" She looked at me and said, "But of course I understand that you'll need more time, so for now I think you should sit here and enjoy the view."

A few seconds later, the robes came off the girls, and I was enjoying the view very much. They went running into the water, where they were hit right away by a big wave, and another and another. They were laughing and shrieking as they dove and swam further out. They didn't come back in for a good forty-five minutes, and while I was watching them Isabelle never let her sister drift further than a few feet from her.

As they walked out of the water and started heading slowly back to me, they were met by two young men who were wearing only their bathing suits. The guys were so tanned that I imagined they lived at the beach. They were muscular and blond, and one was tall and one was a little shorter. They could easily have been poster boys for a magazine like *California Dreaming*.

I overheard the taller guy say, "Wow! Will you look at those two babes? I'd love to ride a wave or two with either one, but the taller one looks more experienced. I call dibs."

"I'll take the smaller one," the other guy said with an ugly laugh. "She might be less experienced, but I'm told I'm a great teacher."

Isabelle had heard the whole exchange. Her body stiffened as she looked at them and said, "What was that you just said?"

"Just admiring the view," the taller one said, as I stood up and started moving toward them. "No crime in that."

"Do you realize you're talking about a fifteen-year-old girl?" Isabelle said. "You both disgust me."

Short guy said, "Fifteen's not that young. And is that any way to talk when all we've done is compliment you?"

"Fifteen *is* young," she spat under her breath. She was trying hard not to be overheard by Rachel, who was about twenty feet away, exploring a little cluster of rocks and seaweed. "What are you both, twenty-eight? Thirty? Repulsive. Wasting your life hanging around on the beach and hitting on girls half your age."

I stood nearby, watching, coiled, not wanting to override Isabelle's skillful handling of the situation, but ready to intervene if things got more heated. The two men stood there, briefly silenced, until something passed between them — a moment of denial, conveyed by electricity — and the switch turned to anger.

"You stuck up bitch," the taller one said as he moved toward Isabelle and went to grab her arm. I was already sprinting at that point, and managed to catch his hand before he touched her. In one quick motion, I slammed his arm down upon my knee. He screamed and lunged at me but I landed a nice solid punch to his jaw that sent him knee-high into the water.

The other one threw a punch that I blocked, and I smashed him in the face with my elbow, punching him so hard that he landed in the water next to his friend, who was by now complaining of a broken arm.

The water around them started turning red as I pulled them both up by their hair and flung them onto the sand. "Learning some manners might stop you two from getting your asses handed to you."

They stood up and limped away, muttering in a pathetic attempt to save face. I stood in the water, hypnotized by the blood that quickly dissipated. I closed my eyes and it all came back…

Suddenly, I was on my knees in the shallow water, staring straight ahead. With my right hand, I reached for the scar from the bullet wound in my thigh. I couldn't speak or think, and I have no idea how long I kneeled there. Isabelle's gentle voice finally pierced my trance. She had taken me by the hand and was saying, "It's okay, Laurence. It's okay," as she helped me to my feet.

CHAPTER SIXTEEN

Laurence

Later that evening at the dinner table, Rachel held her father's hand and told him what had happened at the beach. "Daddy, Laurence was like a superhero. He was so brave."

"So what you're telling me is that Laurence protected my two beautiful girls?"

"Yes, Daddy, but you had to be there to see how amazing it was. If I write a story about it, can you publish it in one of your newspapers?"

"I would love to, sweetheart," Mr. Hamill replied.

"Maybe you can put it next to the story Laurence wrote last night."

"I think that's a fabulous idea."

"Great! I'm going to get started on it right away. Isabelle, can you help me?"

"Of course, sweetheart. I would love to."

She came around the table and grabbed Isabelle's hand and, in a flash, they were gone.

Mr. Hamill looked at me and said, "She just got away without having to help with the dishes."

"Sometimes, the creative process is so overpowering that you forget about everything else."

"I guess so," Mr. Hamill said. "And thank you so much for protecting my girls. If anything had happened to either one of them, I don't know what I would have done."

I knocked on Rachel's door where both Rachel and Isabelle were sitting at a typewriter working diligently on the story.

I asked Isabelle if I could talk to her for a moment in private.

"Of course," she said, then told Rachel, "You keep on working and I'll be right back."

She walked over to me and asked, "Where would you like to talk?"

"Just down the hallway," I said and we walked to the far end of the hall. I turned to her and was struck, again, by how beautiful she was.

She stopped and faced me and asked, "What is it?"

I was afraid of what I had to say, but I fought through my worry and launched in.

"It's no secret that I fell in love with you the moment I met you, and those feelings have only grown since I've gotten to know the caring, loving, and creative person you are."

Isabelle smiled bashfully, then began to look worried.

"Laurence, what are you trying to say?"

I looked down at the floor, then into her eyes. "That it's not going to work between us."

For the first time since I'd met her, Isabelle looked like she had no idea what to say or do next. There was real anguish in her eyes.

"What are you talking about?" she demanded to know. "You're wrong. This is wrong."

"Please, Isabelle, listen to me."

She crossed her arms and turned away. I had to force myself to say the words I didn't want to say.

"I realized it at the beach today, after those two clowns left. I was kneeling in the water and it was like I was right back in Normandy. I was terrified."

"But—"

"I'll never be able to see the ocean the way you do, and to pretend I can change would simply be lying to you. I can never erase what happened on Omaha Beach—"

"But—"

"Please, Isabelle. This is hard enough. Please listen."

She went quiet and looked at me from under hooded eyes.

"I can't erase what happened, and even trying to block out those memories would feel like a disservice to my friends who were killed that day — and to the families they left behind. I wouldn't be able to live with myself."

She looked at me with those mesmerizing emerald eyes as I fought back tears, and a small smile crept onto her face.

"So you're saying you can't learn to love the ocean the way I do?"

"That's right. I'm so sorry Isabelle. I wanted to—"

"Is that all? Is that the whole reason it won't work between us?"

"Yes."

"Laurence." Now she was mocking me.

"Isabelle?"

"You're such a silly boy. Brave, handsome, creative, and caring, but such a silly boy."

She put her arms around my neck and kissed me.

"To think that I would make your feelings about the ocean a reason to break up with you is simply crazy. Such a silly boy."

Joe

The movie reel that was unspooling in my brain came to an end. Laurence and Isabelle were still kissing when they faded into the ether. I looked down at my chinos and my blue short-sleeved shirt, then I reached out to feel the bench I was sitting on. It was there. I was there, on the bench, overlooking the water.

Mr. Laurence had stopped talking, and there were tears rolling down his face. We sat for a few minutes without saying a word. Then, in a low, despairing voice, he said, "Such a silly boy."

He stood up and took me gently by the arm and led me down a set of stairs to the beach. It was one of those typical New England beaches — rough but inviting, with dark, granular sand, boulders covered in barnacles, and long lines of seaweed left behind by the tide. The water was rough and choppy, as though a storm were about to hit, but it was sunny and clear, without a cloud in the sky.

Mr. Laurence was still holding the three roses when he stopped and faced the water. He looked out as though mesmerized, and then, with the strength and agility of a young pitcher, he rotated his whole body back and threw the roses into the ocean.

What happened next was as strange as everything I'd just witnessed in that vision from his early days with Isabelle.

The roses should have dropped into the water no more than fifteen or twenty feet out — but they didn't. They defied gravity and traveled further out over the water than I would have thought possible for anyone, let alone Mr. Laurence. When they finally dropped, they disappeared between two waves and were carried away.

I didn't ask him why he brought three roses, especially after he'd told me the story behind giving a lady two red roses. It was apparent: he wasn't mourning one lady, but two.

We walked back up the stairs, and out of respect I stopped by Isabelle's grave and said a prayer. Then I turned to Mr. Laurence and asked, "Did Isabelle want to be buried outside?"

"Isabelle isn't buried there. No one is."

"She's in the mausoleum with the rest of the family?"

"No," he replied in a gentle, melancholic voice that nevertheless told me that the subject was closed.

We got into the car and I drove out of the cemetery toward home. I was finished asking questions. I had enough to ponder for weeks.

CHAPTER SEVENTEEN

Joe

I dropped Mr. Laurence off at the house and drove toward the women's center, thinking about how strange everything seemed in this place, and wondering what would happen next.

I began making a mental list of the bizarre things that had happened since I met Mr. Laurence.

First there was Isabelle. She seemed to be capable of talking to me, despite being dead. There she was, a female voice hovering near a tombstone where, according to Mr. Laurence, she wasn't even buried. Of course, there were other possibilities concerning her remains, such as cremation, or cryonics. Cryonics was a real possibility, considering how much Mr. Laurence and Isabelle loved each other. Maybe she'd been frozen, and maybe Mr. Laurence planned to follow suit, so that in fifty years or so, when scientists figure out how to bring people back to life, they could be re-united and continue their love affair.

Then the horrifying thought occurred to me that Mr. Laurence could have had Isabelle stuffed, like a hunting bounty or a beloved pet. He could have had a taxidermist remove her organs and use her skin and skeleton to create a lifelike version of the once-beautiful Isabelle. For all I knew, she and her sister could both be stuffed and on display in the big house.

I shook my head to get rid of this image, and instead tried to prepare myself for what might be in store for me at the center. I had no idea which version of Angie might show up today, and it was making me nervous.

I parked in the parking lot, grabbed the two boxes of chocolates and the flowers off the passenger's seat, and walked over to the center. After I was let in, I knocked on Angie's door, and Gloria opened it, looking fabulous in a one-piece white outfit that highlighted every curve. It was impossible not to look.

"Wow," I said. "You must have a hot date."

"No, just entertaining myself with fashion while getting ready for a visit with my middle-aged shrink."

I laughed as she passed her hand over the high-quality fabric that skimmed her hips. "This gorgeous ensemble is compliments of your friend, Mr. Laurence. He left Angie and me a thousand-dollar credit at the clothing store, and since your girlfriend has old-lady taste in clothes, I had enough to pay for this one, in-fashion, Jennifer Lopez-style outfit that the saleslady said she never expected to sell, and wouldn't you know it, it fit like it was made for me."

Of course, it did, I thought as I handed one of the boxes of chocolates to her. She looked at the rectangular box with the large golden bow, and said, "Surely you must be kidding? You think I can maintain this shape eating chocolates?"

"Chocolate-covered cherries," I replied.

"My favorite," she said as she took the box and put it in the refrigerator. "Maybe I'll have one later, but feel free to have all you want, and tell Angie she's more than welcome to them once she finishes off her box. That girl could gain thirty pounds and still be considered underweight." She kissed me on the cheek. "Thank you, Joe. You're a sweetheart."

She walked out the door and when I turned around, Angie came out of the bedroom wearing a simple red dress with a white belt and red ballet flats. The contrast with Gloria could not have been greater, but for me there wasn't a prettier girl in the world than my Angie, even if she dressed like a middle-aged librarian. She had her hair pulled back into a ponytail and her face glowed. I looked at her for a long moment without saying a word.

"Something wrong?" she asked.

"You're just so beautiful."

"Well, thank you kindly," she said, in a less-than-convincing southern dialect.

"My pleasure, Scarlett," I said as I handed her the two roses.

"Only two roses today? No bouquet?"

"Do you know what two roses given to a lady signifies?"

"No, but why don't you tell me, my little romantic botanist?"

"Mutual love," I said, and she broke into the biggest smile. I wrapped my arms around her and spoke quietly into her ear. "I love you, Ang. I can only hope you feel the same way."

"After all this time you still have doubts?"

There was something a little edgy in her voice, but I chose to ignore it. Angie looked at me, then at the flowers, and said, "Let me put these in some water." Then she left for the bedroom and the bathroom, where I heard her running water and rummaging around. Eventually she rejoined me in the living room and we sat together on one of the love seats.

"I put them next to my bed. They'll be the last thing I see when I go to sleep and the first thing I see when I wake up."

That's when I reached down and produced the box of chocolates that I'd stashed next to the love seat. "This is also for you," I said.

She stared at the box, then looked at me with a mixture of panic and anger. "What did I tell you about never buying me chocolates?"

"They're chocolate-covered cherries," I said, defensively.

"My favorite," she said as she cautiously opened the box and looked down at the chocolates like they were tiny grenades. After a long moment she picked one up and took the smallest bite imaginable and then quickly put it back in the box. As she let the iota of chocolate melt in her mouth she closed her eyes in ecstasy. I couldn't help thinking that was the closest I would ever come to seeing her having an orgasm.

Then she opened her eyes, slammed the box shut, and glared at me. "How do you expect me to keep my figure if you keep feeding me sweets?"

"Why don't you forget about your figure and just enjoy them?"

"Is that your plan? You feed me sweets, I get fat, and then you can dump me for some other girl?"

I couldn't believe what I was hearing. I didn't know whether to storm out or scream at her. I was the fool who forgave her for trying to kill me — who saved her from going to jail — and here she was accusing me of hatching an elaborate plan to fatten her up just so I could get rid of her.

I snatched the box back, stood up, and walked over to the trash can. After a couple of attempts to get the foot pedal to work, I emptied the chocolates into the can and stuffed the empty box down on top of them until they were completely crushed.

Angie's mouth hung open. "You didn't have to throw them out. Gloria might have liked them," she said as I looked at her with fury in my eyes.

"Gloria has her own chocolates. I bought them for her and she said thank you, like a normal person," I said. "Goodbye, Angie."

I marched toward the front door, grabbing my coat off a chair and going for the doorknob.

"Where are you going?"

"To a place where I can forget you, make amends with my family, and stop feeling guilty for your mistakes."

"Joe, please, I'm sorry!"

"Just stop it! I'm tired of your excuses, your lies, and your paranoia! I turned my life upside down to help you get through this difficult time, but if I have any hope of staying sane, I can't be around you."

"But Joe, I love you!"

"And I imagine there will always be a certain part of me that's in love with you, but I can't go through this anymore. And besides I seriously doubt you have ever loved me."

"You know that's not true. How many times have I told you that you're the only man I've ever loved, and the only one I want to spend the rest of my life with?"

"Words, words, words. Goodbye, Angie," I said as I opened the door and walked toward the front gate, as her apologies and pleas for me to come back, and her frantic reminders that I was the only one she had in her entire life, evaporated under the late morning sun.

CHAPTER EIGHTEEN

Joe

As I opened the car door, a wave a nausea overcame me. I walked away from the car, fell to my knees, and vomited. I leaned against the car, panting, with my hands on my knees, and my phone started ringing. I looked at the number and it was Angie. She left a message, crying hysterically and begging me to forgive her. It was enough to make me want to vomit again.

I climbed into the car and leaned back in the driver's seat with my eyes closed. As I sat there, my entire relationship with Angie passed through my mind. She was always the victim, which I totally understood, especially considering the family she'd come from. Even after she apologized to me, I could guarantee that in a few days she would turn it all back on me again and say that I'd caused her undue stress by overreacting to her harmless comments about the chocolates. And maybe I had overreacted. I began to wonder. This kind of thing had happened so often that every insinuation from her felt like an attack. She was always ready to believe the worst — always so terrified of being abandoned that she seemed to want to beat me to it and push me away. When she came down from a paranoid rant, she would apologize. But her apologies never stuck, and reassurances had to be repeated constantly — sometimes dozens of times a day — or they would float away.

There was a venomous side to Angie. She was incapable of seeing things or people objectively. She saw everything through the narrow lens of her own insecurity. Yes, I was starting to take in the psychobabble that I'd been hearing about since Angie was locked up. And to tell the truth, it was beginning to make sense. I'd even done some reading to try and understand her fear of abandonment. And I knew enough to know that she wouldn't get better — if I stayed with her, I would always be subject to the same behavior. The lashing out. The black-and-white thinking of a person stuck at the age she was when she was traumatized. The splitting episodes, where I go from being perfect to being a monster, all in her mind.

The worst was the way she put everyone in boxes marked Good or Bad. To Angie, all of my friends were losers because they drank and wanted to talk about sports. Of course, during the few times she'd hung out with us she never once asked any of them a single question that would help her get to know them. She could have asked them what they liked to do or whether they planned to go to college and where, but she just sat there in a corner, scowling, waiting to go home.

When I told her that two of my friends were accepted into MIT, that one was going to Cornell, and that another got into Columbia, she laughed and said I must be joking.

"It's the truth," I'd said. "Why don't we go back and ask them?"

"Even if it's true, it doesn't make them any less a bunch of drunken losers."

Coming from a loving family, I never passed judgment on her. I went out of my way to make her feel protected and loved. I knew she had problems with intimacy, and never once did I even attempt to cross any line. I was content to simply hold hands with her, and to get a goodnight kiss. Strangely, it was she who crossed the line in a big way, that day near the duck pond.

My phone rang and, once again, it was Angie. She'd left a message almost identical to the last one, except she'd added a threat that she had "no reason to live if it was without me."

And then a dark, horrifying dose of reality hit me in the face like a Nolan Ryan fastball. Ever since I'd met her, she'd repeatedly told me that she had contemplated suicide.

She'd repeatedly told me she wouldn't do it because it was a mortal sin, but at one point I got so worried that I researched the subject, and the one thing that stood out in every article was that when a person talks about killing themselves, the people around them have to take what they're saying very seriously. Loved ones tend to brush such talk off, only to regret their indifference when the person actually commits the unthinkable act.

I dialed her number. She picked up on the first ring and started by saying, "I'm so sorry, Joe. Believe me, I love you with all my heart."

I paused. "It's okay, Angie."

"It's not okay. I made you so mad—"

"Angie, I forgive you. I love you." I paused and put on a stern voice. "But tomorrow when I bring you a box of chocolates, I expect you to eat all of them."

She laughed nervously and negotiated a compromise: she would eat half the chocolates when I first got there, and the other half before I left. "I'll get sick if I eat them all at once."

"Yes, that would be fine."

"Are you going to come back today?"

"I never left the parking lot."

I could hear her stifling tears on the other end of the phone.

"Angie, you need to tell me if things are bothering you."

"It's the nightmares, Joe. It's the nightmares."

"I'll be right over," I said as I walked back to the center and knocked on Angie's door. She opened it and was crying hysterically. I wrapped my arms around her trembling body and softly caressed the back of her head.

"It's going to be okay," I said. "I'm here."

CHAPTER NINETEEN

Joe

She was in my arms for at least a half hour before her body went totally limp. I picked her up and gently lowered her onto her bed. The front of her dress was drenched with her tears, but I didn't dare try to take her dress off and put on dry clothes. Hopefully, Gloria would come back soon. She could undress her.

I pulled a chair up beside her bed and sat down and watched her sleep. She had the most beautiful face, and with her hair pulled back, her features looked exquisitely delicate. But she was so thin that it was getting frightening, and with the front of her dress plastered to her skin, I could easily make out her ribcage.

I couldn't recall her ever being so underweight before. When I first saw her back home, she seemed to always be wearing clothes a few sizes too big, as if she was trying to hide her body. When she moved in with my family, she started wearing clothes her size. At the time, I never thought of her as skin and bones. Now she was so light, I could have picked her up with one hand.

I looked at the bureau beside her bed and noticed that the only picture on display was of the two of us, taken around Thanksgiving. The two roses I'd given her were on the bureau, in a large glass filled with water. I was tempted to go through the bureau in search of things I didn't know, but all the proof I needed was right there before me.

As I sat there next to her, my foot hit something under her box spring. It was the library book about US coastal towns. I pulled it out and opened it to the front page, where I found a yellow sticky note that read, "Places Joe and I are hoping to move to where we can be happy for the rest of our lives. Please God!"

She'd placed notes on six pages and assigned each coastal town a number. The number one spot went to Santa Barbara, followed by Laguna Beach; San Diego; Carmel-by-the-Sea in Monterey County; Wellfleet, Cape Cod; and Lahaina, Hawaii.

I guess she was expecting us to get super rich along the way, and who knows, maybe we will. One thing I knew I would never do is discourage her from dreaming. Like the great shortstop for the Chicago Cubs Ernie Banks said, "Once you stop dreaming, you stop living."

I tucked the book back under the bed and looked at her. Her eyes were moving rapidly, which meant that she was dreaming. She started perspiring, and suddenly she just shot up and was gasping for air. I leaned down and whispered, "Everything is okay, Angie. I'm here."

She looked at me and for a few seconds it was like she didn't recognize me, and then she simply said my name and sank back onto the bed, asleep. I wrapped my arms around her and couldn't help thinking, *There is no peace for this child.*

CHAPTER TWENTY

Joe

By 8:05 p.m. I was sitting in the parking lot of the center, gripping the steering wheel and staring through the windshield. I didn't turn on the ignition. I just needed a little more time to process the events of the day. Apart from the short time when we'd been officially broken up, I'd spent the whole day in her bedroom, watching over her. She slept almost the entire time, swatting away demons and suddenly waking up and gasping before falling back onto her pillow. It was by far the worst I had ever seen her, including during her time at Rikers.

I could smell her fear and anxiety all over me like cigarette smoke clinging to my clothes. It would be too simplistic to blame her state of mind totally on our little fight, even though that episode reinforced the fact that this beautiful girl felt completely alone and vulnerable unless I was there beside her. Gloria was great, but she'd only been a part of Angie's life for a little while. Not long enough to build the kind of trust that she and I had.

Angie's nightmares were getting worse, and I had to admit, I was worried. She had to be suffering from some kind of post-traumatic stress, no doubt stemming from that night of murderous revenge and the near-fatal push from behind that sent me tumbling down flights of stairs.

I knew she was nothing like this six months ago when she was living with my family. My little brother would have said something if she'd been having nightmares all the time, and with the walls in the apartment being as thin as paper, I would have heard something. She was so thin that she could play a skeleton in a movie, and the idea that I had an elaborate plan to fatten her up just so I could leave her was another indication of how much she had deteriorated. That was outright paranoia.

I sat there, staring straight ahead, until a streetlight came on and jolted me back into the moment. A guard swung past and gave me a look that told me to clear out, so I waved and started the car and drove back to the house. I parked in the driveway and once again couldn't move for all the thinking I needed to do. Eventually I noticed Mr. Laurence sitting on the porch. I got out of the car and walked over to him and sat down in the chair beside his without saying a word.

He searched my eyes and quietly asked, "Did you … have a wonderful day with your lovely Angie?"

I shook my head. "It was the worst day since that infamous night that set it all off."

I told Mr. Laurence everything that had happened and described the shape Angie was in. I had to tell someone, and Mr. Laurence was starting to feel like the only person I could trust. I cried several times and finished by apologizing. "I'm sorry to hit you with all this. At my age you were storming the beaches at Normandy, and here I am, whining about my girlfriend."

"You're not whining," he said, seriously. "You're trying to save a life."

Nobody had ever put it that way. I hadn't even thought about it that way, but it was true. As I wiped the tears away with my shirt sleeve, Mr. Laurence kept talking.

"Most young men would have walked away by now. A guy as good-looking as you would have had no problem meeting other girls, and no one would have faulted you for leaving. They would have said it was your only choice. But you didn't see it that way. Your ability to forgive and understand Angie's actions is a sign of maturity, empathy, and love. I'm personally very proud of you."

I managed a tearful smile before reaching for a box of tissues that happened to be sitting near us. When I blew my nose loudly, he smiled and patted my shoulder.

"Let it out, Joe. This is what it feels like to do the right thing instead of the easy thing."

"I fell in love the first time I saw her," I said. "If I had my way, we'd already be married. Not much chance of that happening right now. But I won't leave her."

Mr. Laurence patted me on the back of my head and reassured me that everything was going to work out. As I took in the words and felt his mild gaze on my bowed head, I suddenly felt sure he was right.

I opened the door to the small house and walked in. I was physically and emotionally exhausted, but I needed to take a shower. Angie's desperation and fear clung to me like a scent, and I couldn't bear the thought of it eating away at me.

I jumped into the shower and let the water splash down upon my body for a long time before picking up a washcloth and a bar of soap and scrubbing my entire body clean, twice. I put on a pair of pajamas that Mr. Laurence had left for me, and I couldn't believe how good they felt. It had to have been ten years since I'd worn pajamas. Usually, I went to sleep in a T-shirt and shorts.

Hunger was competing with exhaustion, so I went to the kitchen for a bagel, which I slowly ate as I walked over to the sliding glass door that opened onto the pool. The lights from under the water were playing tricks on my eyes and making the pool look even bigger than it was. From where I stood, it looked like the rippling blue water extended outward into a distant galaxy. I finished my bagel, brushed my teeth, got into bed, and fell into a deep sleep.

It was night, and I was still looking at the pool from the sliding glass door, but now there was a beautiful woman in the water, swimming under a full moon as bright as I have ever seen. I felt an irresistible pull to walk out of the house and toward the shimmering blue water. The lady was at the far end of the pool but swimming gracefully toward me. As she got closer, I could see that it was Isabelle. She was so stunning, so perfect, that it was as if she was not of this world.

"Hello, Joseph," she called out. "It's such a lovely night. Why not put on a bathing suit and jump in?"

She flipped over, and instead of her feet breaching the surface, a glistening orange tail rose into the air and came splashing down, soaking my pajamas with pool water. As I watched her glide toward the other side of the pool and then back toward me, I said, "My God, Isabelle, you really are a mermaid."

"Silly boy. Surely, you know mermaids aren't real." She stared down into the water. "Oh Rachel ... please come up and meet Laurence's friend, Joe."

Rachel shot up from the bottom of the pool and hovered in the water beside Isabelle. "Hello Joe, it's a pleasure to meet you. Isabelle has told me about you."

"It's a pleasure to meet you," I said. They both smiled, flipped over, and started undulating toward the other end of the pool. They both had tails, and when they came splashing down into the water it was like being hit by a hurricane.

They came swimming back toward me, giggling, as Isabelle told Rachel that I thought she was a mermaid.

"You're both mermaids," I said, pointing. "You both have tails."

"See what I mean, Rachel? Now he even believes you're a mermaid," Isabelle said as they both leaned against the side of the pool, flapping their tails in unison and smiling at me.

Isabelle turned to Rachel and said, "You know, his girlfriend is one of us."

Rachel looked very concerned and said, "Oh, I'm so sorry."

"I told Laurence that she needs to move in here as soon as possible, and he agrees."

"Good. She'll always feel safe here, and Daddy and Mommy will be so happy. The house has been so empty of late."

"Yes, far too empty. And Joseph, if you want to believe that your lovely Angie is also a mermaid that's okay, because this is the place where dreams become reality."

They swam off toward the far end. In a farewell gesture, they lifted their tails up high and flapped them back and forth like they were waving goodbye.

I woke up, and I wasn't sure if I had been dreaming, or if what I had just witnessed was real. After all, I'd been talking to a tombstone earlier in the morning and Isabelle had spoken back to me, even though she wasn't buried there. I had completely forgotten about that when the rest of the day turned sour. Maybe, the concussion I'd suffered hadn't turned me into a temporary genius after all. I might be having hallucinations and not even know it.

CHAPTER TWENTY-ONE

Joe

The following morning, Mr. Laurence and I drove to the florist. At the cash register, I insisted on paying for the three roses he'd picked out. I didn't leave as big a tip as Mr. Laurence had left the day before, but it was still a nice tip.

We then drove to the confectionery shop, where I bought another box of chocolates for Angie. Once again, I insisted on paying, and it felt good to finally give back a little of what I'd received. I mean, how much could I take from the man? He was letting me live in that beautiful house for next to nothing, and he was paying me three hundred dollars a week for doing what turned out to be a miniscule number of chores around the property. So far, he'd allowed me to water the plants once. On top of that, he'd already paid for flowers, chocolates, and clothing for my girlfriend and Gloria.

I didn't care how much money he had. It wasn't right to let someone pay for everything, and deep down I knew that Mr. Laurence had to feel the same way. After all, we were both brought up in the Bronx. People are generous there, but everyone is expected to pull their weight and give back what they can.

As we drove toward the cemetery, I told Mr. Laurence about my dream. He listened carefully, and to my surprise he didn't find anything strange about it. When I finished describing the scene in the pool, he said, "Well, if mermaids were real, I'm quite sure Isabelle and Rachel would qualify."

"But they seemed to know things that I don't even think I have ever known or thought about."

"That's not surprising. My Isabelle is the smartest person I've ever known, and she and Rachel are inseparable."

I couldn't help noticing that he always talked about them as though they were still alive, and I was starting to believe they might be, in some form or the other.

We drove through the cemetery gates and parked by Isabelle's gravestone. I bowed my head and said a prayer while Mr. Laurence tidied up the little garden in front of the grave. He then took me by my arm and led me over to the bench. We sat there for a while, watching the waves crash against the shore.

I asked, "Did Rachel and Isabelle get their column written?"

Mr. Laurence smiled and said, "Oh yes, and they made me out to be a superhero, when really it was Isabelle who first put the creeps in their place. Rachel insisted that Isabelle's name appear alongside hers, but to avoid the appearance of nepotism, they called it 'A Day at The Beach,' and signed it Annabel and Catherine Poe."

I smiled and said, "Did they get any feedback from readers?"

"Actually, yes. The response was overwhelmingly positive and they went on to write a weekly column about their adventures for many years."

"And how about your piece? Did Isabelle change it as much as you thought?"

"She hardly changed it at all. She re-arranged several paragraphs, deleted a few adjectives, added a few words, and it read a million times better. I told her that I feared she had rewritten the entire column because of all the crossing out and all the side notes she made.

"She told me, 'That's what you get for looking over the editor's shoulder. From now on when you finish a column simply hand it off to me and walk out of the room and if I have a question, I will call you back.' I never again looked over her shoulder when she was editing my work."

"And how was the response to your column?"

"Good. Not nearly as positive as the girls' tale, but Mr. Hamill felt it was good enough to give me my own weekly column."

"And do you remember what your second column was about?"

"I do," he said. "Like the first piece, the images and details in the second one have haunted me my entire life. After we took control of Omaha beach, we made our way up the hills to where the German gunners had their bunkers. Most of the machine-gun fire had died down, and some of the bunkers were taken out by our fighter bombers, but there were still plenty of German soldiers up there.

"The fighting in the hills was fierce and we lost a lot of men. When we came to a bunker, we would usually throw a hand grenade in first, and a few seconds later we would carefully go in and see if anyone was alive. We tried to stay in teams of two or three, but just after we tossed a grenade into this one bunker, we got into fight with a group of German soldiers coming from further up the hill.

"I went into the bunker, as the other two soldiers fought the Germans off. In a fog of smoke, I saw a German soldier rise and take aim at me with his rifle. He was wounded, wobbling on his feet, which gave me just enough time to knock the rifle out of his hand. He grabbed onto me, and suddenly, we were in a hand-to-hand fight, rolling around the dirt floor. I had to punch him at least five times in the face, and yet he refused to give up. He was no older than me. I grabbed his rifle with both hands and used all my strength to pull it down toward his neck. He pushed back on the rifle, his large, dilated, blue eyes looking directly at me, pleading, begging, as his strength receded, and in less than a split second he stopped pushing back and my momentum took the rifle and me straight down onto his neck. I could hear the crack of his neck, despite all the surrounding gunfire.

"God only knows how many of my fellow soldiers, my friends, this boy had killed as we landed on the beach, yet at that moment..." He paused as he looked out over the water. "It's one thing to shoot someone from five hundred feet away, but to kill someone when you're so close to them that you could smell their breath before they die — that's a different story."

I was still taking all of this in when Mr. Laurence stood up and motioned for me to follow him. We walked down the stairs to the beach, then ambled along the shore for about half a mile. When we stopped to look at the ocean, Mr. Laurence said, "Why don't you throw the flowers into the water? Just pretend you're Sandy Koufax. Lean back and let go."

It was so windy on the beach that I was just hoping to throw them far enough that they wouldn't fly back into our faces or float back on the next wave. I leaned back, thought of the great Dodgers pitcher, and threw the flowers as hard as I could. To my amazement, they cut through the powerful on-shore wind and just kept going, sailing about three hundred feet before dropping between two waves and floating peacefully out into the majestic embrace of a rising sun.

CHAPTER TWENTY-TWO

Joe

After dropping Mr. Laurence off at the house, I drove straight to the center. It felt like I was going on a blind date with a girl I'd never met, not a girl I had planned an entire life with. I didn't know who I would find — the sick, skinny waif who kept waking up short of breath, perspiring like she had just been caught in a downpour, a semi-normal Angie capable of flashing the occasional smile, or some combination of the two.

I parked the car in the lot and walked slowly to the center, preparing myself for the worst while hoping for the best. I knocked on the door and I was greeted by a smiling, gorgeous Angie, dressed in a white spring dress, with her hair pulled back and a twinkle in her eyes. Before I could say a word, she flung her arms around my shoulders and kissed me passionately, and suddenly I was the one short of breath.

"I'm so happy you're here, Joe. I love you so much, so very much," she said as she kissed me again and again. I wasn't quite sure which category this Angie fell into, but I liked it a whole lot.

"You look so beautiful, Angie."

"Thank you, and thank you for loving me so much despite all the craziness I put you through," she said as she hugged me around my waist and started crying. Before I had time to wonder if she was going over to the dark side, she said, "Don't worry, these are happy tears."

When I stepped back and looked at her, it was like gazing at an of image of purity and innocence. I had a flash of what her life might have been like if she had been born into a loving and supportive family. This could have been her normal.

I took her by the hand and sat her down on the couch. She pointed to the box of chocolates that I had set down when she'd started in with the kissing. "Are those for me?" she asked, and I handed her the box. She unwrapped it and looked inside. Before she could pick up a chocolate, I touched her shoulder and said, "I don't want you to feel pressured to eat more than you're comfortable with, but I hope you can eat at least two."

She looked at me for a long and confusing moment and then asked, "What's wrong, Joe?"

"Not a thing, but I don't want you to stuff your face just to please me and then get sick. I worry about you, and it's because I love you so much."

She put the chocolates aside, and before I knew it, we were stretched out on the couch, kissing passionately. She paused for a moment and grabbed two of the chocolates. She put one in my mouth and one in her mouth. After we'd finished chewing, we went back to kissing. Then we paused and had two more chocolates. We continued like this until the box was empty. It was better than I could ever have imagined. After gorging ourselves on two of the best things in life — kissing and chocolate — we took a walk, holding hands, stopped by the pond to watch the ducks, and then continued walking, like two newlyweds in love.

It was the best day I'd had with her in so long that it was like I was falling for her all over again, which is strange, because I had never *not* been madly in love with her, even during our forty-five-minute breakup the day before.

CHAPTER TWENTY-THREE

Joe

I parked the car in Mr. Laurence's driveway and walked over to where he was sitting on the porch. Actually, I must have been floating, because when I sat down next to him, he just grinned and said, "Is it safe to say you had a good day with Angie?"

"The best. It felt like I died and went to Heaven."

"That's wonderful," he said. "And it's only going to get better."

"I don't know how it could get any better."

At that moment the door to the mansion opened and a stunningly beautiful woman stepped out. If not for the doctor's uniform she was wearing, I would have guessed that she'd wandered off the set of a Fellini movie. I couldn't stop staring at her smooth, olive skin or her long, dark-brown hair.

"What a pleasure to meet you, Joseph," she said. "I've heard wonderful things about you." We shook hands and Mr. Laurence said, "This is my daughter, Maria. Our pride and joy."

"It's a pleasure to meet you," I said.

"Are you going back to the clinic?" Mr. Laurence asked her.

"Yes, the doctor who was supposed to be on call had to deal with a family emergency, so I'm covering for them for a few hours." She bent down and kissed Mr. Laurence on the cheek and said, "Love you, Dad."

"Love you, sweetheart," Mr. Laurence said as she waved good-bye to us and got into her car and drove off.

I opened my mouth to speak, but before I could ask about Maria, Mr. Laurence quickly patted me on the hand and said, "You look exhausted, Joe. Go get some sleep. I'll see you in the morning."

Inside the small house, I sat down at the kitchen table and thought about what had just happened. I had no idea that Mr. Laurence had a daughter who was a doctor. It was apparent that he didn't want to talk about it, and so I left it at that. Not for nothing, but she didn't look like either Isabelle or Mr. Laurence. She was gorgeous, but more in a Mediterranean way ... perhaps Italian or Greek.

I hadn't talked to my mom in a few days, and I knew she would be worried if she didn't hear from me soon. I knew how the conversation would go, and knew that if I called her, a great day would end on a sour note. But she was my mom, and I didn't want to leave her, or my dad, wondering.

I dialed the home phone and my mother picked up on the first ring. She sounded relieved to hear from me, and I could tell she was in a better mood than the last time we'd talked. She told me she'd looked up Mr. Laurence on the internet, and that he and the family he'd married into had books written about them, about his father-in-law, who was a newspaper tycoon, and about all the charitable organizations they'd started, and how they'd adopted fifteen orphan girls who had been abused as children.

She told me that Mr. Laurence looked like Laurence Olivier — "so very handsome." She was always comparing people's looks to those of screen actors. She couldn't believe the luck I had in meeting him, and I told her I couldn't agree more. We talked about Angie for only a few minutes, and she only compared her to the devil's daughter once. All in all, it was a positive conversation, and we ended it like we always did, by saying how much we loved each other.

Unlike the other nights, I didn't take a shower. Instead, I brushed my teeth and washed my face, then took my sneakers off and climbed into bed with my clothes on. Angie's scent was all over me, and this time it wasn't toxic or sickly, but clean and pure and lovely. The way things were going, I had to soak up the intoxicating beauty that was Angie while it lasted, because by tomorrow or the next day or in a week it could all be toxic.

As I hovered next to sleep, breathing in her scent, I suddenly became aware of her face hovering over mine. It was like she was really there, and I was getting to see her in that confident, happy state all over again. Even in my dream, I was grateful for the chance to relive a day that had given me so much hope for the future. I slept as long as I could, drinking in every minute of Angie's dream-self, who was just as sweet and lovely as she had been that day.

The next morning, Mr. Laurence and I went about our normal routine, picking up three roses, then driving to the cemetery. When we'd paid our respects to Isabelle and Rachel and settled onto the bench, Mr. Laurence apologized for abruptly cutting off our conversation after Maria left the night before. He said he'd forgotten about a telephone call he had to make to someone on the West Coast while the person was still in his office.

"That's okay," I said. "I was just surprised to find out that you and Isabelle had a daughter. I guess I've been talking about myself so much that it never came up."

"Not at all," Mr. Laurence said. "Maria is just a lot to take in sometimes. She's a big personality. I thought it best for you to meet after you'd settled in."

"I see," I said. But I didn't really understand — or not fully — and Mr. Laurence looked at me as though he could tell.

"How is Maria a lot to take in?"

He thought for a moment, then said, "Like all of the women who have passed through the Hamill's house, Maria has suffered abuse. Her suffering was different from Isabelle's and Rachel's, but the effect was similar. Shock. Dysfunction. Recovery. If I've learned anything from knowing Isabelle and Rachel and then helping to care for Maria, it's that suffering rarely just ends, even when a person's circumstances change for the better."

"I think I know what you mean," I said. "One of Angie's doctors said something about that, and Angie tried to explain it to me once."

"What did they say?"

"Something about demons. How we always talk about people having demons, but they're not demons at all." Mr. Laurence nodded encouragingly as I struggled to remember the doctor's phrasing. "I think she said suffering converts to dysfunction. We call it people having demons, but it's really just suffering working its way through and then out of the mind and body."

"That's right!" Mr. Laurence looked surprised. "That's exactly right."

I had seen the process up close, and I had to admit — I had no idea if Angie would ever be completely free.

Mr. Laurence looked at me as though he was struggling to decide how much to say. Finally, he said, "I'm going to tell you something about Maria, and I hope you can put it in the vault."

"Of course."

He explained the situation about Maria and told me about the tragic circumstances involving her biological family. Early in her medical training, when she was still living with her parents and working on her degree, Maria had decided to share something with her parents that she could no longer keep to herself. She calmly sat down with them over a cup of tea and explained what she had known, but kept hidden, for many years: that she was, without any doubt, attracted to women — exclusively. And she shared the great news that she was seeing someone wonderful and couldn't wait for them to finally meet her, since the relationship was getting quite serious.

As soon as she said the words, her parents lost their minds. They screamed and cried, calling Maria a filthy deviant and many other unspeakable things, and moaning about how they would never have grandchildren. Her father led the charge, looming over her and threatening her with terrible consequences if she didn't recant her statement, stop seeing her girlfriend — he couldn't even say the word— and agree to meet with the priest at their local Catholic church. When Maria refused to do any of this, her father kicked her out of the home she had grown up in and banned her from ever contacting the family again, unless and until she was "cured."

All of this unfolded in an astonishingly short period of time. Within ten minutes of broaching the subject, Maria was standing out on the sidewalk, catching a few items of clothing and a couple of teddy bears that were raining down on her from her bedroom window. She had gone into shock and couldn't even remember how she survived that night. She ended up staying in the dorm rooms of a couple of friends from her degree program, but there was never enough room, and she was running out of options, both for housing and paying her next tuition bill, since her parents had immediately cut her off from any financial help. As she bounced from place to place, desperately trying to sort out her finances and her living situation, she started to fall behind on her studies. Soon she was facing the clear prospect of having to drop out of the program and give up on her lifelong dream of being a doctor.

Isabelle, Rachel, and Mr. Laurence had come to know Maria well through her volunteer work at the Pediatric Cancer Hospital. They came to the center every Saturday to visit with the children, and first met Maria in one of the center's play rooms. Before she had been kicked out of her family home, Maria had wandered over to where Isabelle and Rachel were engaging some children in a spirited game of beanbag toss, using a set up that Mr. Laurence had built for the center. Maria was so lovely that they sought her out every time they came to the center, and the four of them had had many friendly conversations. "We used to talk fondly about what a perfect daughter Maria would make, and how happy her family must be to have such a loving, intelligent, and beautiful child," Mr. Laurence said.

"Then one Saturday, she took Isabelle and Rachel aside, and told them the story about her family. She had just started medical school, which her family was helping her pay for, and she had promised to pay them back once she became a doctor. Now, with her family wanting nothing to do with her, she didn't know if she would ever graduate.

"We invited her to move into the house and offered to pay for her medical school and support her during her internship. We made it clear that she didn't have to pay us back, and we only asked that she stay the compassionate and loving person that we knew her to be. 'The perfect child,' as Isabelle used to say. That was over a decade ago, and during that time she became our daughter. She even took the Hamill name."

"The Hamill name? Not Laurence?" I asked, suddenly realizing that I didn't know if Laurence was a first or last name. Mr. Laurence explained that Isabelle had kept her maiden name when they married — a rarity in the mid-1940s — and that both of them had encouraged Maria to take the Hamill name as a way to honor everything that Isabelle's parents had accomplished through their foundation, businesses, and philanthropy. Adopting Maria was a way of celebrating the Hamill legacy and continuing Mr. and Mrs. Hamill's commitment to offering a safe harbor to young women in crisis. And Maria had become a Hamill in every sense.

"Apart from me, she's the only person who knows all of the ins-and-outs of the Hamill Foundation and our affiliated business interests," Mr. Laurence explained. "She'll take over when I'm no longer capable. After finishing medical school and completing her internship, she decided not to go into her own private practice but to join a nearby free clinic that we fund through our foundation. She doesn't receive a salary, but she enjoys all the benefits of being a member of the Hamill family, which far outweigh any salary or amount of money she would have made with her own practice."

I was nodding and listening carefully when Mr. Laurence said something else that shocked me.

"She is the child that Isabelle, Rachel, and I have trusted with eventually running the foundation and business. She's never let any of us down, and hopefully, one day, if you want, you'll join her and help run the Hamill foundation and business that has relieved the suffering of thousands of people throughout the world. In our eyes, you're a younger version of our Maria and possess many of the wonderful traits we originally noticed in our daughter."

I don't remember what I said. I think I just stared at him, stunned. Things were happening with disorienting speed, and I had no way of making sense of the trust this exceptional man was placing in me. The best I could do was to listen and learn.

CHAPTER TWENTY-FOUR

Joe

I parked in the center's lot and couldn't wait to tell Angie about Mr. Laurence's offer to me, which would naturally influence both our futures in a very positive way. I knocked on the apartment door and Gloria opened the door, looking like a million bucks in mauve sweatpants and a matching hoodie.

I talked to her for a few minutes, as the joy I felt in the parking lot slowly diminished. Gloria had to force-feed Angie that morning because she had not eaten since early last evening with me. I walked into the bedroom and found her asleep, fighting off demons as her hands flailed in the air above her.

I sat down in a chair beside her and gently took hold of her. She opened her eyes and then with the force of a thousand-pound gorilla she hit me and send me flying to the floor. She laid back down, closed her eyes and fell back to asleep, perspiring like she'd just run a marathon.

I stayed by her bed all day, and the few times she woke up and was somewhat lucid she accused me of cheating on her and went on to call me names I never thought I would hear out of her mouth. I had to rely on Gloria to force-feed her because she didn't want the cheating son-of-a-bitch to touch her.

For the next several months her behavior was erratic. One day she would be all lovey-dovey, the next day she would bounce between sweetness and paranoia. At her worst, she was delusional and aggressive, accusing me of horrible things from serial cheating to making elaborate plans to abandon her. Then, just to keep me totally off balance, she occasionally had days like this, in which she never got out of bed, and I had to rely on Gloria to make sure she got anything to eat. During stretches like this, Angie missed appointments with the psychiatrist and would go days without bathing.

I did not tell Mr. Laurence any of this, and I felt guilty as hell. He had a right to know. I was convinced that if Angie stayed at the women's center much longer that she would either commit suicide or die from malnutrition.

At last, I broke down and told Mr. Laurence everything. He listened without commenting and then, like he did when I first met his daughter, he abruptly ended the conversation and told me to get a good night's sleep and that he would see me the next day at the usual time.

As we were driving back from the cemetery the next morning, he said, "I'll be going with you to the center today. I just need to stop at the house for a few minutes, and while I'm there you should call Angie and tell her to start packing. She's checking out of the center and coming home with us today."

"She is?" I asked, in shock.

"Yes, and I talked to Gloria last night and told her that once she decides to tell the therapist what she wants to hear, that she will be released. I have a nursing job all set up for her at Stony Brook Hospital. Her credentials are quite impressive."

Mr. Laurence got out of the car and walked into the mansion as I sat there in a state of wonder. I had a thousand questions that I had no intention of asking him. He would let me know in his own way and at the right time.

I dialed Angie's number and she picked up immediately. I asked, "How is the girl of my dreams today?"

"Wonderful!" she said, and I thought to myself, *I hope it stays that way until we get her out of that place.*

"Well, I have news that is going to make your day ten thousand times better. You're being released today and coming to live with Mr. Laurence and me."

"Oh my God! How?"

"Mr. Laurence will have to tell you that, and before you start worrying about Gloria, Mr. Laurence has also hopefully fixed her problem. He has secured a nursing job for her at Stony Brook Hospital, but before she's released, she'll have to tell the therapist what she wants to hear."

"Oh my God. It's like a miracle. I can't believe it!"

"Believe it, and start packing. We should be there in half an hour. I love you."

"I love you so much," she said as she blew me kisses and, in response, I said a *Hail Mary* right after we hung up.

When Mr. Laurence got back into the car, he was holding a simple manila folder. I wanted to ask what was in it, but decided not to pry. I started driving and he asked if I'd spoken to Angie.

"Yes. She sounded like a kid on Christmas morning. She's so excited."

"Great! We're going to make sure she never feels threatened and always feels safe and loved." He paused to look out the side window. "Always loved and safe, especially during difficult times. She's blessed to have you, Joe."

"I think she's blessed that you've taken such an interest in her. It's not me getting her released, it's you."

"I'm just a conduit. The responsibility falls upon both of you, but for now it lies heaviest upon you."

"How did you get her released? It's not like she has been the model inmate…"

"Isabelle, Rachel, and I have contributed large sums of money and time and helped get the center built against some strong opposition. As you know, it was a top priority for the Hamill Foundation to provide a safe haven and other help for girls who had been abused. I didn't tell you earlier because I know the center has done some wonderful work, especially with cases like Angie and Gloria, where the abuse they suffered compelled them to take drastic steps. But when you told me about Angie's behavior and your concerns about her well-being last night, I felt it was time to intercede."

"Thank you, Mr. Laurence," was all I could manage.

CHAPTER TWENTY-FIVE

Joe

We parked in a lot across from the center and walked over to Angie and Gloria's apartment. Mr. Laurence was a towering figure and he not only looked like Olivier, but he was broader around the shoulders and more muscular than the great actor. He usually wore a sports coat, slacks, a dress shirt with no tie, and comfortable shoes. When he walked into a room, or just into the diner where we ate breakfast, every woman looked at him as though he was the only person in the world. Like Cary Grant, he had aged gracefully.

We knocked on Angie and Gloria's door and it flew open and Angie jumped straight into my arms and kissed me. She was wearing a simple dress with a white and yellow floral print and a white belt. The dress obscured how very thin she was, and made her look clean and pure and, dare I say, virginal.

She quickly moved back once she noticed Mr. Laurence standing behind me. Before she could say anything, Mr. Laurence reached out and took her hand and said, "So you're the beautiful Angie that Joe has talked so much about. It's wonderful to finally meet you."

"Thank you so much, Mr. Laurence," Angie said. "It's wonderful to meet you, too."

"So, are you all packed and ready to start anew with the two of us?"

"Yes, sir. I don't know how to thank you. I'm so grateful."

"Well, you can start by thanking your boyfriend, who spoke so glowingly about you that I said we had to get you out of here and bring you home where you belong."

She started crying and I asked, "Why are you crying?"

"They're happy tears. I love you so much!" She kissed me again as I wiped the tears from her cheeks.

"Can we speak for a moment before we go to the office?" Mr. Laurence asked.

"Of course," Angie said as she let us in the apartment and shut the door.

"Just a few things to go over. They agreed to let you go under a few conditions. First, you'll need to see an outside psychiatrist twice a week. I have set that up for you, with a highly recommended female psychiatrist less than half a mile from our house. Next, you'll need to call the administrator of the center once a week, to tell her how everything is turning out. That's not so hard, is it?"

"No, sir," she replied.

"So why don't we get this done?" Mr. Laurence asked. "Joe, you're going to have to stay behind. It shouldn't take too long."

"Joe can't come?"

"No, sweetheart," Mr. Laurence said as I looked at a suddenly nervous Angie. I turned to Mr. Laurence, "Can we just have a minute?"

"Of course," Mr. Laurence said as I took Angie by the hand and led her into the bedroom. She kept her eyes down but I could still see her lip trembling.

"Look at me," I said, as I lifted her chin up. "Mr. Laurence is going to do all the talking. Just agree with him. That is all you need to do. He's the smartest, nicest person I've ever met, so just follow his lead. And please, let me see you smile?"

She forced a smile onto her face, and even though it was manufactured, her dimples managed to shine through. I said, "That's it. I live for that smile. Now, in a very short time we'll be out of here and heading home, and just wait until you see this place."

Angie nodded silently and we went back into the living room. Mr. Laurence took her gently by the arm and said, "We shouldn't be long."

They left and I closed the door and walked into the bedroom to make sure Angie had not left anything behind. I looked down at her bed and thought about how many times I felt like I might lose her. I pictured her there, sweating, gasping for air, literally skin and bones, not being able to sleep for more than half an hour at a time, waking up from nightmare after nightmare. I was not naive enough to think that the sudden change of scenery would put an end to all of that. And then the image of her pushing me over the railing and rolling down flights of stairs came rushing at me. I shook my head as I looked down and saw the book with all the wonderful seaside towns. I picked it up and as I flipped through it, I heard a voice.

"She's your responsibility now. Do you think you're up to it?"

I quickly turned around and saw Gloria sitting on Angie's bed. I said, "I didn't even hear you come in."

"It's all those years of being a nurse and trying to not make too much noise when walking into patients' rooms. So, are you up to it, Joe?"

"I hope so. I sincerely do."

"What's your biggest fear?"

"The same as always. Her committing suicide."

"Is that what brought you back here, day after day, after the way she treated you?"

"Yes, and because I love her, and I've seen what I believe is the real Angie. The caring, loving, and compassionate girl who lived with my parents for six months. I'll do everything in my power to get her back to that place."

"You're such a good-looking kid. In a place like Manhattan or Los Angeles you could easily pass for a movie star. Angie's beautiful, but there are ten beautiful girls on every block in cities like New York and Los Angeles who would be all over someone like you. Yet you stay with Angie. And after the things she has told me, I don't know of another guy who would still be with her."

"Before I ever laid eyes on her, if I was to draw a picture of my dream girl it would have been Angie, and that hasn't changed."

"The abuse she suffered, and the consequences of that abuse, are never going away."

"I know," I said as I looked directly at Gloria.

"I'm not a superstitious person, and I don't believe in God, but I can't help but think that it was not by mere chance that you and Mr. Laurence met. In fact, every time I look at you, I can't help thinking how much you look like him. You have grown a few inches since I first met you, and your hair is wavier than I first remembered, and your cheeks and chin are more chiseled."

"I've had a late growth spurt. At first, I thought I was washing my pants on the wrong setting or that I put them in the dryer by accident, but then a day ago Mr. Laurence bought me new pants that were four inches longer than my older pairs and they fit perfectly."

"He also buys you your clothes?" Gloria asked.

"Yeah, I come home, and I'll find new ones on the kitchen table, and they always fit perfectly, and they're always the type of clothes I like. He can read people better than anyone I've ever known. But I'm certain I'm not related to him."

"I don't think you're related to him either, but I also don't think it's a coincidence that you met, or that your features have changed so abruptly. I mean, it's been barely six months since you two met. Even Angie has noticed, which has made her even more terrified that you were planning on leaving her."

"That would explain some of her more bizarre statements and accusations..."

"And some of her un-Angie like behavior?" Gloria added. "Or maybe we're just looking too hard for an explanation to our recent string of good luck. If you had told me that I would ever get another job as a nurse in a famous hospital I would have laughed, and now Mr. Laurence has promised me just that type of job, and all I have to do is show remorse for killing that son-of-a-bitch."

"Think you can do that?"

"Yes. In all honesty, one of the reasons I didn't just lie about it earlier to my psychiatrist is because I didn't really know what I was going to do once I got out of here. Yes, the center does help you get a job, but it's usually some low-level job in a department store or a supermarket. I graduated college and went two more years for my masters so I would be a highly qualified, specialized nurse. The one thing I know how to do well and get great satisfaction out of is being a nurse and helping people. I may have killed, but I'm no killer! Believe me, I'm not."

"I never thought you were," I said.

"Nor is your Angie, but you need to remember that under the right circumstances a person as timid as Angie can show unusual strength and daring."

"Believe me, I know."

"And it doesn't always have to be physical abuse that sets one off. It could be an unfounded suspicion, verbal abuse, or no communication at all."

"Is this a warning?" I asked.

"Yes, frankly, it's a warning. You're a good guy, Joe, and I know how much you love her. I mean, that's the only logical reason I could think of that explains why you've stayed by her side. You could have washed your hands of her, especially if you pressed charges against her for almost killing you. That would have put her in prison for a good long time. Instead, you didn't press charges and that was enough to wipe away any guilt you might have felt, but you stayed, and now she's walking away totally free after spending only six months in this resort."

"You don't think she should be released?" I asked.

"I didn't say that. It just worries me how dependent she is on you. She told me numerous times that the happiest time of her life, after her mother died, was living with you and your family. But now that your mother hates her, she will never know that feeling again."

"I can't blame my mother, but I don't think it's as hopeless as she thinks. With time I see my mother coming around."

"Do you honestly believe that?"

"No, my mother has a memory like an elephant, and she'll never forgive Angie for trying to kill one of her sons ... But she might pretend that all is well just to keep the lines of communication open. Angie tells me she didn't tell her about pushing me over the railing, but I find that hard to believe. My mother is not a hateful person, but I swear if she ran into Angie, she would be seriously tempted to kill her."

The door to the apartment opened and Angie and Mr. Laurence walked in, but instead of getting up off the beds, we stayed seated. I picked up the book and yelled out, "In here."

Angie immediately walked into the bedroom, followed by Mr. Laurence. She asked, "What are you doing in here?"

"Just talking," I said as I handed her the book. "You have to return this to the library."

She looked down at the book as though she was in a cloud and I asked, "So did everything go well?"

"Everything went wonderfully," Mr. Laurence said. "In just a few minutes your lovely girlfriend will be heading home with us." He turned to Gloria, "And as for you, Ms. Gloria, you know what you have to do. You have far too much to offer the world to remain in here any longer than the next two weeks."

Gloria got up and hugged Mr. Laurence, as tears came running down her cheeks. "I don't know how to thank you. Never in my life did I think that men like you and Joe existed. It's like a dream."

She pulled away and grabbed the book from Angie and said, "I'll take that back to the library. Please, just get out of here before I make a bigger fool out of myself."

I hugged Gloria, picked up Angie's bags, and we walked out of the apartment. I stopped about twenty feet from the apartment and took Angie aside as Mr. Laurence looked on.

I held her gently by the arm and looked her straight in the face and said, "Did you forget something?"

"What? I don't think so..."

"Gloria?"

"I don't know what you mean."

"I think you need to get back in there and hug that woman and tell her how much you love her. She's the only true friend you have besides Mr. Laurence and me."

"I thought I already did that," she said hopelessly.

"You actually didn't," I said. She continued to stare at me in disbelief for a few seconds before turning and walking back into the apartment. I shook my head. Mr. Laurence walked over to me, and I said, "Sorry about that."

"Nothing to be sorry about, but don't let that little oversight ruin what is otherwise going to be a wonderful day."

Angie walked out of the apartment a few minutes later as Gloria waved to us from the door. Angie's eyes were all wet from crying. She stood across from me and said, "I really didn't realize I hadn't said goodbye."

"That's okay, thank you for doing that," I said as I placed my hands gently on both sides of her head. "I love you so much, and this is a new beginning for both of us."

She threw her arms around me, and we kissed, and I couldn't help thinking that this was the beginning of the end of free expression for me, that every reaction I had from now on would have to be censored before it escaped my lips. Gloria had described her as a delicate flower. Well, I couldn't help feeling that the delicate flower was wielding immense power over me.

Angie insisted on sitting in the back of the car, even though Mr. Laurence had told her it was totally fine to sit up front with me. Before starting the car, I reminded her to buckle up. She fumbled with the seat belt and when she finally got it, I drove off.

"Thank you, again, Mr. Laurence. I will never be able to repay you, but always know that I'm forever thankful," Angie said as Mr. Laurence turned around and looked at her.

"I'm the lucky one. I'm an old man who gets to look at such a beautiful girl as you every day. That's luck!"

"That's not true, you're so good looking and kind you could go out with any girl you like. If Gloria hadn't sworn off men for at least another year, she would marry you in a heartbeat. She told me that her crush on Denzel Washington has greatly diminished since meeting you."

"That's very nice of you to say, but I'm just scratching off time until I'm re-united with the one and only true love of my life."

I stopped at a red light and turned to Angie and said, "Mr. Laurence's wife, Isabelle, is the most beautiful woman I've ever seen. When you see pictures of her, I have no doubt you'll agree."

"I don't doubt that one moment," Angie said quietly.

"So, tell me Angie, what's your favorite food?" Mr. Laurence asked.

"Pizza, I guess."

"Oh, I don't know about that. I put a large bag of popcorn between Angie and me when we go to the movies, and before I even get a chance to eat some it's all gone."

"I do love popcorn. I can't help myself. I'm addicted," she said with a little laugh.

"Well then, I think we should have a movie night," Mr. Laurence said. "How about tonight? I'll order the pizza and make sure there's plenty of popcorn for the popcorn fiend here." He winked at Angie and she beamed at him.

"What movie would you like to see, Mr. Laurence?" I asked.

"How about *Casablanca*?" he offered.

"Is that playing at a movie theater around here?" Angie asked.

"Yes, in the main house, where I live. We have a built-in movie theater. It's bigger than most of the ones they build these days, and it even has a popcorn machine. Shall we say, six o'clock, and is *Casablanca* okay with everyone?"

"Yes!" Angie said as she nearly jumped out of her seat. "And you won't get any complaints from Joe because he's in love with Ingrid Bergman. I would be so jealous if she wasn't dead, which is not very nice to say."

I parked the car in the driveway, and we all got out. Angie stared up at the main house with her mouth hanging open. She had never seen a house that big, except in the movies, which were probably sets.

We walked from the car to our little house, and when I opened the door, she took a deep breath and said, "Oh my God, this is where you have been living all this time?"

"Great, isn't it?"

"Incredible," she said as she turned around in the living room, then walked into the kitchen and looked out at the giant pool. "The whole place is so beautiful!"

"A perfect fit for a beautiful princess like you."

"That's the first time you've told me I look beautiful today, but then I understand because today you only had eyes for Gloria."

I don't know how I managed to restrain myself because if there was ever a moment in my life that I felt like ripping into her, it was right then. Instead, I took a deep breath and sighed.

"I'm sorry, I didn't mean that," she said as she realized how mad she had just made me.

I took her gently by the arm and said, "Let me show you the rest of the house." I had told her at least three times how beautiful she was that day, but that was the last path I wanted to go down. I just kept asking myself, *Will this girl ever be normal? Will I have to fend off these jealous attacks for the rest of my life?*

I showed her the three bedrooms, each with its own separate bathroom, and she said, "My God, I've never had my own bathroom."

"Well, now you have two."

"Where will I sleep?" she asked.

"Anywhere you like. I thought you would like the room overlooking the pool."

"Is that where you sleep?"

"No, I sleep in the room closest to the kitchen and living room."

"Are we not going to be sleeping together?"

"That's totally up to you, Angie. I don't want you to feel uncomfortable."

"I'll think about it. Is that okay?" she hesitantly asked, and then suddenly said, "Or is that going to be too tough on you?"

"No, not at all," I said.

"Would it be okay if I took a nap? I'm so tired."

"Of course. We don't have to be at Mr. Laurence's house for another five hours."

Angie sat down on my bed and took her shoes off, then lay down, scrunched a pillow under her head, and immediately fell asleep. I looked at her for a long time, and as I did, bits and pieces of my conversation with Gloria kept coming back to me.

After a few minutes, Angie started swinging her arms over her head in a frantic, sweaty attempt to fight off the enemies that came for her in her sleep. I took off my shoes and climbed onto the bed as gently as I could, until I was lying next to her. I wrapped my arms around her and whispered, "Angie, I promise you — no one is ever going to hurt you again." She opened her eyes and stared at me as I said, "I'll always be here to protect you, I promise." Then she closed her eyes, and I slightly tightened my protective grip around her. She slept peacefully as I looked down on her lovely face until I also fell asleep.

When I woke up, Angie was coming out of the bathroom wearing her red dress from a couple of days earlier. She had taken a shower and was brushing her wet hair as she sat down on the bed. Without warning, she threw her arms around me and started planting kisses all over my face.

"That's for being the best boyfriend any girl could ever pray for." We kissed on the lips, and she said, "And that's to show you that I love you more than anything in this world, and that I'm truly sorry for driving you crazy."

"Is there anything else?" I asked.

"Maybe later, but you have to get up and get ready. It's almost five o'clock, and I'd like to stop by the florist to pick up some flowers for

Mr. Laurence. I don't want him ever to feel like his generosity is taken for granted."

I got up off the bed and started walking toward the bathroom as Angie said, "And one other thing, I've decided on a room to sleep in. The room that looks out onto the pool, but only if you sleep with me and hold me all night long."

"I can't think of a thing I'd like more than to hold you all night long and into eternity."

She smiled and her dimples glowed like orbs of sanctity.

CHAPTER TWENTY-SIX

Joe

Just before leaving the house, Angie said, "Joe, I don't have any money. Can you lend me some to buy the flowers?"

I opened my wallet and handed her three hundred dollars. She looked at the money and said, "I don't need that much."

"I don't want you ever walking around with no money. What's mine is yours, there is no paying back. We might not be married yet, but we will be. There's no way I'm having you slip away."

"And there's no one who will ever take you from me. I've hit the jackpot."

I took her hand and we walked toward the car, as the thought ran through my mind that just a few hours earlier I'd had serious doubts about whether I would ever be able to deal with her. It was almost as if something had changed while we slept. I felt confident, for the first time, that everything was going to turn out fine. It was a subtle change, but a significant one.

She seemed different. Happy. *Normal.* Maybe it was because she'd slept peacefully for several hours. Or maybe it was this place that was already giving her a chance to heal.

Then another thought occurred to me. What if being in this cocoon is what she needed in order to reconnect with the person she was before her mother died? Surely, Angie must have been different while her mother was around to protect her from harm.

We got into the car and drove to the florist. By then, I knew everyone who worked there. I introduced them to Angie, and they were all very friendly and sweet with her. Several of them commented on how beautiful she was and made jokes about how lucky I was, to which I enthusiastically agreed. She blushed and after recovering her voice she asked, "Would it be possible for me to get a bouquet of purple chrysanthemums in a vase?"

"Ooh, good choice," the gentleman replied.

I looked at Angie and asked, "Do chrysanthemums have a special meaning?"

"Yes," she said. "They symbolize friendship and loyalty, and they're the perfect flower to give to a gentleman friend, and knowing how much Mr. Laurence loves flowers, I think he'll like them."

"I'm sure he'll adore them," I said as the man who was helping us put a beautiful bouquet of purple chrysanthemums in a vase on the counter. He handed Angie a card and a pen. Angie thought for a minute, then wrote: *Dear Mr. Laurence, Joe and I cannot express how much we appreciate your kindness, generosity, caring and a million other things. Love, Joe and Angie.*

She handed me the card and I read it and said, "Absolutely perfect, like you."

Angie paid for the flowers, but didn't leave a tip, so when she wasn't looking, I put a twenty-dollar bill in the tip jar. She wasn't aware that Mr. Laurence's generosity had no limits, but I, as Mr. Laurence's apprentice, had the responsibility to keep up his good name.

Back at the house, Mr. Laurence greeted us at the front door and stepped aside to welcome us in. Angie and I crossed the threshold into an enormous front hall. The first thing we saw were two long, curved staircases separated by an enormous crystal chandelier. We looked at each other and smiled at Mr. Laurence.

Angie was so gobsmacked that she forgot to give Mr. Laurence the flowers.

"It's like an enchanted mansion," she said. "I feel like I'm here to meet Sleeping Beauty."

Mr. Laurence laughed and offered us a tour of the first floor, and we both nodded like a couple of eager school kids visiting Disneyland for the first time.

Just off the foyer was a large ballroom, with space for dancing and a baby grand piano. Across from the ballroom was a dining room with a long, narrow table that could easily have seated fifty people. Mr. Laurence explained that the hallways on either side of the two staircases branched off into wings that included ten bedrooms, and we knew there must be more upstairs. Beyond the staircases, at the back of the house, was a study lined with mahogany bookshelves and what looked like at least a thousand books.

The whole time we were walking around the house, Angie held onto the vase of purple chrysanthemums, and Mr. Laurence never said a word about them. When she finally presented them to him, he smiled graciously and set them down on a side table in order to read the card. After he'd read her words, he looked at her warmly and said, "The only thing more beautiful than these chrysanthemums, my dear, is you."

I could see Angie blushing, but she managed to thank him sincerely and we continued the tour.

Eventually we ended up in the kitchen, which was as big as my parents' whole apartment. Two large pizza pies, already sliced, sat on a large stove under a heating lamp. Mr. Laurence moved one pie to the middle of the table and gave each of us a plate. He then put several bottles of soda on the table, along with three glasses filled with ice. One of the soda bottles was grape, which in a bygone time in NYC was common in pizzerias. Every pizzeria used to carry grape soda in the can or out of the fountain.

Mr. Laurence slid two slices of pizza onto Angie's plate, and instead of complaining that it was too much, she just thanked him cheerfully. We each had grape soda that I poured into everyone's glass.

We ate the pizza like real New Yorkers — folding each slice in half between our thumb and forefingers. Angie ate slowly but finished both pieces, and Mr. Laurence asked if she wanted more.

"If I have more, I don't know if I'll have room for popcorn."

"How about you and I split a slice?" Mr. Laurence asked, and Angie, without hesitation, said, "That would be great."

I reached over and poured some more soda into her glass, thinking she might need it to keep down all the pizza. I don't know if I had ever seen her eat so much as she did in those fifteen minutes ... and that didn't include the popcorn that came later.

I picked up the dirty plates and glasses and put them in the sink. Angie wanted to help me clean, but I told her to go with Mr. Laurence, who wanted to show her a 35mm projector from the 1940s and the film can that held his copy of *Casablanca*.

"Are you sure you don't need any help? I'm very good at drying."

"No, sweetheart, but thank you," I said.

While we were all still standing there, Angie turned to our host and said, "You know, Mr. Laurence, Joe is more excited about seeing *Casablanca* than even I am. Like I told you earlier, he's in love with Ingrid Bergman. I bet if she was still alive and my age, he would choose her in a heartbeat over me."

I turned to her and tried to quell a small flash of anger. "That is simply not true. You will always be my first and only choice."

"I have to agree with Joe. In all the time I've known your boyfriend, he has talked about his lovely Angie many times and never once mentioned Ms. Bergman."

Angie blushed and walked over to me and said, "I love you so much." She threw her arms around me, and we kissed as I kept my foamy hands up in the air so I wouldn't stain her dress. A soap bubble floated past us and popped near our heads, and with it, my irritation disappeared.

After I finished cleaning, drying, and putting away the dishes, I walked to the screening room. It was bigger than most multiplex theaters. Red velvet curtains hung from the top of the ceiling to the bottom of the stage, just shy of the floor, and the seating area was filled with rows of plush seats, each with a cup holder.

I entered the theater just as Mr. Laurence was handing Angie an extra-large bag of freshly popped popcorn with her name on it and a soft drink. He handed me a smaller bag, with no name on it and a soft drink, and for himself he had a smaller bag with a bottle of water. He suggested we sit in the middle, so we did. He ran off to dim the lights and start the projector. When he came back, he sat in a seat a few seats down from us. I guess he wanted to give us some privacy, but we both told him we would feel better if he sat next to us, and he did. Just before the movie started, I whispered into his ear, "Once the movie starts, she won't even know that we exist." Mr. Laurence smiled as the movie started.

As I predicted, Angie was transfixed. Even though we'd seen this movie multiple times on TV, it seemed to have a totally different effect on her when she watched it on the big screen. She was like some kind of popcorn-addicted robot: once every ten seconds or so she would reach into her bag of popcorn, take out three or four pieces, and put them into her mouth. She did this repeatedly, without once taking her eyes off the screen. I kept stealing looks at her because it made me so happy to see her leave her worries behind and give herself over to a favorite movie.

After the screening, while Mr. Laurence was wrapping up the leftover pizza for us to take home, Angie kept talking about the movie as though it was the first time she had ever seen it. There was an innocence and unbridled joy that lit up her face and touched my heart in a way I never thought possible.

Back in the smaller house, which we were already thinking of as our home, I put the pizza away as Angie went into her bathroom to clean up and change for bed. I was still unsure about what part I was playing that night. Would I be sleeping alone, sleeping in Angie's bed and protecting her from nightmares, or would we be sleeping together and doing the type of things that couples do? I shook my head and tried to keep that possibility as far away as a person sleeping with the woman of his dreams could possibly keep such a dirty thought from intruding on a perfect night.

In the meantime, I went into my bathroom and cleaned up and changed into pajamas. I walked into Angie's room, and found her sitting up in bed, also dressed in pajamas.

"There you are," she said, as though she'd been waiting.

She pulled back the blankets on the opposite side of bed and tapped her hand against the mattress. "Come, my handsome protector, and love of my life."

I got into the bed and before I had a chance to lay down, her lips were pressed against mine, and then just as suddenly they weren't. "That's for being the best and most handsome boyfriend in the whole world."

She turned over and faced the other way and said, "Did you forget, you promised to hold me all night?"

"No, I didn't forget," I said, and I kissed her on her head and wrapped my arms around her. When one of my hands accidentally landed on her breast, she flinched and I recoiled immediately.

"We're not quite ready for that, but hopefully soon," she said.

"I didn't mean that, I'm sorry..."

She turned and pressed a finger against my lips and said, "I know, Joe, and I know I'm the luckiest girl in the world to have you." We kissed goodnight and then I wrapped my arms around her and we stayed that way all night long.

CHAPTER TWENTY-SEVEN

Angie

I quietly slipped out of Joe's protective grasp and replaced my body with a pillow. It was a little before in six in the morning, and I didn't want to wake him because I knew he usually got up at around seven o'clock, and it was time to give the poor guy a break. He had come every day to visit me for months at the women's center, staying from eleven in the morning to eight at night. I was often selfish and self-centered, and acted as though my problems were caused by him, or like I was the only one in this whole world who had problems. I knew I was doing this, but couldn't stop myself, and I knew I was in danger of pushing him away. I wanted to take advantage of this rare moment of strength and insight to finally give him some space.

I walked into the bathroom, brushed my teeth, and put on a beautiful bathrobe that Mr. Laurence had bought for me. It was big and fluffy — the type of robe you see at fancy spas. I walked into the kitchen, opened the refrigerator, and took out a carton of orange juice and poured myself a glass.

The sun was just starting to come up and the birds were putting on a symphony. I felt beautiful, safe, and secure for possibly the first time in my life. It was as though the chains had been clipped, and the labels dismissed, and yes, I thought, *God does exist.*

I had slept peacefully in the arms of the man who loved me unconditionally. I'd passed a whole night without a single nightmare. This, in itself, was a gift.

I got up, cleaned the glass I'd been drinking out of, and walked out through the sliding glass door to the pool. I dipped my toes in the water and giggled out of sheer amazement at the beauty of it all. Then I did something so clumsy that I blush just thinking about it. As I stepped back, I tripped on a piece of pool cleaning equipment — some sort of leaf removing device that was lying on the ground — and fell forward into the pool. As my fluffy robe took on water and began to feel like a weighted blanket, I stood up in the shallow end, feeling like the world's biggest idiot. I looked across at the sliding glass door and saw Joe looking directly at me. He asked, "Is that a new swimsuit you're checking out?"

"Very funny," I said, stifling a laugh.

"Personally, I think you look awfully sexy."

"Is that so? Well, if I look so sexy, why don't walk in here and prove it to me?"

"Is that a dare?"

"I suppose it is," I said as he walked into the pool — sensibly taking the stairs — with his pajamas on.

He stopped before me, and suddenly we were kissing. When my once-fluffy robe fell off and floated away, our hands started reaching under our pajamas and touching places that neither of us had explored before. Then, just like that, the sound of the Rascals singing, "It's a Beautiful Morning," came blasting through the open door.

We stepped back from each other like children caught with their hands in the cookie jar. Joe let out a yelp and then relaxed when he realized that it was his clock radio waking him up.

We tried to pick up where we left off but started laughing when we looked down and realized that our pajamas had filled up with air pockets.

"So attractive," I said, as I patted the edges of my enormous stomach made of air.

Joe kissed my forehead and said, "I guess I'd better go clean up so I'm not late for Mr. Laurence."

"Guess so," I said with my eyes cast downward as he started to walk away. Then I called out after him. "Hey. Maybe later?"

CHAPTER TWENTY-EIGHT

Angie

I picked up Joe's wet pajamas and put them in the washing machine, along with my pajamas and robe. I didn't know if I would ever get back the softness in my robe, but I was hoping so because it was so comfy. And yet, I had to admit that what had just happened between us was worth it, even if that robe ended up stiff as a board.

I always thought of Joe as good-looking, but lately he seems to have graduated from handsome to drop-dead gorgeous. He's grown at least four inches, and his face has that chiseled look that you see in stars from the 1940s, like Olivier or Errol Flynn. But what's really uncanny is that he looks like a younger Mr. Laurence. He could easily pass for the man's son, and they even have similar dispositions.

I was feeling an excitement that I'd never really felt before. At times when I'm near Joe or he has his hands wrapped around me I'm so overwhelmed that when I touch myself down there I'm all wet. I know it's natural, but I feel so embarrassed.

I walked into the shower and turned on the water and stood there, feeling the temperature climb from cold to warm to hot. I tried to empty my mind as I let the water cascade over my body. After a while I shampooed my hair, then rinsed it and applied a thick conditioner that smelled of lilac. The scent seemed to almost be jamming my senses, and suddenly I found myself wondering why Joe had a floral conditioner in his bathroom. *Could it belong to someone else? Another woman?*

An old, familiar panic crept into my mind, until I was so agitated that the water started to feel like it was punishing me instead of soothing me. I bent down and put my hands on my knees and tried to slow my breathing. That's when I remembered a simple technique that my therapist told me about at the women's center. Breathing steadily, with my head still down, I spoke to myself. *You are safe. You are loved. You are lovable.* I repeated the mantra until it began to feel true, and my heart rate started to slow down.

I pictured Joe's face and reminded myself of how many times in the past day alone he had praised me, told me I was beautiful, or told me that he loved me. They had to number in the dozens. He was doing everything possible to reassure me that I was safe and loved, and although I always seemed to need more and more and more proof, I could feel something shifting. I was beginning to believe him. At the very least, I *wanted* to believe him. I wanted so badly to believe that I wouldn't be hurt or abandoned.

I reminded myself of the feeling of having been in Joe's arms all night while I slept. It felt like a cocoon, and it was the best feeling in the world. My breathing became steady and calm, and I began to feel really good as I continued to replay everything that had happened since I'd arrived at the house. I had to admit that every word Joe had said, and everything he'd done since I'd arrived, had been loving. For the first time in a long time, I felt safe.

Then the visions shifted and I began to see flashes of the two us in the pool, with our hands roaming all over each other's bodies. It was hot — so very hot — to 'see' us from the outside, on the cusp of doing things that we hadn't come close to trying before. As the visions played in my head like a movie, I began touching myself. It was all so instinctual, and the wetness was there already — not the water, but my own wetness, a slickness that I had only allowed myself to enjoy once, maybe twice before — and after a few minutes I felt it — the spasm of heat and intensity that I had only heard about until that moment. Was this it? It had to be. Nothing else felt like this. I kept the water running as I leaned against the tiled wall and recovered.

When it was time to get dressed, I opened my closet and surveyed row after row of new clothes, shoes, and jackets, all gifts from Mr. Laurence. I put on a floral sundress with a wraparound leather belt. The dress was beautifully made, with a hidden side zipper and a delicate lining, and probably cost more than all of my old clothes combined.

I picked up my purse and checked to see if I still had the money Joe gave me. I wasn't used to having more than a few dollars to my name, and having just under three hundred dollars felt exciting and strange.

I walked out of the house and toward the car that was sitting in the driveway. Joe and Mr. Laurence had invited me to breakfast, and how could I refuse? Joe jumped out of the car and opened the back door for me, and I slid in. He leaned in to help me with my seatbelt, and I let him, mostly for the pleasure of smelling his hair and feeling his breath on my skin. Our mouths were just a few inches apart, and I swear I was ready to plant a wet kiss on him, but thankfully his mouth moved away, and he kissed me on the forehead again and said, "You look fabulous."

"Breathtaking," Mr. Laurence added from the front seat.

"Thank you both," I said.

I felt different, and I wondered if they could see a change in me, but if either of them saw anything new, they didn't let on.

CHAPTER TWENTY-NINE

Angie

We parked at Mo's Diner, walked in, and quickly found a table.
Mr. Laurence beat Joe to my chair and pulled it out for me. I gave a
little curtsy in my sundress and said, "Thank you, kind sir," before
sitting down.

"You're welcome, my dear," Mr. Laurence said as our waitress
came over to the table. She was beautiful — the kind of blonde
bombshell one would expect to see walking on a beach in Southern
California, and the tag on her uniform said Diane. Mr. Laurence
introduced me to her as Joe's fiancée, and Diane's too-pretty face lit
up like a fake Christmas tree.

"So *you're* the lucky one," she said, literally giving my
boyfriend — my fiancé — an open invitation to visit her anytime he
wanted ... without me. At least, that's the way I saw it.

Before I could say anything to her, Joe reached over and kissed
me on the forehead and said, "I'm the lucky one."

Diane smiled, handed us menus, and took our drink orders. I
looked down at the menu and at the same time I thought I spotted a
drop of blood, coming up through my panties and quickly spreading
across my dress. I grabbed my napkin and put it over the blood, but
it just as quickly spread across the napkin.

"Angie, are you okay?" Joe asked. I just smiled as he moved toward me and said, "Are you sure?" When he saw me looking down at my dress, he looked there too, and it was like nothing registered on his face. I looked back down and there was nothing, no blood, nothing.

"I'm great, Joe. I have you two sitting beside me. How could I be anything but great?"

I looked at the menu and thought about what to order. Maybe it was that little run-in with our waitress — which she didn't even seem to notice — but I suddenly felt confused. On a normal day, that glass of orange juice I'd had earlier would have been more than enough for my whole breakfast, and yet I suddenly found myself ordering a stack of pancakes, with sausages, bacon and a glass of milk. I was quite sure Diane must have been laughing her head off when she handed the order over to the kitchen staff. At the rate I was going, I would be three hundred pounds and she could have her way with Joe.

Joe and Mr. Laurence didn't say a thing, but they must have thought it strange that the lady at the table had ordered twice as much food as anyone else. I ate slowly, and to be quite honest, the food was delicious, and I came close to finishing all of it. After Diane cleared our plates and gave Joe and Mr. Laurence more coffee, she turned to me and asked, "Would you like some dessert? We have a three-layer chocolate cake that's out of this world. I'm sure the guys would love a bite?"

"No, thank you," I said as it suddenly dawned on me that no one orders dessert after breakfast. She had to have been mocking me. My face went red as I imagined her joking to the line cooks and the other waitresses about the human garburator out in the dining area.

Mr. Laurence paid the bill, and we left. Then we drove back to the house, where we made plans for later that night: another movie, popcorn, and Chinese food for dinner.

As Joe and I were walking back to our house, I said, "That waitress likes you."

"You think so?" he replied nonchalantly.

"Yeah, I think so, wiseass."

"Wow! I feel so special." He turned toward me and we stopped. "The most beautiful girl in the world is jealous that another girl might be interested in me."

"That's not funny," I said.

"Yeah, it is. Diane is married and has a two-year-old son. She'll be graduating from Stony Brook soon and heading to Chicago to attend graduate school."

"I didn't see a wedding ring on her," I said.

"That's because she doesn't wear it at work. It's a sad fact of the world that guys are more likely to leave a big tip if they don't think the waitress is married."

"Mr. Laurence left her a hundred-dollar tip."

"And the next twenty tables she has are more likely to leave her one or two dollars each."

"If you say so," I said. Then I ran into the house and into the bathroom because I really had to pee.

When I came out, Joe was sitting on the couch watching TV. I sat down next to him and asked, "So, my betrothed, when are we actually getting married?"

He took both my hands and said, "I was thinking about asking Mr. Laurence to talk to my mom, who is right now not very supportive of the idea. What do you think? The last time I talked to her she was very excited that I was living with such a famous and rich man. She looked up everything she could find on Mr. Laurence on the computer, and the way she talked about him you'd have thought she was talking about the Pope."

"I don't know," I said. "That might be asking too much of him."

"I think he'd be happy to do this for us."

"But she might tell him that I'm crazy and convince him he's taking a chance even having me live here."

"He knows everything about you, and he thinks you're perfect."

"He thinks I'm perfect? That's the first time anybody ever thought I was perfect besides your little brother."

"I tell you you're perfect all the time."

"You don't count. You're in love with me and overlook all my flaws. Thank God for that, otherwise you'd have been a thousand miles away from me by now."

"I would never allow myself to be a thousand miles away from you. A few miles at most."

"A few miles? And where might those few miles take you?"

"I don't know, maybe to a jeweler to buy you a diamond engagement ring?"

"Don't you dare. We might be living in luxury right now, but we have no money of our own, and don't you ever buy anything as stupid as a ring on credit."

"I do have about ten thousand dollars to my name."

"Wow! You're rich, and now you know the real reason behind my rush to marry you. It's to get at all that money."

"So, you're a gold-digger?"

"Is that what they call a girl who's looking out for her own well-being?"

"Yes."

"Well then, I guess I should be dating Mr. Laurence. He thinks I'm perfect, and he apparently has millions."

"But he's already married to the most beautiful girl, and he would never be unfaithful to his Isabelle."

I started crying — why, I couldn't be sure, but I did — and as Joe reached over and wiped my tears away, he looked into my eyes. "Please don't think I'm crazy," he said, "but I would swear that Isabelle and her little sister Rachel roam this property and go swimming in the pool all the time."

I lowered my eyes, and then I took his hand and said, "I think we should go for a walk."

"You think I'm crazy, don't you?"

"No, I don't think you're crazy. Not one bit. But I would still like to go for that walk."

I picked up a blanket and put it under my arm and we walked out the sliding door and past the pool.

I took Joe's arm and asked, "Have you been out very far past the pool?"

"No further than a few steps past the pool."

"You've been here for months. What have you been doing?"

"Visiting you," he said, and like a fastball hitting me directly in the face I was, once again, reminded of how much Joe had sacrificed for me.

"I'm sorry for saying that Joe. I'm just a selfish…"

He stopped and turned to me and held my arms. "No, you're not selfish. You've been through a hell I wouldn't wish on anyone."

"And so have most of the girls in the women's center, and millions and millions of girls around the world."

Joe closed his eyes and nodded as he kept holding onto me. I could see that it hurt him to imagine the world I came from. A world of girls who fall prey to monsters.

"And of all of those girls, you're the one I love," he said.

That brought tears to my eyes, and I said, "Yes, I'm the lucky one." Then the tears really flowed, and I said, in a low, cracked voice, "I wouldn't be here if not for you. I probably wouldn't be alive."

This got him choked up, and he wrapped his arms around me and nuzzled my neck. "But you're happy here?"

"I've never been happier," I said, drying my tears. "And when you said you were sure Isabelle and her sister roam around and swim in the pool, I have no doubt that they do. I hear voices — happy and friendly and consoling voices. The laughter of children."

I looked up and realized that we were walking on a paved path, flanked on both sides by perennial gardens full of phlox, hydrangeas, and delphiniums in full bloom, and the glossy hulks of spent rhododendrons. I suddenly put my hand in front of Joe to stop him as a mother duck crossed the path, followed by a row of ducklings.

We both smiled through our tears as we let them pass, not wanting to make a sound to disturb their trek to a little pond inside one of the gardens. When the ducks were out of sight we kept walking until we came to the very edge of the property. We looked past the fence and realized that we were looking down at the Long Island Sound. Joe pointed to a staircase that led down to the beach. We picked our way down a steep staircase, holding onto the railing, and walked onto the beach.

The water was calm, and the sand was soft underfoot. I tucked myself into Joe's side and said, "It's like living a dream."

"Our dream," he added as I rose on tiptoe and kissed him. The sun was just shy of its midnoon high, and the water was sparkling and flashing so much that it seemed to be trying to get a message to us. We walked for about a mile without seeing anyone else. It was like being on our own island.

We walked back up the stairs and headed back toward the house when Joe stopped, took the blanket that I had brought from the house, and spread it on the grass. We were not far from where mommy duck and her ducklings passed. We sat on the blanket, and I lay back and rested my head on Joe's stomach. He looked into my eyes, and although I'd never had any real doubts about his love for me, I was now certain that he was God's gift to me.

I looked up at him and said, "This morning in the pool, I wanted to make love to you so much. Did you feel the same?"

"Yes, but now we can always look back when we hear the Rascals' 'A Beautiful Morning' and laugh."

"Afterwards, I thought about it, and I so want to make love to you, but it made me realize that we really do need protection. I don't think either of us is ready to have a baby, and I could never have an abortion. My first appointment with the out-patient psychiatrist is in a few days. Do you think she would write me a prescription for birth control pills?"

"That I don't know. We might have to go to a clinic."

"I really don't want to go to a clinic if I can avoid it."

"That I totally understand. We could ask Mr. Laurence if he knows of a good doctor he could recommend for both of us. We could pay cash."

"And between the doctor and the prescription, half your fortune will be gone."

"I don't care about that. Besides, I think it would only eat up about a fifth of my fortune."

"We'll see. Let's see what happens with the psychiatrist. Do you think it would be okay to tell her everything?"

"Yes, Mr. Laurence assured me that you should tell her everything, and that there is nothing to worry about."

"I don't want her to put me on any medications. Half the girls at the center were either addicted to the medications they had them taking or complaining about side effects. I don't want that."

"I won't let them put you on anything you don't want."

"Will you go with me?"

"Of course, but I won't be allowed in with you. I'll stay in the lobby."

"Thank you. I can't believe how fortunate I've been since that terrible night, and it's all because of you."

"Mr. Laurence has played a very big part."

"But there would be no Mr. Laurence if there was no Joe."

"You're the girl of my dreams. Before you even knew I existed, I used to watch you walk in and out of the building and pray to God to just give me a chance to talk to you. You're my Isabelle."

"That's hard to believe, especially considering the way I used to dress."

"It was your face, Ang. The same face I'm looking at right now, and after I got to know you, it was the whole package."

"Except the insanity I put you through while I was in jail and at the center."

"But we made it through all that, and that's what couples do."

"If you keep on talking like this, protection or no protection, I'm going to throw you in bed, and we are going to make love."

"We will, soon, without the worry of an unplanned pregnancy hanging over us."

"Such a gentleman, my handsome Joey," I said as I reached up and traced my finger around his mouth, nose, and gorgeous brown eyes. "You've grown a lot over these last several months."

"What do you mean?"

"You're so far removed from the person you were when we were living with your parents. You don't even mention your friends."

"I don't even think of them, and apparently they don't think about me much either. I haven't heard from any of them."

"I always thought that after your family, came your friends, and then basketball."

"No Angie, after my family, came you, even if I continued to act like an immature jackass."

"I've put you through hell!"

"No! What you put me through was not hell. You know what Mr. Laurence was doing at my age? He was charging the beach at Normandy, watching his friends die—"

I nodded my understanding, and he looked at me feverishly.

"Taking care of the girl I love during a difficult time is nothing compared to what he and thousands of other soldiers my age lived through during that terrible war."

I sat up and looked at my handsome boyfriend and said, "Please don't judge your behavior by the actions of young men fighting a war over fifty years ago. I'm very happy you weren't born back then, and that I have you all for myself. You're my protection and my love." I leaned in and kissed him just as the mommy duck and her ducklings came walking past us in the other direction.

CHAPTER THIRTY

Angie

Mr. Laurence called us on the phone a few hours before we were supposed to go over and have dinner. He asked if we could come over now because he had several things to discuss with us.

I took the call and asked right away if we'd done something wrong.

"Not that I know about. Did you?"

"Not that I know about," I said, and he laughed.

We walked into the mansion a few minutes later and Mr. Laurence led us into the study. He picked up four plastic cards and handed two each to Joe and me.

"One is for your health and the other is for dental insurance. The plan is accepted everywhere. I hope you don't mind, but I've made appointments with an internist for both of you tomorrow at ten o'clock, so please don't eat anything after midnight because they will probably want to take blood and urine samples from both of you.

"Angie, your appointment is with a highly respected female doctor. I thought you would feel more comfortable with that. And Joe, you have an appointment with Dr. Souter, who is also my doctor. They have offices right beside each other so there shouldn't be much of a wait."

"But we don't have any money," I said.

"Well, thank goodness you're working for a man who provides the best insurance to his employees, at no charge."

He took me by the hand and led both of us into a back room that was filled with old newspapers. They were stacked from floor to ceiling and covered every wall.

"I'd like to offer you a job," he said to me. "You know about computers and how to transfer written documents, newspaper clippings, onto a computer and save them onto a drive?"

"Yes, sir," I replied, as he smiled and turned to Joe. "Do you know how lucky you are to have such a beautiful and smart fiancée"

"Yes sir," Joe replied.

Mr. Laurence looked back at me and said, "So, Angie, I'm offering you a job that will require you to transfer a large portion of these newspapers onto computer drives and disks. Might you be interested?"

"Yes, sir."

"And how much would you like to be paid each week?"

"You don't have to pay me. You already give us everything for free."

"That, young lady, is the wrong answer. How about six hundred dollars a week, and I will pay your taxes and social security separately?"

"Six hundred dollars a week? I haven't made that much in my whole life."

"Well, you have a large job ahead of you. How about you start at eleven o'clock in the morning, Monday through Friday, and quit at four?"

"That's hardly any time at all for that type of money," I said.

"That's for me to decide, and because I know your loving boyfriend wouldn't want his lovely girlfriend to spend all those hours in this room alone, I think it would be quite gentlemanly if he helped. Now, I pay you three hundred a week, and starting next week I will give you a raise of another three hundred dollars, so you'll both be earning six hundred dollars a week. Does that sound about right?"

"Mr. Laurence, that is way too generous. We can't accept all that money, including the free medical, free board, food, clothes, and God only knows what else."

"I want to tell you a story," Mr. Laurence said, and we both settled in to listen.

Mr. Laurence talked about the first time that Isabelle's father tried to pay him after he'd written four columns. He'd been sitting in his room when Isabelle came in and handed him a check and told him he'd been hired.

"I looked down at the check and it was for four hundred dollars," Mr. Laurence said. "This was the most money I'd ever seen. I looked up at Isabelle and said, 'I can't take this. I live here for nothing, eat your food … You buy me expensive clothing, the cost of which I'm afraid to even ask about. And on top of that I get to spend time with the most beautiful girl on the planet.' I handed the check back to Isabelle and she said, 'My father is not going to be happy about this. I give you fair warning!'"

"Ooh," I said, sensing that the encounter didn't end there.

"Ooh is right," Mr. Laurence said. "Isabelle turned and left, and about fifteen minutes later, Mr. Hamill walked into my room and stuffed five hundred dollars in my hand. He said, 'I paid you for work well done — work that received glowing reviews from our readers. How in the world do you ever plan on taking my daughter out to a romantic dinner when you refuse to accept payment for the work you do?'

"It turned out he'd made a reservation for us at Musso & Frank. He told me to dress appropriately, and asked if he should have Isabelle come up and pick out my wardrobe. I told him I thought that was a good idea, and he said, 'That's what I figured.' As he started to walk out of the room, I asked, 'Is the reservation for two or three? I'm guessing three.'

"Mr. Hamill said, 'You guessed right,' and explained that, wherever Isabelle went, Rachel went. Then he really threw me for a loop by saying, 'And by the way, whenever you get up the courage to propose to my daughter, she will only say yes if you agree that Rachel is part of the bargain. Those two are inseparable, and even after my younger daughter gets married, you shouldn't expect anything to change.'"

Joe shook his head and laughed. "So he already knew you wanted to marry Isabelle?"

"Oh, he had my number," Mr. Laurence said. "Any sane young man would have jumped at the chance. So I just said, 'Do you really think Isabelle would marry me?' And Mr. Hamill said, 'Yes, unless you're stupid enough to continue to turn down paychecks.'"

Joe laughed again and asked him if Rachel went with them on their honeymoon.

"Oh yes," he said. "She had her own room, but I must admit, most mornings I woke up I didn't find my gorgeous wife in bed beside me. I found her curled up next to her sister."

He paused as he looked at both of us. "Kids, the first point is that I've lived a life that was like a fairytale. Not the war, of course. But everything else. I married the most gorgeous girl I've ever laid eyes on, and our love for each other never lost its magic. She was not only breathtaking to look at, but she was the smartest person I've ever known. Rachel was a bonus, a caring and loving doll who was very much a part of that magic."

"What's the second point?" Joe asked.

"The second point is that when someone offers you money in exchange for work, you say yes, thank you, and you take it." Mr. Laurence winked. Then he switched gears, looked at Joe, and asked, "Did you by any chance give your mother my phone number?"

"No, I would never give away your phone number. I promise!" Joe replied and I felt so sorry for him.

"Well, she called me up today," he said, and all I could think was, *All good things come to end, but why so soon.*

"A very pleasant lady. She sounded just like my mom, who also came from the Bronx. I told your mother she raised an exceptional young man. I made her cry, but I think they were happy tears." He paused and looked down at me and I thought at any moment I was going to pee my pants.

He continued, saying, "She had her concerns, like any good mother, but after a few minutes she saw things my way. I told her the story of my wife's family, and I said that in Angie I see my lovely wife, Isabelle. The most beautiful, generous, loving and intelligent person I've ever met. One should never judge a person's actions unless one has been in similar circumstances. I never judged Isabelle, and there is never a moment in a day when I fail to think of her or feel her presence.

"Joe's mom said she's ready to make peace with you, and I believe her. I told her you would give her a call in the next day or two, and that if at any time during the conversation she got angry, I would tell you to hang up. I told her I would love to have them over for dinner, possibly on Thanksgiving. She promised to make homemade cannoli and I told her I'd hold her to that.

"Just before hanging up, Joe's little brother grabbed the phone and told me to tell you, Angie, that 'Despite the news that you and Joe are getting married, it's not too late to cancel.' All you have to do is wait seven years until he's old enough to marry you, and he promises that you'll be 'much happier married to him.' He went on to say, that he 'loves you more than the moon and sun combined and even more than Derek Jeter.' Quite an interesting little fellow, with an eye and a passion for beautiful women."

I could see Joe steaming and Mr. Laurence asked, "Is everything okay, Joe?"

"Yes, Mr. Laurence. It's just that no matter how many times I tell him not to say things like that, he simply doesn't listen."

"He's just a cute little baby, Joe. He'll grow out of it," I said.

"No, he's not. He's a ten-year-old pervert." Joe looked at Mr. Laurence. "Sorry, but he is. When I was his age, the only thing on my mind was basketball."

"That was the only thing on your mind eight years later when I met you."

"Not true, Ang. I had a major league crush on you from the moment I saw you. I was just too embarrassed to talk to you. That's why it took six months for me to work up the courage to speak up."

"That and a faulty grocery bag," I said with a laugh.

"True. It probably would have taken me a year if not for that bag."

I walked over to Joe and kissed him and said, "Seven years from now or sixty years from now, you will always be my one and only true love."

Mr. Laurence went about ordering the Chinese food for us without even asking us what we liked. Naturally, he ordered all the things that Joe and I like best: wonton soup, beef fried rice, egg rolls, shrimp with lobster sauce, and the oolong tea that I love.

After Joe and I finished cleaning and drying the dishes — refusing all offers of help from Mr. Laurence — we walked into the movie theater. Mr. Laurence had asked me what my second-favorite movie was, and I'd told him it was *Wuthering Heights*, and of course he had his own 35mm copy in the house, so we were in for a treat.

Mr. Laurence handed me my super-sized bag of popcorn and gave Joe a regular-sized bag. The movie started, and for about the first twenty minutes I was fine. The little boy playing the future Heathcliff (Olivier) thankfully didn't do anything for me, and then Laurence Olivier appeared, and I went from picking up two or three pieces of popcorn at a time to grabbing handfuls and stuffing my face like a pig. And then a switch flipped in my head and I suddenly had to do everything in my power not to throw the bag of popcorn aside and straddle Joe in his seat.

Only a couple of days earlier, the idea of any man touching me made me want to vomit. Now here I was sitting next to my boyfriend, the Olivier-lookalike, and all I wanted to do was to rip off his clothes and make passionate love to him repeatedly.

I must have been vibrating in my seat because Joe looked at me and asked, "Are you okay?"

I just smiled and thought, *This is all your fault, you gorgeous son-of-a bitch!!* Then I resorted to an old Catholic school trick, and started saying one Hail Mary after another, followed by one Our Father after another.

But it was hopeless; the devil had control over me.

After the movie was over and Mr. Laurence turned on the lights, I felt exposed, as if Joe and Mr. Laurence and even the ghost of Laurence Olivier could all read my thoughts. I was beginning to think that I had a hormonal disease. I mean, the girls back at school talked about boys and sex all the time, but I could not think of any one of them going into throes of ecstasy just sitting next to their boyfriends. Then again, I was quite sure none of their boyfriends looked like my Joey.

Mr. Laurence packed up all the Chinese food for us to take back to our house, reminding us not to eat anything after midnight. Without thinking, I hugged him tightly and thanked him for everything. He was so kind, and caring, and good-looking … Oh my God, I really was an out-of-control tramp.

CHAPTER THIRTY-ONE

Angie

As we entered our house, I was a complete bundle of nerves. I just needed to be alone with my thoughts and not feel like I was in a fish bowl. I told Joe I needed to run to the bathroom and off I ran, leaving him to put the food away. I locked the door behind me, even though Joe would never walk into my bathroom without knocking.

I immediately took my dress off and sat down on the floor by the tub and started to cry. After a few minutes, I lay down and fell asleep on the tile, with a bathmat under my head and shoulders. I was so exhausted, so very exhausted.

I woke up to a knock on the door and said, "Yes."

"Angie are you all right? You've been in there for an hour," Joe said, as I tried desperately to get hold of the situation. Could I possibly have been asleep for an hour, naked, curled up like a fetus?

"I'm fine," I said, as I felt myself dozing off again.

"Angie, you don't sound fine. Are you sick?"

Yeah, I thought. *Sick of being a bitch in heat, all because of you. That should make you happy, considering how many times you've told me that you doubted I ever loved you.*

"Angie, open the door!"

"I told you, I'm fine. Just give me a few more minutes. My God, can't I even go to the bathroom in peace?"

I heard him walk away, and without even attempting to get up I fell back to sleep. The next thing I knew Joe was picking me up off the bathroom floor and laying me down on the bed. He started going through my closet and I asked, "What are you doing?"

"I'm getting something for you to wear. I'm taking you to the hospital."

I pulled myself up and drew a blanket over my naked body.

"I'm fine! I don't need to go to the hospital."

"Sure, because it's so normal to sleep on the bathroom floor for two hours straight."

"I know … I'm sorry … It's just that time of the month. I'm sorry for worrying you. I was just embarrassed."

Joe left the closet and stood at the end of the bed with his arms crossed, looking at me. "Angie, you need to tell me these things. I thought I was going to have a heart attack when I saw you curled up on the floor like that."

"It's embarrassing," I said as I started crying and Joe walked over to me and lifted my head up.

"It's human nature, sweetheart. What do you think, that I'm going to find you any less perfect because you have your period like every other woman?"

I shook my head meekly and sat up. Joe handed me a pair of my pajamas and turned around while I got dressed. This, after seeing me totally naked on the bathroom floor.

"I'll make you some tea," he said.

"No, just a glass of water, please."

He brought me a large glass of water and told me to drink it all because I was probably dehydrated.

"Do you do full-body exams, doctor?" I jokingly asked.

"Yes, including rectal," he replied.

"That doesn't sound like much fun."

"It isn't, wiseass."

"You don't have to be so nasty," I said, sipping my water.

"You nearly gave me a heart attack."

"All the more reason to be nice to me," I said, as he sat down beside me. He took the glass I'd just emptied and put it on the night table.

"If anything ever happened to you I'd kill myself. So please tell me when you're not feeling well. There is no such thing as too embarrassing."

"Can I tell you something?" I asked.

"Of course."

"I love you so much it hurts."

"Yeah?" he said, looking at his fingernails.

"Yeah. And I'm sorry for making you worry."

"It's okay."

We kissed and then he got into bed with me and wrapped his arms around me, and I felt safe and clean and loved.

CHAPTER THIRTY-TWO

Angie

We arrived at the doctors' offices a little before ten o'clock and were given patient forms to fill out. Mr. Laurence came up with us and naturally the three receptionists knew him, and they exchanged greetings.

I was called in first, and a nurse greeted me. She took my weight, blood pressure and temperature, and measured my height. She also asked me a bunch of questions that were like the questions on the patient forms.

She excused herself and told me the doctor would be in shortly. I looked around the room, which had several pretty pictures hanging on the walls — a forest scene and a photo-realistic painting of horses — and another wall for her framed degrees. She'd earned her medical degree from Columbia and did her internship at New York-Presbyterian Hospital.

A woman walked into the room and at first I thought it was another nurse, or possibly a supermodel! She was gorgeous, with dark, wavy hair, baby-smooth olive skin, dark-brown eyes, and a small, straight nose. When she smiled at me, her dimples could have lit up the darkest night.

She put out her hand and said, "Hi, I'm Dr. Maria Pesci." I shook her hand and said, "I'm Angie."

"It's a pleasure meeting you, Angie. Mr. Laurence speaks very highly of you."

"Oh," I said, surprised. "That's so nice. I love Mr. Laurence."

"I see that you're originally from the Bronx. I had relatives from the Bronx, from an area called Country Club."

"Were they in the mob?" I asked, like a nervous jackass.

"The mob! Like the Mafia? I don't think so."

"I'm sorry, that didn't come out right. It's just that the part of the Bronx I come from is lower-middle-class, and when someone tells you they live in Country Club, which is absolutely gorgeous, with big houses, you assume..."

"That they're in the mob, because that area is all Italian?"

I hung my head and shook it from side to side. "Now that you say it out loud, it does sound pretty bad."

Dr. Pesci laughed and said, "Well, I'm happy I live right here on the island. I would hate to think that people thought I was in the Mafia."

I was so embarrassed, but she just looked at me kindly and changed the subject. "I understand you're nervous. I read your file and I know some of what you've been through. I also know that being a friend of Mr. Laurence makes you a special person. So let's get you taken care of, shall we?"

I nodded gratefully and climbed onto the examination table, where Dr. Pesci put her stethoscope to my heart. She then ran it across my back and told me to cough, which I did. Then she lowered the stethoscope and started to take my pulse with her hand. After a minute she said, "Your heart is racing, Angie. Are you nervous?"

"Little bit."

"By any chance, does this happen whenever anyone touches your body?"

I nodded and she said, "I understand. I read your chart. Would you prefer to wait a little while?"

"No, it's better if we get it over with."

"Okay," she said, and smiled patiently.

She put down her stethoscope and picked up an otoscope to check my ears, and then used two other instruments to check my eyes and nose. She looked back down on my chart and said, "For someone who is five feet nine inches tall you're very underweight. A young lady with your frame should be at least 135 pounds. The nurse weighed you in at 103. Have you lost weight recently?"

"I'm not sure. Probably."

"Since being ... incarcerated?"

I nodded.

"And would you say the nerves have something to do with your low weight?"

"I think so."

"Being in prison and then in the women's center must have been very stressful," she said casually as she tapped my knees with a rubber mallet to test my reflexes.

"Yes. The past six months have been really hard. But now that I'm living with Mr. Laurence and my boyfriend I've started to eat normally. Believe it or not, I probably gained three pounds last week."

"That's great! So in three months when I see you for a follow-up, I should expect you to be around 115?"

"Maybe even a little more."

"Attagirl!" she said, and her smile did put me at ease.

"Now, if you're ready, I'd like you to take off your gown and lay down on the table. I just want to check your entire body. If at any time you feel uncomfortable just let me know and we'll stop. Does that sound all right?"

"Yes," I said as I could feel my anxiety rising again. I closed my eyes as her hands pressed against the glands in my neck, and then she checked both my breasts, which felt like it took an eternity, and I was seriously starting to freak out. Images of that motherfucker trying to rape me started running through my mind like a movie.

"How about we stop for a short time?"

"No! Just go fast, please! I just need to get it over with, please."

She took my hand and gently caressed it, and the image of my brother faded away. As soon as it did, it was replaced by a memory of my mother. I had no idea why I was thinking of her in that moment, but there she was, sitting on my bed, holding my hand. I must have been five or six. I'd had this memory before and had always noticed her mouth moving, but I'd never been able to make out what she was saying. Now her voice came through loud and clear. She was touching my arm and saying, "It was just a bad dream, sweetheart. Just a bad dream."

For the first time I also heard my own voice. "No, Mommy," I said. "He was here, touching me. Please, Mommy, don't leave me."

Suddenly Maria pressed a spot on my abdomen just above my uterus and I jumped. "Uh-oh," she said. "Did that hurt?"

"Yes!" I exclaimed.

"Have you ever had an injury to that part of your body? Maybe an accident?"

"Not that I can recall."

"When you have sex does it hurt?"

"I've never had sex," I said, as she looked at me with disbelief.

"My brother tried to rape me a few times, but I always stopped him ..."

"I see," she said, thinking. "Did he hit you here?" She gently traced her finger around my lower abdomen.

"Yes, but that was before I met Joe. If I told him he'd been hitting me Joe would have killed him."

"That night when everything came to an end and they transported you to the hospital, the doctor wrote on your chart that you'd suffered severe bruising in this area."

I looked at her blankly. As hard as I tried to put that night behind me, it would always be there. "Yes, he beat me really bad," I said. "I didn't mean to lie..."

"It's okay Angie. It's okay," she said as she covered me with my gown and sat on the table next to me. "You have a really great boyfriend, don't you?"

"The best."

"And the two of you plan on getting married?"

"Yes."

"That's wonderful. And when someone has had the experiences you've had, it's great to have a mate that understands all that you have been through."

"Joe understands. At times I can't believe he's stood by me all this time."

"Why shouldn't he stand by you?" the doctor asked.

This felt like such a strange question. But I could see she had no idea what I was talking about, so I said, "Because I've treated him terribly at times. And he just stays and stays."

I started to cry and said, "My greatest fear is that he's going to wake up one day and say to himself, *What am I doing with this sick basket case?* And he's just going to walk away. He's matured so much and he's so good-looking, he could have his choice of beautiful girls. Why would he stay with me?"

"Well, I can think of two reasons," Maria said. "First, have you seen yourself? I'm pretty sure you're the most beautiful girl he's ever seen."

I laughed and thought, *Well she has a fan for life.*

"But beauty isn't everything," she added. "My guess is he stays with you because you two have already been through so much together that you've formed a bond stronger than a lot of married couples achieve during a lifetime together."

I nodded and thought about this. Then I asked, "Are you married?"

"No."

"Well, it can't be because of a lack of options. When you walked in here, I thought you were a supermodel."

"Wow! A supermodel! I think I need to check your eyes again. I might have missed something."

"Seriously Maria, I doubt there's been a day in your life where some guy hasn't asked you out or asked you to marry him on the spot."

"Oh, I've had a few boyfriends, and I imagine one or two were in love with me, but their interest in me was mainly physical. They pretended to care about my work, but when I asked them to come with me to the pediatric cancer hospital where I volunteer they always had an excuse, yet somehow they were always available to take me out to dinner later that day. And then came the inevitable offer to go back to their place or mine for a nightcap.

"I told them my place wouldn't do because my parents and two brothers, who I lived with, wouldn't be too keen on me bringing home a guy who just wanted to get me into bed. They would always deny it, but eventually they wandered off."

"Did you really live with your parents?"

"Yes, but not anymore."

"Do you still volunteer at the pediatric hospital?"

"I do. Almost every Saturday."

"Would it be all right if I went with you, and maybe if I did okay, they would allow me to be a volunteer?"

Dr. Pesci looked uncomfortable for a second, then said, "I can ask," in as bright and encouraging a tone as she could manage.

I was suddenly embarrassed. "I completely forgot — they probably don't allow people who've been in prison to volunteer."

"Well it would be an obstacle if you were anyone else, but Mr. Laurence and the foundation basically fund the children's hospital, so I think the board will be happy to make an exception, especially when they hear about your circumstances."

I nodded at her and listened.

"With your permission, I'd like to tell the volunteer coordinator about your situation," she said. "I'm fairly certain she'll be delighted to have you volunteer."

"Oh! That's so nice of you. Yes, please."

"Wonderful! I'll call her as soon as you leave. Assuming all goes well I can pick you up at Mr. Laurence's estate Saturday morning and we can go together. I only live a few minutes away."

"I would love that. Thank you so much."

"Thank you!" Maria exclaimed. "You can put your gown back on. I just have to go check on the availability of a machine." She left the room as I put the gown back on and sat up. I tried to drown out my mother's voice as it came back and threatened to overwhelm my thoughts. That was the first time I'd remembered every detail of the scene, and now her words started repeating like a refrain: *It was just a bad dream, sweetheart. Just a bad dream.*

No, Mom, it wasn't just a bad dream. It was you allowing your little girl to be molested by your disgusting husband and son. It was a family affair, and I was the sacrificial lamb.

Maria took me into a room where a female technician was sitting by a patient table and an ultrasound machine. Maria had me lay down on the table as she covered the lower half of my body with a blanket and pulled the gown up to my breasts.

"We're just going to do an ultrasound on that part of your stomach where you were beaten. Nothing to worry about, I just want to see the extent of the scar tissue."

The technician ran a probe over that part of my body as Maria and the tech watched as images of my uterus appear on the screen from several different angles. Maria's concentration was so intense, as she occasionally took control of the probe, that I started thinking that there was something seriously wrong. When the procedure was over Maria pulled my gown back down and took off the blanket.

I stood up and asked, "Should I start making funeral arrangements?"

She laughed and said, "Not for at least another seventy years or so."

I changed back into my clothes, had my blood taken, and peed into a cup. Then I met Maria in her office, which was more like a library. She sat behind a lovely mahogany desk, surrounded by bookcases that were filled with medical books and journals. I sat across from her as she looked directly at me.

"The good news is that you're a healthy young woman who needs to gain at least fifteen pounds. I would be happy if you did that over a period of three months. You need to gradually get your body conditioned to eating regularly. After you achieve that, it would be good for you, both emotionally and physically, to start exercising. Do you swim?"

"Yes, I love being in the water."

"Great, because as you know, Mr. Laurence has a pool that's half the size of the Atlantic Ocean." She looked at the computer screen on her desk as she started playing with the cursor. Looking back up at me, she said, "You have an alarming amount of scar tissue around your uterus and fallopian tubes. We'll have to do further investigation, but this looks like a case of endometrial adhesions from trauma to the uterus."

She turned the computer screen around and pointed to the scarring. "I'm very sorry to say that this means that it would be nearly impossible for you to ever get pregnant, and that if by some chance you did, you would almost certainly have a miscarriage. Do you even have a period every month?"

"When I first started having my period when I was thirteen, I had normal bleeding, but over time it has become less and less, and over the last six months, it has been almost nonexistent … a drop here or there."

"They do perform surgeries where they remove scar tissue around the uterus, and that gives a woman some hope to get pregnant the old-fashion way, but at best it's a fifty-fifty chance. In your case, there is simply too much scar tissue. I hope you don't mind me saying this, but you should have told your boyfriend about your brother. The world, and especially you, would have had one less son-of-a-bitch to deal with a lot sooner."

"It wouldn't have made any difference. He had been beating me for years before I met Joe, and having Joe go to jail for me would have led me to suicide."

"Have you and Joe talked about having children?"

I started laughing, and Maria asked me if something was wrong.

"No," I said. "It's just that one of the main reasons I wanted a doctor's appointment was so I could ask you if you could write me out a prescription for birth control medicine."

"That is funny," Maria said.

"It's just bound to happen. Joe holds me all night long to stop me from having nightmares. It has to be so hard on him…"

"You have a special boyfriend, which doesn't surprise me because Mr. Laurence doesn't take an interest in a person unless he sees something special in them."

"How long have you known Mr. Laurence?"

"For over ten years. I met him and his wife and her sister at the children's hospital we'll be going to on Saturday. His wife, Isabelle, was the most gorgeous woman I have ever seen, especially for her age. She was mesmerizing, and the way Mr. Laurence looked at her, it was like he was falling in love with her again every day. In all the years I watched my parents interact, I never saw anything like that. And Isabelle's younger sister Rachel was always with them. They were inseparable, Rachel and Isabelle, and she was also a beautiful woman, yet she never got married."

Maria started crying as she took a tissue and wiped the tears away, and after a quiet moment, she started crying all over again. She shook her head and said, "I'm sorry Angie. You must be thinking that they must allow every crackpot and crybaby to become a doctor these days."

"That's the last thing in the world I was thinking."

"Well, over the next two years, I used to go over to their place quite often. We'd have dinner and watch movies, and I heard so many wonderful stories from all of them. And I was just in awe of Isabelle and Mr. Laurence's relationship. It was so apparent that he had eyes for only one woman and that was Isabelle. He had the grand prize, and there would never be any substitute, no stand in, no one that could take her place in life or in death.

"A few years after I met them, Rachel was diagnosed with bone cancer. She had been healthy all her life, and it came as a shock. Isabelle had part of the house literally turned into a hospital where Rachel could receive chemo treatments and radiation. They hired two full-time nurses who lived in the house the whole time, and a highly respected oncologist who specialized in that type of cancer who came to see her at least twice a day.

"I used to go over every night after work and bring them food or whatever they might need, and sit with Rachel, Isabelle, and Mr. Laurence for hours. At the beginning it wasn't that bad, and we would joke and laugh and watch TV. Isabelle stayed beside her day and night, and I swear the only time she wasn't there was when she had to use the bathroom.

"But as the disease progressed, and the pain became unbearable, the doctor put her on a morphine drip twenty-four seven. This once-vibrant, beautiful lady who just a couple of years earlier looked like she was in perfect health was reduced to a skeleton, unable to hold down food, conscious only an hour or two a day. Isabelle refused to let her go. She would hold her hand day and night and occasionally got a smile out of her sister when she told a funny story.

"The night she passed away, Isabelle got into bed with her and wrapped her arms around Rachel and would not let go. It was the only time I've seen Mr. Laurence appear hopeless. Whatever he said to Isabelle didn't register. No one was taking her sister away from her, dead or alive.

"I left about four hours later with Isabelle still in bed with her deceased sister and her arms wrapped firmly around her. The next morning, I got a call from the oncologist telling me that Isabelle had died from what appeared to be cardiac arrest earlier that morning, with her sister still in her arms.

"I immediately drove over there and entered without knocking. I walked to the area where the hospital was set up and the equipment had already been removed. The only thing left was the bed with the two sisters on it. I swear, I nearly passed out as Mr. Laurence approached me and said, 'You need to leave, Maria.' He led me to the door as I rambled on about how sorry I was. He opened the door, and before I could turn around and say goodbye, he closed it, and I heard the lock slide into place.

"There were no notices in the newspapers about the deaths, nothing posted about funeral arrangements or a burial ... I tried a few times over the next couple weeks to call him, but he never picked up or responded to any of the messages I left. Every night after work I drove by his house, but the only lights that were ever on were the front porch lights; otherwise the estate was shrouded in darkness. I was ready to call the police, I was so worried. I started having dreams that he'd curled up next to his wife and sister-in-law, cut his wrists, and died. It's hard to explain, but for the longest time, Mr. Laurence, Isabelle, and Rachel were the glue that kept me together while I was going through difficult times. In fact, Mr. Laurence is still that glue."

"When did you finally get back in touch with him?" I asked.

"After about three weeks he called me and apologized for not returning my messages. He invited me to dinner at the house that night, and ever since he's been my tutor, support, and caregiver. I don't know if there's a better man on the planet."

She took my hand and said, "I've probably told you a lot more than I should have, Angie. I know how close Joe and Mr. Laurence have become and I'm sure Mr. Laurence has told him a lot, but probably not about the deaths of his wife and sister-in-law. I'm sorry to have to ask this, but I'm hoping we can keep this between us. I think it would be best if we let Mr. Laurence talk to Joe about all of this in his own time."

"Of course, Dr. Pesci—"

"Maria. Please call me Maria," she said. "Honestly, it's a good thing I work for the foundation's clinic, because as you've just witnessed, I can perhaps be guilty of over-sharing, especially when I sense a kinship with a patient." She smiled at me and I beamed back at her. It felt so good to hear that she liked me.

"Of course, Maria. I won't say a word."

"Thank you," she said. "And since we're busting through boundaries, I have one lie to correct before you leave. I was actually adopted by Mr. Laurence and Isabelle when my family disowned me for reasons I cannot get into now. I use their last name, Hamill, except when I'm here at the clinic. This entire building and its different departments are funded by the Hamill Foundation and the clinic is free to anyone who cannot afford health care. Mr. Laurence paid for my medical school and supported me during my internship. I've lived at the mansion for over twelve years, occasionally taking an apartment close to the clinic on my own to show some independence, but it never lasts very long, and I'm right back at the mansion.

"I've met your boyfriend a couple of times, but never really got to talk to him because we seem to be on opposite schedules; he was either off to see you, or I was off to the clinic. For all practical purposes, Mr. Laurence is my father, and Isabelle was my mother. I'm deeply involved with the work of the foundation, which is far-reaching, not only in the United States but around the world.

"I didn't tell you this earlier because Mr. Laurence and I felt it might put extra pressure on you ... me being a member of the family."

"I totally understand, Maria, and I'm happy you didn't tell me. If you thought I was nervous when we first met, I would have been ten times worse if I'd known."

"I also want you to know that anything we discussed, such as the scar tissue, is totally confidential ... between just you and me and whoever you choose to tell."

Maria walked me out to the lobby where Mr. Laurence and Joe were waiting for us. Maria and Mr. Laurence immediately embraced, and he whispered into her ear, and she smiled. She took my hand and said, "It was such a pleasure to meet you, Angie."

"Thank you so much, Maria," I said.

Turning to Mr. Laurence, Maria said, "Good news, Dad. Angie has expressed interest in volunteering at the pediatric cancer hospital with me. I told her there might be a bit of an approval process, but that they're sure to say yes."

"That's wonderful, Angie," Mr. Laurence said. "I'm happy to put in a good word if that's of any use."

"Yes, that would help. I have a hunch they'll listen to you," Maria said with a smile. Then she turned to Joe and shook his hand and said, "Nice to see you again, Joe. Maybe sometime in the future we can actually have what resembles a real conversation."

"That would be great," he said.

"According to your lovely fiancée, you're the best thing since the invention of New York pizza."

Joe laughed and grabbed my hand and kissed it. "That might be the nicest thing anyone has ever said about me, but it's actually Angie who holds that honor."

Mr. Laurence turned to Maria and said, "So Saturday night, after the two of you get back from the hospital, I expect you to stay for dinner and a movie, and please feel free to bring a friend."

"I would love that," Maria said.

Maria turned to me and said, "Saturday at nine. I'll pick you up out front?"

"Yes," I said as I couldn't help myself and I hugged her and for a few moments I never, ever wanted to let go.

CHAPTER THIRTY-THREE

Angie

After eating a very late breakfast, we arrived back home. Mr. Laurence and Joe had the whole day mapped out, and their plans did not include me. When Maria mentioned that she knew Joe and Mr. Laurence were very close, I wasn't sure if she knew exactly how much time they spent together, and the last thing I was going to do was interfere with their plans. If not for both of them, I would still be at the correctional center, not roaming around this breathtaking estate a free woman.

Joe was definitely not the same person he'd been just six months earlier in the Bronx. He was just as caring and loving and generous as he'd always been toward me and others, but he was no longer rash and impulsive. He'd become contemplative and insightful, and when he looked at me with those big, expressive brown eyes my body tingled all over. He was like a younger version of Mr. Laurence, and whereas I had just recently gone through an obsessive, hysterically jealous stage in which I thought he was interested in every good-looking girl we approached, such as Diane the waitress and my good friend Gloria, I was no longer concerned with any of that nonsense.

Previously, the simple thought that he knew a woman like Maria would have had me sweating and on the verge of a nervous breakdown because, let's face it, Maria was the real thing. She was physically perfect, and a lovely person, to boot. Yet, I never felt jealous or threatened. And why? Because I could feel Joe's gaze always on me like I was the most important thing in the universe.

Joe escorted me up to the house and came inside. He sat down at the kitchen table, and I sat beside him and said, "I thought you and Mr. Laurence have a whole bunch to do today?"

"We do, but a few minutes isn't going to matter. So, tell me everything the doctor told you?"

He was looking directly at me and for a moment I felt like a witness sitting in a witness chair. Then Joe reached over and gently pushed some of my stray hair behind my ear and I suddenly felt relaxed.

"Well, I need to gain fifteen pounds, but Maria told me to go slowly over three months, otherwise if I forced the food down, I could get sick."

"That sounds doable," he said. "Was there anything else?"

I hesitated, then said, "She also told me … I could never get pregnant."

"Never? Why is that?"

"Basically because of all the scar tissue in my uterus. A fetus would have no place to grow, and besides that, my fallopian tubes are blocked with scar tissue, which would make fertilization impossible. The bastard really did a job on me. So, once again, I'm depriving you of something."

"Depriving me? Of what?"

"Of children. Carrying on the family name," I said as I bowed my head. He touched my hand and said, "Ang, it makes *no* difference. I mean it. In fact, I want you all for myself,."

"Really?"

"Yes, and if by chance we change our minds, there are a million children out there who need to be adopted. What I want to know is, are you in pain? And is the scar tissue going to cause you any problems down the road?"

"No, but the first few times we make love it will probably hurt because the scar tissue from the last beating hasn't fully healed."

"So we won't have sex until it fully heals. I'm not putting you through any pain."

"I could ... do things for you that could make it easier. I know it can't be easy, Joe."

"I appreciate the offer, but I want to wait until we can both enjoy it."

"I guess the plus side is that we don't have to worry about birth control," I said.

"Now, did the doctor tell you anything else I should know?"

"No, that's it. I promise. Did your doctor tell *you* anything *I* should know?"

"No, it was no different than any other physical I've had. Promise."

We kissed, and then he ran off to be with Mr. Laurence.

"So we just won't have sex until it fully heals."

He'd said it as though it was no big deal. As if holding me all night was enough. Truth be told, I'd used the idea that it might hurt to put him off until I gained a little weight. I knew he'd seen me naked when he picked me up off the bathroom floor, but then again, he might not have looked very closely. He did turn his head away while I put on my pajamas.

I really didn't know much about sex, except for what they taught us in biology class. I could look at some videos on the internet, but the little I'd seen of them was so disgusting that it actually turned me off. However, that didn't stop me from fantasizing about Joe. When those thoughts took over, I imagined him in control and the two of us entwined as one, with me feasting off his deliciously sculpted body.

I thought about that time by the pond with the ducks, when I took control and tried to get Joe to have sex with me right there. So embarrassing. Why did I do it? I searched my mind for answers and finally realized that it happened during one of my jealous phases, when I was sure Joe was going to leave me. I was so desperate to keep him that I was ready to have sex right there in the open. All of that seemed so irrational now. I decided to just let the sex happen whenever it happened, and not to worry about it so much.

That evening we had dinner at Mr. Laurence's house again. He cooked us New York steaks, creamy mashed potatoes, and steamed green beans. When he put my plate down in front of me, I looked down at this 18-ounce steak and thought to myself, *There is no way I can eat all of this.* I must have looked anxious because Mr. Laurence said, "You don't have to eat the whole steak, Angie. Eat as much as you're comfortable with, and we'll wrap the rest up."

I looked up at Mr. Laurence and said, "Thank you."

"You do have that large bag of popcorn waiting for you," he said. I laughed and cut off a small bite of steak and popped it into my mouth. It was so delicious that I instantly wanted more. Mr. Laurence smiled and said, "I was happy to see how well you and Maria got along, and I'm very proud of you for volunteering. I have no doubt that you and the children are going to get along wonderfully."

"I hope so. I've always been able to relate to children and I seem to get along with them well — at times, better than with people my own age."

Mr. Laurence chose the movie that night: *The Bishop's Wife*, starring Cary Grant, Loretta Young, and David Niven. Joe set up the projector while Mr. Laurence and I sat next to each other.

"So," I said, "you taught Joe how to work the projector?"

"Yes, it took him only a few minutes to catch on. Your fiancé is a very smart young man."

The room went dark, and Joe sat down next to me, and I placed my head comfortably on his shoulder as I ate my popcorn and watched this delightful movie about an angel (Cary Grant) who visits a bishop (Niven) and his wife (Young) and makes the frustrating bishop realize that asking for large donations to build a large expensive cathedral to praise and preach the word of God was not needed; whereas the small church he preached in before was just right.

It takes place during Christmastime, and while the bishop is out there begging for money from a rich patron, the angel shows the bishop's wife what she has been missing since her husband's obsession with the cathedral has taken over: the joy of ice skating, or eating in a French restaurant, or buying a beautiful hat, or once again getting in touch with a charming older man they call the professor.

I clapped when the movie was over and suddenly, I became conscious of Mr. Laurence looking directly at me. He said, "Angie, you have dimples that glow like lanterns that could turn a cloudy day into rays of sunshine. And yet, you doubt your attractiveness to Joe. Sometimes our best qualities, the ones that light up other people's lives, are ones we're not even aware of."

Mr. Laurence handed Joe the bag of leftovers, which included the half of my steak that I couldn't finish. I hugged Mr. Laurence and thanked him for everything. Before I came here, I could not even imagine hugging another man, except for Joe, and yet hugging Mr. Laurence felt so right. Cary Grant might have played an angel in *The Bishop's Wife*, but Mr. Laurence was an angel in real life.

I said to Joe as we were walking back to our house, "So I see Mr. Laurence has taught you how to use the projector. That's so cool."

"It's easy. I could teach you in five minutes."

"Five minutes," I repeated in disbelief. "How long did it take you?"

"About forty-five minutes, but you're a lot smarter. I'll ask Mr. Laurence, but I'm fairly sure he'd love for you to learn too."

"When did I become so smart?"

"You're the one who never got less than an A-minus in any of her courses."

"And what did that get me?" I asked as Joe looked directly at me.

"Don't say that, Angie. None of that was your fault."

"You know, you're right. I am that smart, or that lucky. Otherwise I'd never have you."

CHAPTER THIRTY-FOUR

Angie

I woke up the next morning when Joe reached down and kissed me and told me he was running off to drive Mr. Laurence to the cemetery. I waited to hear the front door shut, and then I got out of bed. I felt unusually refreshed, like I'd had a fantastic sleep. I vaguely remembered some dreams of the X-rated variety involving my delicious-looking boyfriend.

After drinking a glass of orange juice at the kitchen table, I washed up and went outside. There in the pool, under trees filled with birds singing their morning songs, was a rubber raft drifting toward me. I kicked off my slippers and rolled up the hems of my pajamas and, without getting too wet, managed to climb into the raft. I laid back and rested my head on the edge. I swear, it was like floating on a cloud.

Then one of the birds squawked from the top of a tree not far from the pool, and I swear it sounded like my mother. *Just a bad dream, ca-caw. Just a bad dream.*

My eyes popped open, and I stared at the tree, craning my neck. No movement. Then I watched a huge, fluffy cloud float directly over the pool. "Screw you, Mother," I said, and shut my eyes and focused on floating.

As I drifted into the deep end, I made a decision. It was time to put my entire family — mother included — behind me. Two of these miscreants were dead, and wherever my father might be, I really didn't care. Of course, I couldn't put them totally behind me. I had to visit a psychiatrist twice a week as a condition of my release, and the topic of my family would have to come up. Also, I had no control over my dreams, and it would only be a matter of time before the wretched demons re-visited me.

But there was a big difference now. I was in a committed relationship with a young man who loved me unconditionally. My welfare was paramount to him, and his welfare was paramount to me. He had decided to stand by me through all the trials and tribulations, and, for the first time in my life, I felt safe.

I slowly dozed off and woke up to the sound of Joe's voice. "What are you doing, Ang?"

I looked at him and smiled and said, "I'll give you three guesses, gorgeous."

"Floating around in a raft with your pajamas on."

"Right you are," I said, pointing at him. "See? Not just a handsome face."

"Very funny," he said. "Think you can float over here?"

"Hmm, I don't know. What's in it for me?" I was squinting at him now, as the morning sun filtered through the trees, splitting into rays of hard and soft light.

"A kiss from me, and your breakfast order."

"Oooh, a kiss," I said, paddling over. "Why didn't you say so?"

"Thought it was implied."

As I reached the side of the pool, I extended my arms to Joe. "Think you could lift me without both of us falling in?"

"I can do my best," he said. Then he reached down and lifted me out of the raft like it was nothing.

"Wow," I said, as my bare feet landed on the pool's tiled edge. "Now where is that kiss?"

He bent down and kissed me for what felt like a full minute. "There," he said. "Will that do?"

I giggled and said, "Very satisfactory."

"And now your breakfast order?"

"How about a plate of pancakes with scrambled eggs and bacon."

"Good choice."

He kissed me again and started toward the house when I called out to him. "Joe, I have to see the psychiatrist today. Will you be able to come with me?"

"Of course I'm going with you," he said, and blew me a kiss.

I walked back into the house and picked up my phone and called Gloria.

She answered with, "So chicken legs, how are you doing?"

"Haha, wonderful!" I said, too happy to bother questioning her latest nickname for me. "Better than I could have imagined. This place is a paradise."

"Is that so. Well, I'm happy for you, cupcake."

She did sound happy, but also wistful and a bit distracted. I got to the point. "I'm calling to remind you not to let your pride get in the way today when you visit the psychiatrist. Tell them what they want to hear and get your butt over here."

"Don't you worry. Gloria is all about repentance today. I want a piece of that paradise."

"Good. Don't forget to call me after you're finished repenting."

She laughed and said, "I will, cupcake. I love you."

"And I love you."

As soon as we hung up, Maria called.

"How's my favorite patient?" she asked, right off the top.

I laughed and said, "I'm well, Maria. How are you?"

"Great. I was wondering if you'd had time to talk to your boyfriend about what we discussed yesterday?"

"Yes, I did, and in typical Joe fashion, he was only concerned about me and whether the scar tissue could cause me future problems."

"What a prince," she said, sounding genuinely impressed.

"I know. He said it makes no difference to him at all that we can't have children, and that if we ever decide we really want to be parents there's always adoption."

"Amazing. Hang onto that boy."

"I fully intend to!"

"And were the two of you finally intimate?"

"No..." I said. "I told him if we made love, it would probably cause me pain for at least the next couple of months, until the scar tissue completely healed."

"Is that the real reason you didn't want to have sex?"

"No, I just wasn't ready. I don't want him to see me looking like a skeleton."

"Ah," she said, then thought for a moment. "And when you gain some weight, you'll feel comfortable?"

"I hope so."

"But you're not sure?"

"Not really," I said. "I've seen videos... you know ... of couples having sex..."

"And?"

"And even with the guy trying to be as loving and compassionate as possible it seemed so rough on the woman."

"Considering everything you've been through, it's only natural that you'd be hesitant. I just hope you'll remember that in the context of a loving relationship, sex can be great."

"Thank you so much, Maria. I'm working on believing that."

"How's the weight gain going?"

"I ate half a huge steak last night, and for me that's amazing."

"That's so great!"

"Thank you. Are we still on for tomorrow?"

"Of course, I can't wait. I'll meet you outside the house at nine o'clock."

"Yes, and thank you, Maria."

"Thank you, sweetheart."

I sat down at the kitchen table and thought of how caring it was for Maria to check on me. But then everyone in Mr. Laurence's orbit was caring and loving. It made me think that there really are nice people in this world. There was a time when I didn't believe such people existed.

I suddenly jumped as Joe put down the bag with my breakfast inside. I hadn't even heard him opening the door, and I swear I thought I was going to have a heart attack.

"Are you okay?" he asked.

"Yes — sorry, I was lost in thought."

"What about?"

"Gloria. She has her meeting with the psychiatrist today."

"Ah."

"She promised me she was going to tell them what they wanted to hear, but you know her, and how her pride can get in the way."

"So I've heard."

"I was also thinking about everyone I've met since I came here and realizing that there really are nicer people in this world than I ever thought. Of course it helps that they're in Mr. Laurence's orbit."

"Yes, Mr. Laurence's standards are very high," Joe said. "And yes, Gloria is a proud lady, but this time I'm fairly certain she's going to say what she needs to say to get out of there. Mr. Laurence talked to her yesterday, and she promised him she'd do what she needed to do."

"And no one goes against Mr. Laurence?" I said, a little sarcastically.

Joe looked at me as though I'd committed a crime.

"You wouldn't be sitting here right now if it wasn't for Mr. Laurence. Nor would I be living in this lovely house if not for his generosity and compassion."

"Joe, I was only kidding. It was just a dumb thing that flew out of my mouth. It sounded funny in my head but it wasn't so funny out loud. The only person I love more than Mr. Laurence is you."

"You should eat your breakfast before it gets cold," he said, as I took the container out of the bag. I took off the lid, and the pancakes, bacon, and scrambled eggs were all there with syrup and a knife and fork." I felt guilty just looking at it. I'd accidentally besmirched the name of the nicest man on earth, and here he was, giving me pancakes. But Joe was already moving beyond my faux pas.

"Would you like something to drink?" he asked.

"Just a glass of orange juice, but I can get it," I said. I started to get up, but he gently stopped me by putting his hand on my arm, then went to the refrigerator, poured a glass of orange juice, and brought it to me.

"Thanks."

When I started eating, he sat down about a foot away and watched me.

I finally glanced up into his dark, large brown eyes and said, "Is there something wrong?"

"No, why do you ask?"

"Because it feels like you're looking at me as though I've done something wrong..."

"Not at all," he said, beaming at me. I'm just making sure you're real." He reached out and poked my forearm with his finger.

I laughed. "What do you mean?"

"You can't possibly be real."

"Joe—"

"Deep down, I can't believe how lucky I am to have you. You're the most beautiful girl I've ever seen."

"I think I might have to get you a pair of glasses."

"No, my eyesight is quite good and what I see quite clearly is the most beautiful girl in the world."

I blushed as I stood up from the table and leaned over to kiss Joe, and then suddenly I covered my mouth. "I have a sticky mouth from the syrup," I said as he removed my hand and he kissed me anyway.

"Tasty," he said as he ran his tongue around his lips. "More syrup, please."

We kissed again, this time more deeply. I pushed my breakfast aside and pressed my whole face against Joe's chest. Then I got up and sat on the table and allowed him to slide me onto his lap as we kissed with a fiery intensity. I was speaking into his neck when I finally said, "Make love to me, Joe."

"Are you sure?"

"I've never been more sure of anything."

He looked at me with such love and gratitude that I blushed. Then he picked me up and carried me into the bedroom and laid me on the bed. He slowly took off my pajamas — so slowly that I laughed and joked that we'd be there all day —and then he took a long time to kiss and caress and explore my whole body with his eyes and hands and mouth. Once he was inside me, he was very gentle. I did feel a little pain at first, but it quickly transformed into pure pleasure, and amazement, as he rocked into me and kissed me deeply at the same time.

I remember being briefly frozen while he was on top of me, and then I remember my mind going somewhere else, as I focused on his breathing and mine. From there, I became aware of a remarkable sensation; I'd been a separate person, and now I was joined with another body that belonged to the person I loved most in the world.

When his gentle rocking turned to rhythmic thrusting and he came inside me, he looked surprised and quickly asked if I was okay. Boy was I — right on the cusp of my own orgasm, but still maddeningly on the other side of it, and in desperate need of help. He seemed to know what to do, but he was new to my body, and so was I. Amazingly, I felt no shame, self-consciousness, or worry. All of my repressed feelings exploded at once, and I felt free and unconstrained and fully loved by the one person who was always there to protect me. And my God, was he good-looking.

After we were finished, Joe had his legs chained to the bottom half of my body. He looked down at my face and gently caressed it as he pushed loose strands of my hair back behind my ears.

"Did it hurt?" he asked.

"If it did, I can't remember."

"So it felt good?"

"I was in ecstasy." Joe smiled and held me tighter. I looked up at him and said, "By the way, how did you get so good at making love? Have you been practicing with some other girls I don't know about?"

"Today was my first time, and I swear to that on my grandma's grave."

"You know, you're not supposed to swear."

"I know, sorry. I did take Biology 101 and 102."

"So did I, but I don't ever remember learning about any of that…"

He looked down at me with those big brown eyes that seemed like they could penetrate my very thoughts.

"Did you spot a pimple?" I asked.

"No, what I'm looking at is perfection," he said as he lifted the blanket I'd thrown over my body. "Yup. Perfection from head to toes."

I laughed as I switched positions and straddled his hips. "Now it's my turn to study your body more closely."

And study him I did, for another hour, at least.

CHAPTER THIRTY-FIVE

Angie

After taking a shower, I put on my bra and underwear and looked in the mirror. Joe made me feel so beautiful, and after we made love, he made me feel not only beautiful but special.

Joe had changed so much. The teenager who loved playing basketball ten hours a day and hanging out with his friends seemed to have evaporated and been reincarnated as this near-perfect man. He was always kind and protective, but the rough edges were always there too. I guess you could say such traits were bred into most boys from the Bronx. It was a survival mechanism.

Mr. Laurence had gone off to war, seen his friends be killed, and been wounded himself, and he came home a man. Joe's war was closer to home. Against his family's wishes, he refused to give up on me. He helped lift me out a bottomless pit, and in doing that, he went from being a teenager to being a man in less than a year. Of course, there was no real comparison between the two situations, but in my mind, both Joe and Mr. Laurence were heroes, in their different ways.

I put on my favorite red dress and tied back my hair in a loose ponytail. I walked into the kitchen where Joe was reading what looked like a very old newspaper. I peered at it and saw the date: 1946. He looked up at me and said, "Wow! Just when I thought you couldn't get any prettier."

"You like?" I asked as I twirled around.

"Stunning!" He stood up and took me in his arms. "I'm one lucky guy."

We kissed and then we walked to the car and drove in the direction of the psychiatrist's office. I turned toward Joe and asked, "Is there anything I shouldn't tell the psychiatrist?"

"I asked Mr. Laurence, and he said you should tell the psychiatrist whatever is on your mind. That it's all confidential and you don't have to worry about anything."

"So it's okay if I tell her I'm the happiest girl in the world?"

Joe laughed. "Yes, that's certainly something I would tell her. While you're at it, you could also tell her that I think you're the most perfect girl in the whole wide universe."

"You don't think that might be stretching it just a little bit?"

"Not one bit."

We took the elevator up to third floor, got off, and entered the psychiatrist's office. The receptionist gave me a form to fill out. It asked all of the usual questions, about medications, drinking, anxiety, and suicide — whether I'd attempted it or thought about it.

I scribbled away, then handed the form back to the receptionist and gave her my insurance card. She made a copy and handed it back to me and I went back and sat next to Joe. I put my head on his shoulder and he asked, "You okay, angel?"

"I'm perfect!" I said as the receptionist told me that the doctor was ready to see me. I kissed Joe and followed the receptionist into Dr. Nicole Piaget's office. Dr. Piaget stood up behind her desk and we greeted each other by shaking hands. She was quite stylish, pretty, in her mid-thirties, and she had a smile that instantly put me at ease. She said I could sit anywhere I felt comfortable, on the couch or on one of the leather back recliners. I sat on the recliner closest to her desk, and she asked if I would prefer to have her sit across from me. I said I was perfectly okay with her sitting behind her desk.

"I've been going over your file. I'd say you've had a pretty rough life. Does that seem like a fair assessment to you?"

"Yes, that's fair."

"How do you feel now?"

"The best I've felt in my entire life."

"And why is that?"

"Because I feel secure for the first time ever. I'm living in a beautiful place and I have the best boyfriend — fiancé — in the entire world. He's been my protector and support system. He's kind, generous, patient, and…"

"And?"

"Drop-dead gorgeous. You can see for yourself. He's out in the waiting room."

She laughed and said, "Drop-dead gorgeous is always a nice bonus, especially when someone possesses all the wonderful traits you mentioned. You said he's patient. How so?"

"Well, he's always known I have problems with intimacy, and he's never once pushed me, let alone forced me, to do anything that would make me feel uncomfortable. We've been going out for a year and a half and we only started kissing last month."

"He sounds like a very considerate and caring boyfriend."

"He is, and for a long time I never knew how lucky I was. The truth is, I wouldn't be alive right now if not for Joe."

Dr. Piaget closed her eyes, and when she opened them, she asked, "Does he know your entire history behind the sexual assaults you have endured since you were how old?"

I stared at her face without seeing, and a bird call came through the window as though there were no glass there. Suddenly, images of my mother began floating in my vision.

Mother, making a sandwich before school. Mother, brushing my hair. Mother, sitting on my bed, talking about the dream. Telling me that I was a creative child with a big imagination. Maybe someday I could be a writer! But that the things I was trying to tell her couldn't be real. The foul breath, the sweat, the heaviness on top of my tiny frame. Density, crushing my bones. My mother's mouth moving, forming words. *It was just a dream.* My truth, not real. My senses, my body, my mind, *wrong.*

"Is something the matter, Angie?"

I squirmed in my chair and began to cry. Dr. Piaget produced a box of tissues and I took a handful.

"Sorry," I said.

"There is nothing for you to be sorry about," she said. "You're safe here, and crying is good. It's very good."

When I was out of tears, I spoke.

"My mother died when I was twelve. And until I met Joe, I always thought she was the one person who ever protected me."

"She wasn't?"

I shook my head. "Lately I've been remembering things…"

"And did you remember something just now, when I asked you if Joe knew about the abuse you suffered as a child?"

I nodded and started to cry again as Dr. Piaget handed me more tissues.

"Can you tell me what you remember?"

I noticed a potted tree in a corner of the room. Its light-green leaves were each about the size of a child's palm. Dr. Piaget finally said, "That's my ginkgo. Do you like it?"

I nodded and kept staring at it until I could speak.

"I've been seeing her sitting beside me. It's late at night and I'm in bed. She's sitting a few inches away, and I'm upset."

"How old are you in this memory?"

"I'm little. Maybe five. I'm trying to tell her something, and she just keeps saying 'It was a just a bad dream. It was just a dream.'"

"And was it? A bad dream?"

I shook my head, and Dr. Piaget leaned forward. "If it wasn't a dream, what was it?"

I hesitated, and finally choked out the word, "Real."

"Right. What happened to you was real."

I pursed my lips and stared at her, and for once I didn't cry. I could feel a kind of shimmering sensation —a liquid energy — flowing from my chest to my limbs, all the way to my toes.

Dr. Piaget was watching me closely.

"What is it your mother didn't know, or didn't want to know?"

"My father … and brother —" I brought my hands up to my face. I realized I'd been tearing at a wad of tissues and digging the fingernails of one hand into my other forearm.

"It's all right. You don't have to talk right now. But I'm going to just say one thing now. Is that all right?"

I nodded.

"From everything I can tell — from your history and from your reaction today — I believe you were sexually assaulted. That this wasn't attempted assault, but true sexual assault, beginning when you were too young to remember."

She held my gaze and spoke slowly.

"These were not dreams. And you did nothing to deserve what happened to you. You didn't consent, because a child can't consent to sex. You tried to tell your mother, and she failed you."

"Why?" I asked. The word came out like a strangled cry.

"Some mothers can't admit to themselves that they've put their child in danger. Some put self-interest ahead of their child's safety. Many, many times, they're complicit."

I just sat there, trying to take in the words and their meanings.

"I need to ask you again. Does Joe know about the abuse?"

"No, it was just after remembering these things that I had

decided to put it all behind me, and so I didn't tell Joe. But it's never going away. It's always going to be there, forever and ever."

CHAPTER THIRTY-SIX

Angie

I walked out of the doctor's office feeling like I was dragging a pair of anchors on my legs. Joe popped out of his chair to join me at the reception desk and immediately looked alarmed when he saw my puffy face and red eyes.

"What's going on?"

I raised one finger to ask him to wait and turned to the receptionist to book my next appointment. I was having trouble making myself heard. My voice just wasn't coming out at full volume. Once I finally had a little appointment card in hand, Joe and I walked into the hallway and waited for the elevator. He turned to me sort of frantically and asked, "Are you okay?"

I burst into tears. The elevator doors opened, but instead of us getting on it he took me by the elbow and led me down the hallway to a small leather couch. I buried my head into his chest and continued crying while he held onto me and rocked me and gently patted the back of my head. We stayed like that for a long time. When I finally pulled away I could see that the front of Joe's shirt was soaked.

"Joe," I said, "do yourself a favor and just leave me."

"What are you even talking about?"

My voice had returned and I felt a little stronger. I looked at him and said, "I'm talking about your sanity. You shouldn't have to be with a basket case like me. You're way too good a person."

He looked stricken. "Sweetheart, what is going on?"

"I'm broken!" I got up and started pacing the hallway. He watched me for a few seconds before he got up and gently took me by the shoulders and led me back to the bench.

"What happened in there? These institutional psychiatrists … What did she do to you? We need to find you someone else."

"No!" I stamped my foot. "Dr. Piaget is perfect!"

"Okay…"

"You're not listening."

"I'll try to do better. Just please explain what's happening. What are we talking about?"

"Everything! Just everything!"

"Sweetheart, you're going to have to help me here—"

"You don't get it! My past is always going to be with me! And the more I remember, the worse it gets!"

"I do get that. I do. And as I always say, we'll get through this together. Do you want to tell me what has so upset you?"

I looked around frantically and eyed the elevators, and then the door to the stairwell. I was already on the move when I said, "I have to get outside. I need to get out of here."

I ran down three flights of stairs and out the front door of the building to a little landscaped area outside the foyer. Joe was right behind me and caught up with me under a maple tree. I plunked myself down on the grass and leaned against the trunk, and he sat next to me.

"Ang. You're kinda scaring me here."

I turned on him. "*I'm* scaring *you*? You think *this* is scary?"

"No — I mean—"

"You have no idea what it's like to be scared."

"You're right, I don't. That was a stupid thing to say," he said, then quietly added, "I mean, you did push me down a flight of stairs. That was pretty scary."

I glared at him and he retreated instantly, saying "You're right, you're right. What do I know? Stairs. Pfft. Just please tell me what this is about."

I leaned against the tree and felt the bark against my back. Thick, ridged, solid.

"My mother."

"Your mother? Is that what you talked about with Dr. Piaget? Are you missing your mom?"

"No."

"You're not?"

"No."

"What, then?"

"Remember I told you that she was my only protector, and that once she died, it became a living hell, until I met you? Well, that's not true."

"It isn't?"

"Not exactly. Maybe it's what I wanted to believe."

"I don't understand."

If I looked at him, I wouldn't be able to speak, so I focused on a patch of ground off to the side of where he was sitting. A small winged insect was climbing a blade of grass like it was Mt. Everest.

"She was as guilty as my father and brother. She knew, and she let it happen." I started to cry as I worked up the courage to say the next part. "And they did so much more than you know! Sickening beasts!" I couldn't bear to see his face in that moment, so I avoided his eyes and just kept talking.

"I would scream for her in the middle of the night and tell her that they were hurting me and touching me all over, and she always used to say I was dreaming. She flat out denied that any of it happened." I had my head in my hands now and was spitting out the words. "She *let* them—"

Joe was making a slight choking noise as he fought back tears. He rose to his knees and wrapped me in his arms. I let my forehead rest against his chest until I suddenly had to escape the cocoon — to keep letting this river of bile flow out of me.

I shook off his embrace and looked at him dead on. "What kind of mother would do that?"

Joe was speechless. He shook his head mournfully. "And to think, I've been saying prayers for her. I hope she's burning in hell."

Joe held me until the fury gradually drained out of me. Then he took my face in his hands. "Your mother might not have protected you," he said, "but I will, until the day I die, and that's a promise."

We kissed and sat still for a while with our backs against the tree. It was all so exhausting.

"Today was such a perfect day until all this happened," I said.

"I know."

"Dr. Piaget wrote me a couple of prescriptions to help with the anxiety, but I don't want to take any medications. I saw what it did to some of the girls in the women's center and I don't want to go down that path."

"Then you won't. You've been doing much better, so I think it would be wise to continue on the path you've been on. Whatever happens, we'll face it together."

He took me by my hand and we got up and brushed off our clothes. That's when Joe told me that he'd promised Mr. Laurence that he would pick up something in the mall.

"Think you have the energy to come with me?" he asked, and I nodded and slipped my arm in his.

Since the place he needed to go was in the same complex, we walked. I didn't ask what he had to pick up. I didn't want to interfere in their relationship. It wasn't like Mr. Laurence was anything like Joe's drunken friends back in the Bronx. If Mr. Laurence asked him to pick something up, he had a good reason.

We walked through the sliding doors of the Smith Haven Mall. The mall at this hour was relatively quiet, and after walking about halfway through we stopped in front of a jewelry shop. Joe glanced in the window and said, "Yes, this is it."

We entered the shop and the saleswoman looked at us as though we were there to rob the store. Joe's shirt was all wet from my tears, and I looked like I'd just been in a fight. I caught a glimpse of myself in a mirror and was briefly horrified. My hair was all over the place and my cheeks glowed red under puffy eyes.

"Can I help you?" the woman asked.

Joe looked at her and said, "I hope so, Michelle. Mr. Laurence recommended I come here. He said the service is great, and that he's certain I'll find exactly what I'm looking for."

She perked up at the mention of Mr. Laurence and suddenly couldn't do enough for us. She asked how she could help, and leaned forward to listen carefully as she held onto a set of keys.

"Well, I need to gather a little information first," Joe said. He turned to me and asked, "If you had a choice between a bracelet and a necklace, which would you choose?"

"Well, since I've never had either I think I would go with a necklace so I wouldn't have to worry about getting it wet every time I washed my hands."

"That makes sense. What type of pendant would you choose for the necklace?"

I thought and said, "Your birthstone."

"Don't most women pick the birthstone that corresponds with the month they were born?"

"Probably, but if you were never born, I don't know how I would have survived. Besides, there are far too many times I wish I was never born."

Joe cringed and wrinkled his forehead. "Please, Angie," he said softly, "never say that."

"I'm sorry."

"Okay, back to the necklace and pendant. Michelle, would you be able to show us a gold necklace that would hold an oval-shaped Alexandrite stone, the birthstone of the month I was born, with a yellow gold mantle?"

"Certainly. I can put together some different combinations and you can tell me if you like any of them."

"Thank you."

I was standing by in mute amazement and finally spoke. "Excuse me, Michelle, I just need to talk to my boyfriend a minute."

"Of course."

I took Joe by the elbow and led him out of the store and said, "Are you buying this for me?"

"Yes."

"Are you crazy? We could put down a down payment on a house with what this is going to cost."

"I think that might be an exaggeration. Besides, we already have a house."

"We don't own it. We don't own much more than the clothes on our backs, and most of those come from Mr. Laurence too."

"Please, angel, just pick out the necklace and pendant you like most."

"I'm walking away. This is crazy."

"I wouldn't do that unless you want me to pick it out for you. I would much rather have you choose the one you really like. Please, Angie, trust me."

We walked back into the store and Michelle had put together five combinations and laid them on a velvet background on top of a glass cabinet. The middle one caught my eye, and I was thunderstruck. The Alexandrite stone changed colors and the gold mantle and chain reminded me of something Princess Diana would have worn.

"Michelle, can I try on the middle one?"

"Of course," she said as she came around the counter and carefully placed the necklace around my neck. "Your fiancé has exquisite taste."

I walked over to a full-length mirror and looked at my reflection.

"Do you like?" Joe asked.

"What's not to like? It's lovely."

"But not as lovely as the girl wearing it," he said as he kissed me on the neck, sending a shiver down my spine.

I asked, "How much is it, Michelle?"

"Give me a moment and I'll add it up." She walked back around to the counter as I stood there, unable to take my eyes off the necklace. Then I nearly had a heart attack when she said, "It's normally forty-two hundred dollars, but since you're friends of Mr. Laurence you automatically get a fifteen percent discount. So the new total would be three thousand, five hundred and seventy."

Then I nearly had another heart attack when I heard Joe say, "We'll take it," as he pulled out an American Express platinum card — *The* Platinum Card — handed it to her and asked, "When do you think it will be ready?"

"In a couple of days. Our jeweler will start working on it first thing tomorrow. We'll give you a call. How about an inscription, Angie?"

I finally turned away from the mirror and walked over to the counter and wrote down on a pad Michelle gave me, "Whatever our souls are made of, his and mine are the same."

"How beautiful," Michelle said as she re-read the quote out loud.

"Emily Brontë," Joe said, and I just stared at him.

"Who are you and what have you done with my Joe?"

"What?" he asked, pretending to be offended. "I read."

"I guess you do," I said.

Michelle wanted to know if she should add something more personal, as well. "Something like, *To Angie, with love from Joe?*"

"Yes, especially that," I said as Joe signed the credit card receipt and handed Michelle a three-hundred-dollar tip, which she tried to hand back but which Joe refused to take.

I handed Michelle back the necklace and we finally left the store and started walking toward the entrance to the mall. I put out my hand and stopped Joe and said, "Please explain."

"Mr. Laurence gave me the card, a business card in my name, and he said, 'I want your first purchase to be a gift from you to Angie. Something that can come close to matching her beauty.' He gave me the name of the store and told me to spend as much as I needed. Do you like it?"

"I have never looked into a mirror for such a long time in my life. Yes, I love it."

We walked back to car and sat in the front seat for a few minutes, watching people pass by. Joe was deciding if he should call

Mr. Laurence and offer to pick up dinner. I couldn't help myself and did exactly what I told myself I wouldn't do: I asked Joe what he did for Mr. Laurence besides driving him to the cemetery.

"It's not what I do for him, Ang. It's what he does for me. He's teaching me how to run the foundation when he decides to step down, and while he's teaching me, I'm helping him with the paperwork and learning the history of the Hamill family and its empire."

My eyes must have gone as wide as saucers. He explained that the foundation has assets of over fifty billion dollars and helps millions of women and children around the world who have been victims of abuse.

"It has board members who make recommendations and draw up plans to help get the needed resources to the women and children, without the looting and corruption you find in so many nonprofits. Mr. Laurence has the final say. He either approves the operation, rejects it, or modifies it in some way."

"And when he steps down he's going to leave these decisions to you?"

"Not entirely. I'll be part of a team that'll have a say over proposed projects. Right now the only member of the team that I know of is your doctor, Maria. She's been working with Mr. Laurence since his wife passed away. For a time she was living at the mansion while attending medical school and doing her internship. You probably haven't heard this yet, but her father threw her out of the house she grew up in when she told them she was a lesbian. She told them she planned to marry the girl she'd been seeing for over a year and that they wanted to start a family. Sadly, her relationship with that girl went sour and she never got married.

"Her father called her a freak and a disgrace to the family and literally threw her out of their house and stopped helping her with medical school costs. Mr. Laurence ended up paying for her program and kept supporting her during her internship, and she also got to live at the mansion."

I was sitting there with my mouth hanging open, just trying to keep up, as Joe kept going.

"Maria knows the ins and outs of the foundation, and once Mr. Laurence steps down she'll become its president. When I turn twenty-one I'll become her assistant and share in the final approval of all projects. But Mr. Laurence has made it clear that Maria is in charge. She'll make the final decisions."

"And will we have to move into the mansion?" I asked.

"No, Mr. Laurence said that the house we're living in is for all practical purposes our house. He's already bequeathed it to us in his will. He's hoping that the job you start on Monday is the start of your apprenticeship and that eventually you'll become a major part of the foundation."

"I thought you were going to be working with me?" I asked, totally baffled at what my fiancé was telling me.

"I'll be working next to you but on different material."

"But I was planning on going to college next year."

"And Mr. Laurence is hoping you do. In fact, he's hoping you'll consider going into medicine like Maria. He's already put the money aside for your education. I only hope that you don't go too far away for school. I couldn't bear to be away from you."

"How could you even imagine me doing that? You're my entire life. No, I'll have to go to college somewhere close by."

"Good," Joe said. "And that reminds me of two things you said today that greatly upset me. The first was outside the doctor's office. You called yourself a basket case and told me to just leave you because I'm 'too good a person' to stay. Please Angie, don't ever say such a thing. I'm the one who doesn't deserve you. Every day I have you next to me it's like a miracle. You were my dream girl before I ever met you. How many guys can say they went out with, and married, the girl of their dreams?"

I started to speak but he put a finger to my lips and said, "Please let me finish. The other thing you said was that you didn't want your birthstone attached to the necklace because there are so many times you wish you were never born. If you were never born, Ang, I never would have had the opportunity to meet the most perfect girl in the world. You're the strongest person I know. What you had to put up with for eighteen years of your life, I never could have done. I would have been lucky to make it through half that time. The memories of those years are never going to completely go way, but we're already on the way to making wonderful new memories and we'll continue on that path until our wonderful memories far outpace the terrible ones."

"Am I allowed to speak now?" I asked as I desperately tried to hold back tears.

"Of course."

"I love you so much it hurts!" I exclaimed as I literally attacked him, jumping on his lap and pinning his head against the driver's side window, running my hands through his hair, down along his body, and pushing my tongue deep into his mouth. If it wasn't for the fact that he told me we'd attracted an audience, I would have ravished him right there. I was that turned on.

CHAPTER THIRTY-SEVEN

Angie

After the audience dispersed and I was back on my own seat, I turned to Joe and said, "Want to go to a motel or back to the house and pick up where we left off?"

He looked at me as though that was the most ridiculous thing I'd ever said. "Don't give me that, Joe. You were as turned on as I was."

"Of course I was. I get turned on just looking at you."

"So, what's the problem?"

"When I saw all those people watching us, I thought I was going to drop dead. Granted, I would have died happy, but we have too many good times ahead of us to check out now."

We both laughed, but I wasn't going to let it go. "Motel or house?" I said again.

"How about the house after we have dinner with Mr. Laurence? It's almost five."

"But then he'll want to see a movie," I said.

"True. But remember, it's Mr. Laurence…"

"…the man responsible for giving us a future we never could have dreamed of in a million years."

"Right."

Joe called Mr. Laurence and we all decided on Chinese food. We drove to the restaurant and put in a large order. While waiting we walked outside and my phone rang. It was Gloria. For once she had put her pride aside and told the psychiatrist what they wanted to hear. She had already called Mr. Laurence and told him the good news. He had informed her that within a week she would be out of the center.

I was all giggly and excited when talking to Gloria, and she was onto me right away, asking, "Has my little cupcake been a naughty girl?"

"What?" I replied.

"Well that just answered the question. How long has this been going on?"

"A couple of days," I lied, because I felt stupid saying it just started that morning. I looked back to make sure that Joe was out of earshot. He wasn't the type to go bragging about sex, and he surely wouldn't want me talking about it to other people. I whispered into the phone. "It was *so* good. I can't believe how many orgasms I had, especially since I've heard other women complaining that they never have orgasms during sex."

"Maybe it's because you have a super-hot boyfriend who for whatever reason loves you more than anything in this world."

"Do you really think that might be it?"

"Possibly, or maybe he made love to you like every woman would hope a man would make love to them … patiently, lovingly, exploring every part of your body and touching you in all the right spots."

"He definitely did that. I'm so lucky to have a boyfriend like Joe."

"Wow! Cupcake, you finally figured out what's been obvious to everyone who's ever seen you together. That boy looks at you like you're the only person in the world."

I blushed and told her I loved her, and she told me she loved me, and I said I couldn't wait until we could all be together again.

I walked back to Joe and excitedly shared the news that Gloria had done what she needed to do and would hopefully be released next week.

"That's so great," Joe said. "She's a really wonderful person. That makes me so happy."

I looked at him closely, and suddenly I remembered the day at the women's center when I accused Joe of cheating on me with Gloria. Afterwards, it seemed insane, but just now it didn't seem quite so insane anymore.

"What's wrong, Angie?" Joe asked, but I didn't answer and so once again he asked in a louder voice, "Angie, what's wrong?"

"What makes you think there is something wrong?"

"Because you're staring at me as though there's mud on my face."

"I was just wondering how long it's going to take you before you start cheating on me, if you haven't already?"

He took a step toward me, and for the first time I thought he was going to hit me. But instead he said, "I'm going to pretend you didn't say that, Angie." He then turned and walked into the restaurant as I slumped against the wall and started crying.

A few minutes later he walked out holding a bag filled with food. He reached down and helped me up. "I'm sorry," I said. "I don't know what came over me."

"It's okay," he said as he opened the passenger side door for me, and then went around and got into the driver's seat. I took the bag from him and put it on the floor between my legs. "It smells so good."

Joe picked up a mini package of tissues that was sitting between us and handed them to me. "You might want to fix your face, Angie. It's all smudged from crying."

I pulled down the sun visor on my side, flipped open the small mirror, and used a tissue to wipe away some eyeliner that was giving me raccoon eyes. Then I reached into my purse and found a mini blusher and applied a little pink to both cheeks. I turned to Joe and asked, "Better?"

He looked at me and said, "Yes, you look beautiful." Those were the last few words we said to each other until we pulled into the driveway of the mansion.

CHAPTER THIRTY-EIGHT

Angie

Inside Mr. Laurence's kitchen, Joe placed the bag on the table and took out his phone. He showed Mr. Laurence some pictures he'd taken of me with the necklace on and Mr. Laurence said, "The only thing more beautiful than that necklace is the young lady wearing it."

I blushed and said, "That's so kind of you, Mr. Laurence. Thank you."

He looked at me for a long moment as though he'd noticed something was wrong. The man has better instincts than anyone I've ever met. Maybe it had to do with working for his father-in-law, the newspaper tycoon. "How did your session go with the psychiatrist?"

It just came rushing out of my mouth like the sour taste of lemon juice and even Joe looked up at me, somewhat shocked, as I told Mr. Laurence everything.

"I broke down, and she prescribed a bunch of medication for me that I don't want to take. What can I say? I'm a mess."

Mr. Laurence looked at Joe and said, "I'm going to take your lovely fiancée on a little tour. You can get everything prepared so that when we come down, we're ready to eat. It really does smell good."

I didn't even look at Joe, but inside I felt that this little tour could not have been something he envisioned or wanted. Mr. Laurence took me by the arm and led me up the staircase to the second floor. "You've never been up here?"

"Joe said it was off limits."

"I don't know if I would put it like that, but no one is allowed into the rooms." He took me down the east wing first. In front of every door was a red roped barrier like one sees at movie premiers. Each daughter had their own room and attached to each door was a gold nameplate. We paused before each room and Mr. Laurence bowed his head.

We then walked over to the west wing, which was similar to the east wing, except for the fact the Isabelle and Rachel's room had one long barrier that stretched across both rooms. I could see tears form in Mr. Laurence's eyes as he stayed there with his head lowered for a long time. After we had stopped before each room, we sat down on a couch just to the left of the staircase and against the wall.

"In Mr. Hamill's will, he left instructions that these rooms should never be used again or even changed once the daughter had passed away. It was a testimony to their memories. It was here that young girls like you found a home where, for the first time, they felt safe and secure, and where they were unconditionally loved by their adoptive parents. Each girl, regardless of where they were in the world and what condition they were in, found her way back to the mansion and their room when their demise was certain, and death was but a step away. It was in this mansion that they learned that life could be beautiful, and it was here, the place where it all began, that they came back so their souls would always be present in the home where they first experienced the miracle of true love and security.

"Many of the guests over the years have told me they hear giggling and laughing and footsteps running back and forth, and they're not sure where it's coming from. I tell them it's nothing to worry about. That it's just the sound of happy young girls. Many of the girls who came here, like Rachel, were much younger than you. Others were closer to your age, like my Isabelle. It took all of them a different amount of time to finally feel safe and secure and loved, but once they did, this place became their haven, the place that would spring them forward into careers in medicine, science, travel, TV and movies.

"Mr. and Mrs. Hamill had the patience of monks. No matter how busy they were, the girls came first. The first time I met Mr. Hamill was in Los Angeles, where he had rented a house while he was working on the final sale of a newspaper he wanted to buy. Rachel, who was fifteen at the time, had promised him that she was going to cook a gourmet French dinner for him and the family. Sadly, she burned everything, and the roast was scorched so badly that it looked like a little piece of volcanic rock. Rachel was terribly upset. Not even Isabelle could calm her down. She went running into Mr. Hamill's study, where he was busy going over contracts and new layouts for the newspaper. He took one look at her and put aside all the paperwork so he could find out what was wrong and give her comfort. She hugged him and cried and kept saying how sorry she was for destroying the French dinner she'd promised him."

I stared up at Mr. Laurence and pouted my sympathies with Rachel, and he flashed me a smile as he continued the story.

"He calmed her down and gently wiped away her tears and told her how proud he was of her for trying something new. He reminded her that almost no one succeeds at something they're trying for the first time, and that with the proper training he was positive she would become a great French chef. For the next several hours he didn't touch his work, but concentrated entirely on his young, distressed daughter."

"He sounds like you, Mr. Laurence," I said as I started to cry, once again.

"He taught me a lot, but I could never be half the person Mr. Hamill was. He and Mrs. Hamill were both extraordinary. They started the home for the girls after they got married. Mr. Hamill had just come back from covering World War I for the newspaper he was working for as a reporter. A little later he purchased that newspaper, which was on the verge of bankruptcy. In a short time, he turned it into the biggest morning paper in New York City. She was working as a copy editor at the paper, and according to them, it was love at first sight. He learned about the severe abuse she'd suffered as a child, and he promised her that when they had enough money, they would create a refuge for girls who had been abandoned or survived abuse. A few years later, with her help, he was on his way to be becoming a newspaper tycoon along the lines of William Randolph Hearst. And instead of using his money to collect art from around the world like Mr. Hearst, he and Mrs. Hamill worked with orphanages and social service agencies to find a group of girls who desperately needed care, and gave them a home and the miracle of security and unconditional love.

"You have been here for less than two weeks, and already I've seen so many positive changes. You're more relaxed, less guarded, and that beautiful face and spirit you possess has at times glowed with the medicinal power to heal. Yes, you are going to have setbacks, but you are stronger than you think, and your fiancé is dedicated to helping you deal with any problem that might come your way. In all the time I've spent with him, he has never said a bad word about you. He's expressed his concerns, and it was those concerns that convinced me to intervene and have you released from the women's center."

"It's just that I rely on him for everything," I said hopelessly.

"And one day he'll rely on you. That's how healthy marriages work. There is always a back and forth."

"I hope so, but it seems like I'm always the one who needs help. In the psychiatrist's office I had a total breakdown. I've been remembering all kinds of horrible things lately. I've realized that my mother wasn't the protector I thought she was. I know now that she actually knew about the abuse and allowed it to happen. She sat on my bed and told me it was just a bad dream."

I told him about the afternoon — how I'd run away from Joe and told him that he should find someone else, because he deserves to be happy and not chained to someone who will never be free of her past. I described Joe's reaction — how he listened carefully and then told me that our wonderful memories together would far outnumber the bad memories, and that when the bad memories did occasionally come back, we'd face them together.

I stopped talking as tears flowed down my face, and Mr. Laurence took out his handkerchief and gently wiped them away. When I finally caught my breath, I continued. "Then we went to the jewelry store, and when I looked in the mirror with the necklace on, I felt beautiful in a way I never have before. I was so happy. It was like what happened in the doctor's office was behind me.

"And then when we were waiting for the Chinese food I looked at him and thought to myself that someone like Joe would never remain faithful to someone like me. He could have his choice of beautiful girls who won't burden him."

Mr. Laurence looked like he was about to speak, but I needed to get the worst out, so I talked over him, spilling the rest of my confession. "Then he said something nice about Gloria — Gloria, who I love and trust — and that's when I lost my mind and asked him how long it would be before he started cheating on me…"

"Oh."

"… and I might have implied that he could already be cheating."

"I see."

"I know it was crazy," I said, speaking quickly now. "I think I knew it then. I didn't have one shred of evidence to prove any of what I'd said. And he was not happy."

"What did he say?"

"He stepped very close to me, and for a second I thought he was going to hit me … another absurd idea considering how kind he is, and how many times he's told me he would never hit a woman … and then he said, 'I'm going to pretend you never said that.' He then went into the restaurant and picked up the food and we drove back here in almost complete silence."

Mr. Laurence had been listening carefully and waited until he had made sure I was finished speaking. After a pause, he said, "And now you have to explain to him why you said what you said. Joe possesses one of the greatest gifts given to man, and that is the ability to forgive. For a person so young, he has an astute knowledge of human behavior and how fragile it can be at times, especially under stressful conditions. No one knows this better than you, Angie."

We sat silently for a short while, and suddenly I saw myself pushing Joe over the railing and down the flight of stairs and nearly killing him. Not only did he forgive me for that, but he lied to protect me and keep me from going to jail.

Mr. Laurence looked at me and said, "Why don't you go help your fiancé. I'll be down in a few minutes." I hugged Mr. Laurence. The girl who couldn't stand another man touching me not so long ago had become a hugger. But then, Mr. Laurence was no ordinary man.

I walked into the kitchen as Joe was just finishing setting the table. "Can I talk to you for a minute?"

"Where's Mr. Laurence?"

"He said he'd be down in a few minutes."

Joe pulled out a chair for me and sat down in a chair a few feet away. He asked, "What would you like to talk about, sweetheart?"

"Until I met you, I don't think I ever experienced any type of luck. And now I'm suddenly engaged to this super-handsome, loving, caring and generous guy who I couldn't dream up in my wildest dreams. So, it shouldn't come as a surprise that I'm always worried that my luck is going to run out. Today, when I looked at you in front of the restaurant, I couldn't help thinking that there is no way that someone who looks like you and who is as stable as you are is going to want to stay with me long term, or stay faithful. Not to a girl who is burdened with a thousand issues. I'm sorry for the things I said. I wasn't thinking straight, and it wasn't fair to you."

"That's kind of funny, because as I was setting the table, I was thinking how unbelievable it was that the most beautiful girl in the world, the girl of my dreams, could possibly think that I would cheat on her and find someone else." He pointed to himself, and then to me. "Me, cheat on you? I mean, come on."

"Really? So you forgive me?"

"Of course I forgive you, and no, your luck is not going to run out." Then he eyed me and said, "I just hope *mine* isn't going to run out."

"What?" I said, surprised that he would even suggest I might be interested in anyone else. I just looked at him like he was the biggest dummy in the world, and of course he laughed and leaned over to me and we kissed.

Mr. Laurence walked in shortly after and we ate dinner, then washed and dried the dishes and put them all back in their proper place. Joe then showed me how to use the projector. It took me about ten minutes to learn, but I stretched the session out to about twenty minutes just because it was fun to be close to him.

Mr. Laurence chose the 1938 Frank Capra film, *You Can't Take It with You*, starring James Stewart, Jean Arthur and Lionel Barrymore. It was about an eccentric family and their beautiful daughter (Arthur) who falls for a banker's son (Stewart). There were plenty of fireworks — including the literal kind — and a lot of laughs. I loved the film so much that I gave it a standing ovation.

Like always, Mr. Laurence gave us the leftovers to take home and I hugged and thanked him. After taking a few steps toward our house, I turned back and gave him another long hug and thanked him repeatedly for his kindness and generosity and words of wisdom.

CHAPTER THIRTY-NINE

Angie

Joe and Mr. Laurence came back from the cemetery just before nine o'clock, but they didn't go straight to the diner, because Joe wanted to make sure Maria showed up to go to the pediatric cancer center at nine o'clock. Joe was always very protective of me back in the Bronx, at the women's center, and now at the mansion. I gave up arguing with him long ago, once it dawned on me that it was nice to know that someone loved me enough to want to protect me from harm.

I kissed him for at least ten seconds as Maria pulled up beside us. Joe opened the car door for me and looked at Maria and said, "Please take care of my girl and get her back here safely."

Maria laughed in his face. "What do you think is going to happen to her? Worried a bunch of five- and six-year-old cancer patients are going to beat her up?"

Joe laughed, even though I could tell he was a little thrown by her tone. "You never know — if enough of them get together they could do some damage."

"Bye, Joe," Maria said with a smirk as she drove off and I waved goodbye.

When we were a little ways down the road, Maria said, "It must be nice to have someone who cares about you so much."

"It really is, and one day you're going to find someone who cares about you just as much. Hopefully today."

"Wow! Look who's the optimist now." She looked at me while driving, and I must have been glowing because she suddenly looked like she'd figured out a secret. "Did something happen between yesterday and today that you might want to share?"

I smiled and shook my head.

"Oh, oh, oh! Should I pull over? Do we need to talk?"

"Keep driving! No time for gossip!"

"There is always time for gossip. But let me put it another way — was it good?"

I paused and then looked over at her, dying to spill my guts. "It was unbelievable! So good that we did it a bunch of times!"

Maria laughed gleefully, then looked serious. "That's so great, but did you have any pain?"

"Maybe just a little at the beginning, but then it was amazing."

She was grinning like a maniac, and I suddenly wanted to change the subject. "What about you? Any promising dates on the horizon?"

"No, and you don't have to pretend you don't know. When I told you about the boyfriends, I'd forgotten that Joe probably knows everything and has no doubt told you that I'm a lesbian … a freak, according to my father."

"Joe did tell me, but only because he was telling me about the house and the foundation and its mission to help women and girls, and he mentioned how you came to live with Mr. Laurence and Isabelle and her sister. I hope that was all right."

Maria waved her hand. "It's completely fine."

"I'm so sorry your dad said that to you. I'd hoped the days of people holding those opinions were far behind us."

"What can I say? He's a dinosaur."

"It must have been incredibly painful."

Maria glanced at me. "It was."

"Have you spoken to your family since it all happened?"

"Very little. My father hasn't talked to me in nearly ten years. Same goes for my two brothers, who I always thought of as my protectors. The only one I still talk to is my mom."

"That's something, I guess."

"It would be, but every time I talk to her, she asks me to go see a priest."

"A priest?"

"I'm pretty sure she's banking on an exorcism to rid me of my *deviant tendencies*," she said with a laugh.

"Oh no. Oh dear. Well, it's good you can laugh."

"It's better than cryin' — and believe me, there was plenty of that, especially in the beginning."

"Joe said you were in medical school when it happened, and that you almost had to drop out because your family withdrew their support?"

"I came this close to losing everything," she said, lifting one hand off the wheel to hold her fingers about an inch apart. "I never would have been able to finish school if not for Mr. Laurence and Isabelle. They swooped in like a couple of angels and paid for everything."

"Amazing."

"It was. I owe them my life. They saved my medical career, but really, they saved my life."

"Funny, I was just saying that about Joe — that I owe him my life. And both of us could say the same about Mr. Laurence. I have no idea where I'd be if he hadn't met Joe and taken him in. Or — I do know — I'd be at the women's correctional center."

"I know what it feels like to be rescued by these wonderful people. I lived at the mansion for ten years, and Mr. Laurence never let me pay for anything. The only thing he expected of me was to help with the dishes after every meal."

I lowered my eyes and held tightly onto the notebook I'd brought along with me. Maria was gorgeous, intelligent, and compassionate, and anyone who didn't know her story would think her life must be an effortless and charming adventure. I finally raised my eyes and looked at her. She was trying not to cry as she sputtered, "And to think that for the longest time I'd always heard that Italian fathers treated their daughters like princesses. I guess my father drew the line at my sexuality. I often think that the biggest mistake I made was telling them the truth. It would have been easy enough to hide, especially on a doctor's busy schedule. But I always wanted a family, and it wouldn't have been fair to my partner. So I told them the truth, and was exiled."

I paused and said, "It's one hundred percent their loss," and Maria looked across at me appreciatively.

She shook her head as she came to a stop at a red light. "It's at the point now, that if my father accepted me and wanted me to come back, I wouldn't. Mr. Laurence is my father, and Isabelle is the beautiful mom I only knew for a few years because she died so young." Maria stopped suddenly and looked at me with guilt in her eyes. "I'm sorry to lay this all on you, especially with the horrific things you've been through."

"That's okay! To tell you the truth, it's nice to hear about someone else's problems. I've been such a mess lately."

"That's the trauma," Maria said. "It comes in so many forms, and it's a persistent bugger, always trying to hijack your life."

"So true."

Then Maria brightened. "But we have to focus on the good. For example, I'm a freaking doctor — nice, right? — and *you* have your freedom and a super-hot boyfriend who would jump in front of a speeding train for you. I'd say we're doing all right."

"I'd say you're right. Now we just have to work on getting you a super-hot girlfriend." Maria laughed out loud. "The only problem is that I don't know if there's anyone out there as beautiful and loving as you."

"You're so sweet, Angie." She looked at the notebook I was clutching and asked, "What's that? You plan on taking notes?"

"I just don't want to mess up. These kids have it tough enough. The last thing I want to do is to make anything worse."

"You're going to do great. The kids are going to love you."

We parked in the lot outside the building and just as Maria predicted, everything went great. The children *did* love me, and I felt so happy that I could cheer up their day.

CHAPTER FORTY

Angie

We drove back to the mansion at five o'clock and found Joe and Mr. Laurence hunched over papers at the kitchen table. I caught a glimpse of a notary seal and a sheet with formal letterhead. As soon as we walked in, Joe and Mr. Laurence scooped up the documents and moved them into a folder. Apparently, whatever was in the documents was not for us to see.

I sat down next to Joe, and he asked me about how everything went at the cancer center. I told him everything went great, and Maria added, "She's a natural. The children loved her."

Mr. Laurence asked Maria if he could talk to her in his study. She readily agreed and as she was passing by, she said, "Don't forget to show him the pictures."

I took out my phone and went through the forty or fifty pictures I had taken of the kids. "Let me tell you, Joe, they are a lot braver than I could ever be, and they seemed to have so much energy for children going through treatment. And the great news is that the cure rate for some of the cancers is very, very high, over eighty percent and climbing." Never once did Joe take his eyes off me or the pictures I was showing him. He was completely focused on what I had to say and show him. After I finished my presentation he stood up and hugged and kissed me repeatedly on the head and said, "I am so proud of my beautiful, beautiful Angie. None of those handsome little guys made a pass at you?"

"Joe!" I exclaimed. "Well come to think of it one … only joking."

Suddenly, there was a loud slamming of a door and Maria walked into the kitchen crying. She opened a cabinet and took out a flashlight. I asked, "Is everything okay?"

"Nothing a few bottles of wine won't cure," she said as I followed her downstairs to a wine cellar that was dark and damp and contained at least five hundred bottles of wine. It was the type of wine cellar that I'd only seen in movies. She was still crying as she tried to read the labels on the bottles. I asked, "Is there anything you want to tell me?"

"No!" she said. "I prefer not to share this type of misery." Then she grabbed two bottles of red and thrust them at me, telling me to be careful because they might be slippery.

We walked out of the cellar and when I looked down at the labels one read Lafite Rothschild 1900 and the other Château Lafite Rothschild 2010. I was no wine expert, but I could somehow tell that these were expensive bottles. I asked, "Are you sure you want these ones? They look super expensive."

She pointed the flashlight on the bottles and said, "Yes, they're expensive. Maybe fifteen thousand dollars for both."

She continued walking and I asked, "Should you talk to Mr. Laurence before opening them?"

She looked at me really hard and said, "I don't need his permission."

We walked back into the kitchen, and I looked at Joe with wide eyes as I waved the bottles in front of him. Maria asked, "Do either of you drink?" We both shook our heads, and even though I knew Joe drank I didn't want him mixed up in this possible disaster, so I was happy he said no. She took the Rothschild 1900 out of my hand, and with a simple corkscrew she opened the bottle, breaking the cork three times trying to get it out. She filled a regular wine glass to the rim and drank it down like she was drinking a beer. She re-filled the glass and said to me, "Want to at least taste it?"

"No, I really don't want to."

"Don't be such a baby, Angie. Take a sip…"

Mr. Laurence walked into the kitchen and right away it was clear he'd overheard. "If she doesn't want to, don't you force her, Maria," he said.

"She has to grow up some time."

"That child has done enough growing up already."

"Whatever," Maria said as she downed another glass of wine and poured what was left from the bottle into her glass.

"Have you eaten today, Maria?" Mr. Laurence asked.

She looked at me and said, "Have we eaten today, Angie?"

"Yes, we had lunch around 12:30," I said as Maria took a sip for a change.

Mr. Laurence looked at Joe and asked him to order a couple of pizzas and a dozen cannoli, saying, "They're Maria's favorites."

"I'm not hungry," she said angrily.

"You're going to get sick," Mr. Laurence said.

Maria glared at him and downed the remainder in her glass in one gulp. "Did you forget? I'm a doctor. I'm quite capable of treating myself. I can even write myself a prescription. Lucky me."

She put her empty glass down and picked up the second bottle, but Mr. Laurence reached over and grabbed it out of her hand. "You've had enough!"

He looked at her with an expression that would've had me peeing my pants. She backed off and started to walk away as Mr. Laurence grabbed her by the hand, pulled out a chair, and told her to sit down before she fell down. She grabbed the back of the chair and sat down a little unsteadily.

By the time the pizza and cannoli arrived, Maria was slumped over the kitchen table with her head resting on her arms. At Mr. Laurence's request, Joe picked her up and carried her down the hall to her room, while Mr. Laurence followed. I went along, and when we got there, I pulled back the sheets on her bed and Joe gently placed her down.

Mr. Laurence was standing beside the door with sad eyes transfixed on Maria. I wanted to say something, but I didn't know what. If I ever had any doubts that he thought of Maria as a daughter, they dissipated at that moment.

The room was large, with an attached bathroom. One wall was lined with mahogany bookshelves filled with medical books, novels and poetry. Teddy bears, dressed like doctors and nurses, were scattered throughout the room.

She slept peacefully, and I hoped she wouldn't remember much about the night. We left the door open and tiptoed back to the kitchen. Mr. Laurence, without looking at the label on the bottle of wine she'd finished in record time, simply placed it in a trash can.

We then sat down and ate the pizza and each had one cannoli. Mr. Laurence asked me about the children at the hospital and I told him everything I'd told Joe. He mentioned how proud he was of me and what a great feeling it was to know that for at least a short time I made a positive difference in the lives of the children.

Mr. Laurence and I periodically checked on Maria, who continued to sleep peacefully. Joe and I left after a while, and I could only hope that the worst that would come out of the episode was a hangover in the morning.

CHAPTER FORTY-ONE

Angie

Back in our house, while I put away the leftover pizza, Joe went into the living room and sat down. He was deep in thought when I sat beside him. I picked up a cushion and placed it on his lap, then stretched out on the couch and put my head on the pillow.

"I don't mean to be nosy, but I have something I need to ask you," I said.

He ran his finger along my nose and said, "You do have the cutest little nose, so you're allowed to be as nosy as you like."

"Why did you and Mr. Laurence put away the papers you were reading when Maria and I came in the kitchen? Was there something in them that you didn't want us to see?"

"No, not at all. We were just going over the paperwork, summaries, and petitions submitted to Mr. Laurence from his representatives across the globe. They were from organizations asking the Hamill Foundation for contributions."

"And that was all?"

"Yes, if there was more, I'd tell you, and if Mr. Laurence told me it was privileged information, I'd just tell you I couldn't talk about it. I won't lie to you, Angie."

"So, there was nothing in that paperwork that would have set Maria off, had her slamming doors, crying, and drinking a twelve-thousand-dollar bottle of wine?"

"No. In fact she'd already read and initialed most of the material we were going over."

"Did Mr. Laurence say anything about being upset with Maria?"

"Ang, Mr. Laurence loves her as much as any father could love a child. He's so proud of her and everything she's accomplished. He's placed her on a pedestal, and the only two people above her are Isabelle and Rachel."

"And where are you in this row of pedestals? Just below Maria?"

"Nowhere near Maria. They have a long history together, and I could never override that. Nor would I want to."

"Well, if it makes you feel any better, you're at the very top, the highest level, in my ranking order."

"Funny you should say so, because that's exactly where you are in mine. Tippy top." We kissed, and for a few sweet minutes I forgot all about pedestals and paperwork and even Maria.

I got up to use the bathroom, and after I was finished, I stopped by the sliding door. In the distance, by the pool, I could see Mr. Laurence sitting by himself. A solitary figure, beneath a canopy of stars and a full moon, with his hand cupped just below his mouth, alone with his memories.

I watched him for a few minutes and then went back toward the living room and suddenly stopped as I saw Joe, still sitting on the couch, motionless like a statue with his eyes lowered and his hands cupped under his chin. I cleared my throat so as not to surprise him. He turned toward me as I approached the couch, and I said, "Sorry it took me so long."

"That's okay, a lot of times bathroom visits turn out to be longer than we expected."

"I was only in the bathroom for a short time. I was watching Mr. Laurence. He's sitting outside, alone, beside the pool, and seems to be deep in thought."

"He does that quite a bit."

"Well, I'm going to go outside and see if he'd like a little company."

Joe looked at me as though I was ready to infringe on something sacred.

"Unless you think I'm going to disturb him?"

"No, of course not. I'm sure he'd love to talk to you. Please be sure to take your phone."

"Why would I need my phone? Surely, Mr. Laurence would never let anything happen to me."

"That's not it, Angie. I always worry about you when we're not together. I thought about you all day while you were at the cancer hospital. I can't help it."

"Would you rather we went to bed?"

"No, go talk to Mr. Laurence. He's had a rough night and might appreciate it."

"I won't be long," I said as I leaned down and kissed him.

I opened the sliding door and walked outside and toward Mr. Laurence. I was happy that he turned and saw me coming. I didn't want to shock him. I asked, "Would you mind a little company?"

"Not at all," he said, patting the chair next to him. "It would be a pleasure."

"It's a lovely night. Do you often sit out here at night?"

"It usually depends on the type of day I've had."

"It was a tough evening," I said. "I don't know what happened, but I felt so sorry for Maria. In the short time I've known her, she's been so sweet and has gone out of her way to support me."

Mr. Laurence smiled and said, "She's a very special person."

"Yes, she is. I often get the impression when talking to her that she not only thinks of you as a father, but as a life saver."

He looked directly at me and said, "What makes you say that?"

"Because it's not only her relationship with her biological family that haunts her, but the idea that she's different. One would think that in this day and age it wouldn't have such an effect on her, but that's simply not true. It only takes one or two people to label you and treat you horribly, and suddenly you realize how far we still have to go.

"Surely Mr. Laurence, enough people have told you the effect you have on them. You see someone in pain, and you have the unique ability to alleviate that pain and to give them hope and a desire to live. You've done that for Maria, and if you weren't there for her, she would slowly sink."

"I think you're underestimating Maria. She can stand on her own."

"I hope you're right, and if you don't mind me asking, do you think Joe can stand on his own?"

"Your fiancé was standing on his own before he ever met me. He stood by you. A lot of young men would have run the other way. He has one of the greatest traits any person can possess: the ability to forgive. You're fortunate to have each other."

"You're so right. In all honesty, I don't believe I deserve him, and that's why I sometimes get jealous and suspect him of being unfaithful, with absolutely no proof."

"Joe loves you the way I love Isabelle. There was no distraction. No other woman was even in the same ballpark as my Isabelle. That's exactly how Joe feels about you."

"I knew Joe for almost a year before you met him, and he was always there to protect me and to make me feel beautiful and important, but if you'd have told me that he would turn into the man he is today after such a short time I would have laughed. He's like a younger version of you, and I don't think I could pay anyone a higher compliment. Your mentoring of him is beyond anything I could have imagined. And he knows it. He says he doesn't even want to think about where he would be without you."

"I don't know if Joe told you, but I grew up in the Bronx like you two. I left college after a couple of years and joined the marines, and I was part of the invasion force that attacked the beaches at Normandy. I saw so many friends die that day. After I was discharged, I wandered the streets, wondering if I had the right to live, when those boys who'd become my best friends were all gone."

"And if they were here today, they would thank you for leading the life you have led — helping others, using the time they were denied to aid in the recovery of the country they died for, and at the same time finding supreme happiness with a loving, caring, and beautiful woman who might not be physically here today, but who you will eventually spend eternity with."

Mr. Laurence didn't say a word as he looked at me with a profundity that was unnerving. "I'm sorry for talking so much," I said. "I'm usually the quiet one."

"Don't be sorry," he said. He continued to look at me, and then he sat up and helped me to my feet. "How about we go check on Maria?"

We walked into the mansion and rushed toward Maria's room when we heard her shouting from the end of the hall. When we entered the room she was slamming her pillow with her fists and screaming in her sleep as she fended off an invisible opponent. Mr. Laurence sat down on the bed next to his sleeping, frightened daughter and said, "It's okay, Maria. It's okay." He softly rubbed her back and repeated the words until she finally settled down.

She opened her eyes and smiled as she wrapped her arms around the man who had supported and loved her unconditionally and said, "Mr. Laurence, don't ever leave me." Then her arms went limp and she fell back to sleep peacefully.

"I can stay with her if you like," I said. "It's no problem."

"No, sweetheart, you go back to Joe." I started walking toward the door and Mr. Laurence said, "Thank you, Angie."

"You're welcome, Mr. Laurence."

When I got back to the house, Joe was still sitting on the couch. He looked at me and said, "You were gone a long time. I was getting worried."

"I'm sorry. Mr. Laurence and I had a very nice talk."

"And what did you talk about?"

"It's privileged, Joe. I'm sorry."

"That's fine, but is everything okay?"

"Yes, everything is well," I said as I bent down and kissed him and then went off and got ready for bed.

CHAPTER FORTY-TWO

Maria

I woke up with the worst headache. Very little was clear to me after I opened the first bottle of wine. I'm not much of a drinker, and I can usually nurse a glass of wine for a couple of hours, but I went way overboard last night and was now paying the price — all while suffering terrible uncertainty over what I might have said or done.

The room that was my bedroom for nearly ten years was as familiar as ever. My teddy bears were all over every flat surface, still dressed in their white coats and nursing uniforms, some with stethoscopes, others holding little thermometers. I'd rescued a couple of them from my childhood bedroom the night I was kicked out. The rest I'd collected as an adult. It's a bit of a strange hobby, but these furry friends have always made me feel safer and more secure in the world. In this moment, though, they were all looking at me, and I couldn't help thinking that any one of them would be more qualified to practice medicine than me.

I got up from bed, took off my clothes, and jumped into the shower. I put on a pair of pajamas, certain that in a short time I was going back to bed, and then put on my comfy robe and walked out of the bedroom and into the kitchen where Mr. Laurence was sitting reading the morning paper.

"Good morning, beautiful," he said. "Why don't you take a seat and let me pour you a cup of coffee?" I nodded painfully and he put a hot cup of coffee before me and asked, "How do you feel?"

"Physically terrible, emotionally like a fool."

"Well, I have something to cheer you up." He opened the refrigerator and took out two cannoli and placed them before me.

"Oh my God, when did you get them?"

"Last night, but by the time they arrived you were already sound asleep with your head on the kitchen table."

"I'm so sorry about last night. The little I remember wasn't very pleasant, and the rest I can only hope wasn't that bad."

"Sweetheart, you were out cold within fifteen minutes of opening the first bottle. You weren't awake long enough to do any damage, except to express your profound love, and that only made me feel overjoyed."

"I do remember what started it and..."

"Please, totally forget what we talked about in the study. It's not going to happen, period, and that is a promise."

I jumped up from my seat and hugged Mr. Laurence as tears of love and happiness poured down my face. "What changed your mind?" I asked as I sat back down.

"The unexpected wisdom of a little angel," he replied.

"Isabelle?" I asked.

"No, not Isabelle, but I'm certain she's in full agreement with my decision."

"Was it Angie?" I asked as I bit into the first cannoli.

"Yes. What began as a polite conversation beside the pool turned into a moving picture about my life and purpose."

"How did she find out? Did you tell Joe?"

"No, I doubt she knows anything about our now-aborted plans. Like Isabelle and you, she simply sensed that something was wrong and acted upon it."

"I knew that girl was special."

"Indeed."

"This is going to sound strange, but every time I look at her, I get this overwhelming desire to dress her up in a red petticoat, with the white-trimmed fur. She should be holding a candle, with her long hair curled and draping her lovely face. Like a Christmas doll…" I smiled as I lowered my eyes and for an instant I remembered the tragic circumstances of Angie's life. If only it was that simple: To dress her up like a doll, with candle and petticoat, forever erasing the scars and the recurrent nightmares.

"What is it, Maria?" Mr. Laurence asked.

"I was just wondering if it would be okay if I moved back into my room?"

"Of course! I would love nothing more."

"Would today be too soon? It's not like I have much to move. Just some clothes and a few boxes of books that I never opened. Angie and I could move it all in one trip."

"Yesterday would not have been soon enough," Mr. Laurence said as he stood up and walked over and gave me a big hug. "You know, of course, that Isabelle and I thought of you as our daughter. God couldn't have created a more perfect creature than you, and I'm quite certain Isabelle is thinking the same thing right this moment. She might have left me prematurely, but she knew I had you, and that we would manage wonderfully." He kissed me on the head and naturally I couldn't stop crying.

He left to go meet Joe and drive off to the cemetery. I finished my coffee and licked the delicious cream from the cannoli off my fingers. I cleaned the coffee cup and coffee pot and put them away, then wrapped my robe a little tighter around my waist and took a little tour around the mansion.

I entered the parlor, where Isabelle, Rachel, and I would sit and talk after dinner. They would usually sit on the couch, and I would sit across from them on one of the chairs. I was remembering a time when I had just finished an introductory letter that I wanted to send off to hospitals where I was interested in doing my internship. I gave it to Isabelle to see what she thought. She produced a typewriter from inside an old desk and pulled a pencil out of thin air. As she read the letter at the desk, she seemed to be crossing out everything I had written. I knew it wasn't perfect, but I didn't think it was that bad.

After she was done with the pencil, she fed a sheet of paper into the typewriter and proceeded to rewrite my letter in under ten minutes.

She handed me her version, and I read it carefully. Never before had I seen such smooth and compelling prose in a simple application letter. "This is perfect, Isabelle. Simply perfect!"

"All I did was change a few words and rewrite a few sentences."

I re-read the letter a few more times and she was right. She had changed a few words and re-arranged a few sentences but kept everything I wanted to highlight in the letter.

"You're a genius," I said.

"No, it's what an editor does," she replied as Mr. Laurence entered the room. She looked up at him as he looked at the typewriter and the crossed-out pencil marks on the original letter and said, "I see she gave you the same lesson she gave me when we first met."

"How does she do it?" I asked.

"I don't know, even after all these years. But I do know that Isabelle is a walking lesson in the importance of having a good editor — and I've never come across one as good as her."

"You just say that because you love me so," Isabelle said.

"Well, there is definitely that, but truth be told, you are the best." He then leaned down and kissed her.

I looked at a portrait of Isabelle hanging over the couch and said, "Please don't be mad at me for keeping him a little longer." I could hear her gentle laughter in my head and knew all was well. In fact, I could feel her relief. She couldn't have approved of his talk of joining her sooner than God, or nature, intended. However much they might want to be together again, that wasn't the way.

I walked into the screening room and went to the area where the movies were kept. I picked out the can labeled, "Isabelle's Wedding and Santa Barbara."

I was the only person who was allowed to screen these homemade movies, apart from Mr. Laurence. The reason being that before

Isabelle and Rachel passed away, we had watched them together numerous times.

I threaded the film into the projector and started it running, then sat down. Before the picture started, the background music came through the speakers. The song was "Moonlight Serenade," sung by the great Frank Sinatra, who I think was at the wedding.

The picture opens on Isabelle and Mr. Laurence dancing. Isabelle is wearing a white flowing gown, and Mr. Laurence is in a handsome black tuxedo. If I've ever seen a more beautiful couple, more in love, I seriously doubt it. They never take their eyes off one another, even as they execute a flawless waltz.

The camera pans left and we see Rachel, the maid of honor, with a veteran and dear friend of Mr. Laurence from World War II, as his best man. They are also dancing — a little haltingly, as the soldier is missing a leg — but wonderfully all the same. The music continues as we get a wide shot of all the guests, who numbered almost a thousand. The wedding is taking place at the mansion, outside by the pool, which at this time was only about one-third of its current size.

Mr. Hamill enlarged the pool when Isabelle and Mr. Laurence told him they were coming back home to live at the mansion. Mr. and Mrs. Hamill had bought the newlyweds a home in Santa Barbara when it looked like Isabelle would run the newspapers out west. But after Isabelle reviewed the operations and the ideas of the chief editors and staffs of the newspapers, she decided that all of them were more than capable of running and expanding the publications without her, so she and Rachel and Mr. Laurence had opted to stay in Long Island.

Truth be told, Rachel and Isabelle would have missed their parents too much if they had settled out west, especially since all the other children had grown up and moved away from the Long Island estate.

From images of the wedding, the movie switched to a beach scene. The footage of Isabelle and Rachel walking along the shore at Santa Barbara in their bathing suits was a sight to behold. They were a couple of hotties! Mr. Laurence was seen only in the pictures taken at the house. The ocean brought back those terrible memories of Normandy, and it would take him a very long time to make peace with the sea.

The picture ended and the screen faded to black, and for a few minutes the only sound in the darkened room was Mr. Sinatra singing to me about tomorrows.

CHAPTER FORTY-THREE

Angie

Joe leaned down and kissed me. I was still in bed and before he could run off to take Mr. Laurence to the cemetery I reached over and grabbed his arm and pulled him back toward me and kissed him passionately. "Must you go right now?"

"Yeah, I have to drive Mr. Laurence to the cemetery."

"He wouldn't really mind if you were a half-hour late, would he? I'm sure he'd understand."

"I wouldn't feel very comfortable explaining it to him," he said with the innocence of child, and I started to laugh.

"What's so funny?" he asked.

"It's that you're so adorable, my silly little boy."

"Can I get a rain check?"

"You can have as many rain checks as you like," I said as he reached down and kissed me again, then escaped out the door.

I got up from bed, put on my robe — which had recovered most of its fluffiness since taking on pool water and going through the wash — and walked into the kitchen. I poured myself a glass of orange juice and drank it as I stared through the sliding doors out at the pool. In the distance, coming from the mansion, I could hear a man singing. I listened more closely and recognized it as Frank Sinatra singing "All My Tomorrows" — a song that Joe's parents used to play around the apartment.

I picked up my phone and called Joe's mother. I had put it off long enough. Joe and I, with advice from Mr. Laurence, had decided to put off our wedding for a year. I wasn't so thrilled at the time, but now I could see the logic. It would take away any talk of us jumping into marriage on impulse. Of course, before the notorious night, Joe's mom would have been glad to see us get married once we turned eighteen — even though back then we had decided to wait until we graduated college. Everything had changed, and it was time to face my future mother-in-law.

I dialed the number and she picked up. I'd been hoping to start off with Joe's father — who according to Joe still thought I was fantastic — or his baby brother, who was madly in love with me, but the Band-aid came off as soon as I heard her voice.

God must have been looking down upon me, because before I could finish saying hello she jumped in and didn't stop talking for the next ten minutes. "Oh how wonderful it is to hear from you, Angie. I've missed you so much, and I was just thinking that if that young lady doesn't call me by tomorrow, I'll just have to go back on my promise to Mr. Laurence to let you call me first. You know, Mr. Laurence and I have become quite friendly, and he's simply falling in love with you and my Joe. He tells me that he's the lucky one to have found you two. Can you believe that? Such humility ... so unusual for a man in his position..."

I didn't even try to interrupt her. I just let her go on and on about how wonderful I was, and how lucky Joe was to find Mr. Laurence, and how impressed he was with both of us. Finally, I heard Joe's father say to her that they had ten minutes to get to church. That gave me a chance to say, "It's been so great talking to you, but I don't want to make you late. Love you a bunch."

"Love you a bunch and then some," she said and finally I was able to hang up. To think that just a few months ago I was the devil's daughter, and now I was Saint Angie again. Whoever said money can't buy you love? It certainly can, especially when the fortune can be counted in billions. But I resolved to be grateful, and silently thanked Mr. Laurence for pulling off another miracle.

A few minutes later Maria called and asked if I could help her move a few things from her apartment back to her bedroom at the mansion. She was coming back to her rightful home, and I was only too happy to help.

CHAPTER FORTY-FOUR

Angie

I met Maria as she was leaving the mansion and we walked over to her car and got in. She handed me a small bag and said, "A little gift." I peered inside it and saw two beautiful cannoli laying on a little cardboard tray atop a white paper doily. "Oh my God," I said, "I'm so happy I haven't eaten breakfast yet. Would you like one?"

"No sweetheart, they're both for you. Besides, I already had two for breakfast."

Pretty soon we were buckled in and on our way. After driving in silence for a couple of minutes, Maria turned to me and said, "I want to apologize for acting so stupid last night."

I had to swallow a big bite of creamy cannoli, but as soon as I could speak, I said, "Maria, please. You have nothing to apologize for … even though I think you might have set two records."

She laughed and asked, "And what might those be?"

"First, you finished an entire bottle of wine in under ten minutes, and secondly you fell asleep with your head on the kitchen table in about five seconds, and there was no waking you. Joe and Mr. Laurence had to carry you into your bedroom."

"It took *two* men to carry me into my bedroom?"

"Well, Joe could have easily done it himself but there was no way I was letting that happen."

"I don't believe you…"

"Hey, one has to protect what one has. I don't want Joe calling out, *Maria, oh Maria* in his sleep, even if you're unlikely to ever return his affections. The only thing I want to hear coming out of his mouth is, *Angie, oh Angie.* Sorry, I'm just a jealous bitch."

She smiled and said, "What you *are* is a wise and beautiful little angel. If you don't believe me just ask Mr. Laurence. That's how he described you this morning."

"Why would he say that?"

"You don't need to play coy with me," she said as she stopped at a red light. She reached over and patted my leg and said, "I love you, my sweet little angel."

"And I love you, my record-breaking, gorgeous mama lush."

We both laughed as we parked in front of her apartment building.

I followed Maria into her apartment, which looked like she had never moved in. Apart from the furnishing that came with the place, the only signs of life were three boxes of books, two teddy bears, and some clothes draped over a chair. Maria gathered the clothing into a bag, then went to clear out the bathroom.

When she finished, we sat on the couch in the living room, and I asked, "So you never planned on staying here very long?"

"I guess not," she said.

I looked at the mantle above the fireplace and saw a framed picture of a very pretty young woman with light brown skin, corkscrew curls, and a huge smile. I pointed to it and asked, "Did that also come with the apartment?"

She smiled and said, "No, that's my ex."

"Ah," I said.

"You probably think it's strange of me to keep carting her picture around."

"No…"

"Oh come on, you do."

"No! It's not strange. But it does make me wonder how long it has been, and whether you still miss her a lot."

Maria got up and went over to the mantle, then picked up the photo and stared at it. "It's been hard to let go. We had our whole life planned! House, kids, jobs, everything. We were happy!"

"What happened?"

"Bigotry and impatience — that's what happened. I came out to my parents, and they were complete monsters about it, and she couldn't deal with the fallout."

"That's awful. She should have supported you."

"I think she tried, but it was too much. When I told her what happened, she said our only choice was to move as far away from my family as possible. She said she didn't want to live near anyone who still held such 'antiquated views.'

"I told her that moving away wouldn't solve the problem. That there are people who think that way everywhere, and it was unrealistic to think we could find some sort of utopia where prejudice doesn't exist."

"That's unfortunately true," I said. "But was that really why you didn't want to move away with her?"

Maria shook her head a little guiltily. "No, probably not. By the time she started pressuring me to leave with her, I was living with Mr. Laurence, and Isabelle was gone. He was alone, and I owed him everything. So I tried to convince her to stay in the area, but I think she wanted me to take a stand — to make a dramatic break from my family. And I guess she lost patience. One night she was just gone. I haven't heard from her since."

"Did you love her?"

"I really don't know. I missed her terribly for a long time, but I never made any effort to get in touch with her. I do remember how nice it was to go to bed with her and wake up beside her. Truthfully, I don't know if I've ever loved anyone the way you and Joe love each other, or the way Mr. Laurence and Isabelle loved each other."

"You'll meet someone," I said, as Maria shrugged. "I think what happened just proves that she wasn't the one."

"Maybe. I don't exactly do a lot to get myself 'out there.' I've never let it be known that I'm a lesbian or told anybody I went to medical school with or did my internships with. I'm sure some of the doctors I know are lesbians, but it's not like we all know who's in the club," she said with a laugh. "People tend to downplay their orientation, at least to their peers in medicine."

"You must have male doctors hitting on you all the time."

"It's not unheard of," Maria said with a laugh.

"How do you handle that? It must be so annoying."

"Kind of, yes. I wore a wedding ring for a while, but that didn't deter all of them. I don't know how many advances I've had to fight off, including some *really* inappropriate behavior from a few colleagues, but I never reported them because I didn't want to put a spotlight on myself or my personal life."

"Can I tell you something I've never told anyone else?"

"Of course. I won't tell anyone, I promise."

"Before I met Joe, I used to sit in this park by myself after school and just think … *how am I going to make it through another night with my father and brother?* So many terrible thoughts went through my mind that I'm almost ashamed to mention them … ways to fight them off, ways to poison or castrate the sick sons-of-bitches. It came to a point where men seriously disgusted me. I could never picture getting married and living my life with one of these hideous creatures. On the other hand, I clearly wasn't gay or even bi. I was pretty seriously attracted to a lot of the old movie stars like Paul Newman, Robert Redford, Cary Grant, and Laurence Olivier. Maybe it was easier to fantasize about them because most of them are gone. Even so, I learned to despise men so much that I thought if I was ever going to live with anyone when I got older, it would have to be a woman. Unlike the men in my life, including a few priests, no woman ever threatened me like boys did.

"Then one day, that all changed. I dropped a bag of groceries, and they scattered all over the ground. Before I had a chance to react, this sixteen-year-old boy helped me pick them up and insisted on carrying them up to my apartment. I barely looked at him until my brother came out of the bathroom and asked me who he was and accused me of bringing him up to the apartment to have sex with him."

Maria rolled her eyes and groaned.

"Disgusting, I know," I said.

"So what happened?"

"He went to hit me, but before he could land the punch the boy deflected it and went on to beat my brother to a bloody pulp ... screaming at him the whole time that only cowards hit girls."

"Wow. How did you react? That would have been intense."

"It was. It felt like I was watching a movie. That's the only place I'd ever seen a man come to the defense of a woman. Then the boy grabbed my hand and pulled me out of the apartment and onto the elevator and I finally realized that it was really happening. Of course, the boy was Joe." Maria clapped her hands and beamed at the revelation, and said, "I knew it. What a hero."

"One hundred percent. He was my hero. And I remember lowering my eyes and saying, 'Thank you. That's the first time anyone has helped me.'"

"Amazing."

"I think I've been falling in love with Joe in stages. When we lived in the Bronx, we would always say we loved each other, and we made plans to get married after college and move to a coastal town like Santa Barbara. But I think it was when he came to visit me at Rikers Island, after he was released from the hospital, that I began to truly love him."

"What changed?"

"He forgave me. I don't know how he did, because I nearly killed him that night. He lied to the police so I wouldn't have to spend time in a real jail. He understood my situation, and that in itself was incredible, because it's not like he had experience or knew other girls who had experienced abuse. He comes from a loving family. This is all so new to him. They took me in for six months, and it wasn't until that deadly night that his mother turned on me, and who could blame her? Since then, with help from Mr. Laurence, we've had a sort of reconciliation."

I stopped talking and collected my thoughts. Maria had returned to the couch and was curled up at one end, where she listened intently to my rambling story. I looked at her and said, "I'm starting to understand that Joe lives by a moral code. And he won't cross it — not for all the money in the world. He knew how upset his mother was that he insisted on seeing me and moving to Long Island, but that didn't stop him from calling her every night and telling her how much he loved her.

"It took me a long time to appreciate what I had. Any other guy would have walked out on me a dozen times, especially after the kinds of things I accused him of while I was living at the women's center."

Maria said, "But in the end everything turned out perfectly, and it's not only you who's benefited from the relationship. The way that boy looks at you, it's like you're the only person in the universe… "

I smiled, and said, "Thank you. It's just important to me that he never thinks I take him for granted."

It took two trips to bring all Maria's belongings down to the car. When I picked up the picture of her ex and offered it to her, she said, "I think it's about time I let go." The picture remained on the mantle, face down.

We drove back to the mansion and naturally Joe was waiting for us in the driveway. With his help, it took only one trip to move all of Maria's belongings from the car into her room, which was bigger than the entire footprint of the apartment she had just left behind. Mr. Laurence walked into the room as we were opening the boxes of books and starting to place them on the bookshelves.

Maria turned, smiled, and said, "I'm back."

"And I could not be happier, my princess," Mr. Laurence said as he hugged her and kissed her on the top of her head.

"Does that mean I'm allowed to have sorority parties?"

"You can have whatever you like."

"How about a pool party for the children at the cancer center?"

"Absolutely. Just be sure to get the parents' permission and line up enough lifeguards and a couple of nurses just in case."

"Do I have a budget?"

"Yes, whatever it takes to make them all feel special," he said as he looked at me and said, "And I want to thank *you* for your enlightened conversation last night. You made a bigger difference than you could possibly know." This was both mysterious and thrilling, and I just flashed him a huge smile, having no idea what he might be talking about.

Mr. Laurence had just started to walk out of the room when he stopped, turned around and looked at me. "I have an idea," he said. "Instead of starting that job for me tomorrow, how about you work as Maria's assistant, helping her with the arrangements for the party? Maria, would that be okay with you?"

"Yes, as long as she stays my assistant after the party. You have Joe, why shouldn't I have Angie?"

"Would you like that, Angie?"

"I would love that," I said enthusiastically.

"Then it's settled. I have no doubt that the two of you will make a great team," he said as he looked at Maria sitting cross-legged on her bed, holding one of her teddy bears. He continued, "It's so great having you back home, Maria."

Mr. Laurence left the room and suddenly I had a flashback to the night before when we came running in here and Maria was having a nightmare, punching a pillow, and yelling at an invisible opponent.

Maria must have noticed a change in my expression, because she asked me if I was having second thoughts about being her assistant.

"No!" I said. "Are you crazy? I was just thinking about how much Mr. Laurence loves you."

"Oh! That's a nice thought."

"Do you ever think — and I know this might sound insane — that your tragic situation with your biological father was a blessing in some ways?"

"It doesn't sound insane at all. Even before the final blow-up with my family, Isabelle and Mr. Laurence had showered me with more support and love than my parents had in many years. They never neglected to mention that I'd become a financial liability, even though I promised to pay them back many times over once I started my practice. My mother would tell me how proud she was of me, and then ... without fail ... she'd say that with my looks it would just be easier to marry a rich man."

"So backwards," I said. Maria started fiddling with the teddy bear she was holding, and I asked, "Does he have a name?"

"Oh gosh, yes. I can't believe I haven't introduced you two. Dr. Laurence, meet Angie. Angie, this is Dr. Laurence." I laughed and reached out to shake Dr. Laurence's little paw and said, "I should have known."

Suddenly Maria reached out and hugged me and said, "We're going to make such a great team."

I looked at her and smiled as it dawned on me that I should tell Joe about my change of jobs. I didn't want him working on all the preparations only to find out that I'd been reassigned. When I told Maria about my concern she started laughing.

"All the preparations? They would have consisted of him putting a stack of newspapers from before World War I in front of you and telling you to read them and write anything interesting down. Mr. Laurence would occasionally ask you if you'd read anything interesting, and there is no right or wrong answer. After two weeks, if you're on newspaper duty and you haven't complained about the ink, he'll give you a cash bonus and find something else for you to do."

"The ink?"

"When you handle newspapers off the presses, the ink from the print dirties up your hands, and when you look at yourself in the mirror, you'll discover that your face is covered in little splotches of ink, too. You'll have smudges everywhere. Stay silent about it, and you get a bonus ... complain and you get to keep on reading. Joe didn't tell you about this?"

"Of course not. He's the only teenager I've ever known that went every morning to the only newsstand and bought a print copy of *The*

New York Times. I used to laugh at him, and he'd tell me it was the only way to truly read a newspaper. I guess it's just another reason why he and Mr. Laurence get along so well."

She laughed as we went back to placing her medical books onto the bookshelves, with Dr. Laurence overseeing the operation.

CHAPTER FORTY-FIVE

Angie

I sat in bed, in my pajamas, and read several pamphlets on pediatric cancer that Maria had given me. She thought it was a good idea for me to learn as much as possible about the types of treatments the children were going through and the medical devices they were fitted with. Since I would be dealing with many of the children, especially at the party we were planning, she wanted to make sure I knew the symptoms that could be warning signs that something was not right.

Joe got into bed with me and rested his head on my lap as I put the pamphlets aside. "Difficult reading?" he asked.

"Yes. It's hard to fathom the bravery of these kids. They're so little, and they're fighting such a terrible disease. It really has a way of putting everything into perspective," I said. He gazed up at me as I added, "But I like the idea of doing something to help. It feels good to know that we'll be able to give the kids and their parents a fun and carefree atmosphere to enjoy, even if it's only for one day." I looked down at my handsome fiancé and could see from the tears brimming in his eyes that he was sincerely moved.

"Sweety!" I said, and Joe looked at me and replied, "I know, I have something in my eye."

I laughed and said, "I guess you mean both eyes." He smiled and wiped away a tear that escaped down one cheek.

I looked at him and said, "Hey, I have a question for you, and please tell me the truth, even if it might hurt. Do you ever feel like I take you for granted?"

He thought for a moment and said, "In all honesty, no. It's like Mr. Laurence says: Whereas you might be relying on me more during your very difficult situation, there will come a time when I'll rely heavily on you. It's what people who love each other do."

"I have another question. Why didn't you tell me about the ink?"

"What ink?"

"You really don't know, do you?" He shook his head and I said, "Before I switched jobs today, I would have been reading newspapers dating back to before World War I, taking notes on whatever interested me, and if I didn't complain about the ink from the newspapers dirtying my hands and face, I'd get a bonus after two weeks."

"So that's why Mr. Laurence gave me such a big bonus after two weeks of reading those fascinating news stories. I never once thought about the ink from the presses dirtying my hands. I've been reading the—"

"Yes, I know. You've been reading the print edition of *The New York Times* your whole life, so the smudges seemed natural to you. I think you should at least split your bonus with me. It's simply part of a loving relationship."

"That's fine, but why don't I just deposit it into our joint bank account?"

"We have a joint bank account?"

"We will if you decide to go in on it with me. They're waiting for your signature and your permission at the branch."

"Exciting! I never thought about sharing a bank account."

"It's what loving couples do."

"I can think of something else loving couples do."

"And what's that?" he asked as I reached down and started to undress him.

CHAPTER FORTY-SIX

Angie

Joe left for the cemetery at his usual time. I left a few minutes later, with pamphlets and notebook in hand. I was excited. The idea of helping children really made me feel like I was doing something important. I had depended on Joe for so long that just the idea of doing something independently of him was a welcome change.

Maria opened the door to the mansion. She was dressed in her doctor's uniform and held a small plate of cannoli. I followed her into the kitchen, where she had my breakfast — two cannoli and a glass of orange juice — ready on the table. I sat down as she poured herself a cup of coffee and walked around chattering like the morning person she was.

"Mr. Laurence ordered the cannoli last night without me knowing," she said. "It was a welcome home treat, even though I also had them for breakfast yesterday."

"That was so sweet of him," I said.

"I know, I know, but I had to make him promise that he wouldn't order any more without my permission. I have absolutely no will power against these creamy devils, and if I eat one I always have to eat two and eventually I'll have to work out five hours a day just to burn off the calories." I was already on my second cannoli and feeling absolutely no guilt. After all, I'd been told by my lovely doctor to gain at least fifteen pounds in the next three months, and I was on my way.

We walked into her bedroom, which we were going to use as our office, and she had me sit at her mahogany desk. On it was a list of everything I was expected to do, along with instructions. She also handed me a book, *The Emperor of All Maladies: A Biography of Cancer*, by Siddhartha Mukherjee. She said it was a must-read and that it was written for the average person to understand, and that since I was above-average, she expected me to have no problems. She left me a phone number in case I needed to reach her, and she hugged and kissed me and off she went.

I was reading her instructions when I thought I heard footsteps from above, followed by what sounded like giggling. Seconds later, I heard doors opening and closing. I thought to myself, *But of course it's the ghosts of Mr. and Mrs. Hamill's daughters.* I shook my head at that insane idea, as the noise intensified. I got up from my chair and walked out of the room and into the hallway and looked up to the second floor where all of the giggling and running back and forth was coming from.

I stood in the hallway and yelled, "Is there anybody here?"

The running stopped but the chorus of laughter grew louder. "I can hear you," I called. "Who's there?"

"Wow!" a voice said, "she's pretty, *and* she has excellent hearing."

"Yes, but apparently her eyesight isn't too good," another voice said.

"What a shame," the first girl said. "Her boyfriend is so gorgeous, and a real gentleman. I wonder if she can even see him?" A chorus of laughter followed.

I crossed my arms and stared down the hallway. I briefly wondered if I was losing my mind.

"I can see him," I called out, only to have them ignore me.

"She probably has no idea how lucky she is," the second girl said.

"Not a clue," said the first.

That's when I yelled, "Be quiet! You don't know what you're talking about."

"And so rude, a stranger telling us how to behave and what to say," the first girl said and suddenly, the voices and the laughter died down and all I could hear was the sound of one pair of feet walking confidently across the hallway from above.

"Oh shit, it's Isabelle, the crusader," the second girl remarked.

"I heard that!" Isabelle said. "And why are you treating a guest in our home so rudely?"

"We're only playing, Isabelle."

Isabelle! It was Isabelle! She sounded so confident. I listened in rapt fascination.

"Have you even introduced yourselves?" she asked.

"No, isn't it customary for the guest to introduce herself, first?"

"No it is not," Isabelle said. "Have you even made yourselves visible to her?"

"That would have taken all the fun out of it."

"And how do you think our father would react to this type of behavior?"

"Daddy loves for us to have fun…"

"But not to be rude," Isabelle scolded. "I think you owe Angie an apology."

There was a pause, and a chorus of female voices called out their apologies. Some of them even sounded sincere.

Suddenly Isabelle appeared beside me, wearing a long green dress and leather ankle boots. "Welcome to our home, Angie."

I stared at her a little too long, taking in just how beautiful and full of authority she seemed. Finally, I said, "Thank you."

Isabelle smiled, and I could feel her trying to put me at ease. "Why don't we all meet in the ballroom for a proper welcome?"

Isabelle took my hand and said, "Come with me, Angie." Suddenly, with a flip of the wrist she twirled me around and we were in the ballroom where the Beatles song "Penny Lane" was playing and fourteen girls danced in a circle, laughing and singing to the music. "You see, they just love having fun. Shall we join in?"

We joined the chain, with Isabelle on one side of me and Rachel on the other. I felt like a bird flying high, free from all the tragedies of my life, soaring higher and higher as "Strawberry Fields Forever" started playing and nothing felt real and it was like a wonderful dream. I passed through a lovely patch of clouds and continued to soar into the heavenly blue stratosphere until I unexpectedly collided with an asteroid and started tumbling downward, following Joe as he fell hopelessly down a circular staircase, his head splitting open as it smashed against the concrete stairs, and his shattered body coming to a rest at the very bottom and I, draped in a white gown, landed on top of him and very slowly the blood from Joe's wound seeped into every inch of the gown, turning it red, and I screamed and that was the last thing I remember until...

I woke up in the middle of the ballroom, covered in sweat. I opened my eyes and saw Joe and Mr. Laurence. Joe was rubbing my arm and saying my name over and over again, while Mr. Laurence was looking at me intently from a little further away. I reached up and ran my hand across Joe's face. Then my arm dropped and at that moment it felt like the easiest thing to do was just to die. I closed my eyes and went completely limp.

The next thing I knew I was lying on the couch in the living room with my head elevated and Maria beside me.

I asked, "What are you doing home?"

"I came by to see how you were doing," she said as she touched my forehead. "Do you remember what you were doing in the ballroom?"

"Dancing," I mumbled.

"Huh."

I looked past her and saw Joe and Mr. Laurence again. I tried to wave to them, but my hand felt like an overcooked noodle. Maria put a glass of water to my lips and told me to drink, which I did. She then turned to the men and said, "It's time for you boys to get lost for a while. If I need you, I'll yell."

Joe hovered for a moment, then came over and kissed me on the head. After he and Mr. Laurence left the room, Maria took out her stethoscope and checked my heart and lungs, took my blood pressure and checked my pulse, and then shone a light in my eyes.

"Does everything check out?" I asked.

"So far. Do you have a headache?"

"No."

"Do you faint often?"

"It's happened a few times."

"What happened here after I left you? Tell me everything you remember, from the beginning to now."

I did as she said, recalling everything as though it was just happening. Everything the girls said, the running up and down, the giggling. Isabelle finally bringing about order. I told her about the dancing, and recited the exact words to "Strawberry Fields Forever" and "Penny Lane." I couldn't help feeling how happy that would make Joe — a huge Beatles fan. And finally, Joe falling down the circular staircase and me falling on top of him. It was so strange because Maria never once flinched. It was like she'd heard this story before. In fact, she didn't comment on anything I told her. Instead, she said, "We have to get you out of these clothes and into bed."

"I feel a lot better now and could use a shower, but I need to get back to work."

"No, you don't."

"What, am I fired?"

"Don't be silly. I'm counting on you to do a fantastic job — just not today. Do you feel strong enough to walk back to your house?"

"I think so. Otherwise, Joe can carry me."

She called the men back into the room and before I could try standing, Joe swooped me into his arms and carried me home. Maria and Mr. Laurence followed.

Maria stayed with me while I took a shower and helped me put on pajamas. She then helped me into bed and brought me a glass of water, then stood there while I drank it. After that she reached into her doctor's bag and pulled out a needle and a vial filled with medicine that she extracted into the hub of the needle.

"I don't want any drugs…"

"You don't have a choice. You're much too valuable to me. I'm not taking any chances."

Before I could object again, she stuck me with the needle, saying, "It's going to help you relax."

Those were the last words I heard before completely falling out.

CHAPTER FORTY-SEVEN

Maria

After giving Angie a sedative, I walked back to the mansion with Mr. Laurence. I had no doubt that Joe would keep an eye on her the whole time she slept and would immediately get back to me if anything seemed out of the ordinary, like her vomiting in her sleep.

I sat down at the kitchen table as Mr. Laurence put on a pot of tea for us.

"I should have known better than to leave her here by herself, but she's been in and out of this mansion so much that I didn't even think about it."

"Neither did I," Mr. Laurence said.

"But you were smart enough to skip breakfast and come right back here."

"I got a warning, Maria," Mr. Laurence replied.

I smiled and said, "That child has been to hell and back, just like all the other girls who became members of Mr. and Mrs. Hamill's family. You don't have to answer, but did Rachel go through something similar to what Angie went through?"

"Yes, and it took nearly two years for Mr. Hamill and Isabelle to get her to fully trust them. Mr. Hamill loved all his daughters, but he had a very special place in his heart for Rachel. I don't think there was a thing in this world that made him happier than to see Rachel laugh and play around and tease Isabelle. And you saw the relationship Isabelle had with her. They were inseparable. And together they made my life a living dream.

"It's impossible to express the joy and happiness Mr. and Mrs. Hamill felt when they learned we were coming back here to live. The thirteen other girls had already moved away, and the quiet was driving them crazy. As you know, the girls were a pretty rowdy group once they got started, but never once did I ever hear either of them raise their voices at any of their daughters."

Mr. Laurence stopped speaking, and it was during these quiet, contemplative moments that I could feel the true depth of his pain. The loneliness and despair he could never let go of and always carried around inside him, and suddenly I felt like the vile doctor who had purposely prolonged his suffering.

"Why do you think Rachel never married? It can't have been a lack of suitors."

Mr. Laurence thought for a moment and said, "I think it was a matter of trust."

When I stayed silent, Mr. Laurence said, "It's not what you're thinking."

"That's not what I was thinking," I replied.

"There's no need to lie to me, Maria. I know exactly what you were thinking."

"Fine," I said with a laugh. "It's not like they, we, didn't exist back then."

"Of course not, but that wasn't the reason," Mr. Laurence said. He put a cup of tea down before me and sat down. "Rachel never got married because, after what she'd been through, she could never trust any men except for Mr. Hamill and, because she trusted Isabelle's judgement so much, me. It's no different with Angie."

"If Joe ever left her, or God forbid something were to happen to him, I don't know what would become of her."

"Joe's not leaving her, nor is anything going to happen to him."

"A boy with those looks and that personality…" I suddenly put the brakes on because I knew I was heading into dangerous territory.

Mr. Laurence loved this boy, and he never would have put so much faith in Joe unless he had total confidence in him as a person. Besides Isabelle, I have never met anyone with better instincts about character.

"Besides, if anything were to happen, she'd always have this place as her home," Mr. Laurence said.

"I know that, but that doesn't keep me from worrying. She's smart and insightful, but she's not even close to processing the entire tragedy that was her life until a month or so ago."

"You're right, Maria, but she has a support system now. All of us — Joe, you, her friend Gloria, and I — are invested in making sure she gets through every day."

I nodded silently, but I must have looked like I needed more convincing, because Mr. Laurence continued. "She has made wonderful memories since coming to live here. That, plus the knowledge that she has people who love and care about her, will make all the difference."

"But it would be so easy for her to backslide—"

"We'll always have to be vigilant, to be sure. No matter how much time passes, we must always be alert to the things that she says, even if they sound totally innocuous, and to her actions and mood swings. But we're here for her. Never forget that she's loved and surrounded by supporters now. We can do for her what Mr. and Mrs. Hamill did for several of the girls, who might have committed suicide if not for their love and support."

That's when I remembered something that Isabelle had told me, and I shared it with Mr. Laurence. "I remember asking Isabelle if there were any men she trusted, besides Mr. Hamill and you. She said, 'It depends on the situation. If there are a lot of men and women in the room acting as a buffer, then I have more trust in the men's behavior. If I'm alone in a room with a man, I never let down my guard for a second. I can't say all men are pigs, but I've never met one besides my husband and father who I totally trusted, especially if they've been drinking.'

"I asked, 'So the only men you totally trust, besides your husband, are dead men?' And she said, 'Don't be foolish, Maria — dead men are often the most dangerous. It's after they're dead that all the dirty secrets and disgusting behavior come to light, and that's enough to make you want to vomit.'"

"That was the news reporter in my wife," Mr. Laurence laughingly replied.

"What made her choose you so quickly?"

"That was the editor in her. The best I've ever known. Editing is about selecting from among possibilities, and I guess she saw something in me that she felt was worth keeping," he said, with the smile of someone who knows he won the lottery.

"I guess she did," I said.

"And let's not forget, it took us more than a year to finally get married, and I can assure you there was no hanky-panky during that time. But all the same she was a great kisser, and that was more than I could handle at that time."

"No, hanky-panky, but a great kisser," I repeated happily.

"Do you have anyone you're seeing?" he asked.

"No! Maybe if I advertise … *Lonely, mansion-dwelling lesbian, daughter of Mr. and Mrs. Laurence, desperately seeks female companion…*" I stopped talking, and immediately started crying.

I heard Mr. Laurence sigh and could feel him staring at me. He reached over and put a tissue in my hand. I wiped my face and blew my nose and said, "You see, you raised a crybaby."

"No, we helped raise the most perfect daughter imaginable."

I grabbed another tissue from the box. "You know, it's not like I *have* to be lonely. There are clubs where I could meet girls, and a few female doctors in my cohort who could be gay. I've been asked out by women I find attractive and intelligent, but I always come up with excuses, like I'm too busy, or I'm seeing someone."

"And why is that?"

"Honestly, because I don't think I got over my last relationship. It was like we were married. We shared everything, told each other our deepest secrets, planned on having children, and then when the first bit of adversity hit, she picked up and left. I wish I had your ability to read a person's true character."

"You're a little older now and wiser, and believe me, you'll meet someone, when you least expect to, who is going to be the perfect companion to my perfect daughter."

"Do you really think so?"

"I know so."

"A sign?" I asked.

"More like a message, from a messenger with a very high batting average," he said with a knowing smile. "Are you going back to work?"

"No. We had nothing on the books today, and if anyone comes in, the other doctors can handle it. Besides, I have a very important patient right here."

"Yes, you do."

"Mr. Laurence, do you think it's strange that I think of Angie as my daughter? I don't want her to feel like I want to replace her mother."

"Showing her the love, support and protection of a wonderful mother is exactly what I think a doctor would prescribe for such a patient."

"Like what Isabelle did for me."

"Exactly," Mr. Laurence said as he bent down and kissed me on the head.

CHAPTER FORTY-EIGHT

Maria

I decided to go for a swim, which I hadn't done since moving out of the mansion. I was a little worried my bathing suit might be tight, especially after all the cannoli I'd eaten in the few days prior. I was relieved when it slipped on as easily as I remembered. I put my robe on and walked out to the pool and looked out at the water.

I cautiously walked into the shallow end, then kept walking until the water was up to my hips. As usual, it was the perfect temperature. I swam slowly toward the other end of the pool, doing the breaststroke. At about the halfway mark, I was interrupted by nine ducklings following mommy duck across the water. I stopped swimming and treaded water softly, lowering my face into the pool until only my nose was above water, as I watched the ducklings cross the width of pool. I didn't start swimming again until the last baby jumped out and they all continued to march across dry land.

When I reached the end of the pool, I lifted myself out of the water and walked about a hundred feet to the edge of the cliff that overlooked the Long Island Sound. I sat down on one of the benches and soaked in the beauty of the place. It was easy to see why Isabelle had been drawn back here, and how much she loved being near the water and nature. It was as though every aspect of nature's beauty was embodied in her. Its by-product was the creation of a woman so beautiful that not even death could conquer her.

I yelled, "Isabelle, are you out there?"

A few moments later I could see the bright, silvery flash of a tail flapping back and forth, appearing and disappearing between the waves. "Are you mad at me for keeping your husband with us longer than expected?" I asked.

Just then a spout of water erupted from the place in the water where I had just seen the flapping tail. "I guess that's a yes?"

Suddenly, I could feel her presence inside my head, and I heard her saying, "Maria, Maria, my beautiful Maria. How could I ever be mad at you? I love you so. Besides, my husband has unfinished business he still needs to take care of before I get to torture him throughout eternity." She laughed a laugh that seemed to escape from inside my head and echo off the surface of the water where a flapping tail appeared and waved goodbye for now.

When I couldn't see her, I walked back to the pool and dove into the deep end and swam underwater for as long as I could. I swam back toward the other end, treading water once again as the same family of ducks got back into the pool and crossed back over to the opposite side. When I finally reached the other end, I got out of the water, dried myself off, and put on my robe.

I knocked gently on the sliding door of Joe and Angie's house and Joe let me in. I asked, "And how is my lovely assistant doing?"

"Still sleeping."

"Comfortably, I hope?"

"Yes, as comfortably and peacefully as I've ever seen her sleep."

I followed him into the bedroom and looked at Angie, who was curled up on her side. Next to the head of the bed was a chair. "Would you like me to leave?" Joe asked.

"Just for a few minutes," I said. He left the room, and I sat down in the chair I was quite certain he had just vacated. On the night table, a copy of *David Copperfield* lay face-down. Mr. Laurence had given me that book and told me it was essential reading, and I was quite sure he'd said and done the same for Joe.

I looked at Angie, and if I didn't know better, I would have mistaken her for a child. The only thing missing was a teddy bear sleeping beside her. She had a face that emitted innocence and purity and she was sleeping so peacefully that you could imagine all of her dreams being fairytales; and yet for the first seventeen years of her life I doubt she had a handful of peaceful nights.

I entered the mansion and knocked on the door of Mr. Laurence's study. Inside, I found him sitting at his desk, going over paperwork. I sat across from him and said, "You know, I could help you with all of this stuff."

He looked at me and smiled. "How was your swim?"

"Wonderful, but I did have to stop twice and tread water as a family of ducklings crossed my path both coming and going."

He laughed as he asked, "Did you check on your own duckling?"

"Yes, she was sleeping peacefully, and of course Joe was sitting on a chair at the head of the bed, watching over her."

"I'd expect nothing less," Mr. Laurence said.

"I've decided to change Angie's work hours," I said, "so she's never here by herself. Surely, you and your assistant wouldn't mind her joining you for breakfast after your morning visits to the cemetery?"

"Not at all. She's been out to breakfast with us numerous times."

"So that would make her hours ten to four, with plenty of breaks in between to see her boyfriend. Did Mr. and Mrs. Hamill take in many girls as old as Angie?"

"No, almost all of them were younger than ten, except for Isabelle, who I think was fourteen, and Rachel, who was eleven. Why do you ask?"

"Because Angie told me she planned on starting college next fall, and after studying her, I don't see how she could manage it, unless Joe takes the same classes as her. She stiffens up around groups of people. It's really sad. She already has severe anxiety and a tendency to faint.

She needs an extended bridge of support and caring like Mr. and Mrs. Hamill provided to the girls before having them attend schools."

"Joe will not be attending college, at least not in the foreseeable future. With Angie we'll have several choices. She can start off taking online courses or we could hire an accredited female tutor so she'll immediately start building up college credits toward a diploma."

"Those sound like wonderful ideas," I said as I paused and thought about the next question I wanted to ask. Joe and Mr. Laurence's relationship was a tricky subject, and I still was not totally clear on how much of a role he was going to play when it came to the foundation and other business interests.

"What's bothering you, Maria?" he asked.

"What makes you think something is bothering me?"

"Because when uncertainty enters that brilliant brain of yours, you exhibit telltale signs that ring out, loud and clear."

"And would you mind telling me what those telltale signs are?"

"Absolutely not. That would be like showing my hand in a poker game. What's the question that's rolling around in that brain of yours?"

"How much does Joe know?" I asked cautiously.

"Less than half of what he needs to know. He's very smart and picks up complex things quickly, and he's not afraid to ask questions — but he's not you. You set a very high standard, and you are, and always will be, the chosen one ... the one in charge. It was Isabelle's wish, and I'm quite certain Mr. and Mrs. Hamill would be in total agreement, as am I. Joe will be a great help to you, and as he matures, you would be wise to ask his opinions. But you're the boss."

"Thank you..."

"If I gave you any other impression, I'm sorry."

I shook my head, and then walked around his desk and hugged him for a long time. "That's all right. I'm just happy to be here where I belong and happy we're not arguing. I can't stand to be mad at you or have you be mad at me." And Mr. Laurence — that most remarkable human being, patted my arm as I held onto him and said, "I know, sweetheart, I know."

CHAPTER FORTY-NINE

Maria

That night we ordered Chinese food and ate dinner in Joe and Angie's house for a change. We bought extra wonton soup because it was Angie's favorite. After dinner and cleanup, I took her by the arm and told the men that we were going for a walk.

Joe looked at me like I was planning some type of theft and I said, "Don't worry, I'm not going to steal her … at least not tonight."

"I wasn't thinking that."

"Oh yes you were. No need to lie," I said, and then laughed.

"Okay, maybe…"

We walked out the sliding door, and I took Angie under my arm as we walked along the pool's edge.

"That boy is crazy in love with you."

"I'm pretty sure he sat beside my bed for over eight hours while I was passed out. I really don't deserve him."

"Don't you ever let me hear you say that. You already said it enough times and I don't want to hear it anymore. You both deserve each other, and that's that. Got it?"

"Yes," she said meekly.

"When I had my falling out with my family, Isabelle became the mother I wished for. She listened, supported me, and graciously accepted me for who I was, and showed me the love and caring that I was always looking for and not getting from my actual mother. I love you like a daughter. In fact, I tell Mr. Laurence all the time that if you were twelve or thirteen, I'd adopt you, and then he reminds me that when Isabelle took me under her wing, I was twenty-four. What I'm trying to say is that I'm here to support, love, and care for you, and if you ever need to talk, I'm here. I love to think of you as my daughter and hopefully you can think of me as your adopted mother. There are certain issues that women only feel comfortable talking to other women about and I never want you think that I'm too busy and don't have the time because for you there will always be time."

Angie, who had been listening closely, started to cry. We stopped walking and I took her into my arms and hugged her as her tears ran through my shirt and touched my heart.

Angie agreed with the changes we made to her schedule. Instead of arriving at the mansion at eight, she would go to breakfast with the boys and start her workday at ten. I also left open the possibility that once she learned more of the secrets hidden inside the mansion, she could move back to eight o'clock. I reminded her that all of Mr. and Mrs. Hamill's daughters were friendly and lovable and would never harm her. At times, they just acted like children and teenagers because that's the ages they were when they were first adopted.

Angie understood, and said her goal was to work on the party for the children from the cancer hospital. She said she felt most at ease when she was around children, and I assured her that she would be around plenty of children for quite a long time.

Then she blurted out that she didn't always want to be seen as "the helpless one."

"That's the farthest thing from any of our minds. In fact, Mr. Laurence is astonished by how quickly you've adapted, and whatever that conversation was about a few nights ago, he came away as impressed as I've seen him in a long time."

"I didn't say very much…" Angie began.

"Well, you must have said something that moved him, because you changed some plans that he told me about years ago. After so much time had passed, I'd forgotten about those plans, or maybe just repressed my memory of them. When he called me into his study that night, he reminded me that the date those plans were to go into effect was quickly approaching, and that's when I had my meltdown.

"I couldn't change his mind, no matter how much I begged, but after talking to you that night, and then consulting Isabelle, he changed his plans, and for that I will always be grateful."

Angie started to speak, and I put my finger to her mouth and said, "What you talked about is between you two."

CHAPTER FIFTY

Maria

A couple of days later Joe and Mr. Laurence drove to the Women's Correctional Center and picked up Gloria and brought her to the estate. I stayed behind with Angie, prepping Gloria's room and pulling together a little snack for when she arrived. My schedule at the office was very flexible, and everyone who worked there was officially a volunteer, even though Mr. Laurence and the Hamill Foundation insisted on compensating everyone who did work on the foundation's behalf, including the volunteer doctors, nurses, and receptionists. Everyone was generously rewarded.

As for myself, I had an unlimited bank account at my disposal. I could literally take out one-hundred-and-fifty thousand dollars and buy myself a new Ferrari with no questions asked. The only condition was that I told no one about this, and I never have. It helps that I like to live simply, and would never dream of using the foundation's money on a Ferrari!

The boys arrived with Gloria, and Angie ran over to her, and they fell into a long hug.

"Cupcake!" Gloria said, rocking Angie back and forth.

"I really need a nickname for you," Angie said, when they finally separated.

"Hmm," Gloria said. "Gloria mundi? Lady of the Manor?"

"Let's think about it," Angie said.

"How are you?" Gloria wanted to know.

"I'm great, and I'm so happy you're finally out of that place."

Gloria leaned in and whispered in Angie's ear. "Have you put on weight, or is that an adult diaper you're wearing?"

"Gloria!" Angie exclaimed. "I don't wear diapers."

Gloria cracked up and said, "Cupcake, you're so cute, but you're seriously in need of a sense of humor."

"I'm friends with you — doesn't that show a sense of humor?"

"Touché, angel."

I'd been hanging back, admiring Gloria's incredible sense of style. How anyone managed to dress so fashionably while living in a correctional facility I had no idea, unless every piece of clothing she wore came from Mr. Laurence, and I suddenly realized that that was a distinct possibility. She carried it all off with natural authority and what could only be called a regal bearing.

I finally moved a little closer and introduced myself. As her velvety smooth hand slipped into mine, Gloria said, "You must be Maria — the doctor with the teddy bears! Cupcake has told me so much about you."

"Cupcake?" I asked. "That fits — especially since she's been told to eat cannoli and cupcakes so she can gain fifteen pounds." She laughed and I continued, "It's wonderful to meet you, Gloria. Angie has told us about how you helped her deal with life at the center, and I, for one, am so grateful that you've been a great friend to her."

"Angie makes it easy to be her friend, don't you, cupcake?" Gloria said, turning to Angie, and then back to me and finally to Mr. Laurence, who was standing a few feet away. "Thank you, and thank you, Mr. Laurence," she said, looking at him. "I don't know how I can ever repay you for welcoming me into your home. This place is like a palace. In fact, it is a palace."

Angie and I followed Joe as he carried Gloria's luggage into her room, which was next to mine. He then turned to us, and said, "I'll leave you girls alone."

"Thank you, Joe."

"Great to see you out of that place and here with us, really great!"

Gloria looked at Angie and said, "You might be as bony as Olive Oyl, but you hit a grand slam with that boy." She looked around the room, checked out the bathroom and the closet space and said, "This feels like a version of my parents' house in the Hamptons, only about a third bigger and much, much friendlier."

Angie and I helped Gloria hang up her clothes, which she said were mostly gifts from Mr. Laurence. Gloria said that she appreciated the clothing, since her parents had cut her off and she'd been unable to work in the center. She asked Angie about the house she shared with Joe, and Angie said it was nothing like this, but perfect all the same. "We thought you might be staying with us, but Mr. Laurence said he wanted to give you the royal treatment."

"So, you don't get the royal treatment?" Gloria laughingly asked.

"Oh, cupcake gets the royal treatment all right. She just has to walk fifty feet," I said.

Gloria looked at me and asked, "So you're practicing medicine in town?"

"Yes, I'm a GP with the free clinic that's part of the Hamill Foundation."

"That is amazing, and so nice of you," Gloria said.

"It's no sacrifice. I love the work, and I'm generously compensated, even though all of us who work at the clinic are technically volunteers," I said. "You can see I lack for nothing."

"I can see that," Gloria said, smiling.

"And you worked as an ER nurse in a hospital in Harlem?"

"Yes, at times the most rewarding of jobs, but often very depressing. Young kids, fifteen, sixteen, seventeen years old, rolled into the ER with gunshot wounds, stabbings, beaten to a pulp. Too many of them took their last breaths in the ER in the first five minutes and were rolled off to the morgue. But others made it, and it was those few that got me through it."

Angie, who had been watching us like a ping pong match, said, "You two have so much to talk about. I'm so glad you came here instead of trying to go home to your parents, Gloria."

"Oh cupcake, that was never a real possibility."

"They wouldn't have taken you in?"

"No, they made it quite clear that I wouldn't be welcome."

"I don't understand," Angie said. "How could they side with your boyfriend after everything he did to you and all of those other young women?"

"They're not siding with him, exactly," Gloria said, as she sat on the end of the bed and gestured for us to sit on some nearby chairs, which we did. "They just don't want to be anywhere near such a messy scandal."

"Even if it means hanging their daughter out to dry?" Angie said.

"My dad's an investment banker, and my mom is on the boards of several Fortune 500 companies. I was the only one who went into a helping profession. Being in any way associated with my case is bad for business, I guess. Even though Darian was a monster, and even though I was defending myself and standing up for his other victims."

I'd been listening closely and finally spoke up. "It's amazing how many different types of prejudice and self-interest there are out there," I said. "My family wasn't rich, but they still managed to cut me out of their lives. Angie's right. I think we do have a lot to talk about, and not just because we're both in medicine."

Gloria smiled and said, "I look forward to that."

Since it was Gloria's first night with us, she got to choose what she wanted for dinner, and everyone was happy when she picked Chinese food. Like Angie, she was crazy about wonton soup. We bought six large containers of the stuff, along with a variety of other dishes. There was plenty of food left over, but not a drop of the soup remained, and everyone went to bed happy and full.

CHAPTER FIFTY-ONE

Maria

A few days later, after Joe and Mr. Laurence returned from the cemetery, they drove Gloria to her interview for the nursing job in Stony Brook University Hospital's ER. The chances of her not getting the job were zero. The Hamill Foundation had been major contributors to the university and hospital for fifty years, and both the hospital and the university had grown simultaneously into world-renowned institutions.

I drove Angie to her appointment with the psychiatrist. She told me about her first appointment and her breakdown over her mother's role in her abuse. I told her that all psychiatrists wish they had such a breakthrough on a patient's first visit.

"Don't go in there today and decide to act normal. You need to tell her what's troubling you. That's how you get better."

"What about the situation in the ballroom with Mr. Hamill's daughters?"

That one threw me for a loop, but after thinking about it, I said, "You don't want her to think you're schizophrenic. That might have you residing in a psych ward. You can tell her about the last part of that episode like it was a dream."

"She gave me prescriptions, but I didn't fill them. I don't want to take any drugs, especially after seeing so many of the women at the center on medications. They were like zombies."

"Then let her know that. It's your choice. If she strongly believes you need medication, she can always revisit the issue later. For now, hold your ground. She should support your decision to focus on lifestyle changes and talk therapy. Those things take longer to work, but the effects can be just as powerful as meds, and they carry no side effects. Eating well, getting plenty of sleep, surrounding yourself with loving and positive people, getting exercise — all of that is medicine, too."

I looked at Angie as she kept nervously playing with her hands. "Sweetheart, what's wrong?"

"What happens if she thinks I'm really crazy and trying to cause trouble by not taking the medication? She might send me back to the women's center."

"There is absolutely no chance of that happening. I would have a better chance of becoming Leonardo da Vinci," I said. As soon as the words came out of my mouth, I realized that they must have sounded a little random.

"Why would you say that?"

"Oh, I don't know."

"Joe thought he had become Leonardo da Vinci or, should I say, the second coming of Mr. da Vinci. After he fell down the stairs and while he was recuperating in the hospital, he was suddenly able to draw these beautiful pictures. When he came to visit me at Rikers he wanted me to pose for him and he was going to paint a portrait of me that would be as famous as the Mona Lisa."

"And did he?"

"No, when it came time to paint the portrait, he'd lost his artistic gift. I think he was still suffering from the concussion."

"Fascinating," I said.

"You know, Maria, it really seems unreal at times. It was just over six months ago that I was locked up at Rikers Island, and if it wasn't for my boyfriend lying to the prosecutors for me, I could be spending the next fifteen-to-twenty years behind bars. I guess that's what you call true love, and yet there are still times when I get so jealous when I see other girls looking at him, or when I think there's even a chance that he *might* be interested in someone else. He was always nice-looking, but now he's become super good-looking. He could get any girl he wants."

"But he's chosen you, and it's not like you couldn't also get any guy you want."

"No, that's not true. Any guy with half a brain would be out the door in half a minute after meeting me."

"That is absolutely not true. You're beautiful and smart and you have a wonderful personality."

"No, Maria," she said, her voice rising and constricting, "you're beautiful and Gloria's beautiful and you're both smart and amazing. I'm a scrawny, weird looking basket case!"

I parked in front of the doctor's office and looked at Angie. "What's got into you? You're very beautiful, and that's only one small part of why Joe's lucky to have you. He's *lucky*, and he *knows* it. I can't understand why *you* don't know it."

"I don't feel beautiful," she said as I turned away, speechless, as we both got out of the car.

We walked into the lobby and Angie signed in as I took a seat. She took a seat next to me and asked, "You're not mad at me?"

"I could never be mad at you," I said as I gently touched her face. "I love you so much."

The receptionist told her the doctor was ready to see her and Angie thanked me for being there and then walked into the doctor's office.

I sat back, with my head against the wall, and could feel the anger build up inside me. It was the same anger that I felt every time I read a dossier on one of the girls who had found refuge at one of the Hamill Foundations across the world. But it was different with Angie. The girls I read about were not a part of my life; I had never met them or discussed the abuse they suffered. I had concentrated more on the pediatric side of the foundation. The side that provided medical care and research for children with terrible diseases like cancer or cystic fibrosis, but not so much with girls like Angie.

Joe was Mr. Laurence's project. He was shaping and re-shaping and eventually molding the young man into an individual who he could honestly say Raphael would have been proud to add to his famous painting *The School of Athens.*

Angie was my project, and when I see her with my eyes closed, I see only a young woman's face, beautiful with dark, tousled hair, like da Vinci's sketch-like painting, *Head of a Young Woman with Tousled Hair.* It's up to me to complete the picture, not just by filling in her physical characteristics but more importantly by contributing to her mental and spiritual makeup. In essence, to banish the demons of abuse and bring forth the glowing divinity inherent in the mind and soul of this very special young person.

Angie tapped me on the shoulder, and I opened my eyes and asked, "Finished already?"

"Yes, after the first session all the other sessions are only half an hour. Were you asleep?"

"No, I was thinking of you," I said.

"Well, that can't be good. Thinking about taking back your offer of being my adoptive mother?"

"Absolutely not, thinking about your intrinsic radiance," I said, so earnestly that she started to laugh.

"Are you sure you're not on any medications?" she asked, and I couldn't stop myself from chuckling. "Or maybe you stashed that other bottle of wine in your purse?"

"I'm as sober as the day I was born. Somber as a judge. You're radiant."

Angie didn't know what to make of this, so she just stared at me and said, "If you say so," and laughed again.

We took the elevator down, and after exiting the building we walked toward the mall. "I know of a really good Vietnamese restaurant," I said. "Would you like to try it?"

"Love to," she said as her phone rang and it was Joe. I grabbed the phone out of her hand and motioned for her to be quiet.

"Hello," I said.

"Hello ... Angie?" Joe replied.

"No, it's Maria. Angie can't talk right now. Her bags are going through airport security, and she's about to get frisked by a good-looking customs officer. We're going to Maui for a week. I thought I told Mr. Laurence but I must have forgot. Sorry about that."

"Angie would never do that without telling me," Joe said anxiously.

"Sometimes girls just need to be girls. That's all there is to it."

"No, I can't believe Angie would do that without telling me. Please, Maria, let me talk to her."

I looked across at Angie, who was stifling laughter. "I'm sorry, but she's going through security. She can't talk to you." I held the phone away from myself and made a beeping noise like an airport metal detector, then returned the phone to my ear.

Joe went silent, then asked, "What airport are you at?"

"Kennedy, at Delta airlines. We're departing shortly, so don't waste your time trying to get here before we leave. Definitely don't try reenacting one of those movie scenes where you run through traffic to get to the airport so you can catch your girlfriend before she gets on the plane."

There was confused silence on the other end. "I ...won't?"

"This short separation will be good for you. Absence and fond hearts and all that. And it'll give you and Mr. Laurence even more time together. The second we land I'll have her call you. Aloha!"

I hung up the phone and handed it back to Angie, who looked simultaneously amused and worried. "You know he's going totally crazy right now, right?" she said. "I have to call him back."

Angie dialed the number and said, "Joe, I don't have much time. We're taking off in ten minutes. What do you need?" She winked at me and I threw my head back in silent laughter.

"Angie, I don't believe this. How could you leave town without telling me?"

"I was so excited I guess I just forgot. Don't you want me to have fun?"

"Of course I want you to have fun, but you could have at least let me know. I'm going to go nuts worrying about you."

Angie laughed long and hard into the receiver and said, "Joe, love of my life, when did you stop having a sense of humor? Maria was just playing with you. We're going to eat lunch at a Vietnamese restaurant beside the mall. I'll be home in about an hour and a half."

"What? Seriously? Oh, okay, you can tell Maria she got me this time. Hawaii … sheesh."

"Didn't it all seem a little outlandish to you?"

"Well now it does, but she's very convincing, and so are you, by the way," he said, sounding almost impressed. "So, you're not on your way to Hawaii?"

"No, we're going to Vietnam instead."

"Very funny," he said. "Well, my beautiful little wiseass, I was calling to tell you that the necklace is ready, and that since you're down there you can go pick it up and make sure it fits properly. Then, later tonight I can put it on you and tell you how beautiful you are and how much I love you and how I'm the luckiest person in the world to have you."

Angie started to cry, but I could tell they were happy tears, and she said, "I love you so much and I promise I'll never go to Hawaii or Vietnam without telling you first. I could never go to any of those places without you anyway. I could never survive being away from you for so long."

"Promise?"

"Yes, I promise. Was there something else you wanted to tell me?

"I just wanted to make sure everything went okay with the doctor."

"Everything went exceptionally well."

Angie hung up the phone and looked at me as tears continued to roll down her cheeks. "He loves me so much. I can't believe I could be so lucky, especially…"

I put a finger over her mouth and said, "And he can't believe how lucky he is that you love him so much. So, you complement each other perfectly."

CHAPTER FIFTY-TWO

Maria

Before going to eat, we went to the jewelry store to pick up the necklace. Michelle helped her put it on and Angie declared it perfect. The colors matched her complexion beautifully and they had managed to fit the entire Brontë inscription on the back of the pendant in tiny cursive: "Whatever our souls are made of, his and mine are the same."

Michelle put the necklace into a custom-made box, and then into a glossy little shopping bag with velvety rope handles. We left the store and headed to the Vietnamese restaurant.

The lunch crowd had already cleared, and we were able to choose a big table near a window. I ordered a Bird's Nest cocktail, which consisted of Grey Goose vodka, Southern Comfort, *salangane* water — from edible bird's nests — mandarin juice, lime juice and sugar syrup, tossed and served with three onions. It was one of my favorite cocktails, and one was my limit.

Angie ordered soda, then told me to choose her food for her because she'd never tried Vietnamese cuisine. I ordered goi cuon (spring rolls) as appetizers and bun cha (grilled meatballs) as our entrees.

She kept eyeing my drink, and finally said, "That looks really delicious."

"It is, and if you like you can have a tiny sip." She nodded and I handed her the glass and she took a sip and said, "Yummy!"

She was about to take another sip and I reached over and took the glass away. "Mean mommy," she said.

"No — concerned mommy. One of these drinks is all I can handle, and I'm quite sure I've had much more drinking experience than you. If I ever brought you home drunk, I would get such a lecture from Mr. Laurence."

"Mr. Laurence loves you so much, I doubt he's ever even reprimanded you!"

I had to think about that for a moment and couldn't come up with anything. "He doesn't have to yell or scold to make a point," I said. "He just exudes a quiet authority."

"Oh is that right?" Angie said laughingly as the waiter brought our appetizers. She took a bite of spring roll and said, "Yummy! Oh please don't take these away from me."

"Keep acting like a little wiseass and I will," I said as I took a bite of my spring roll.

"Mean mommy," Angie said with a giggle, and I gasped in mock horror.

"That's it!" I said, and snatched the last spring roll off the plate and raised it to my mouth. Angie let out the cutest little shriek and I threw my head back in surrender and handed it over.

"I give up," I said. "You're too adorable. I guess I'll just have to spoil you rotten and always give you the last spring roll and everything else you want."

"Yay," she said, looking pleased with herself and like she was having fun. But the glee only lasted for a moment. "I do sometimes feel like I'm being spoiled rotten," she said, a little more seriously.

"Is it the necklace?"

She nodded and leaned across to whisper. "Do you know that it cost over three thousand dollars? That's more than I've spent in my life on clothes, books and occasional gifts for Joe, combined. With that money I could have bought all the children at the hospital a gift.

I made a list of all the gifts they would love most, and those three thousand dollars would have covered it, but Joe told me that Mr. Laurence insisted, so I bought the necklace." She lowered her head and took another bite of spring roll.

I looked at her and thought about everything that this child had been through, and marveled at the fact that her first instinct was still to help children with cancer before helping herself. I touched her hand and said, "Mr. Laurence wanted you to have the necklace. Did you forget that he gave us an unlimited budget for the party? We'll get the children the gifts they wanted. I promise."

"Thank you, Maria. If the foundation gives out all this money and doesn't accept outside contributions, won't it eventually run out of money?"

"No, and the reason is that the foundation's advisory team has been smart and has diversified across a range of industries. When Mr. Hamill sold his publishing empire, he didn't sell it all. He kept several well-known magazines that are still very popular today, and several TV stations he had bought when TV first came into existence, and six newspapers. The Hamill trust still owns them, and the money they bring sometimes triples the amount that the foundation gives out. The foundation also bought some major media companies, including a couple of streaming services that have done exceptionally well, and it has holdings in non-media companies, too, including investment banking and insurance. Then there's the Santa Barbara estate that Mr. Hamill bought for Mr. Laurence and Isabelle when they got married. God only knows how much that's worth today. The foundation and the trusts have a small army of lawyers and accountants working for them to keep all of the balls in the air."

"And, God forbid anything happens to Mr. Laurence, who inherits all the private businesses and real estate?"

"It will all stay the same. The money from the private investments will continue to go into the same accounts, and the foundation will continue to run like it always has, with some changes that are already underway. We're expanding the mission while centralizing the area of the foundation. The mission, which was originally to help abused and orphaned children, has now expanded into research and affordable health care for children suffering from cancer, cystic fibrosis and other deadly diseases or disabilities. Our area of operations will be more community-based, like the health clinic I work at, or the pediatric cancer center we visit, and contributions to hospitals such as Stony Brook and many in the cities that deal with pediatric disorders."

"And eventually you're the heir apparent?" Angie asked as I took a sip of my drink and looked curiously at the child.

"The heir apparent, is that what you think?"

"Well, doesn't there have to be an heir apparent, once Mr. Laurence steps down? And with no offspring from any of the other adopted daughters, who else could it be? You're the adopted daughter of Isabelle and Mr. Laurence. There is no doubt in my mind that Mr. Laurence adores you, and from what he and you tell me about Isabelle, she also adored you."

"Mr. Laurence wanted the Hamill name carried on and he was the one who asked me if I would like to change names. It was the easiest choice I ever made," I said, and then asked, "And what part do you get to play, my gorgeous child?"

"I don't know if I get to play a part. I'd love to, especially when it comes to the children. I'd love to contribute if I'm not too much of a burden."

"A burden? More like a godsend."

"Thank you," she said. "And what about Joe? Was he also a godsend?"

"Joe was chosen," I replied as I took another sip of my drink.

"I don't understand."

"And for now, it's better that way, and I would appreciate it if you don't mention anything to Joe about this."

"He's not in danger in any way, is he?" she asked, seriously.

"Do you actually believe that Mr. Laurence would put any of us in the least bit of danger?"

"No, of course not. But Joe…"

I reached across and put my finger over her mouth and said, "We're all going to make a great team, just like the twenty-seventh Yankees."

"Who are they?"

"Seriously Angie, and you're from the Bronx. The Bronx Bombers. The New York Yankees, Babe Ruth, Joe DiMaggio?"

"They're a baseball team?" she replied hesitantly.

"Yes, probably the most famous team in America. I know your boyfriend loves sports because I've heard him have long conversations about different teams and players with Mr. Laurence. How did you manage to corral that boy without knowing anything about his favorite teams?"

"I got lucky."

I ordered some food to bring home to Mr. Laurence and Joe. The waiter brought the order to go, and I asked for the check. I paid and left an oversized tip. Angie picked up her bag with the necklace in it and I picked up the bag with the food. She hesitated a minute as she looked down at the table and said, "You only finished half your drink. Can I have the rest?"

"Only if you want to get your first spanking by your adopted mother."

"Mean mommy," she replied and started giggling like a child.

CHAPTER FIFTY-THREE

Maria

I pulled up to the mansion and before I'd parked, Joe was out in the driveway to greet us … or more accurately to greet Angie.

He kissed her and took her bag as I said, "You are really one jealous boyfriend."

He looked at me, and then ran over and took the food bag out of my hand like a real gentleman. "Fiancé," he said, "and you've got me there. But it's just because I'm so in love."

"Well, that's understandable, especially since every guy we passed today did a double-take when looking at her."

"Don't believe her, Joe. If any guys were doing double-takes it was because they were gawking at *her* — poor, misguided souls."

I had to laugh at that, and shrugged as if to say, *Can I help it if I'm every straight man's dream*?

As we entered the mansion, Mr. Laurence greeted us and asked, "Did you girls have a good time today?"

"Wonderful," I said as I kissed Mr. Laurence on the cheek and kicked off my shoes. "And we bring gifts of food from the Vietnamese restaurant we love so much."

"And did you have your one Bird's Nest cocktail?"

"I did," I said. "It was as delicious as ever."

"She only drank half of it and wouldn't let me have any more than a sip."

"Is that so?" Mr. Laurence asked.

"That stuff is potent," I said, and reached out and touched Angie's cheek. "And this little chickadee is too precious to end up under the table."

"That she is," Mr. Laurence said. Then he looked at Angie and said, "But you do look even more radiant than usual, my dear. Are you sure you stuck to one sip?"

"Not even a full sip. More like a thimble full."

We left the boys in the kitchen with the Vietnamese food, and Angie and I went into my room to work on the party. She sat in the chair next to my desk, and I dictated while she typed in the information for the party on a spreadsheet.

As her hands flew over the keys, she said, "I've never worked on a computer this fast and this nice."

"I'll get you one because you're going to need it, especially if you plan on working for the foundation."

"Maria, you've already bought me too much. I can use Joe's old laptop."

"You have no say in such decisions, my lovely child. I will spoil you as I please, and you really will need a new computer."

"Whatever you say, Mommy," she said, and started giggling.

Joe and Angie went back to their place at about eight o'clock. It was the unveiling of the necklace, so it was a big night for my little girl. I walked into the kitchen where Mr. Laurence was opening a bottle of Château Lafite Rothschild 1969. "I was just coming to get you," he said as he put two wine glasses on the table.

I sat down and he poured a smidge of wine in my glass for me to smell and taste. I said, "You know I can't tell the difference between a ten-dollar bottle and this one, which probably cost as much as a small car."

"I'm not much better, sweetheart. I imagine I was supposed to let the wine breathe for a while before just opening it up and pouring."

I swirled the wine around in my glass, sniffed, and shrugged. Then I brought a little bit of the wine to my lips and tried to concentrate. I had to admit, it was pretty special.

"You do have wonderful taste," I said, and Mr. Laurence thanked me and refilled our glasses. Then I got him reminiscing about the old days by asking him a question that I already knew the answer to — whether Mr. and Mrs. Hamill were really such teetotalers, despite owning a huge collection of expensive wines.

"I'm not sure I would call them teetotalers," he said, "but it's true that they mainly drank wine at Thanksgiving or Christmas. That wonderful collection in the cellar all came to them as gifts. Mr. Hamill enjoyed an ice-cold beer or two while watching a ball game, but they steered away from drinking alcohol when the children were around because so many of the girls had been abused by drunken parents, relatives, and friends."

"That was very thoughtful of them."

"Their daughters always came first. Mr. Hamill could be talking on the phone to the secretary of state and if one of the girls was in distress he'd say, 'I'm sorry, I have an emergency to attend to,' and ask to call them back later."

I put on my best listening face, and to my delight he kept sipping wine and telling stories.

"But the girls were never spoiled. There were no maids or cooks, except if they were throwing a big party. The girls did the cleaning, but Mr. and Mrs. Hamill did have a butler—"

"Adam, right?"

"Exactly. He was also their driver, and a close friend of Mr. Hamill from World War I. A very nice man who was there that day when I first met Isabelle. And they had an army of gardeners and groundskeepers. The girls had the run of the place, and they were always out playing croquet and badminton on the lawns, or picking flowers for the table, or just sitting and talking on the wrap-around porch. This house was so full of life."

Without warning, as I listened, my eyes brimmed with tears. I raised my glass and said, "To wonderful parents and happy children," and Mr. Laurence clinked my glass and we both drank.

He stopped talking as he looked closely at me and asked, "You had a really good day today, didn't you? You've been glowing ever since you came back with Angie."

"She's such a doll, and when she laughs it's more like a giggle and it just makes me feel so good. And you were right — Joe is never going to abandon her. You should have heard him on the phone today when he thought I was whisking her off to Hawaii."

"He mentioned that," Mr. Laurence said with a laugh.

"He was ready to get in the car and drive to Kennedy airport!" I said, beaming. "Were you like that with Isabelle at first?"

"I never stopped being like that with Isabelle. It's always been like a dream, like I've been comatose for fifty years and dreamt this whole thing up. Like Joe and Angie, I'm just a kid from the Bronx who lived with my parents in a two-bedroom, one-bathroom apartment. To meet Isabelle on a street in Los Angeles was shocking enough, but to be invited into her parents' home and then to marry her ... well, I was blessed."

"And nothing has changed, has it?"

"You know the answer to that better than anyone."

"Yes I do, and it's definitely the most beautiful of dreams."

As I swirled my wine and breathed in its black raspberry scent, I wondered if I would ever come to close to having the type of relationship that Mr. Laurence and Isabelle enjoyed, or that my adopted daughter and Joe were now enjoying.

I asked, "You and Isabelle tasted perfection. But I'm wondering — do you have any regrets?"

He looked thoughtfully down into his glass. "Just one. I can't square the fact that I survived Normandy and so many of my friends perished ... I think of those young men and of their families every day. I can't regret keeping my own life, because without it I wouldn't have had Isabelle, or you," he looked at me and smiled, "but I do feel terrible guilt at having come out of that day intact and gone on to be happy."

He wiped tears from his eyes and before I could speak, he asked, "And you, Maria. What do you regret?"

I thought for a moment. "I regret allowing myself to hate my biological parents and my brothers. If forgiveness is the greatest gift a person can bestow, then I've failed miserably."

"And in a sense so have Isabelle and I, because it's that sense of betrayal you feel toward your parents and brothers that gave us the greatest gift we could ever imagine…"

I started to cry, which was truly becoming a habit that I couldn't control. I took a gulp of wine and Mr. Laurence eyed me suspiciously. "It really is good wine," I said.

He refilled my glass and I asked him how Gloria's interview went.

"Exceedingly well," he said. "They were so impressed that they gave her the job and started training her immediately. She'll be working four long night shifts a week, with plenty of opportunity for overtime."

"It's incredible that you were able to get her out of the center."

"Well, she had a lot of support. I'm told that at her criminal trial, half a dozen community leaders testified on her behalf. Back at the hospital in Harlem she helped save dozens of people who'd been badly wounded, so they were eager to vouch for her. A local politician, an addiction counselor and a police officer all volunteered to be character witnesses for her in court."

I nodded and said, "Doctors get the credit, but it's the nurses who do the heavy lifting and see that patients fully recover."

"So is that why you became a doctor and not a nurse? An aversion to heavy lifting?"

"Very funny."

"Gloria told me that for the first couple of months at the women's center, she was very worried about Angie. She said if it wasn't for Joe being there every day, she was certain she'd come back to the apartment one day and find her dead."

"I have no doubt about that. She's fragile, but she's slowly getting stronger and more confident and physically healthier."

Mr. Laurence looked at me and said, "What would you say to taking a few weeks off at the clinic so you can keep an eye on her? You could help her prepare for the party, take her out to lunch, maybe drive out to Port Jefferson or the Hamptons."

"I was going to ask you for exactly that. In fact, I was going to ask you if I could greatly limit my time at the clinic in order to spend time with her. Thankfully, we're well-staffed. If I need to, I can always go in and help."

"That sounds perfect."

"But you'd better check with Joe and make sure he's okay with it. I don't want him to think I'm kidnapping his fiancée."

"I'll talk to him," Mr. Laurence laughingly replied.

CHAPTER FIFTY-FOUR

Maria

Back in my room, I straightened a line of teddy bears, then walked over to my bookshelf, where I took down an art history book about the Renaissance. I opened it to my favorite page: an unfinished da Vinci painting — a painted sketch, as some have called it — known as *La Scapigliata*, or *Head of a Young Woman with Tousled Hair.*

This piece had fascinated me for years. It's haunting in part because you can't tell if it's a sketch or a painting; the young woman's skin and hair and coloring are all suggested rather than rendered in detail, which leaves the viewer to fill in the missing information.

Like the girl with the tousled hair, Angie was caught between states of being. Her future had yet to be written, and so much depended on her ability to face her own demons, with and without help from Joe.

I heard the front door open, and before I could turn around, Gloria was lightly tapping on my bedroom door, which I had left ajar. She poked her head into my room, and I turned to face her.

"Gloria! Come in."

"I hope it's not too late."

"Not at all," I said, as I lay the book on my desk. "Come tell me all about your interview. I heard you were a hit."

She swished in, somehow looking stunning in her scrubs. I tried not to stare, but it was difficult.

"Yes, they were all so nice," Gloria said, "and having Mr. Laurence sitting outside their offices certainly added to their enthusiasm."

"Well, I'm sure your experience and charming personality helped a lot too. How was the first day of training?"

"Great! Everyone was super supportive and helpful — even some of the male doctors," she said. "It's so different from where I worked before. Stony Brook is much better-equipped. And the visitor's area is so deluxe — all that's missing is a bar."

I laughed and gestured for her to sit on an overstuffed chair next to my bed, while I perched on a swivel chair at my desk. She picked up a teddy bear that was sitting on the end of my bed and held it in her lap. "Cute," she said. When she stared down at the bear and went quiet, I asked, "What's wrong?"

"Nothing!" she said, looking around the room and then back at me. "I mean ... it's all just too incredible."

"The hospital?"

"The hospital. Mr. Laurence. You and Angie and Joe. Being welcomed into this beautiful home. The fact that I'm *free,* and working again in the field I love ..."

"Welcome back, Gloria," I said. "I hear you were missed."

"Thank you," she said, suddenly a little tearful. "You know, I never thought I would work as a nurse again. I was sure my training would go to waste. The fact that Mr. Laurence would use his influence to help me is just..."

I nodded and said, "I get it. I really do," but she wasn't quite finished making her point, and didn't really seem to hear me.

"It's just that ... you know, I'm used to power," she explained. "I grew up around investment bankers and CEOs. I've seen how often people gain power on the backs of others, then discard anyone who doesn't serve their interests. Mr. Laurence has all the influence in the world, and he just wants to use it to do good. I don't know how I can ever thank him enough. And on top of it all, to be living in this beautiful home with four of the loveliest people I've ever met—"

"Oh, that's so nice. And I know — it's all a little overwhelming at first — to be so sure that all is lost, and that your life will never be the same, and then to find that you're safe. I've been there. You can relax. This is your home now."

Gloria hesitated, lowered her eyes, and said, "I know you've been through a lot too. And look how far you've come!" She beamed at me, and I felt my stomach do a little flip. "Do you have your own practice?"

"No! I volunteer at the free clinic and the pediatric cancer center, and I help run the foundation."

"Would you ever want your own practice?"

"I might have at one time, but when I met Mr. Laurence and his wife and sister-in-law, all that seemed to change."

"I've heard a bit about this from Angie, but not much. Was there some sort of break with your family?"

"Yes, you could say that."

"Don't feel you have to tell me—"

"No, it's okay," I said. "I feel like I can talk to you."

"I feel like I can talk to you too," she said, and with that I launched in, telling her about the night when I came out to my family and the aftermath, including the parts about my ex, and the fact that I almost had to drop out of medical school.

"That sounds incredibly painful," Gloria said. "I'm sorry."

I paused and looked down at the da Vinci sketch, then up at Gloria. "Thank you," I said. "I guess you could say I misjudged my family's love for me, and underestimated how backward looking they still were when it came to sexuality. When I told my parents I was planning on getting married, they asked, 'Who's the boy? Is he a medical student, or better yet a doctor?' I told them 'he' was a female accountant at a law firm, and that we'd been seeing each other for nearly two years and were very much in love.

"My father asked me if I was joking, and I assured him I wasn't. Then my mom and my brothers just stood there while he screamed at me for ten minutes, calling me 'a fucking freak,' and 'a disgrace to the family,' then went up to my room and started throwing my stuff out the window. Shoes, clothes, records, coats, everything. That bear you're holding."

"Unbelievable," Gloria said.

"Oh, it got worse. When he came back downstairs, he grabbed me and shook me so hard I thought he was going to break my arm. He opened the front door and literally flung me out of the home I was raised in. That was ten years ago, and I haven't been back since. I occasionally talk to my mother, whose advice to me is to talk to a priest."

"Oh my God," Gloria said. "Does she think they can get the gay out with an exorcism?"

"That's what I said! She claims she just wants me to hear the Lord's opinion of gay people from a priest, but I wouldn't put it past her to sneak in a quick exorcism."

Both of us laughed at that, but the mood quickly turned somber again when Gloria said, "It's sick the way some parents punish their children for being themselves."

"So true," I said. "You're very perceptive."

Gloria smiled at me and said, "Well, try being a Black woman in America without being perceptive, and see how far you get."

"Of course. God, I'm such an idiot."

"Why?"

"Going on and on about my life. Calling you perceptive. Forgetting that you could easily have it hard every day, whereas I had one terrible day and some difficult years."

"Yeah, I won't fight you on that. And if you want to talk about racial discrimination and the lives of Black women in this fine country of ours, we can talk. But you'd better block out a couple of days," Gloria said with a wry smile. "Right now, we're talking about you. And you were telling me about a girl who suffered a horrible rejection by the people she loved and trusted the most. That's not one bad day. That's a trauma, good as any other."

"Thank you," I said. "I can't believe how good it feels to talk about all of this. And I seriously would like to hear what you have to say about race in America, even though I realize that it's not your job to teach me."

"I appreciate that. It's tiring as hell to teach stuff to white folks who don't want to see their own privilege. But it does help to talk, and I happen to like you," Gloria said. "So talk when you're the one talking! What happened next? Your father showed you his real self, and your mother and brothers showed you that they're just fine with you being bullied. Did you marry that girl?"

"I did not. I wanted to, but the whole fiasco with my parents put a wedge between us. She wanted in-laws who would accept us both and help raise the kids we planned to have together. One day she left without even leaving a note."

"Ouch."

"Tell me about it."

"So how did you meet Mr. and Mrs. Laurence?"

"At the pediatric center. They were regular visitors there, and we'd already spoken a bunch of times before my parents kicked me out. I was still trying to volunteer and keep my life together and stay in med school, but I was kind of coming apart, missing shifts, spacing out from lack of sleep and horrible stress."

"Good old cortisol," Gloria said, and it struck me what a pleasure it was to talk to another medical professional who knew the terms for such things as the chemicals that course through our bodies when we're stressed. I laughed and said, "Yeah, I was swimming in the stuff.

"Isabelle knew. One day she took me aside and asked me what was wrong."

"What a doll."

"Right? I broke down and told her the whole story. That's when they took me in and became what I consider to be my parents. They covered my tuition, paid off all my loans and even gave me a weekly allowance so I'd never be without money."

"And they never asked for anything in return?"

"Not a thing. After Isabelle and Rachel passed away, I started helping Mr. Laurence with the foundation, and when I became a doctor, I started working at the clinic that the foundation built and fully finances."

Gloria looked intrigued. "And in the future, if I wanted to work at the free clinic or the pediatric center, do you think Mr. Laurence would be okay with that?"

"I think he would be overjoyed, and so would I," I said. "Is that what you originally wanted to talk about?"

"Yes. Harlem General might have been underfunded, but I loved being able to help people every day. I would come home exhausted, but with the overwhelming satisfaction of knowing that I had contributed to the community."

"I know that feeling," I said, "and it's worth everything."

"I'd like to continue working at Stony Brook Hospital for now, because they were nice enough to give me a job and I wouldn't feel right quitting after one day of training. But when the time is right, I hope I can talk to you and Mr. Laurence about working for the foundation ."

"We would love nothing better," I said as we both stood up and hugged. Gloria started walking out of the room when she turned and asked, "How'd my little cupcake do today?"

"She did wonderfully, and afterward we went out to eat at a Vietnamese restaurant and she loved it."

"Nice," Gloria said. "You know, when she first came to the center, the first thing I noticed was her face. She has the face of a Christmas doll you might see in a display window, and then when I looked at the rest of her, I saw a child who was seriously underweight, timid, and barely able to force a smile.

"I didn't think she had much time left. Her body looked like the body of a drug addict, yet she was always polite to everyone, except Joe. It was like she took all her anger out on this boy who was only trying to help her. She clung to him, didn't give him any space, and if he showed up late, she'd accuse him of everything under the sun.

"I talked to her about her behavior and at first she said I was imagining the whole thing, and that Joe loved her more than anything in the entire world. I looked at her and said, 'Your boyfriend can get any girl he wants and does not have to put up with your neurotic antics.' I told her she'd better smarten up or she'd lose the best thing she had.

"I could not believe that Joe came every day and stayed with her until closing. I couldn't understand why he just didn't walk away. She nearly killed him, and here he was, lying to the prosecutors so she wouldn't have to go to jail. His own mother begged him to leave her, yet he continued to show up every day."

"And why do you think that was?" I asked.

"Because he saw in her what we're now witnessing ... a caring, loving, intelligent girl who was so badly abused that it was only natural that it would take a lot of time to just get to where she is today."

"Bingo," I said. "I guess Joe is pretty perceptive, too."

"Oh, there's not a day that goes by that I don't acknowledge what that boy has done for her and for me. Neither of us would be where we are now if it wasn't for his undying loyalty to her. In the end, that was the reason he met Mr. Laurence." I nodded my understanding and she asked, "What did Mr. Laurence see in Joe that allowed him to trust Joe so easily from the start?"

"I think he mainly saw himself."

Gloria smiled and said, "I had a feeling that was it. Thank you Maria, it was great talking to you. I hope you have a good night."

After she slipped out the door, I flopped onto the bed and held my chest. What was it about being in the same room as that woman that set my heart on fire?

I moved to my desk and turned back to the da Vinci painting and stared at it for a good minute. Then I held my hand up to the center of the woman's chest and traced a big heart with my fingertip. My heart was suddenly so full! I couldn't wait to see Gloria again, and Angie — well, she was becoming the compassionate, caring, and loving young woman she was always meant to be.

CHAPTER FIFTY-FIVE

Maria

The following morning Angie and I worked on the party, sent out consent forms for the parents to sign, and made arrangements with the hospital so that all necessary precautions were in place before the children arrived.

We then took a ride to beautiful Port Jefferson, about twenty minutes from the mansion. We walked along the dock and I pointed out to Angie that directly across the port was the state of Connecticut. She was surprised to learn that Connecticut was so close. I asked her if she had done any travelling and she replied, "I was a guest at Rikers Island for a month."

"Very funny, wiseass," I said. "Besides that?"

"Joe took me to Manhattan a couple of times. We walked around and went to a few museums and saw a double feature. We wanted to see a Broadway play, but they were too expensive."

"Well, going to a Broadway play is definitely on our to-do list."

"Joe always wanted to take me to nice places, but I didn't want him to spend his money because I knew how hard he worked for it. He always had a job, delivering newspapers or working at the neighborhood candy store or the supermarket across the street. He said he was saving for our honeymoon."

"And where was that going to be?"

"Most likely Santa Barbara. I've always wanted to go there. It looks so beautiful, and I love walking along the ocean. Sadly, before meeting Mr. Laurence, I think Joe spent most of his money trying to save me from myself. He would never admit it, but he's made all the sacrifices, whereas…"

"Whereas…"

"You don't have to say it, Maria. I know, I'll get my chance."

"So, you have learned a few things since coming to live with us."

"I've learned a lot of things, none more important than to trust and love Mr. Laurence, Gloria, and you. I might not have been lucky with my first mom, but I've hit the jackpot with my new one."

We ate at a seafood restaurant overlooking the water. I asked Angie if she'd ever had lobster, and when the answer was no, I ordered two three-pound lobsters for us to split.

The waiter tied plastic bibs on us and Angie asked, "Am I really going to need this?"

"Yes, especially since it's your first time." The waiter placed the two massive crustaceans and some little pots of melted butter in front of us and refilled our iced teas.

"You don't really think I'll be able to eat all this, do you?" Angie asked.

"It's all shell. You'll see. Just watch me and do what I do." I picked up my knife and lobster fork and cut a piece of meat from the tail and dipped it in the hot butter.

She did the same, cut a piece of meat from the tail, and dipped it a little too hard into the butter and it went splashing all over her. I couldn't help myself and started laughing. "You see? That's why you need a bib."

She wiped her face with a napkin and I said, "Don't worry about it. It happens to everyone. Go ahead and try the lobster."

She put the delicate white meat into her mouth and chewed. At first she looked surprised. Then she closed her eyes and chewed some more, and mumbled "Oh my God," as she finished her first bite. She did okay with the rest of the tail, but when it came to cracking open the claws and scooping out the meat with the skinny lobster fork, she had a fight on her hands. Butter went everywhere and she nearly turned over the table. I eventually took the claws away from her and scooped out all the meat and handed it back to her.

"What a mess," she said. "I'm sorry."

"Don't be sorry. It takes practice. You'll ace it next time."

"I think I've put on a few pounds. What do you think?"

"Most definitely."

"That's what you want, right?"

"Yes, angel. That's exactly what the doctor ordered."

"I asked Joe last night, and he said he thought I had. But then Joe will never disagree with me if he thinks it might upset me."

I looked at her and smiled. She had butter in her hair and more dripping down her chin, and she simply looked adorable.

CHAPTER FIFTY-SIX

Maria

The day of the party arrived and two busloads of children, parents, nurses, and two doctors arrived at the mansion. The party was scheduled to take place mostly outside by the pool, where tables were set up with refreshments, food, and enough toys to put Santa Claus out of business.

Mr. Laurence allowed our guests to walk through the mansion and into the pool area, and gave everyone complete access to the home's seven bathrooms. The children were only allowed to go into the pool up to their waists. The risk of infection was always a big concern, and even though our pool could not be cleaner, one never wanted to take a chance, especially since almost all the children were receiving chemotherapy.

The house was basically child-proof. After all, fifteen girls had lived there at various times. Mr. Laurence, like Mr. and Mrs. Hamill, knew what the important things in life were, and they were not possessions. An expensive lamp or a five-thousand-dollar couch could be replaced, but a child's life was precious, and their happiness and well-being were paramount.

Angie was self-conscious about wearing a bathing suit. She thought that even the one-piece suit she'd purchased for the party showed off too much of her body and because she was so thin it made her look sick. I reminded her that most of our distinguished guests were going through chemo and at present had the bodies of skeletons. She thought about that for a moment and started to cry.

She said she hated thinking only about herself, and that "God would not look kindly upon her egotistical behavior."

I replied that "God had more important things to think about than a teenager's ego." I tied her hair back in a ponytail and her face glowed.

As the party got underway, Angie came to life in a way I'd never seen, even during our visits to the cancer center. She led the children in sing-alongs in and out of the pool. They jumped rope and played tag, and she took special joy in handing out gifts to all the children at scheduled times so that they would last the entire party. There were at least fifty gifts and ten children, and each gift was individually wrapped and labeled. Angie made sure that each child got the gifts they had asked for when we visited the hospital. In short, she was a superstar.

The children left happy, and the parents could not have been more grateful. Mr. Laurence talked with all of the parents, and as they were departing, he handed each set of parents an envelope with five thousand dollars inside, to be used however they saw fit.

When the last child had left to return to the pediatric center, Mr. Laurence and Joe came up to me and Mr. Laurence said, "You've done a marvelous job with your adopted child."

"She's always had it in her, but now she's finally having a chance to shine."

"I've already told Joe that he has some fierce competition for the girl he plans on marrying. At least three of the boys at the party said they want to marry her," Mr. Laurence laughingly said.

"It just shows they have great taste," Joe said. "Thank God they're a little too young."

It was no secret how much Joe loved Angie, but the smile on his face was, for once, one of relief and not worry.

CHAPTER FIFTY-SEVEN

Maria

The next big occasion was the impending arrival of Angie's future mother-in-law and the rest of Joe's family. She was so nervous that I threatened her with an injection of the tranquilizer I gave her after we found her passed out in the ballroom.

"You don't understand, Maria," she said. "Joe's family took me in. They gave me a safe place to be, away from my brother and father. And what did I do in turn? I nearly killed their son."

"It's not like you did it on purpose," I said.

"That's not how his mother sees it, and who can blame her? If my son was still planning on marrying the girl that tried to kill him, I wouldn't be so overjoyed with the idea."

"You talked to her numerous times on the phone, and didn't everything go well?"

"Yes, but that was over the phone. She might take one look at me today and decide I'm the devil's daughter. Apparently that was her nickname for me when I was in the women's center."

"One look and she'll see you for the angel that you are."

"I wish I was as confident as you, Maria."

"Mr. Laurence assured you that everything would go smoothly; that should be all the reassurance you need."

We decided to work on her outfit for the visit, as a way to help manage her nerves. I picked out a simple red dress with a black belt and a pair of black flats. I pulled her hair into a ponytail, like at the party for the children, and all one could see was her angelic face.

"You look like a creature that God made with his own hands," I said.

"Seriously Maria? I think you might have mistaken me for you."

"Would your mommy lie to you?" I asked.

"Yes, if she thought it would make me feel better," she replied as I looked at her suspiciously. She then hugged me tightly for a long time and said, "I love you so much!"

Mr. Laurence greeted Joe's family at the door, and as I stood off to the side, I could immediately see how impressed Joe's mom, Mary, was with my adoptive father. He was tall and majestic, and his manners and demeanor were perfect, and she lit up in his presence.

Mary was middle-aged, about five foot seven, and quite attractive. She spoke with a heavy Bronx accent, as did her husband, Richard, and younger son, Stephen.

After Mr. Laurence, Joe was the next to greet them, and when he hugged and kissed his mother she almost seemed unsure who he was. "My God, has it been that long since I've seen you? You've grown another two inches and become better looking than you already were. Richard, look at our son."

Joe hugged and kissed his dad and his father said, "Your mother's right. You look great, son."

"Thanks, Dad," Joe replied, and then he shook his younger brother's hand and eyed the boy suspiciously. "I heard about the message you wanted passed along to Angie," Joe said, "and you can forget it. She's mine." When Stephen pouted openly, Joe shot the boy a stern look and pulled him in for a hug.

Mr. Laurence stealthily reached over and put Angie in front of Joe's mother and said, "And, of course, you know this beautiful and charming young lady?"

Joe's mom and Angie hesitated and then, just like that, Mary reached out to hug Angie and kissed the girl on both cheeks. Then she held Angie by the shoulders and studied her face. "My God," she said, "you're more beautiful than ever."

"Thank you. It's so good to see you again. You look great," Angie said, then she quickly moved over and hugged Joe's dad, and shook Stephen's hand to avoid giving the boy even a shred of hope.

Mr. Laurence introduced me as his daughter, and Gloria, who was off from work, as a dear and close friend of the family. I could be wrong, but Stephen looked as though he might have been checking out both Gloria and me. He was a good-looking little fellow, but God, was he creepy.

It was at that point that Joe came over to us and whispered, "If that kid offers to show you his baseball cards, just say no. Tell him you hate baseball, even if you have to lie. Trust me on this."

Mr. Laurence had ordered a selection of appetizers, including shrimp cocktail, clams on the half shell and fresh oysters. For dinner, he'd ordered five porterhouse steaks, steamed lobster, and vegetables. Mary brought homemade cannoli for dessert.

Partway through the evening, Mr. Laurence asked me to go down to the wine cellar and pick out a couple of bottles of wine. He said, "Maria is our closest thing to a wine connoisseur." I looked at him and was about to laugh out loud, but decided that would be rude. I grabbed Angie's hand and took her with me.

We walked down stairs and I asked, "Are you doing okay?"

"I guess so. The whole time she was hugging me I thought she was going to take a knife out and stab me in the back."

"Too many people around for that. Stay close and I'll protect you."

"Thank you, Mommy."

I turned and looked at her and asked, "Do you know how happy you make me?"

"Happy enough to open a bottle of wine and give me time to drink it before going back upstairs?"

"Happy enough to give you a sip or two of my wine when we're upstairs."

"That works," she said as I handed her two bottles, and I took two bottles. She continued, "Don't you even look at the labels?"

"Why bother? I don't know one from the other."

"But any of these bottles could be worth tens of thousands of dollars."

"Not my problem."

"But how about Mr. Laurence?"

"It's not his problem either. These were all gifts to Mr. and Mrs. Hamill from various VIPs," I laughingly replied. "They hardly drank at all, to avoid triggering the children, since most of them had been abused by drunken parents and relatives."

"The Hamills were really special people," Angie said.

"They would have to be, to adopt fifteen young girls and take care of them the way they did. Each one of them was treated like the most precious gift in the world. That's why it's so important that we carry on the work of the foundation."

"Am I really going to play a major role?" she asked.

"You already have, organizing the party for the children and keeping them all happy and entertained. How many of those little boys asked you to marry them?"

"A few, but then I was the one handing out the gifts," she laughingly replied.

"Joe's little brother is a little, um, precocious, isn't he?" I said.

"Stephen is actually a sweet boy. We were roommates the whole time I stayed with them. His baseball cards are his true love."

"Then why did you shake his hand, instead of hugging him?"

"Nothing gets past you, does it?"

"A mother watches her daughter very closely," I said, boring my eyes into hers until she laughed.

"I shook his hand because Joe asked me to. I felt bad, but Stephen has to know I'm marrying Joe and not him."

We started up the stairs, and I pulled lightly on Angie's ponytail. She looked down at me and I said, "I was dead serious before when I said you would play a major role with the foundation. Mr. Laurence is tutoring Joe and I'm tutoring you."

"But you're still my mommy?" she asked nervously.

"Of course, and like a great mommy I'll always be here to protect my girl."

"Thank you," she said in a tone that revealed that, despite all the love and caring bestowed upon her by Mr. Laurence, Gloria, me and Joe, she still harbored doubts. And who could blame her?

We walked into the dining room and Mr. Laurence and Joe's parents were discussing the Bronx, and how the demographics of that borough had changed so much over the last twenty years with so many Italian, Irish, German, and Jewish people moving either to upstate New York or to different states.

"Wow! We were wondering if you were ever coming back," Mr. Laurence jokingly remarked.

"Well, there is such a wide selection that we wanted to make sure we chose correctly, and hopefully to everyone's delight."

"Such a conscientious connoisseur," Mr. Laurence said, with only enough mischief in his voice for me to notice.

I put the bottles on the buffet and turned to him with a smile. "I'll let you choose what we have first," I said, then sat down next to Angie and Joe.

Joe's mom looked at me and Gloria and said, "Mr. Laurence has told us that you're a medical doctor, Maria. That's wonderful! I could have sworn that you and Gloria were actresses or models."

Gloria smiled a little wearily, and I said, "Thank you, but we both work in the medical field … so no need for Halle Berry or Angelina Jolie to worry. Gloria is a highly skilled ER nurse."

"That's wonderful," Mary said, and quickly turned her attention back to me. "Do you have your own practice?"

"No, I work at the free clinic and the Pediatric Cancer Hospital, which are both funded by the Hamill Foundation." I looked at Gloria as I put my arms around Angie and said, "And we're a growing family enterprise. Gloria has expressed interest in working for the clinic in the future, and this beautiful child" — I squeezed Angie in close — "is my sidekick."

"Wonderful!" said Richard, who had barely spoken up to that point. He looked at Angie ."What does a sidekick do?"

"I just do … whatever Maria needs me to do," she said softly.

I could see that she was starting to feel overwhelmed, so I jumped in. "Angie is irreplaceable," I said. "We had a party here for the children and parents at the hospital and she arranged the whole thing. She was amazing with the kids and was also the star of the party. All the little boys fell in love with her."

"I fell in love with her first!" Stephen blurted out as his mother looked at him like she was ready to slap him.

"One more word about that and you'll spend the rest of the day in the car," she said. "Do you understand?"

"Yes," he said sullenly. Then he turned his attention to Gloria, smiling at her creepily across the table. Gloria leveled him with a gaze that said, *Oh is that right, little man? You think you can handle this?* All of this drama was invisible to the rest of the table, but Gloria and I shared a silent moment of amusement at the kid's behavior. To his credit, he actually seemed to get it. He stopped flirting and pulled out his baseball cards.

Mr. Laurence opened a bottle of wine and poured a little into Joe's mom's glass. She swirled it around, held the glass to her nose, and took a taste. "Wonderful! What is it?"

Mr. Laurence looked at the label and read, "Château Lafite Rothschild, 1967."

"My God, that must be worth a fortune!" Joe's mom exclaimed.

"I wouldn't know. Maria, how much would you say?"

"Well, 1967 wasn't a particularly great year, so I would say on the low side of fourteen or fifteen thousand."

Angie softly kicked me under the table, and I tapped her shin with my toe. Mr. Laurence filled the glasses of all the adults, and I asked him to give a little to Angie, which he did. I said, "I want my beautiful assistant to appreciate the finer things in life."

Joe's father said, "Well, I think it's great, Angie. You always told us that you felt most comfortable with children, and working with children who have cancer makes your role all the more important."

Joe, who had been holding Angie's hand, raised it to his mouth and kissed it.

Angie was beaming at Joe and squirming in her seat when Mr. Laurence raised his glass and said, "How about a toast? To our beautiful, loving, caring Angie!"

We all drank up as Angie blushed and forgot to pick up her glass. Joe handed it to her and said, "Take a sip, sweetheart."

"Oops. I'm not used to people toasting me. Thank you."

Mary, who had been gazing at her future daughter-in-law, said, "You look angelic, Angie. Like a young Audrey Hepburn."

I perked up at the mention of one of my favorite movie stars and asked Mary if she was a film buff.

"Maybe not a buff," she said, "but I do love them. Richard and I used to go to the movies quite a lot. It was a cheap night out. Now, you can just watch it all on your TV, but it's not the same for me. There's no replacing the atmosphere of a theater. If you can believe it, there's not a single movie theater left in the Bronx. The last one just shut down."

"That's a real crime," I said. "We have a theater right here in the house. Maybe, the next time you come and visit we can watch something. Mr. Laurence has a vast collection."

"You mean, you might invite us again?" Mary said as though she never expected another invitation. Mr. Laurence stood behind both Joe and Angie and gently touched their shoulders.

"Anybody who could raise a son like Joe will always be welcome here. Your son is a unique young man. Not only does he possess a moral compass that is rare in any individual, and especially rare in someone so young, but he's also intelligent, eager to learn, loving and caring. Most importantly he understands and practices the most important virtue of all: *forgiveness*."

It was Joe's turn to feel color rushing to his cheeks as he took in the words of his incredible mentor.

Mr. Laurence took his hand off Joe's shoulder and placed both his hands gently against Angie's head. "And you invited this precious young lady into your home, shielding her from an abusive family. Yes, it would be our pleasure to have you all over more often."

There was no one like Mr. Laurence. Not only was he physically imposing, but he could put anyone at ease. That little speech about Joe and Angie terminated any anxiety that might have interrupted the evening. Besides a jealous Stephen, the entire evening was perfect. Dinner was delicious, and the cannoli were out of this world. There was no doubt in my mind that Joe's mom and dad left the mansion relieved and happy. As they drove away, I turned to my beautiful daughter and said, "Mr. Laurence assured you all would go well, and that was all you needed to know."

Angie hugged me as tears of relief flowed down her face. She then turned to Mr. Laurence and hugged him and repeated, "Thank you, thank you..."

Mr. Laurence patted her head and said, "Thank you, my lovely child. Having you in our family is a blessing from God."

Gloria, who had been standing off to one side, came up to me and locked one arm in mine and said, "Well, that was a successful evening." I was briefly paralyzed, frozen at being touched by such a beautiful woman, but I managed to say, "Yes, yes it was."

We all formed a line in the kitchen and washed, dried, and put away the many dishes we had used while entertaining Joe's family. No one would dare ask why we didn't just hire a maid and servants, or even buy a dishwasher. If it was good enough for Mr. and Mrs. Hamill and their daughters to do all of the work by hand, then the tradition would live on in us.

After everything was cleaned, Joe and Angie went back to their house and Gloria, who had to work in a few hours, excused herself and went back to her room for a nap. Mr. Laurence and I stayed in the kitchen and opened another bottle of wine.

Mr. Laurence filled my glass and then his own. "I just want to compliment you once again on the wonderful selection of wines you chose to go with the food."

"Very funny! Just so you know, I picked them without even looking at the labels."

"I figured that," he said. "So blind luck was your secret?"

"I guess you could say that." We clinked glasses. "To blind luck!"

"So, tell me, my beautiful and charming daughter, what are your plans this week?"

"To continue to tutor my lovely daughter and catch up on some paperwork for the foundation and clinic."

"How would you feel about taking a trip out to Santa Barbara?"

"Why?" I was immediately suspicious.

"I need you to check on the house and sign some paperwork the lawyers have waiting for you."

"If that's what you need, no problem."

"Take the kids with you. I doubt either one has been on a plane yet, and I'm sure they'd love to see Santa Barbara. You can take them up and down the coast if you like."

I looked at him really hard and said, "Come to think of it, this week would not be good. In fact, no time soon would be good for me. The lawyers can fax the paperwork like they have been doing for the past ten years. Sorry!"

"From no problem to no way. That was quick."

"You promised me a significant amount of time. I don't consider a couple of weeks significant."

"It's not what you think, and the idea that you think I'm lying to you is insulting."

I studied his face. "Sorry, it's just a selfish feeling. Please don't make me feel any guiltier than I already do."

"How about you take Angie with you, and I keep Joe here?"

"Okay but I'm not going to be the one to tell Joe. That boy guards her."

"He guards her like I guarded Isabelle, and you will eventually do the same when you find the perfect partner."

I took a large gulp of wine and said, "Isabelle is probably cursing me right now, and probably has already put a hex on me, so no woman will ever find me attractive or interesting or even think about falling in love with me."

"Isabelle will never fault you for loving your adoptive dad as much as you do. She gets it, and she can wait a little longer."

I looked at him and smiled. He always knew the exact right thing to say.

CHAPTER FIFTY-EIGHT

Joe

I came out of the bathroom and looked at Angie, who was still asleep in our bed. She looked so peaceful. It was quite a contrast to the troubled girl that I had to hold all night long so that she felt safe.

I walked into the kitchen and sat down as images from the last two years passed through my mind. Images of me playing basketball and getting drunk with my friends, of life with my parents and brother before Angie moved in. The first day I actually talked to Angie, helped her with the groceries, and then beat the shit out of her brother.

The Christmas Eve night that Angie came charging into the bar where I was drinking with my friends and demanded I leave right then. I had promised her that I wouldn't drink that night and ruin the occasion for my family.

The way we argued as we walked past the basketball courts on our way to the apartment. Her pushing me over the coffee table and coming at me with a ceramic figurine and me pushing her aside just as she was going to smash it over my head.

Her running out of the apartment and me chasing her up the stairwell of the building where her brother and father lived. Me begging her not to go into that apartment. Her screaming at me that it couldn't be any less safe than me beating her up in my parents' apartment.

Feeling, the very next night, that something was desperately wrong. Finding the door to her family's apartment open, and her father passed out on the couch, with the TV blasting in the background. And then the slashing sound of a butcher knife repeatedly passing through the dead body of her brother and the final blow of the knife slicing through his limp genitals. The sight of him there, motionless and covered in blood, with his pants partially down.

Her getting up and coming at me with knife in hand, as though she was ready to slice me up next. Me pleading with her to put the knife down as she pushed me aside and went toward her father. Me, grabbing her from behind and taking the knife out of her hands just as she was about to stab her father.

Her desperately trying to get the knife back and me trying to fend her off without hurting her and finally opening the door to the stairwell and flinging the knife down below.

Turning around and seeing her charging at me with eyes wide open, eyes blank with fury, ferocious, like a bull charging at the sight of blood, and then her pushing me over the railing with the force of said bull. Her eyes … wide open … angry and ferocious…

I snapped out of it as the wind started howling outside. I got up and walked over to the sliding door. I opened the door and looked out at bouquets of red roses whirling violently around like giant insects. I swatted at the bouquets as the thorns from the stems pinched at my face and hands, puncturing me, drawing little points of blood to the surface of my skin. I continued walking, along the pool and past the gardens, as the bouquets seemed to lose their power and fell at my feet.

I got to the end and looked down at the ocean and at the waves crashing violently against the shore. In the whirl of the wind, I could hear a scream. The same scream over and over and as I turned, I saw Angie running toward me, calling my name.

When she reached me she threw her arms around me and held on tightly as she asked, "Joe, what are you doing out here? My God, you scared me. The wind woke me up and when I went into the kitchen the floor was littered with roses and the door was wide open and when I couldn't find you, I thought I was going to die."

I lifted her head off my chest and looked into her worried eyes. Her loose hair blew wildly, as did mine. I bent down and kissed her for a long time, and then picked her up and carried her into the house and into our bedroom and placed her on the bed.

We once again started to kiss passionately as we ripped our clothes off, exploring each other's bodies in a way we had never done before, making love three times during the night and finally falling asleep wrapped in each other's arms.

I woke up at my usual time, and even though I slept very little during the night I felt rejuvenated, and as I looked down at my sleeping fiancée I felt like the luckiest person alive. I got out of bed and walked into the kitchen, where just last night the floor had been covered with red roses, and now, they were all gone. I looked at the sliding door that was partially open and as I looked out at the pool, I saw a swirling vortex of red roses rising and twisting and heading out to sea.

CHAPTER FIFTY-NINE

Joe

I walked over to the mansion and was greeted by Mr. Laurence and Maria. I told Maria that Angie was running a little late and Maria said, "So am I, so that works out perfectly."

Mr. Laurence and I drove first to the florist to pick up three red roses and then went off to the cemetery. I thanked Mr. Laurence again for treating my family so wonderfully, and he said it was his pleasure. Then he told me he had a favor to ask.

"Whatever you like," I replied.

"Maria will be flying to Santa Barbara tomorrow to check on the house and sign some papers with the lawyers. She'll be gone four days and I'd like Angie to accompany her."

"Would it be okay if I also went?" I asked.

"No, we have some important things to go over these next couple of days and I need your help."

I was in a state of shock, and I started thinking that I wasn't the only one who was in love with Angie. Mr. Laurence seemed to read my mind, and said, "Maria would never let anything happen to Angie. She likes to think of herself as Angie's adoptive mother. She loves that child as though she'd given birth to her."

"Has Angie agreed to go with Maria?" I asked.

"Maria was going to talk to her this morning."

It was all but set. I knew Angie couldn't say no to Maria.

"Well, Angie's always wanted to visit Santa Barbara. This will be like a dream come true for her. It's absolutely okay with me, Mr. Laurence."

"Thank you, Joe. I know you'll miss her dearly, but she'll be back in your arms before you know it."

We passed through the cemetery gates and parked in our usual spot. I stopped at Isabelle and Rachel's gravestone and said a couple of prayers ... even though there was supposedly no one buried there. Then I joined Mr. Laurence on his bench.

I asked, "Mr. Laurence, have you ever thought about what your life would have been like if you didn't meet Isabelle on that street in Los Angeles?"

"Not really. If it hadn't been that street corner it would have been somewhere else. So the question of what my life would have been like without her is moot. I was always going to find Isabelle, and Isabelle was always going to find me."

"Did you feel that way from the start?"

"No, the shock of meeting her and then Rachel and her father and being invited to stay with them was overwhelming at first, but it then it dawned on me that it was my destiny to marry this amazingly beautiful lady who also happened to be a genius. She felt the same way — that it was her destiny to marry me."

Mr. Laurence sat quietly for a moment, then said, "Why do you ask?"

"Last night I was sitting alone in the kitchen thinking about my life before Angie, and about everything that's happened since we met. The time she spent living with my family, then that dreadful night, and me tumbling down the stairs and not getting seriously hurt, and all the doctors saying it was a miracle that I was still alive. And a year later, here I am, living here, being mentored and supported by you — a man unlike any I've ever met. You're exactly the kind of man I want to be like. And when I think of what you've done for us — and it all happened so automatically. Do you think all that was destiny?"

"You were chosen, Joe."

"Chosen? I don't understand."

"Sure you do. Think about it."

I cast my mind back to that first day we met. The heat of the day, the greenness of the grass as I sat down to rest and look at the few listings that I hadn't already seen and found too expensive. The way Mr. Laurence suddenly appeared behind me. And from that point on, the way doors kept opening for me. Being offered the home behind the mansion for less than it would have cost to rent a closet anywhere else. Angie meeting Gloria and beginning to learn from her what she needed to do to change her life. Angie remembering everything that had happened to her as a child, and her mother's role in letting it happen. Maria entering her life as a mother figure, eager to bestow on Angie all of the love that Angie missed out on. It was all uncanny.

"Were you expecting me that day when I sat on your front lawn?"

"Yes!"

"But how could you know?"

"The same way I knew that Angie was unconscious on the floor of the ballroom and that we should stop at the mansion before going to eat breakfast."

"I don't understand. Are you … do you have some sort of supernatural ability?"

Mr. Laurence seemed to struggle with this part. "Not exactly—"

"Is it Isabelle?"

He smiled. "It's always Isabelle."

"Yes of course, but how?"

"Dear boy, if I could explain this, I would have the answer to all of the mysteries of the universe."

I was struggling to keep up and thought it might help to bring the conversation back to his original request. "Is that why you're not going to Santa Barbara and sending Maria instead? Do you have to stay close to Isabelle?"

Mr. Laurence looked at the sea. "It's strange, isn't it? I'd always prayed that I would pass before her. Instead, as usual, she was many steps ahead of me. She could edit my mind like she could edit my words."

"I thought she died from grief over Rachel's passing?"

"She did, but we knew for a long time that Rachel was terminal. Rachel knew, and late at night I would hear the two sisters talking and Rachel begging her not to stop living once she was gone … telling her that I needed her. And I heard Isabelle tell her that when I died, she would be left alone. She said, 'My husband is stronger than I could ever be, and I will still be able to guide him, the way Mom and Dad have guided me since they passed.'"

I sat in silence, absorbing this idea of a multi-generational spiritual continuum leading from the Hamills to Isabelle to Mr. Laurence to me.

Mr. Laurence watched me puzzling it all out, and said, "She was wrong about one thing. I wasn't the stronger one, and I've never gotten over the loneliness of not having her physically beside me when I go to bed at night or hearing her laugh early in the morning. But she *has* continued to guide me."

Mr. Laurence looked down at the roses in his hands and then across at me. "Does that explain more fully how I knew?"

"Yes," I said as he handed me the roses and asked me to walk down the stairs and toss them into the water.

"Aren't you coming?" I asked.

"No, you go ahead. I'll be right here," he said.

I walked down the stairs and along the beach, and as usual the waves came crashing against the shore. I looked out at the water, at the sun rising in the distance from beneath the ocean's depths and shedding its light on an avalanche of red roses riding the crest of a wave and heading straight toward me.

CHAPTER SIXTY

Joe

I had decided before we even left the cemetery for breakfast that I would act happy for Angie. She had always wanted to go to Santa Barbara and now she was getting her chance. I knew she could never say no to Maria. It was insane for me to think that Maria had any romantic feelings for Angie. Mr. Laurence was right, as in all things. Maria really did see herself as Angie's adoptive mother, and Angie readily accepted Maria as her mother.

I parked the car in the driveway, and Mr. Laurence and I walked into the mansion. I found Angie and Maria working beside each other at a desk in Maria's bedroom.

I knocked on the frame of the open door and said, "Good morning, ladies."

Angie turned and stood up, and for a moment it was like I was looking at the sickly, troubled girl at the women's center. I asked, "Can I talk to you for a moment sweetheart?"

"Of course," she said, and we walked into the parlor and sat down on a couch. I held her hand and said, "Mr. Laurence told me the good news. You're finally going to see Santa Barbara. I'm so happy for you."

"I wish you were also going," she said, looking guilty.

"There will be plenty of times for us to go together, but for right now Mr. Laurence needs me here," I said. "But I have one thing to ask of you."

"What's that?"

"That you call me ten times a day."

"Ten times a day! Don't you think that's a bit much?"

"No. If I was the one going away you would want me to call you fifteen to twenty times a day."

"That's not true. Twelve at most."

"How about we compromise and say five?"

"That sounds reasonable, even though I'll probably call you more like seven times a day."

"Fair enough," I said. "Oh, one other thing — please promise me you're not going to meet some surfer guy and run away with him."

She looked at me as tears started running down her cheeks and she suddenly hugged me and said, "You're the only guy for me. The only one."

I wiped the tears from her face and said, "And you're the only girl for me. The only one." We kissed and the whole time all I could think about was how difficult it was going to be to be away from her for four days.

CHAPTER SIXTY-ONE

Joe

The following morning the four of us had breakfast together and then drove to MacArthur Airport in Central Islip, Long Island, where a private plane that belonged to the Hamill Corporation, not the foundation, waited for Angie and Maria. Two pilots met them by the boarding stairs and carried their luggage into the plane, and the four of us followed them. It was a luxury aircraft, with leather seats for up to nineteen passengers and a wide cabin lined with TVs and dining tables. It also came with a lovely stewardess. The crew all knew Mr. Laurence and Maria.

Angie had never flown before and was visibly nervous. Our discussions the night before about planes being much safer than almost all other forms of transportation didn't really alleviate her concern.

I turned to the stewardess and asked for a glass of red wine for my fiancée. After the stewardess left to fill the request Angie turned to me and said, "Isn't it a little early?"

"Not for you, angel," I said as the woman returned with a glass of Malbec. "If you drink the entire glass you'll pass out and wake up in California. There are benefits to being a lightweight."

She laughed and took her first big gulp of wine. I held her other hand and said, "I'm going to miss you terribly, but I'm so happy you're getting to fulfill a dream of yours." As I reached across her lap and started to buckle her in, she started to cry. Maria sat next to her and noted, "Boy, you're starting early."

Maria then asked the stewardess for a glass of wine for herself. "I hate to see someone drinking alone." Angie laughed and I took that short opportunity to kiss her and tell her how much I loved her. I then quickly turned, because I was just about to start crying, and walked down the aisle and exited the plane with Mr. Laurence.

We waited for the plane to take off, and then we got into the car and drove home.

Mr. Laurence and I walked into the mansion, and even though we were used to being alone there, it seemed unusually quiet and lonesome. We walked into his study, and he pulled a file from a cabinet and handed it to me. It was labeled Santa Barbara Home.

Inside were hundreds of pictures of the Spanish-style house with its meticulously maintained grounds that included a pool and a tennis court. Isabelle and Rachel were in many of the pictures, and it didn't matter how many pictures I saw of Isabelle; in every one, her astonishing beauty never failed to take my breath away.

I never for a moment doubted Isabelle's presence, or her guidance in Mr. Laurence's life after she passed away. In fact, I felt her spirit everywhere in the mansion, in our small home, around the pool, and in the gardens. Now I was seeing the other place where she had held sway.

"You've never been back since Rachel and Isabelle passed away?" I asked.

"No, but as you can see it's a beautiful home with a magnificent view of the Pacific and the boardwalk, and there are plenty of great restaurants and the town looks like something out of a movie." Mr. Laurence paused for a few moments and then continued, "But it was never home for Isabelle and Rachel."

"But all the other daughters left…"

"But in the end, they all came back, and throughout their lives they all came back for long visits. Mr. and Mrs. Hamill wanted them to have lives of their own, to get married, see the world, pursue professions they enjoyed. Isabelle and Rachel were the youngest, and in their parents' mind I think they always thought that if there was to be a successor to carry on the business and foundation it would be Isabelle."

"Yet they gave you the home in Santa Barbara to live in with Rachel."

"Yes. They didn't think it was right to put the burden of running the business and foundation on Isabelle and Rachel. It was my wife and her sister's decision to come back here to live. Isabelle was most like her daddy. Ink ran through their blood. But it was much more than that. Their lives weren't whole unless they were close to their parents.

"Mr. and Mrs. Hamill set up trusts for all the girls, yet none of the girls spent even half of the money in their trusts, and when they passed away the money went back into the corporation and the foundation.

"After all the girls and Mr. and Mrs. Hamill passed away, the responsibility for running the foundation and corporation fell to Isabelle, Rachel, and me. When Maria entered our lives, it was like a blessing from God.

"Maria, like you, was a great student and eager to learn, and my wife, who could spot a phony from ten thousand miles away, was as confident as ever that Maria possessed all the qualifications and morals that Mr. Hamill taught her to look for in individuals. And she was right."

I thought about this, then asked, "Did Isabelle see the same things in me?"

"You wouldn't be here if she hadn't."

"And none of the sisters had any children that wanted to be part of the foundation and corporation?"

"None of the sisters had any children of their own, nor did they adopt any children."

"That seems so strange, all those girls and no offspring."

"Not really. Just look at the situation with your fiancée," he said. "It's very hard, physically and emotionally, to consider having children after a legacy of abuse.

"Maria and I both hope that somewhere down the road, when and if you and Angie feel ready, you'll consider adopting. And Maria wants to try in vitro fertilization, but she's still hoping to meet someone before she goes down that road."

"She's already been a great mother to Angie. I can't see her being any less nurturing with kids of her own," I said.

"Yes, she definitely has a strong maternal instinct. She can often seem overly emotional, but that's because she cares so deeply. The way her biological family abandoned her was a shock to her, and the pain will always be there. I think it's helping Maria to be able to care for Angie as much as it's helping Angie to have a new mother figure in her life."

"Did Isabelle ever talk about her childhood or the time before she was adopted by the Hamills?"

"No, and I never brought it up. It was as though her life began when she was adopted, and everything before that was consigned to a black hole."

"But she knew all about Rachel's past?"

"Yes, but she never brought it up with me. She was very good at keeping secrets. She was built like an investigative reporter, like her father. The only difference was that she knew where the investigation was going before she even asked a question. Lucky for me, she sized me up in a couple of minutes," Mr. Laurence said with a laugh.

Later that evening when Gloria came back from work we ordered her favorite again, Chinese food. Mr. Laurence opened a bottle of wine, and they drank it during dinner. Gloria was quiet. When I asked her how her shift went, she briefly talked about a sixteen-year-old girl, from a so-called good family, who'd been rushed to the ER. She had overdosed on drugs and they'd pumped out her stomach and done everything they could to stop the cascade of symptoms, but she'd died right there.

"The mother burst into the ER just after we lost her. I'll never forget the look on her face," Gloria said. "The parents were this normal, working couple — the mother teaches at a local college and the dad works for a small tech firm. One of the doctors knew them. I can't even imagine what they're going through right now."

"That's just awful," I said. "And it's hard on you."

She nodded and wiped away a couple of tears and took a sip of wine. None of us spoke until Gloria broke the silence.

"So my little cupcake is on her way to California," she said, forcing herself into a better mood. "She was so anxious about flying, but I told her she had nothing to worry about. God forbid something did happen, she'd just float back to earth like a feather, she's so light. She'll be absolutely fine."

CHAPTER SIXTY-TWO

Joe

Just as I opened the door to our house, Angie called. She was all excited. When I asked her how the flight was, she said she didn't know because she slept the whole way. "That wine really did the trick. I woke up just as we were about to land, but the landing was so bumpy that I thought I was going to die, and I nearly peed my pants."

"Where are you now?"

"In the back of a limousine! It was waiting for us at the airport."

"That sounds like fun," I said. Through Angie, Maria let me know that she'd already called Mr. Laurence to tell him they'd arrived safely, so I didn't have to bother him.

After a short conversation we said a bunch of sweet goodbyes, and after only a couple of rounds of "You hang up; no, *you* hang up," we let each other go.

I sat at the kitchen table and reflected on all the things Mr. Laurence and I had talked about. It was so obvious that he missed Isabelle and it didn't take a great imagination to understand why.

It made me think about things that I really didn't like to think about. The inevitability, the loss, that every living creature would eventually have to go through. It made me think of a phrase from the famous poet William Butler Yeats, who refers to, "Whatever is begotten, born and dies."

My phone rang again, and it was Angie. They'd arrived at the house and before even going in she was looking down at the Pacific Ocean and the boardwalk. She described the view and said, "The only thing that could make it better is if you were here."

I promised her that I would be standing in the same spot with her one day, holding her and gazing out at the ocean together. I looked down at the phone as she hung up, and she was about to walk into the house. She sounded so childlike and happy that I was suddenly thrilled for her. I knew all that she had been through, and how much I had given up for her, and at that moment I felt a sense of rejuvenation and renewal, not only for myself, but especially for her.

The abuse Angie had suffered put her in a terrible club, to which no one would ever choose to belong. And yet the Hamills had made it their mission to help girls and women in exactly her situation. Like so many whose lives had crossed paths in this place, Angie had been violated by those closest to her. She'd arrived here essentially orphaned and screaming for help without emitting a sound. It was only natural that it took her so long to trust me, and that no matter what I did or how much I sacrificed, she saw it as a ruse. She always expected good things to disappear, because she had never known goodness to stay.

I recalled looking at the pictures of Isabelle in Santa Barbara earlier that day. I wondered if her spirit occupied that house like it did the mansion, our house, and the surrounding grounds. And then it suddenly all seemed so silly. Isabelle's spirit, her presence and essence, would never abandon the home and family that gave her life. This was why Mr. Laurence never ventured very far from the mansion ... "from his darling —his darling — his life and his bride."

The phone rang again, and it was Angie. I answered by saying, "Yes, my darling."

EPILOGUE

Mr. Laurence sits alone in the movie theater looking at the footage from his wedding. Suddenly, the arms of his darling Isabelle encircle him from behind. "Silly boy," she says, wrapping her arms around his broad shoulders, "what does a girl have to do to get her guy to dance with her?"

Mr. Laurence turns around and looks at his beautiful girl and says, "Not a thing, my darling. It would be my greatest pleasure to dance all night with you."

She takes him by the hand, and they walk out of the theater and toward the ballroom where the glorious sound of an orchestra plays "All My Tomorrows," sung by the incomparable Frank Sinatra.

They enter the romantically lit ballroom and find it empty except for the orchestra. They dance a slow waltz as he looks into her wondrous face. He gazes into her emerald eyes as tears roll down his cheeks, and Isabelle asks, "Why are you crying, my sweet boy?"

He shakes his head and replies, "I miss you so much."

"I know, but have I not always been here for you?"

"Yes, my darling …" He takes her face into his hands, and they kiss, and once again they start dancing as the violin and piano hit a crescendo and Isabelle says, "You still have two brides to give away."

"Two?" he asks.

"Yes, our daughter and Angie."

"Maria is going to meet someone?"

"Not just someone — her perfect match. And she won't have to wait long or look far. When she gets home, you'll see. There will be so much to learn, and it will be glorious, if you catch my meaning," Isabelle said with a laugh. "After that it won't be too long before all our tomorrows will be spent together, along with Rachel, all of my sisters, and mom and dad."

"It sounds perfect, and may I ask — when did the plot change?"

"It's not like all an editor does is change a word or two, switch a sentence, or correct punctuation. Sometimes an editor must change the narrative. You know how much I hate sad endings, and our daughter deserves all the happiness the world has to offer. So, please try to enjoy the time you have remaining with the children. They so adore you."

"I will definitely try."

"No, you have to promise."

"I promise, my dear. I promise."

She smiles as her emerald eyes reflect the majestic love they share. Two souls, entwined, never to be dissevered.

THE END

"Close Friends"

(An excerpt from Joseph Sciuto's forthcoming collection of short fiction)

It was another lovely, sunny day in southern California when I parked in front of my friend Dave Martin's house in West Hollywood. Dave had been diagnosed with lung cancer about nine months earlier and it had spread throughout his body. I'd visited him many times during his battle with this terrible disease, but I was quite certain that this would be the last time I would see my close and fun-loving friend of over twenty-five years.

The gentleman sitting in the passenger's seat was another cherished friend, Rod Lynch. We had met at the restaurant where I worked with Dave a little less than twenty-five years ago. He was an extremely successful businessman and, unlike many in Hollywood, he didn't choose his friends by their status or the size of their bank accounts, but by their beliefs, morals, and capacity for fun. On top of that, if you had a fondness for Irish coffees, it worked in your favor.

We got out of my car and knocked on the front door of Dave's house. Margie, his loving girlfriend of many years, opened the door, and right there beside her was Dave in his wheelchair, dressed quite dapper, and wearing a Gatsby flat hat. He was a mere skeleton of his former self, but dressed that way he looked like quite the charmer.

We waved good-bye to Margie and walked to a nearby restaurant that Dave had frequented before getting sick. Rod took the handles of the wheelchair and steered the apparatus holding our friend from the time we left the house until the time a young waitress sat us at a large table not far from a window view of the boulevard.

We all ordered Bloody Marys — one of Dave's favorite drinks — and a few appetizers. Rod sat next to Dave, and I sat across from him. Rod and I tried to steer the conversation to the good times we'd had, but Dave kept coming back to Margie. He was concerned about her future and prayed that she would be able to manage once he was gone. We tried to assuage his fears, but he kept bringing it up. He was having difficulty talking, and Rod kept having to pick up a napkin and gently wipe the spittle from Dave's chin.

Rod and I finished our Bloody Marys, but Dave barely touched his drink. We ordered another round and then Rod started telling stories that made us all laugh. Naturally, we ordered more drinks, and when I looked across at Dave's first Bloody Mary it was quite apparent he was not going to be able to get through it. At any other time and place I would have been extremely worried if I noticed Dave had not even tasted his drink, but considering the circumstances it made sense.

After about an hour and a half, Dave said that he was getting tired and needed to go home. I asked for the check, and the waitress asked if we wanted the appetizers wrapped up to go because we hadn't touched them, but I simply shook my head.

While she tallied up the check, Rod took hold of the handles on the wheelchair and said they would wait for me outside. The waitress gave me the check and I paid with a credit card and left a generous tip. As I got up to leave the waitress stopped me and said, "I'm really sorry about your friend." I looked at her and replied, "Thank you, that's very sweet of you to say." I took one more look at Dave's drink that he'd never touched and then walked outside and couldn't find Rod and Dave.

I started walking back to the house and figured they got tired of waiting and left without me. As I turned the corner onto Dave's block, I still did not see any sign of them. Surely, they could not have made it back to the house that quickly?

I continued on my way to the house and simply assumed that they would show up eventually. I opened the gate to the front door and looked back one last time and saw Dave racing down the hill in his wheelchair toward the house with Rod steering from behind. They were laughing hysterically and as they slowed down Dave raised his arms up triumphantly like the winner of a marathon, and I couldn't help feeling that he'd lived life on his terms, doing it *his way*, as Sinatra put it, and Rod ... well, Rod was just being Rod ... different in the best of ways, exhibiting and practicing the virtues that are the very best in a human being and until this day still drinking those Irish coffees.

Acknowledgements

To my dear friend Ken Givens, who is fighting a difficult battle, thank you for your support and kind words about all my books.

To my cousin Carmela Greco, thank you for your support, love, and for being such an avid fan of my books.

To the wonderful crew at Iguana books, Cheryl, Greg, etc., thank you for always doing such a superb job. And to Ruth Dwight, thank you for enhancing my books with your beautiful artwork.

www.ingramcontent.com/pod-product-compliance
Lightning Source LLC
Chambersburg PA
CBHW020841020726
47497CB00005B/1195